I0667496

Ophiuchus Cube
book 1

Hendrik de Jong

Published by: Rinke Publishing.
Copyright © 2014 Hendrik de Jong. All rights reserved.

ISBN for paperback: 978-0-9927692-0-8
First paperback edition printed 2014 in the United Kingdom.
A catalogue record for this book is available from the British Library.
ISBN for mobi: 978-0-9927692-1-5
First published in mobi format in 2014.
ISBN for epub: 978-09927692-2-2
First published in epub format in 2014.
ISBN for PDF: 978-0-9927692-3-9
First published in PDF format in 2014.

Designed and Set by: Rinke Publishing.
Cover design by: JD&J.com

If you would like to be informed when the next instalment in this series is published, follow or contact the author, or be added to the mailing list, please visit:
www.ophiuchuscube.com

Warning: This book contains scenes of sex, violence, sexual violence, swearing, drug taking and blasphemy, and is suitable for readers 18 and over only.

Acknowledgments:

Thank you to:
Paul Butler, Martin Deutz, Christopher Hamilton,
Alastair Pont, Harry Trevelyan, Richard Watson, Mr Oakley
and Eduardo Sant'Anna.

Thank you to Dave from JD&J book design for a great cover.

Thank you to my excellent editors: John and Alicia Makin.

A special thank you to Bill McElyea, who heard my story
first and encouraged me to write it.

And thank you to everyone else: my family and dear friends
for supporting me throughout the madness that is writing a
novel.

And I would also like to thank the very friendly staff at
Notes on St. Martin's Lane in Covent Garden, who have
always made me feel welcome with their great coffee and
food, and were happy to for me write there as often as I
wanted.

Pronunciation:

Ophiuchus: [of-ee-yoo-ku*h* s]

Contents:

Prologue.

Old testament, Isaiah Chapter 13

9 Behold, the day of the LORD cometh, cruel both with wrath and fierce anger, to lay the land desolate: and he shall destroy the Sinners thereof out of it.

10 For the stars of heaven and the constellations thereof shall not give their light: the sun shall be darkened in his going forth, and the moon shall not cause her light to shine.

11 And I will punish the world for their evil, and the wicked for their iniquity; and I will cause the arrogancy of the proud to cease, and will lay low the haughtiness of the terrible.

12 I will make a man more precious than fine gold; even a man than the golden wedge of Ophir.

13 Therefore I will shake the heavens, and the earth shall remove out of her place, in the wrath of the LORD of hosts, and in the day of his fierce anger.

2. Biblical Times.
(January year 2)

"Good evening. This is the six o'clock news from the World Wide Live News Channel. These are today's main headlines.

"Gunmen coordinated attacks on 26 major cities worldwide, killing more than 5,000 people, with most casualties in Paris and New York. Followers of the Children of Abraham are suspected of being responsible, although their leader has strongly denied any involvement. Police forces throughout the world are on high alert in anticipation of more attacks.

"The London Metropolitan Police is out in force tonight at the Children of Abraham rally in Trafalgar Square, where thousands of protesters have gathered, waiting for their spiritual leader, Simon Waltz, to address them.

"Stock exchanges around the world suffered huge losses today, wiping over 120 billion US dollars off share prices.

"Riot police in Jerusalem killed at least 400 people at the Wailing Wall after clashes between Jewish and Muslim protesters against followers of the Children of Abraham who were staging prayers.

"In India, the army shot dozens of rioters outside a food processing factory. Food shortages have plagued the country for months and it is estimated over 6 million people have died so far as a result.

"The border control agency in Texas has stepped up its patrols and has adopted a shoot to kill policy against Mexicans illegally crossing the border. This decision was made after Mexican gangs had raided several farms near the border. In the last seven days 50 farmers have been killed during these raids.

"The Prime Minister has announced measures to stop the rise of the — my apologies, we are now going live to

9

Trafalgar Square, with reporter Anne Goodman, where Simon Waltz is about to speak. Hello Anne, what can you tell us?"

"Yes, hello. I am here at the Square and the atmosphere is electric. I can hardly hear myself speak. There are thousands of Children of Abraham gathered here. The crowd has been waiting here for hours in anticipation of their charismatic leader Simon Waltz, who is about to give his keynote speech. Yesterday he announced he had a very important message from God. Ah, here he is —"

Hearing Simon's name made Rick Favier and Paul Jenkinson feel uneasy and they were about to *see* him again. Simon meant trouble, and especially to Rick and Paul. An excited crowd filled the Square, thousands of hands and arms reaching out to the sky, frenzied, as if they wanted to grab the stars and pull them down. Placards were being waved with ferocity above the crowd, and the air seemed turbulent and strong enough to tumble trees. The scene created the illusion of an angry, stormy sea, the waves threatening to drown the empty stage.

Living close to the Square, Rick and Paul heard the shouts and cries from the crowd through their flat's windows, as well as via their television speakers.

"I don't like this. Those lunatics sound very angry," Rick said. "I'm scared they'll come for us tonight. They're so close. Why do they always try to attack us? I'm fed up with him blaming me in every interview, as if *I* made it happen. I know Simon is going to blame me again for everything, as soon as he opens that big mouth of his. It's bloody sickening!"

"Relax. The police are outside protecting us." Paul grabbed his hand and pulled Rick towards him, giving him a gentle hug and a soft kiss on his cheek. "Besides, if they knew we lived here, they would've come for us already.

And I'm here to protect you. I love you. And I won't let anything happen to you."

Even though he trusted Paul, Rick wasn't happy. He knew armed police were outside, but a mob of a few hundred people, willing to die for their cause, could overrun them.

***

The reporter, Anne Goodman, estimated around 20,000 people had congregated in the square. Her voice was barely audible over the chanting and shouting crowd. They held placards, explicitly warning people they would burn in Hell unless they repented and became Children of Abraham. The camera panned to the main stage and a man came into view. A colossal cheer and applause ensued, the crowd seemed to go berserk at his arrival. They knew who he was: the charismatic Simon Waltz, their spiritual leader, their Saviour, their Second Coming. His long, blond hair waved in the light breeze, giving him the same Jesus-like appearance that Michelangelo had painted in The Last Supper. His hypnotic blue eyes pierced straight through the camera. Was there a knowing smile on his face? His attention shifted to the crowd as he walked up to the front of the stage, his pristine white robe flowing, giving the impression he was floating. The winter cold seemed not to bother him. He stared into the crowd, his eyes scanning the Square. A big grin appeared on his face. Clouds in the sky partially obscured the moon; the dim light gave his face an eerie and haunted look.

"Silence!" Simon said. "Children of Abraham. Look into the sky. I can see God's anger. I do not need heathen instruments to see him, I have faith. God is angry and Armageddon is upon us. Look up and see him for yourself — Can you see Him?"

The crowd roared, its arms reaching for the sky. The sea

was angry again, fiercer now, the waves bigger and more menacing, turning into a tidal wave threatening to engulf the stage.

"Silence — You all know that heathen faggot Rick Favier," Simon said, his voice low and full of disgust. "This abomination is the one who tipped the balance. He is the one who changed God from loving man to God hating man. He was chosen by God and given the sign in the sky to warn us, but he had the audacity to deny God and deny the existence of God's sign. Because of him we all have to face the consequences. He, and the other deniers, must suffer the consequences soon." Simon paused. He pointed towards the Houses of Parliament and faced the crowd again, grimacing now, his eyes burning in their sockets with anger. "Children of Abraham. I stand here before you in these troubled times. Armageddon is approaching. We have six months left to make every soul on God's Earth see the light and repent. And Britain has become a filthy, godless country and you all know who's responsible for this. A godless Government rules us and tells us we cannot spread our gospel. It is time to show them we will not take their oppression anymore. It is time to take control. It is time to tell them they are not in charge anymore. Children of Abraham: you know what to do. The time is now!" Simon walked towards the edge of the stage. As he walked down the steps, the crowd parted in front of him like the Red Sea parting before Moses. These were biblical times indeed.

With an almost invisible hand gesture the crowd was given a sign, and as one Simon's followers moved towards the hundreds of police officers cordoning off the Square. Rick and Paul looked in horror as they saw the police being overrun and beaten up by the angry mob who were now heading towards Parliament. What they didn't see was a group of around 50 men going in a different direction — into their street.

Police constables Shaw and Thompson heard the frantic cries through their radios: their colleagues were being beaten up, probably worse. The sound of shooting guns came from the Square and made them look at each other in horror, the shock visible on their faces.

"This isn't happening. This is *not* how I want to spend the last months of my life. I need to be with my wife and kids," Shaw cried; wide eyed and ashen.

Thompson looked at him, "Stay calm, they are lunatics, a minority. We're safe here. It's not the end of the world for us." He almost added the word *yet*, but knew the realisation would make Shaw even more frightened.

They had been stationed outside the entrance to the flat and had been ordered to stay there no matter what was happening elsewhere. Thompson struggled though: hearing the cries for help from their colleagues on the Square made him want to run off and help them. He became aware of shouting at the end of the street. He looked towards the noise and saw a group of men running towards them. "This isn't good, grab your gun," he said, praying he would get through to the police station when he took his radio out. "HQ. This is Thompson. There's a crowd running towards us. I need back-up now! We're going to retreat inside the building." He hoped there were officers nearby to help them. Shaw had already opened the main entrance and was shouting at him. One last look down the street made him shiver: the group of men were less than 20 metres away. A hand gripped his arm and before he realised he was inside the building. Frantically they barricaded the door. Just in time. The crowd was shouting outside. Kicks juddered the door: there was no way the barricade would hold. Running up the stairs, they heard the noises grow louder. On the top floor, outside the entrance to Rick and Paul's flat, Shaw started banging on the door, and shouting, to get their attention. When he heard Paul's voice behind the door, Shaw told him to barricade the door and wait for further instructions.

When he heard a loud cracking noise, Thompson looked down the stairs, and he watched in horror as he saw the door cave in and an angry mob push through. He saw them kick in the doors to the downstairs apartments and he heard a woman scream as the men ran in. Thompson imagined the woman being attacked and probably killed. He saw other men running up to the next floors, also kicking in doors and entering apartments. The screams made his stomach turn. He knew in a few moments the men would be up here and confront him and Shaw. "They're almost here," Thompson said, taking out his gun and checking the safety was off. "Shoot as many as you can. And Shaw — you're not only the best colleague I've worked with, but it's also been a privilege to call you my friend." Tears ran down Thompson's face. He did not want his life to end like this, but as he heard the approaching men, now less than ten steps away, he knew he was never going to see his wife again. Fists punched him in his face and chest. A sharp pain in his stomach: someone had stabbed him with a knife. He was on the floor. Someone took his gun out of his hand. Thompson closed his eyes and imagined sitting with his wife. He looked into her brown eyes and smelt her perfume. She was laughing. In the distance he heard his own gun fire.

***

"Quick. Come, help me barricade the door. They're here," Paul said.

Rick felt real terror. "I hate this. Why are they coming for me? I didn't cause this. It's not *my* fault. Fuck. I really don't want to die."

For weeks they had trained for this moment. The Metropolitan Police had approached them after they'd received intelligence that the Children of Abraham wanted to kill Rick; since then they'd had 24 hour protection, making them prisoners in their own home.

Rick tried to barricade the door, as they had practised many times, though his hands were shaking too much this time. After they put their shoes and coats on, Paul picked up their emergency rucksacks and took out their knives and pepper spray. They waited. Rick listened to the growing noises outside their front door, the shrieks and gunshots frightening him. He thought of his mum, he needed to call her and tell her he loved her and that she shouldn't worry. He imagined she was holding him, stroking his hair, telling him everything would be fine. He wished he was a child again; he missed how simple the world had been then. The commotion outside the door returned him to reality; he had no time to make that call. She would have to wait until this was over. He heard screams, shrill and high pitched, like pigs being slaughtered. He almost vomited.

"Come on, let's go upstairs to the living room. It'll give us more time if they break the door," Paul said.

Rick was amazed how calm Paul appeared. He felt sick and scared, unable to move, let alone run up stairs.

Paul had his phone pressed to his ear, talking to their friend Martin, who had helped them many times before out of sticky situations. Rick could not hear the whole conversation, but knew Martin would send help. A cracking noise came from the downstairs corridor and straight after he heard men cheering.

"Shit. Paul, they're in. Get out!" Rick ran out onto the terrace, into the cold, pulling Paul with him, who was shouting into his phone now. "This is it. I hate those fucking lunatics," Rick said, locking the terrace door from the outside.

Paul looked at him, putting his phone down. "Me too. We'll be fine, they're on their way to help us. I love you."

"And I love you too," Rick said and looked at Paul. They kissed each other quickly. Noises from inside made them turn their heads: their living room was full of angry looking men. One of them stepped forward, pointed a gun at them, and shot a bullet through the window, shattering the glass. The bullet missed them. Paul and Rick pepper-sprayed the men who were trying to get onto the terrace through the broken window, then they turned away and ran down the fire escape, the men close behind them.

"Look. The police, they're here. We're safe now," Paul said, his breath heavy in his voice.

"Run. Now," yelled an approaching officer. "We'll cover you." He held a gun in his hand.

Paul and Rick ran down the remaining four floors as fast as they could. A dozen police officers passed them, going up. Several shots were fired and the noise was deafening. Rick felt a bullet fly past his ear. When they reached street level, an officer bundled them into a police van, which sped off, away from the danger. Shaking with fear, Rick noticed he had pissed himself.

"I think we need to go to the hospital," a pale Paul said, holding his left leg. Both looked at a spreading red patch on his trousers. Blood dripped on the floor. A few seconds later, Paul had lost all colour in his face and fainted.

To the hospital, quick. Rick heard from the front of the van. There was Martin, looking perplexed, but calm.

Six months earlier.

3. A Starry Night.
(July year 1)

Meteorological Office: London Weather Forecast.
"The last few days have been gloriously hot and sunny. Temperatures reached the high twenties and we expect the same weather for next week. Tonight there will be clear skies, with a slight south-westerly breeze, making it feel slightly cooler. Minimum temperature will be around 17 degrees Centigrade, or 66 Fahrenheit. Sunset is at a quarter past nine and sunrise will be at five."

Rick had not felt in such a good mood for a very long time; this morning, after Paul had left for Paris to attend meetings, he had found a big package in the living room, with a note attached. *Have fun tonight. I love you, Paul.* Inside the carefully wrapped box was a telescope, which had taken him most of the day to set up; the accompanying manual was thicker than a telephone book, but he managed and soon the sun would set and then he would be looking at planets and stars. He was pleased Paul had left him this present, but he was also glad Paul had gone away for work: there would be no interruptions. Even the best loving relationships required *alone time* sometimes.

Since childhood, Rick had had an interest in the stars, watching every astronomy programme on television and spending many afternoons in the library looking at pictures of the universe in numerous books. As an adult his interest had been sparked again by all the information available on the internet, and he felt the same amazement and excitement again that he had so many years ago.

Rick had dug up his old charts of the constellations, and now all of them were spread out on the living room floor. His laptop displayed pages explaining where to look for planets, and his telescope stood ready on the terrace. All he had to do now was to wait for the sun to go down.

Rick was only 40 and already a cancer survivor. He had endured a nine month struggle of chemotherapy, radiation therapy and surgery to get rid of the damn disease. After a long recovery he had become depressed, and became addicted to the morphine intended for his physical pain, and to the anti-depressants for his mental pain. He had been unable to lose the nagging guilty feeling of having survived the cancer. The sick leave from his government post turned into leave of absence and Rick realised he would never return to his job. And he had found more reasons for feeling low: he had let Paul down, but also his best friends Isadora and Martin, whom he had known since university; all had offered their support, but he had rejected all help. Rick had tried to convince himself he was having a midlife crisis when he also started drinking, but he knew he had found just another excuse for his bad behaviour. Rick had taken a long time, but he had managed to beat his depression and drug addictions, and his drinking was down to a level where he would enjoy a few glasses, but not end up legless. Recently he started to feel focused and happier again. Astronomy would help him recover faster. *Thank you Paul*.

The sun had disappeared below the horizon. Rick poured himself a whisky and went out onto the terrace to his new telescope. The radio played classical music in the background and made him feel very content; he had not felt this way for a long time. He smiled as he took a sip of his whisky and looked around the dark sky. "A toast", he said. "A toast to all the stars in the sky. May we have a long and happy relationship." Rick thought of Paul, and he took out his mobile phone to call him, but realised Paul would be with his colleagues, so he messaged him instead, thanking him again for his present and wishing him a good night and good luck for tomorrow's meetings.

The evening sky looked dark enough and Rick decided he was ready to start. He looked into the telescope to gaze at the stars. "Hm, I can't see a thing." He frowned, still talking to himself. "It's all black. Let's move it around a bit." Wow! Rick couldn't believe his luck when he saw his first stars, all of them looked so sharp and bright. He scanned the sky and felt more amazed when the full moon came into view. The sight was breath-taking: the bright white light almost hurt his eyes. He loved seeing the details on the craters. Rick felt very excited: he wanted to see more. Everything!

"Okay, okay, okay, let's find Mars," he said, as he walked over to his laptop, with the displayed page to guide him through the sky. After several attempts, one toilet break and another whisky, Rick finally found Mars. Actually, Mars found him, and he couldn't believe how bright and red this beautiful globe was. "He-he, I am *such* a geek," he said out loud, sheer joy on his face and feeling as happy as a child who was running around in a sweet shop without adult supervision.

Rick decided to look for the big three summer constellations which should be easy to find in the July night sky. He had read on the internet that the key was to locate Ursa Major — also known as the Great Bear, or the Big Dipper. After a few clumsy shots he identified the seven stars. Next up was Ursa Minor: known as the Little Dipper, so he could find Draco and the North Star. Rick had difficulty finding Hercules, even though being one of the largest constellations; there were too many faint stars.

"All right then, no Hercules tonight. Next up is Ophiuchus. Let's see if I can catch that snake bearer." Rick adjusted his telescope: pointing at Antares; Ophiuchus would be situated north. Containing the second closest star to Earth, Ophiuchus could prove to be a most interesting constellation. Rick took another sip from his whisky, but noticed his glass was empty. "A refill my friend. And then some more star gazing."

***

Isadora Silva looked around her gallery. She loved being alone in the evening when there were no distractions; just her and beautiful paintings. She had organised an exhibition for a new up-and-coming artist, Conny. 20 great looking paintings were hung on the newly painted pristine white walls and Isadora was confident she would sell at least half of them on tomorrow's opening day; not often had she had this much interest in an exhibition. Isadora felt very proud of the work she had done in the last few weeks. And the preparations had been a good diversion after her separation.

From upstairs she heard her dog barking. "Sally," she said, "come down darling, don't wake up the kids, I'll take you for a walk." Isadora enjoyed walking her dog, around her neighbourhood in East London. Her street was quiet tonight, but tomorrow, with the flower market on, would be buzzing with the tradesmen selling their flowers and the many visiting tourists. She hoped her gallery would also be busy. Sally had run down the stairs, so Isadora could put the leash on.

"Come on then, let's go." She noticed the warm night, but a slight breeze stopped the air from getting sultry. She looked at the clear sky and saw the stars and the moon. Isadora thought of Rick and remembered how excited he had sounded when he had called her earlier to tell her about his telescope. She realised it was quite late, but she knew Rick well enough to figure out he would be up till dawn tonight; so she decided to send him a text message. *So mister. How's your new toy? You discovered any new stars yet? Will you have a star named after you and will you become my most famous friend? Sally woofs hello! X Isadora.*

She let Sally run free at the local park, so she would be tired later and wouldn't wake Isadora too early in the morning. Isadora's phone buzzed. *Having a fab time! No new discoveries made yet, LOL, but night still young. Wish you were here, it's beautiful! X Rick.*

Sally ran back to Isadora and sat at her feet: she was done running around. "Oh come on then, let's go home." Isadora said, putting the leash back around her neck. Noticing the time; she hurried home, wishing she was already in bed. Before she turned in herself, she checked up on her sleeping children.

***

No, no, no, this can't be. This isn't right, Rick thought, looking through his telescope at the Ophiuchus constellation. Tonight started off so well, but had he broken his telescope already? No, something else had to be wrong. *Let me double check.* He became so excited that he spoke out loud to himself. "Okay, don't fail me now internet." He looked at his laptop screen, comparing the image there with what he saw through his telescope and they did not match. "Oh buggery bollocks!"

***

Isadora woke up from her telephone ringing. *Oh God, who could this be?* She switched on her night light and looked at her phone: Rick. *Why on earth would he be calling now?* Reluctant, but worried, she picked up the phone. "Hey,

21

what's going on? You all right?"

"No, I'm not," Rick shouted through the phone. "No, yes I am, well, I don't really know. I think I found something. I'm not sure, but I think it's quite big."

"What do you mean?" Isadora asked him, properly waking up now. "Do you know what time it is? I was already asleep."

"Oh, yes, I see. Sorry about that. I tried Paul, but his phone's not on. I really need to tell someone. I'm excited and scared at the same time. I think I've discovered something. I think I saw something was missing in the sky. Well, it's hard to explain, but I was looking at this constellation and then I saw that this big star in it was missing."

Isadora sat up, wondering what Rick meant. He didn't make much sense to her, but obviously this was something very important to him, so she would let him talk more before interrupting.

"I — I, looked at this star, well at the place in the sky where it's supposed to be, but it's not there, the sky is black there. I compared it with pictures that were taken in that region, from different sources and it all checks out. There should be a star there. I'm quite baffled and don't know what to do."

"I don't know what it means to be honest, but maybe you've discovered something important. You should let others know of your discovery, have other people check it. Email all the people from your work, and Martin too," Isadora answered, wanting to go back to sleep. "Hey, let me and the kids come over to you tomorrow after I close the gallery. We'll fire up the barbecue and have a look through your telescope and you'll explain everything. And get some rest. I need some."

"Oh yes, I forgot, you have the opening tomorrow. Good luck. And for us, I'll get burgers and beers. Night-night."

Isadora had not seen Rick for a few weeks and she missed him. Tomorrow would be a good chance to catch up and for the kids to see their only English uncle again. Her youngest, Karen, had just turned 13 and would love to look at the stars: she was a science buff. And Thomas, her eldest, 17, who was born autistic, would hopefully be happy watching the sports on television. Isadora had taken a few years to realise that Thomas was *different*, and the problems he had caused had created a lot of stress in her marriage. Her husband had rejected Thomas for years and he kept on reminding her Thomas was not his child anyway. He did grow to love Thomas later and even ended up adopting him, but that had happened before their marriage had started to fail. She hoped Thomas would behave tomorrow, because he was very unpredictable: sort of a hit and miss, although he behaved himself most times when around Rick. She needed to stop worrying and go to sleep. She kissed Sally and switched off her light.

***

Cleaning his place had kept Rick busy all afternoon, not that the flat was dirty, but messy: dishes where everywhere, and all over the flat was clean laundry: ready to be ironed and folded. After he finished clearing up, he checked his emails. Last night, before going to bed, he had followed Isadora's advice and sent out an email. Already he received replies from former colleagues and astronomers: his email had been forwarded to many people. He realised he had become an on-line sensation when he read the dozens of messages sent to him. There was a real buzz on scientific boards. Other astronomers confirmed his findings and they speculated what could have happened. Many suggested Rick should send his findings to NASA and ESA for verification. He hurried writing the request to both space agencies, as Isadora and the kids would be arriving soon.

Today's weather was great: hot with a clear blue sky, and tonight would be the same, so he should have no problem showing them his discovery. Karen certainly would be interested. Rick was busy preparing the barbecue when his phone rang.

Paul's voice was on the other side. "Hey, how are you? Everything okay? I got your message after my meetings finished. I'm a bit pissed off that I had to work on a Sunday, but hey, I get to be in Paris. So tell me all about it."

"I'm great. I made a discovery last night. In the Ophiuchus constellation a star is missing."

"What do you mean?" Paul asked.

"Only blackness where a star's supposed to be. First I thought the telescope was broken, but the other stars were still there. All very strange. So I emailed people and, officially, I made a discovery."

"That's great. Make sure they put your name on it."

"I will, don't worry. So, your plans for the rest of the day?"

"Preparing for tomorrow's meetings, dinner with colleagues and then bed," Paul said.

"I have Isadora and the kids coming over. I'm preparing the barbecue now."

"Your evening will be better than mine. I'm spending it with boring bankers. Give my love to Isadora and the kids. And baby, I can't wait to see you tomorrow and your discovery. I love you."

Rick put the phone down and prepared the food for the evening. He would leave the cooking up to Thomas, who always wanted to be in charge of the barbecue, to keep him happy and busy whilst the others would be looking at the heavens and discussing Rick's discovery.

Rick checked his emails again, but there was no reply from either NASA or ESA yet. The boards on the internet were very busy though; people from various countries verified his findings and some of them posted before and after pictures, clearly showing the missing star. Identified as: Beta Ophiuchi, also known as Cebalrai. Rick wrote several thank you messages for all the compliments he had received. Around seven o'clock Isadora, Karen and Thomas arrived.

"Uncle Rick. You're famous," Karen yelled, as she walked in. She gave him a big hug. "I've been on the internet all day and everybody is talking about you."

"Well, you can help me set up the telescope, and when it gets dark you can see for yourself," Rick said, smiling. "Hey Thomas, you all right mate?"

"Yeah. We brought beer to celebrate. I'll put them in the fridge and open a few of them now," Thomas said, heading for the kitchen.

Isadora waited her turn to say hello. She knew not to compete with teenagers for attention. "So tell me all. I was a bit sleepy when you called."

"It's spinning right out of control. I'm all over the internet now. My 15 minutes of fame have started. But tell me first, how did the opening go? And — how are the kids coping with the separation?"

"The opening was a success, I'll tell you later. And Karen's fine, you know her, she's always happy as long as she has her books."

"And Thomas? He seems happy today. I was worried he wouldn't adjust."

"He's okay actually. Much better than I expected. No more dramas than the usual."

"I'm glad," Rick said. He and Isadora did not have to mention Thomas's autism and all the accompanying challenges: they had grown used to the episodes, and for them Thomas was just him, and they loved him the same.

When they got to the living room, Thomas was watching

the sports on the television with a beer in his hand and Karen sat in front of Rick's laptop.

"Thomas, you want to fire up the barbecue and cook the burgers?"

"Sure mate, but I want to see the football scores first," Thomas said.

"No worries, we've plenty of time, *mate*," Rick said. He smiled when he thought how Thomas used words like mate when he felt comfortable and happy. There should be no problems tonight.

Rick and Isadora sat down on the terrace and, over a beer, Rick explained what had happened.

Isadora was impressed. "I can't believe that on your first night you already made a discovery like that. You have any idea what this means? What do people say about this?"

"Well," Rick said, "they don't really understand it either. Some say for a star to disappear, it would've been a super nova, but others believe that would have been picked up by the whole astronomy world, as they are quite rare and this star is close enough to Earth to light up the sky when that happens. So basically people are baffled by this. I know I am."

"So what happens next?" Isadora asked.

"I'm not sure. I wrote to several space agencies to have it verified, but I haven't heard back from them yet. They have massively strong telescopes and can see things better than I can. Anyway, maybe I'll get a mention in *Scientist Monthly* and that'll be the end of my fame."

"What's that?"

"Oh, it's the leading science magazine. If you're mentioned in there, you've made it."

"Well, let's drink to that," Isadora laughed, and raised her bottle. "To Rick, getting a mention and a Nobel Prize too. And now, let's eat, I'm starving after my busy day."

Thomas started cooking the hamburgers on the barbecue,

whilst Karen and Rick were realigning the telescope.

Isadora sat in front of the laptop, reading up on Rick's discovery on various forums. "Hey Rick, there's some guy on the forum who claims to be from NASA. He wrote you should check your emails. Can I have a look?"

Rick was stunned and ran to Isadora. "Yeah sure, open it. NASA? Already? Cool. So, what does it say?"

"It starts pretty standard. They thank you for your email, blah, blah, blah, oh, here it is: *After receiving many more emails, including pictures of the region, we have decided to allocate resources to investigate your findings. As soon as we can verify your findings we will give you full credit for this discovery.* And then it goes on about legal stuff and also requests to various other people to investigate this too. It's a very long email. You'll need to read this yourself. But, hey, this is great!"

"Yes it sure is. It's going to be an exciting time. Let me give Paul a ring. He should have finished dinner by now. Karen, give me a minute and I'll help you again setting up the telescope."

"Uncle Rick, Mum, Karen," Thomas shouted. "Dinner's ready. Don't take too long."

After dinner Karen couldn't wait to have a look through the telescope. Rick showed Isadora and Karen pictures of what the constellation should look like, and pointed out the star that was missing. When Karen had all the information she needed to start, Rick let her try to find the stars herself. After a few minutes she told him she had the stars in her sight, but also that something was different again. "Uncle Rick, Mum, you should have a look at this. I think there's another star missing."

Rick stared into his telescope and couldn't believe what he was seeing. South-west from the first missing star: Beta Ophiuchi, another star was missing. He let Isadora look at the stars too and went to his laptop to figure out what name the star had. Isadora told him this one was called Gamma Ophiuchi.

Rick wondered what the meaning of all this was. He looked at the sky, which was now black, and with his naked eye he could see all the stars and the sky did not look any different from how it was supposed to look, but he knew something was wrong. He looked again at the constellation through his telescope. As he was looking at the bright sparkles, another star disappeared. This time he *saw* it happen. Black where white used to be. Black where white should be. He had no doubt now he was seeing something very peculiar and important happening. Rick felt alarmed and frightened. "Guys, another star has gone, that makes three."

5. Tensions in Downing Street. (August year 1)

NASA press release, August.
Subject: Anomaly discovered in Ophiuchus constellation.

"In July, British amateur astronomer Rick Favier discovered the star Beta Ophiuchi in the Ophiuchus constellation had gone missing. Upon receiving notification, NASA directed various telescopes towards the region and confirmed the findings. Within the next 24 hours the stars Gamma, and Mu Ophiuchi also disappeared from the constellation. Between Mr Favier's discovery and the issue of this August press release, NASA confirms that 12 more stars have gone missing from this area. NASA does not know the origin, nor the cause of this phenomenon and is actively investigating its possible causes. NASA is aware of rumours about extra-terrestrial activity in this area, but observations have so far failed to establish any exoplanets capable of containing life, nor evidence of any extra-terrestrial activity in this region. In addition, NASA does not answer theological questions."

"Rick, you getting ready or what? Martin just called, your car is almost here," Paul shouted down the stairs. "You've been in the bathroom for ages."

"I can't get this fucking tie tied and my hair looks shit. And my beard is too scruffy. I look like a mad scientist," shouted back Rick. "I need to cut my beard, can you tell him to wait?"

"Are you kidding me? No. You look fine. Just get on with it," Paul said.

Rick stared at himself in the mirror: dark rings around his eyes. He was very nervous and tired, all night he had kept waking up. He noticed his hands were shaking. *Okay, get a hold of yourself.* Martin would be here soon and he could not arrive late at his own press-conference. Journalists from all over the world would be there and about a dozen television stations would be broadcasting the event live.

Rick's discovery had set many things in motion: everything humankind thought they knew about the universe had been proved wrong and now action had to be taken. Martin Germain, as the Cabinet Secretary, had been appointed by Prime Minister Christopher Marchant to be in charge of the Ophiuchus Task Force, an inter-departmental and inter-governmental advisory and executive body, analysing data and preparing for any eventuality. Martin had decided they needed a sympathetic face and spokesperson, and that person was going to be his good friend: so he had sent Rick an invitation to give a statement and answer questions at today's press conference at 10 Downing Street.

One evening, a few weeks ago, Rick's doorbell had rung and Martin came in for a chat. They had known each other since university. Rick had studied physics and Martin politics. They had first met in a debating group, but because Martin was gay, and Rick was straight and dating Isadora, they had different interests and different lives, so they had only considered each other close acquaintances. After university they had lost contact, but ran into each other again when they both started working for the Government, Rick as a director of the Council for Science and Technology, and Martin as the Cabinet Secretary. By then Rick was gay too and they had been very good friends ever since.

During the chat, Martin had explained that the Government had suspended due process and he was, by virtue of emergency legislation, authorised to appoint any scientist or specialist, and he had appointed Rick. In fact: the British Government had declared a state of emergency, but Rick had to keep *that* information to himself. Rick's main job would be to keep the public informed with declassified information and keep the public happy and calm. That was, of course, if he would agree to do it. Rick initially protested: he was on sick-leave and did not feel ready to get back to being a professional, so how could Martin expect him to work for the Task Force? Martin insisted though: it still hurt him having seen Rick fighting cancer and subsequently falling into his depression. He felt Rick would be feeling much better after he started working again. Paul had agreed too.

The following weeks Martin had come round regularly, coaching Rick on what to say to journalists and how to behave in front of a camera. A week before the press-conference, Martin had handed him the statement and additional information, so Rick could prepare himself. Martin also made him sign the Official Secrets Act.

So, today was the first time Rick would be part of the Task Force and whether or not he would stay in all depended on his performance. The doorbell rang: Martin was waiting; no more procrastinating.

***

Whitehall was chaotic because of the mayhem the protesters caused, and outside 10 Downing Street the car almost could not drive through the crowd. A bewildered Rick looked out of the windows: hundreds of people had gathered on the road and many of them looked angry, waving their placards. Rick saw a scuffle between riot police, and what looked like men dressed as priests. The bizarre scene felt very surreal to him.

As the car was waiting for the main gate to open, a tall man with long blond hair banged with his big fists on the windscreen, he made Rick jump. The man walked around the car to the door next to Rick. He pounded the window. "You're scum. You're hiding the truth. You should all die. The truth will come out." Before Rick realised what was happening, the man had opened the door and was pulling him out. Rick felt a sudden pain in his left eye. The man had hit him. Rick could not understand why. The surprise attack left Rick paralysed for a moment. He looked at the man, his face was full of anger and his piercing blue eyes were open wide.

"I recognise you. You discovered God's sign, but you're hiding the truth, just like them," the man said, pointing at 10 Downing Street. "All of you should die."

Rick managed to punch the man in his stomach, before police officers grabbed the man by his hair and pulled him away. "Oh fuck, that was scary," said Rick, jumping back into the car.

"Are you okay?" Martin asked. "I can't believe we forgot to lock the doors. He sure was crazy, and fast. Blimey. Sorry I wasn't quick enough to help. I'll make sure he spends the night in a police cell."

"No problem. He caught us off-guard. He's weird. Did you see his eyes? Like an animal. And my eye is hurting. I'll probably have a black eye soon, and for the whole world to see. That's just great."

"Don't worry. We have make-up artists. I'll tell them to put an extra thick layer on your eye. Ah we're here. — Rick, we have a lot to do and we're on a tight schedule," Martin said as they stepped out of the car, into the courtyard. "We'll have to go through security first and straight to the press-conference. When we've done that, we'll drive up to Chequers, where you'll meet the Prime Minister, a few Presidents and the rest of the Task Force. Come on, let's do this."

***

Rick walked into a full and stuffy press room. Bright hot lights from the camera crews pointed at him. The prospect of facing the world and having to answer awkward questions made him feel nervous. And the *extra* information he had also received from Martin about the anomaly in Ophiuchus's constellation made him nauseous. He felt he was not supposed to have been given that information. Maybe not yet? Or at all? But it was there, in the documents. He couldn't figure out whether Martin had made a mistake, or had leaked the information. But Martin never made mistakes. Were they testing him? He would not betray his best friend though, but what if the press would see through him, and figure out he was hiding something? He felt awful.

Martin instructed Rick to sit in the middle of the table and to read out the press release written by Martin, and only answer questions when prompted by Martin. Martin began the conference. He introduced himself and the other scientists, made a brief statement and finally introduced Rick.

Rick's eye hurt and his cheeks felt hot. Everyone in the room went silent and looked at him. Panicked, he glanced at Martin, who smiled at him and gave him a quick wink: indicating everything would be fine.

"Good afternoon Ladies and Gentlemen. I am Rick Favier and the Prime Minister has asked me to give you information and the plan of action by our Government. As you all know by now, I was the first person to notice something had changed in the sky. Last month I observed the constellation Ophiuchus through my telescope, and I noticed a star had gone missing. I contacted various people in the Government and NASA to confirm my findings. The next evening another two stars had gone missing and my findings were confirmed by NASA. Between then and today, over a dozen stars ceased to be visible.

"We are aware of the rumours and conspiracy theories regarding this discovery. This is one of the reasons why we organised this press conference: to provide you with accurate information. Our Government has decided to work together with the American, Chinese and Russian Governments to explore what could have caused this anomaly.

"I can announce that in four hours from now a rocket will be launched from Russia. This rocket is different from any other ever launched. It carries no satellites, but the rocket itself is equipped with telescopes and devices to measure infrared, heat and radio activity. The rocket itself will be travelling at high speed towards the region and will be sending back pictures and readings.

"This is not a science fiction scenario: the rocket will not get there soon — actually it will never reach that region, as it is many light years away. Its only purpose is to give us more information.

"As I mentioned before; many rumours have been spread. They do not originate from us and we will not speculate, or theorise either. However, we can confirm this is not an act of God, nor is it the beginning of Armageddon. There is not a big alien ship coming our way. And no government on Earth has any type of weapon capable of extinguishing stars. This concludes our statement. Thank you very much."

Rick felt as if he had not been breathing for over an hour, speaking in public certainly was not his thing. He listened to the other scientists and the questions asked by the press. He was happy nobody seemed interested in him and he drifted off in his own mind, trying to calm down. All of a sudden he felt as if someone was trying to wake him up.

"Mr Favier, again I ask you. What do you think of the fact that the Pope said in his statement that this is a sign from God, in response to the sins of mankind?"

The reporter looked at him. Rick saw everyone in the room staring at him. Martin had only prepared him for scientific questions.

"I — I, well uhm, I don't know, I don't believe in a god, so I — I," Rick stammered.

Before he could continue Martin interrupted him. "Let me answer this. Mr Favier discovered the anomaly, a purely scientific discovery, that's all. Nobody *caused* this. God did not cause this. In fact, it is certain not any of the over 3,000 existing gods have any involvement. This press conference has ended and we will not answer any more questions. Thank you ladies and gentlemen. On your way out you will receive our briefing pack. Goodbye."

The room erupted with journalists shouting and people getting up, running out as fast as they could. Martin ushered Rick and the other speakers through a back door out of the building and into their cars.

***

The journey to Chequers would take them an hour. The increasing throbbing in his eye, the worrying new information in the documents, and the abrupt ending of the press conference had made Rick grumpy. Martin tried to lift his spirits by telling jokes and commenting on the classical music on the radio. He told Rick the press conference had gone better than he had expected and he didn't need to worry about not acknowledging God; the religious would be proved wrong very soon and that should shut them up once and for all. Martin was certain of that. Rick chose not to challenge Martin, or ask him about the leaked information: he did not want to start an argument. But, thanks to Martin, at the end of the journey, Rick did feel much happier.

Rick was welcomed by the aroma of freshly made coffee

when he entered the meeting room at Chequers. There were plenty of people inside, but Rick was not interested in talking to anyone: first he needed caffeine and something to eat. He caught sight of the table with the coffee and sandwiches and made his way, but someone grabbed him by the arm. When he turned to see who was holding him, he was stunned to find himself facing the President of the United States.

"Oh, hello Mr President."

"Ah Rick, you don't mind if I call you Rick? At these meetings you can call me by my first name. We all do around here. I'm William, or Bill for short."

"Yes, okay, thank you — Bill," Rick said.

"I want to thank you for the fantastic job you did explaining our next step and for not divulging any classified information. I know under pressure one can make big mistakes. I know I have. Anyway, I see you're on your way to the refreshments. Don't let me keep you, the meeting starts in a few minutes."

Rick smiled, but he was puzzled by the President's remark. Why had he mentioned the classified information? Rick needed to find out what was going on. He gestured Martin to join him for a coffee.

"Quite a bunch of powerful people here. Don't you think?" Rick asked.

"Yes, I'm happy we have them all together. It's really important we get all the cooperation we can. There's so much to do."

"The President is nice. He told me I could call him Bill. But he also told me something very interesting." Rick hoped to see a reaction, but Martin showed no emotion.

"What's that then?" Martin asked.

"How I kept my cool and didn't *divulge* classified information. How come the American President said that? What's going on Martin? Did you put those classified documents with my speech?"

Martin's face went pale. He looked at Rick and sighed.

"I'm sorry. It wasn't my idea. They wanted to test you. I objected, but without it, I wouldn't be allowed to hire you. And I wanted you here," Martin said.

"I'm glad I passed the test. But I've been worried sick over this press-conference. I really thought I would screw up. Don't ever do this to me again."

"I did it because of our friendship. Please don't be angry. Friends?"

"Sure. I'm a bit pissed off with you right now, but I'll get over it. I need to use the bathroom before the meeting starts."

"Rick — you did really well earlier. I'm proud of you." Martin's face pleaded for forgiveness.

"I'll see you in a moment," Rick said and walked off. He felt let down by Martin and needed a moment alone, to avoid starting an argument. And he needed to call Paul.

"Hey you, how are you?"

"I'm good. I saw you on television. You looked a bit stressed, but you read out the statement really well," Paul said.

"Thanks, the statement was easy to read. I practised a few times before the conference. I was terribly embarrassed by that guy that asked me that God question though," Rick said.

Paul agreed. "Yes, he was bang out of order. I'm not happy with this God label the gutter press tries to give to the anomaly. It makes people scared. Oh, and why do you have a black eye?"

"You noticed. Ugh, yes, my black eye, this guy punched me outside Downing Street, but I hit him back. He'll be spending the night in a police cell. I'm fine, don't worry. Listen. I don't have long, another meeting is about to start, and I can't let the others wait for me. But, I have something important to tell you and you must keep it to yourself. The documents they gave me. It had confidential information added, because they wanted to test me, see if I could be trusted. Anyway, about that information — my statement was a lie. There *is* an object and it *is* coming towards us."

Paul sighed. "Crap."

7. Bad news bears?
(September year 1)

Home Office and Ophiuchus Task Force joint press release.

The Soyuz rocket: the Serpent Bearer has transmitted useful data to Earth and scientists have been busy analysing it. After they were satisfied with their conclusions, they released the following information:

Since the discovery of the anomaly, over two dozen stars have gone missing in the constellation. It has now been confirmed that the anomaly is caused by an object. This object is between the stars and Earth: thus obscuring the stars. Observations so far have shown that the object appears to be a square and is thought to be around 50 by 50 kilometres, however the object might be cube shaped. Data received so far suggests no energy is emitted from the object; there is also no evidence of a propulsion system.

The origin of this object is not known, as no habitable planets inside the Circumstellar Habitable Zone, or Goldilocks Zone, in the constellation have yet been discovered. It is estimated that at the current speed the object could enter our Solar system in approximately 12,000 years.

The Soyuz rocket named Serpent Bearer was successfully launched from the Russian site in Kazakhstan last month. Mission control confirmed the rocket had left Earth's orbit and has set course towards the Ophiuchus constellation to investigate the anomaly, which two months ago was discovered by amateur astronomer Rick Favier, who was the first to report the missing star Beta Ophiuchi.

When more data is analysed, additional information will be released.

Simon Waltz reread the press release. The evidence was

right in front of him; he didn't need more proof, even the authorities knew, though they were trying to hide the true meaning. They had even sent the *Serpent Bearer* to greet that thing. *Oh, the irony.* Was he really the only one who could see that the Cube was sent by God, and the serpent was hiding in there? God was sending the Devil, who would descend on Earth and start Armageddon. He was certain of that. The blatant lies in this article annoyed him. He knew the object would arrive soon, in his lifetime even. He could feel its presence in the sky right now. They mentioned Rick Favier in the article and Simon's stomach turned. How he hated that guy. Yesterday, when he recognised him in the car, sitting there with that smug look on his face, he instinctively knew Rick was his enemy, part of the conspiracy, so he did what he had to do and had confronted him. Simon had spent the night in a police cell after the incident, and after he had been released he found out Rick had denied the existence of God at the press conference. *How dare he?* He wished for Rick to disappear from the surface of the Earth.

Reading the word Goldilocks made him think of his daughters and he felt sad for them: their lives would be cut short. But they would go to Heaven with him. He did not care about his wife though. Diane, lovely Diane, stupid and thick, but loyal to him, and even after he had been having an affair, she had forgiven him. For God's sake, the only thing she had ever done that meant anything was giving birth to his three beautiful, blonde, blue eyed daughters. Diane would also go to Heaven, like him, but he would make sure she would be right on the opposite side. She drove him crazy and eternity with her would be Hell for him. Divorcing her was out of the question of course, a very *un*-Christian thing to do, but God would make sure now he would not have to endure her for much longer.

Simon's phone rang. It was his good friend Aziz. "What's

up bro?" he asked.

"You must come to the community centre, my friend. I'm here with a few guys and we saw on the news what you did yesterday to that Rick guy. We liked it and we have a very interesting proposition for you," Aziz said.

***

A roaring applause welcomed Simon at the centre. A smiling Aziz waved at him, gesturing him to come to the front, but he could hardly move through the crowd; they all tried to shake his hand and touch him. Simon didn't understand why they acted like that. He noticed rabbis and imams were staring at him, and praying.

Aziz walked up to him and slapped him on the back. "Dude, you're a hero!"

"Why?"

"Because you spoke the truth yesterday. You confronted Rick and called for the truth. And when those police officers pulled you away grabbing your hair, that was just classic man. The video is already on the internet and it's gone viral, the people love you. They agree with what you said and they demand answers too. So we've come up with an idea you might like," Aziz said to him, gesturing him and the others to sit down. "Okay, we're getting organised. My imams at the mosque got together with several rabbis and priests and they decided to work together to get as many people back into believing in God again. We all believe in the same God and because the end of our days are approaching, we need to set aside our differences and save as many souls as possible."

Simon thought this was a very interesting idea, but wondered what Aziz was going to say next.

"Anyway," Aziz continued, "a rabbi came up with the perfect name for our group, the Children of Abraham. And we want you to become our spokesperson."

Simon was surprised. "Thank you, but what will that mean for me?"

"Well, you'll speak on behalf of us, do rallies, go to churches, mosques and synagogues. You'll do television interviews and stuff. So what do you say? Will you accept the position?"

Simon considered for a moment. His felt his career was going nowhere and it sounded like a good excuse to see less of his wife. Everyone stared at him, they were silent, waiting for him to answer. He stood up. "You know what? You made the right decision in choosing me. I will be perfect for the cause. Yes, I accept. I shall be your leader."

The crowd stood up again and cheered and applauded.

After the crowd had calmed down, Aziz led Simon to a small room, so they could talk in private. "Thank you for accepting Simon, but you'll be called our spokesperson," he said, "so, this is the plan. We'll start by making a website and we've arranged a television interview for you later today with the International News Agency, the INA. You're going to be busy. Now, let's go over what you're going to say at the interview. We wrote a statement earlier, we were going to put it as an ad in the newspapers, but now we have you, it will be much better live on the news. Here it is, read it and let me know what you think."

Simon read the piece of paper. The statement was badly worded and lacked any passion. Simon felt disappointed. "I'm not going to read this out loud, it's terrible," he said. "I will rewrite this, because there is no anger and no fear. I must appear more aggressive. If I'm going to unite the believers, I need to give them not only the carrot, but also the stick. Mussolini knew how to make a speech. He's one of my heroes. Leave this with me and tonight you'll be blown away. You just make sure I have that interview tonight."

***

Simon's appearance blew INA reporter Anne Goodman away. She had to be careful not to be taken in by his charming ways: Simon was charismatic, but very dangerous.

Before the broadcast her producer had taken her aside and had warned her about him.

"This man is very radical and has an explosive speech prepared. I need you to stay focused and hit him with hard questions. Stay professional."

The warning had disappeared from her mind, the instant Simon took a seat next to her. She wanted to hear him speak. She wanted to be with him. She wanted to drown in his deep blue eyes. She noticed she licked her lips and she felt a tingling between her legs. Under her desk, she manoeuvred her leg, so her knee touched his. Simon put his hand on her knee and gently squeezed, making the hairs on her neck stand up.

Simon gave an impressive speech. He told the audience how God was angry with those on Earth and would come to claim His souls and send the non-believers to Hell. He spoke into the camera, his smiling face full of confidence, as he delivered the good news for the faithful and the bad news for the rest. He gave a vivid account of what Armageddon was going to look and feel like, and he made that fateful day sound extremely scary. He urged believers of all faiths to sign up for his Children of Abraham movement and all non-believers to join him too, while there still was time, and despite what lies the authorities had told them, there was not much time left: a few months at most.

Anne did not say anything after he finished. She stared at him, mesmerised and excited. She was not afraid of the future anymore.

"We're live, you fucking stupid cow," her producer

43

screamed in her ear-piece. "Say something. Don't just fucking stare at him as if you've fallen in love with him. Confront this freaking lunatic. — Oh, forget it. Fuck you bitch, you're fired. Get off my set."

"Mr Simon Waltz, thank you for your speech. Everything is clear for me now. I believe you. You've taken away my fear and I'll follow your lead on our path to Heaven. Thank you so much." She wanted to add: *I want to sleep with you so bad.*

***

Simon smiled, he knew the Children of Abraham had made an explosive launch and it was his speech that had made it happen. In a few weeks he would re-launch himself from spokesperson to leader, but tonight he would fuck Anne.

The producer appeared on the set. "We've gone to commercials. I want the both of you the fuck out of here."

***

"I loved your speech. Please tell me how you can save me," Anne said, as she kicked off her shoes and sat down on her sofa. After the interview Simon had asked if they could have a drink together. She had agreed and directed the taxi straight to her home; she had noticed the sexual tension between them and did not want to waste any time.

"All you have to do is believe in God and He will look after you," Simon said.

Anne poured them a glass of wine. This was time for a celebration; okay, she had lost her job, but God would take care of her *and* she had Simon in her living room.

Before their glasses were empty Simon's hands were on her breasts. He looked eager and, judging by his bulging trousers: ready. She stood up and took his hands, ready to lead him into her bedroom. But first he made her undress herself. When she stood naked in front of him, she felt vulnerable. *Please be a nice guy and don't hurt me like the other men always do.* "Take me, here, now. I'm horny for you."

"Anne. Look at you, your skin is virgin white, you are pure. I really like you. You're a beautiful and strong woman and it's an honour to make love to you soon, but first I need you to do something for me."

She was confused. Did he not want to fuck her? Was he into perverted sex games? *Are you going to hurt me?* The thought alarmed her and her hands covered her breasts and vagina. Staring into his blue eyes, she heard herself say: "I'll do anything for you."

"I need you to use your influence as a presenter and journalist to make me look good to the world. And I need you to gather information on the Cube and on a few people for me. Will you promise to do whatever I ask you from now on?" Simon pushed her hand away and stroked her between her legs and played with her pubes.

"But I got fired today."

"I'll get you a new job, don't worry. I have connections."

"Thank you, and yes, I told you already, I'll do anything for you," she said, as she moved closer, ready to kiss him.

Simon smiled at her. "This was a great day and tonight will be even better. I love eating pussy and yours looks delicious."

God, that's big. There really must be a God, Simon is blessed, Anne thought, as she watched him lower his trousers.

11. Life's a beach.
(September year 1)

NetInfoSearch result for: Fermi Paradox.

The Fermi Paradox is the apparent contradiction between the high probability of many technologically advanced extraterrestrial civilisations populating the galaxy, and the lack of contact and observational evidence to support it.

In 1950 Enrico Fermi was having lunch with fellow scientists and the conversation turned to extraterrestrial life. They thought it was reasonable to assume life on Earth was not atypical and thus the universe and our galaxy should be teaming with life and many sophisticated societies should be populating the galaxy.

Fermi realised some of them might have spread out. A civilisation with modest rocket technology and a bold amount of drive could easily colonise the whole galaxy in ten million years. This sounds a long time, but compared to the age of the galaxy, which is ten thousand million years old, it is very short. However the lack of any evidence prompted Fermi to ask an obvious question: "Where is everybody?"

Since Fermi asked this question, many attempts have been made to find evidence of extraterrestrial civilisations. Several false alarms have been raised, the most famous being the discovery of Pulsars and Seyfert Galaxies. And the 1977 WOW! signal at the SETI project caused media attention due to its artificial nature, but the signal was never repeated. To date, natural explanations not involving intelligent life have been found for all such observations.

Gustavo Branco sat alone on a nearly deserted Ipanema beach. He had finished reading the morning newspaper and now he had only his thoughts to keep him occupied. The sun touched the horizon, the orange and pink colours in the sky were strong and crisp, but Gustavo did not notice them; he stared at the white sand in his hands, playing with the grains for minutes, deciding if he should stay a bit longer, but he felt tired: not only physically, but also emotionally, empty and lonely.

Before he had come to the beach; he had finished another night of playing tricks. He was sick of being a professional boyfriend. Why did rich American or European women not visit Rio de Janeiro any more? Nowadays the few rich people interested in him were fat and old American men. He didn't want to do gay for pay really, but men paid him a lot better than women did.

Gustavo felt life treated him unfairly. He had lost his job over a year ago, but he couldn't face telling his mother. Since she had been hit by a car five years ago, she had been unable to work. She needed him to bring home money and he tried his hardest to pay the rent for their home and pay for food and other bills. Gustavo was her only child and he had never even met his father. Sometimes he felt so ashamed of himself, he wanted to walk in the sea and let himself float away on the waves, but the thought of his mother all on her own kept him going. This morning he felt the same again, wanting to get away from his life. Last night had been very rough on him: his so called *boyfriend for the week* insisted on having sex with him.

"I've given you all these gifts, taxi money, taken you out for dinner, you owe me boy!"

Gustavo had taken the condoms out of his pocket, but the man had insisted on doing it without them.

"I'll give you two hundred dollars now and more after," he had said.

A reluctant Gustavo turned over and put his face in the pillow, so the man would not see his grimace. He hated this part of his job. The American was obese and not attractive at all, and turned out to be selfish during sex, but he had been very generous all week and Gustavo needed the money. The man had taken less than five minutes to reach his climax. Afterwards he had told him he had loved the sex with Gustavo and wanted it every night from now on. Paid for, of course.

Yes, Gustavo was feeling really low this morning. He needed a shower. He felt dirty, but he did have plenty of money to take home today. Next week he would do his usual sob story at the airport and as always he would get the address of the boyfriend, but more importantly, he would get more money. Quite often he would write letters asking them for more, and some of them would send him a few notes, once or twice maybe, but then he would never hear from them again. Being a professional boyfriend was hard work and he had to do the same routine again and again.

In the distance he heard laughing and Gustavo watched two girls running into the sea. He looked around him. The beach was quiet. He loved the time before the new hectic day started. Seeing the girls in the sea made him hope he would see *her* again today: the most beautiful girl in Brazil. Most mornings around six, she would stroll along the beach, her shoes off, the tips of the waves touching her feet, and he would see her jump and dance with the waves.

For the last few months he had watched her and smiled at her. She had light brown skin and the most amazing long wavy hair. She was always dressed in stunning short and tight dresses, made of fabric so thin, he could see her hips and her full breasts. She used to be unaware of the world around her, but recently she had noticed him and had smiled back.

He gazed down the beach, to the place where she always appeared, and after a few minutes, in the distance, he saw her. His mood lifted in an instant and he felt his heart beat faster as she walked closer to him. Finally, for the first time ever, he had the courage to wave at her as she walked past him. When she waved back, he got up and walked towards her, trying, but not succeeding, to look casual.

She stood with her bare feet in the water, smiling. Today, she wore a little red dress and had red shoes in her hand. *Oh God, she is so beautiful*. This was the first time he saw her eyes: they were light green, emphasised by her light brown skin and her dark wavy hair.

"Hi, I'm Gustavo, I'm so happy to finally say hello to you. I —" Too overwhelmed to speak more, his mind went blank and he felt his face turn red as he looked at her.

She smiled at him. "Hi, Gustavo, I'm Zaira. I'm glad you did. I've been wanting to talk to you for a while. I have a bit of time now. Do you want to go for a coffee?"

"Sure, I know this little beach bar on the boulevard. I hope you like."

***

The bar was buzzing: every morning office workers mingled with the party people who did not want to go home yet, giving the place a smart and fun ambiance. Zaira had never been here. This was the usual hangout for Gustavo: his second home and sanctuary, and he hoped she would love the bar as much as he did; giving him an indication if she could fit in his world. The coffee had never tasted this sweet: it had to be the company. Gustavo had fallen in love with her there and then. She probably had no idea how beautiful she was.

Zaira was chatty and funny. She told him she was a biochemistry student and worked as a cleaner in a hotel to fund her studies. She loved to walk the last part of her commute over the beach each morning, and yes, she had noticed him on many mornings.

Gustavo told her he liked to sit on the beach every morning when he finished his shift in the bar where he worked, and enjoy the peace and quiet before the tourists came back. He didn't want to lie to her and he did intend to look for a real job again, but he needed to save up a lot of money, so he could move his mother out of the slums, the favelas. Soon he would have enough and then he could lead an honest life.

Zaira told him she was having a great time chatting with him, but could not stay much longer. She was already late for work, although her boss wouldn't mind: he was her uncle. Not that she abused that perk, no, of course not: she was almost never late.

Gustavo could only smile as she tried to apologise.

"Can we meet again tonight? I would love to get to know you better," she said. "I can meet you here after work, at seven, and then we'll have time to chat before you start work."

"Yes. That would be lovely."

Both looked to see what was on the television when the bartender turned up the volume. Everyone had stopped talking. A report about the *Anomaly in the sky, hurtling towards Earth* played.

"I'm not too worried about it. I don't believe it's aliens coming for us, there must be a reasonable explanation. The media loves to sensationalise everything," she said.

Gustavo was impressed by her rational and calm behaviour. "Even if they were aliens, which I also doubt, they'll take thousands of years to get here. So we should be fine."

Gustavo panicked when he saw an obese, pale man waving at him. It was *him*, from last night, he had walked past the bar, noticed Gustavo and now he was making his way in towards him, still waving. Zaira was watching the television, unaware the man was approaching them.

Gustavo leapt off his chair. "Hang on for a moment. I have to talk to someone. I'll be right back." He gave her a smile and a wink. Zaira looked at him and at the waving man, she looked confused.

"Hello Gustavo." The man had wet patches under his arms and in his crotch.

If you weren't so fat, you might sweat a bit less, Gustavo thought. The disgusting sex he had to endure only a few hours ago, replayed in his mind. He had to look casual, otherwise Zaira might ask awkward questions: she seemed very clever. Gustavo forced a smile. "Hello, I didn't expect to see you up this early."

"I couldn't sleep. I felt fantastic after our lovemaking. It's good to see you. I want to meet you earlier tonight, not just for sex, but also for dinner beforehand. Pick me up at seven tonight." He reached for Gustavo's hand, but Gustavo pulled his away.

"Sorry, I have plans for the evening. I can still do midnight, as we agreed."

"No, you don't understand. I want you to come at seven."

"I can't. Midnight, and we can have dinner tomorrow."

The man looked unhappy and changed his tone. "Boy," he said, "if you do not show up at seven then we are finished. There are plenty of your kind around on the beach."

Gustavo shook his head and walked off. He didn't want to be around this disgusting man, he wanted to be with Zaira.

"Who was that? He looked angry," she asked when he sat down.

"A disgruntled customer," he said. Not that far from the truth.

"From the bar? Ah, don't worry. I have to deal with the same horrible Americans at my job."

Gustavo was relieved she did not need to know more. She liked him, he could feel that. He didn't want to mess this

52

up, he would treat her like a princess and be the perfect gentleman.

Zaira was ready to leave. "So I still see you here, tonight? At seven?" She leaned over and gave him a soft kiss on his cheek. The touch of her lips gave him goose bumps. Off she went, smiling.

Gustavo hurried home. On his way he stopped to buy two bunches of roses, one for Zaira, the other for his mother; she would be pleased with his news. Life felt great again to Gustavo, and he couldn't wait for tonight.

13. Life(long) Changes.
(September year 1)

Kim Sook sat at the dining table opposite her husband Jiang. They had married four months ago, and on this as on every evening since then, she had cooked dinner, but had made an extra effort this evening. She had to soften up Jiang before she could tell him her big news. For over a month she had felt sick every morning, including half an hour ago whilst chopping the vegetables, and that meant the one thing she expected it to be: she was pregnant.

But Kim knew her husband wanted to wait several years before having a baby. Life in Hong Kong was expensive; they had recently moved to their newly built apartment and they had little spare money every month. Jiang desperately needed his promotion. A baby could ruin all their plans and Kim realised that they might have to move in to her parents' house. No, Jiang would most probably be unhappy to say the least. They ate their dinner in silence, glancing out of their windows, with the busy skyline of Hong Kong as their only entertainment.

"Erm, honey, I have to tell you something," she said, looking straight at him. He kept eating, not looking at her. Was something bothering him? Did he suspect anything? She didn't know him well enough yet to understand his facial expressions. She could not make up her mind. A wave of anxiety went through her and made her shiver. Her dream of a happy life could be over even before it had really started, but they loved each other so much — he would forgive her, she hoped. She tried to keep another wave of nausea hidden from him.

"Jiang, honey, is everything all right?" Her husband looked at her. His eyes a silent stare.

Oh God, she could not take his silence anymore, she felt

she needed to scream. Her pregnancy had made her very emotional. Suddenly a big grin was facing her.

"What, what?" she asked in a loud voice.

"Baby, I have great news," Jiang said, as he got up from his chair and walked towards her. Kim stood up too and he held her in a gentle embrace. He stroked her hair, kissed her on her lips, on her cheeks and on her lips again. "I had my promotion today. I'm the new chief scientist at the research lab. I'm leading a team of scientists to look at the anomaly in the Ophiuchus constellation — it is called the People's Republic of China Ophiuchus Project. My salary will be good enough for us to have our baby."

Kim felt happy her husband was holding her; otherwise she might have fallen on the floor. Could today be better than the day they were married? Or the day she had met him? She remembered when she had seen him for the first time many months ago: this handsome young man walking towards her, their eyes locking. She remembered the moment vividly.

You are beautiful, he had said, *please be my wife.* Although she thought he was very forward, he did make her smile, so she told him she needed to get to know him first. From that day on, he would pick her up from work every day, with a flower for her, and walk her home, telling her about his poor and simple childhood in the small mountain village where he had grown up. After two weeks, she agreed to go on their first date, that night they had their first kiss, and one month later they were married.

"Jiang", she whispered, "I have something to tell you too."

Her husband looked deep into her eyes and kissed her again. "You're going to make me the happiest man alive right now, aren't you?"

Kim cried, but her tears were from happiness now. "Yes, Jiang, you will be. We are — we're pregnant."

56

***

Jiang walked around his office; he had only been head of the Ophiuchus Project for a few days, but he already felt at home, as if he had never worked anywhere else. The team of scientists assigned to him were the smartest in the country. Being a member of the Communist Party had finally paid off: all his requests for resources had been approved by the Central Committee. He had come a long way from his small village, Nyalam Town in Xizang. When he was growing up there, his childhood place still had the old name of Tsongdu in the Tibetan language, but he was not allowed to use that name any more. His family had been resettled there by the Party soon after he was born. As an adolescent, all he wanted was to get away from there: he had always resented the fact that the Party had made him grow up in a backwater. But the Party had never forgotten the sacrifice he and his family had made for the country. Now, they were repaying their debt to him.

The scientists were busy analysing the data they had received from the Russians and sent Jiang regular updates. The reports worried Jiang, and he was unhappy with the fact that he was not allowed to share the real conclusions with anyone, not even with his wife. But in a way that was good: Kim had more important things on her mind right now. She should not be stressed, as that would be bad for their baby. For now he kept her occupied with the redecoration of their new, bigger apartment and all the baby stuff.

Jiang sat at his desk, ready to write his daily report to the Committee, but first he needed to answer the deluge of daily emails. When he checked his in-box he noticed one strange email, originating from India. *I have important information for you from the Indian Government regarding*

Ophiuchus. Do not email me back, but delete this email. I urgently need to meet with you in person. Tonight at 8pm I will be standing at the exit of Chai Wan Station of the Island line. I will find you. Pranit. PS: If you love your country, you must show up.

Jiang reread the email a few times and wondered what he should do. He was under strict instructions never to talk to foreigners; he and his wife could be jailed if he broke the rules. But it was his job to gather as much information as possible about the Cube. And this email fed his suspicions about the amount of information the Russians were giving them. He deleted the email and decided he had to go: for the benefit of his country.

***

Jiang rubbed his sweaty palms on his trousers as the train slowed down and entered the station. The driver announced they had reached the end of the line.

The end of the line for me too, if this is a trap by the Committee, he thought to himself. Feeling nervous, he looked around. He had no idea what a secret agent would look like, but he did not see anyone suspicious in the carriage. He felt reluctant to get off the train, but he could not go back now, so he got up and walked to the exit of the station; the clock read 7.45pm. He had arrived early and felt annoyed he had to wait.

Pranit. An Indian. I should easily recognise him if he is really here. He looked around. Everyone appeared Chinese to him. This area had seen better days; buildings looked worn and many needed a lick of paint. Litter and old newspapers were strewn around in corners. Stray dogs were scared off by the commuters who were running along the street trying to catch their buses. Street traders were selling food. The strong smell of pork and fried garlic made him hungry. Jiang decided to buy noodles from the vendor outside the station: it was where the good smell came from. "May I have one portion please?" he asked the vendor.

"Of course you can, Jiang," the vendor said looking at him, a slight smile on his face.

The hairs on the back of Jiang's neck stood up. "How do you know my name? Are you here to arrest me?"

"Relax," the man said. "It's me, Pranit. I'm the one who contacted you."

"You don't look Indian. How can I trust you?"

"I am very much Indian. And — can we trust each other? That is the true question. For now, you have no other option but to trust me. Let's go somewhere less public," Pranit said.

"Good point, but what about the stall? And how did you know I was going to buy food here?" Fear had changed to confusion.

"Don't you worry about any of that. Let's walk, I have a place nearby. By the way, the noodles are on the house."

Jiang did not know what to think. Should he fear for his life? If they wanted to kill him they would have done that by now. If the Committee was setting him up, he would certainly find out at the end of their walk: he was not looking forward to stepping into a building with this stranger.

The building turned out to be an abandoned restaurant, overlooking Junk Bay.

Pranit led Jiang in and gestured towards a table with chairs, and a single laptop. "Let me start, we don't have much time," Pranit said. "Last week we received information from our contact in Lahore that the Pakistanis are expecting an alien attack on Earth. They want to pre-empt this by attacking the Cube before it enters Earth's orbit. Our contact informed us the Pakistani Government will approach our Government soon with a proposal for co-operation, but our agents have already obtained the documents. The Pakistani Government feels the Russians are not providing them with all data and therefore want to work with us, not only to convince us they are not attacking us, but to have more firepower with our combined nuclear arsenals."

"That's terrible. So they assume there are aliens on their way to attack us?" Jiang asked.

"Yes, they do. We keep an open mind, but our Government wants to be prepared for all possible scenarios."

"But, what is it you want from me? I'm not willing to betray my country, so don't ask me to spy for you," Jiang said. He believed he had become an actor in a spy movie, convinced that any moment men in black suits would crash through the windows and arrest him. He had lost his appetite and the smell of the garlic and noodles made him feel sick. Kim would be worried; he had forgotten to call her, telling her he would be working late tonight.

"I'm not asking you to spy for us, please listen to me," Pranit said. "We have a plan. You must convince your Committee that you have come up with a contingency plan, in case of an imminent alien attack, using China's nuclear arsenal to attack and neutralise the Cube. You must also convince them the idea is yours and then you should make them contact our Government for co-operation. We will pretend we are grateful for the Chinese offer and work with you on the plan. We'll then tell your Government we contacted the Pakistanis and have secured their co-operation too. Our combined nuclear arsenal will have over 400 warheads."

"And there really is no spying for me to do?" Jiang asked.

"Nothing. I promise you. Life on Earth might end and we have no time for petty games. Look, I have all the documents ready, outlining the attack plan. All technical data is here for you. You can rewrite this and present it to your Government as your plan."

"Why me though?" Jiang needed to know.

"They trust you. You're a communist, that's why."

Pranit's remark sounded like an insult to Jiang and he was immediately annoyed with him. He stood up, ready to leave. "Hand me those papers. I'll help you with your plan. Yes, I *am* a communist and I'll do anything for my country. I'm going home now, to my wife."

"I'll contact you soon," Pranit shouted as Jiang hurried out of the building.

***

Where have you been? Do you know what time it is? I've been worrying all evening, was what Jiang heard from his wife as soon as he walked through the door.

"People are searching for you. Jiang, I was so worried," Kim said, hugging him.

Jiang was confused and alarmed: "What do you mean? People are searching for me? Who? And why?"

"When you didn't come home for dinner, I waited and when it got very late I phoned your office. When the security people said you had left hours ago and I told them you weren't home yet, they started a search for you," she said, tears running down her cheeks. "Oh baby, I was so worried. I'm so sorry; I hope you won't be in trouble. But I'm so hormonal now and I panicked."

"Oh crap, this is not good. This is really, really bad Kim."

"What's going on? What did you do? Are you in trouble?" Kim asked, her voice trembling.

"I met this man from India, I don't know, I think he's a spy or something. He gave me information. They have plans for the Ophiuchus Cube. They want to work with us and asked me to make it happen."

"Are you a spy?"

"No!" Jiang answered. How could his wife even think that of him? "I'm not. But because the Committee now knows I was missing, I need to think of something to cover myself."

"Tell them the truth, it's the only way. You know they always find everything out," Kim said.

"I think you are right. You are very wise, my wife." Jiang hugged her: "I'll do that first thing tomorrow. Let me call them and tell them I'm safe at home. And — is my dinner still waiting? I'm famished."

***

The following morning they made him wait in a tiny, badly lit room with dirty green walls. Two uncomfortable, wobbly chairs and a desk with coffee stains were the only items in there. They had taken everything from him: his laptop, phone and watch, even his shoe laces and belt. Every emotion went through his head, but mostly panic. After what felt like, and probably was, four hours, a man walked into the room. Jiang looked at him. The man was around 50 years old, overweight and had a greasy comb-over that could not hide his bald patch. Jiang noticed two yellow stained fingers, evidence of decades of smoking. The man wore a cheap grey suit, clearly two sizes too small. And when he opened his mouth, Jiang found out the man was certainly a fan of garlic: the smell was overwhelming.

"Mr Jiang Sook. I am agent Tuan. We are very pleased you came to us with the plan. I had a look at it and I am impressed. So here is what happens next. You will be dealing with me from now on. You will do what the Indian asked you and at the end of that process we will go ahead as they expect from us and contact them. It is very important for you to act normally and do not mess this up.

The Committee will be monitoring your every step and provide you with assistance when necessary."

Jiang felt relieved. He had phoned the Committee office that morning and told an agent what had happened to him the night before. The agent had been very pleasant and asked him to come to the office, but when they processed him and made him wait for such a long time he had expected to be treated as a traitor during the interview.

"I have developed a schedule for you with instructions. You will give your scientists their tasks and in one month you will have a full report and proposal ready for us," agent Tuan continued. "After that we shall take over from you. There is a car outside to take you to your office. The People's Republic of China thanks you for your patriotism."

17. That left a bad taste in my mouth. (October year 1)

NetInfoSearch result for: Children of Abraham [chil-druhn] [uhv, ov; unstressed uh   v or,   especially   before consonants, uh] [ey-bruh-ham, huhm]. Is a description for an organised group of religious people who believe the end of all life on Earth is imminent. After the discovery of the object (the Cube) in the constellation of Ophiuchus, leaders of the three Abrahamic religions (Judaism, Islam and Christianity) came together and formed this new religion.

Their beliefs are mainly based on the scripts of the Old Testament, except for the Book of Revelations: predicting the Apocalypse, which is found in the New Testament.

The Children of Abraham refer to the coming event with the Hebrew word Armageddon.

Their claims of Armageddon are considered highly ambiguous; they do not mention the correct Biblical terms, but claim God is sending Satan in an object (the Ophiuchus Cube) from Heaven to destroy the world. All the non-believers and sinners shall be sent to Hell and all believers shall go to Heaven.

The Children of Abraham are highly controversial, from various Islamic countries come reports of forced conversions. Attacks on Churches and Mosques are daily occurrences in Europe, the Americas and the Middle East, and are claimed by followers of the religion.

Their appointed spiritual leader is Simon Waltz from London, UK. Simon has been very successful in converting people to this new religion: an estimated 500 million followers worldwide. Simon Waltz is married with three daughters.

The Children of Abraham blame the Sinful societies of the world, the worst offenders being: The United States of

America, Great Britain, Israel, Saudi Arabia, India and China. In these countries the Children of Abraham are most actively recruiting.

Only one person is named as the agitator for the coming Armageddon: Rick Favier, an amateur astronomer from the UK, who discovered the object, but would not acknowledge the object was sent by God, or the existence of God. Since then he has often been referred to, by Simon Waltz, as the Anti-Christ.

Paul and Rick did not have to look at the menu when the waiter came to their table to take their order: they knew what they were going to eat. This restaurant had been their favourite for years; Paul had even proposed to Rick here. The lamb dish was *to die for*, so they always ordered that, together with a bottle of red wine. And tonight was no exception.

The Children of Abraham had found a hate figure in Rick and they had spread rumours about him on the internet and during interviews, resulting in a constant barrage of hate mail and threats on the streets. As a result Rick seemed close to becoming depressed again, so, to cheer him up, Paul had decided to take Rick out for dinner and then the theatre. Paul noticed Rick was not enjoying himself and looked on edge, constantly fiddling with the cutlery and his napkin.

"The show has really good reviews. It was very hard to get tickets. I'm looking forward to seeing it," Paul said as cheerfully as he could.

Rick shrugged. "I'm keen to see the show too, even though I don't know which one, you've been so secretive. When the food arrives, I'll feel better, I promise. There's nothing like a bit of comfort food."

The waiter came and two big plates with food arrived. The lamb looked as delicious as always.

Paul tucked in, but as soon as he had his first bite, he spat it out. "Fuck, what the Hell?" he shouted, anger making his voice tremble.

"What's wrong?" Rick asked.

"This tastes foul. Are they trying to poison us or something? I've never tasted anything this bad."

"I'll try some from my plate," Rick said, as he took a bite. "Crap, this is bad too. Paul, spit it out and wash your mouth. This food is poisoned." Rick spat out his food.

"Waiter. Here. Now," an annoyed Paul shouted across the room. When the waiter arrived, Paul told him to try the lamb.

"I'm so sorry Sir," the waiter said after he tasted a piece himself. "I've no idea what happened. I'll inform the manager now. Please accept my apologies." The waiter ran off towards the kitchen and disappeared. A few minutes later he returned together with the manager. Both of them looked angry.

Giovanni, the manager they had known for years, seated himself at their table. "I'm terribly sorry, you've been great customers for so long and now this happens." He leaned forward, his voice a whisper now. "I've spoken to my chef and am very disturbed by what he said. He saw you come in and decided to cook you the food you deserve for being the Anti-Christ. He made your meal taste as it would in Hell."

"Oh for fuck's sake" Rick exclaimed. "What the hell is up with these people? I haven't done anything wrong."

"Sir, I'm on your side," Giovanni said. "I made him explain himself and he told me he's a Child of Abraham. I never knew. I fired him and literally kicked him out of the building. He'll never work here again. I've no time for these animals who force their religion upon us. I'd like to offer you another dish, on the house of course."

"Uhm, thank you, but I think I've lost my appetite," Rick said. "I want to go. Paul? You coming?"

Paul nodded and both of them got up.

"Of course I won't charge you for this meal. Please come back again soon and I'll make sure you'll have our best dishes, on the house of course," Giovanni said as Paul and Rick hurried out of the restaurant.

"Well that was a bit of a disaster" Paul said. "You fancy a burger instead?"

"Yes, I'm still hungry, but you'll have to order it at the counter and I'm staying outside, in case another crazy one decides to spit in the burger sauce." Rick felt more relaxed, now they were on the street, surrounded by people.

After Paul returned, they walked to the theatre. Ketchup and meat juices dripped on Rick's hands each time he took a bite. He licked his salty fingers when he finished eating: nothing was more satisfying than a good burger.

***

They had amazing theatre seats: second row and in the middle. They sat so close to the stage they would be able to see the sweat on the actors' faces. Rick felt excited: he loved the theatre.

The lights dimmed and the show exploded on the stage. When the main character came on, Rick shrieked. "Ha ha ha, there's Nikki."

"Yes, that's why I got these good seats. She arranged these for us. I did think you would cheat and peek when we walked in. I'm glad you didn't," Paul whispered, he had a big grin on his face.

Nicole Hamilton was a dear friend and they tried to see her in every show she starred in, and this role was her best yet. Rick was sure he saw her wink at him when she looked in their direction. All was good again.

"After the show, Nicole and the cast are going for drinks and she's invited us. We're lording it up tonight," Paul said.

During the interval Rick and Paul went to the lobby for refreshments. They stood in the slow moving queue when Rick felt a hard tap on his shoulder. When he looked to see who was trying to get his attention, he was perplexed. Simon Waltz stood right there, his angry blue eyes staring at Rick. Only that one time in Whitehall had they actually met, and seeing Simon's face so close was a total shock for Rick. Here in front of him was the reason why he was hated by millions of people. "What the hell are you doing here? Are you following me? Trying to harass and intimidate me?" Rick asked, trying to control his trembling voice and conceal his fear.

"You should not be here. You should be in Hell. Get out and rot, you Anti-Christ!" Simon shouted, repeatedly poking Rick in the chest.

That was the last straw for Rick; he had endured months of hate and abuse and now *he* was here in front of him: touching him and shouting. Hate, anger and frustration overwhelmed Rick and he lashed out at Simon, landing his left fist in his face. The force of the blow made Simon fall backwards on to the floor. "Don't you ever come near me again and touch me. You hear?"

Simon licked the blood off his lips and spat in Rick's face. "I'll get you for this. Mark my words. You Anti-Christ."

Three ushers grabbed Simon, kicking and screaming, and dragged him away from Rick towards the exit, and threw him out. A woman with three small girls ran after them; she looked at Rick, mouthing *sorry* before she left.

"My apologies," a man said, when walking up to Rick. "I'm the manager here. I'm very sorry about what just happened. Nicole told me you were in and I was on my way to say hello and saw the whole thing, but your fight was over before I could help you. Luckily our ushers were close. I'm sure he didn't expect a left hander to hit him that hard. Well done." He smiled. "Let me get you guys a drink. And I have a message from Nicole to meet her and the cast backstage after the show."

"Thank you, it's been a very exciting evening, but not entirely in a good way. We could certainly use a glass of red wine," Rick said.

After the show finished, Rick and Paul met Nicole.

"Rick, sweetie darling," she said in her mocking posh lady voice, "I heard you out-staged me tonight. Apparently you have a fierce left hook. How are you my darling?" They hugged. She air-kissed them; she was always pleased to see them.

"Ha ha, you could say that." Rick smiled. "He had it coming. And he got kicked out too. I'm relieved, but ouch! My knuckles are hurting."

"Let me take my make-up off and then we'll find you some medicinal alcohol to soothe the pain," Nicole said.

***

The streets were busy, as always, after the theatres in the West End had finished their shows. The evening was exceptionally warm for mid-October and the pavements were filled with happy people drinking, smoking and laughing. Rick loved these evenings and had been one of the reasons why they had moved to the centre of London. He looked at the group of actors that were in his group, about 15 of them. They were all so young and seemed so alive, and not at all concerned by that thing lurking in the sky. A short walk took them to the pub where most of the West End theatre actors hung out. The place was too crowded and stuffy inside, and after they had ordered their drinks they decided to stand outside. They were all having a good time and made fun of Rick, nicknaming him Boxer Boy.

Nicole started singing a song from her show, making passers-by stop to hear her; she loved the attention. Rick thought there was something unusual about the crowd though: behind the smiling people he saw several angry faces of men who were clearly not enjoying her singing. That was when he heard a soft chanting from the back. *Anti-Christ, Anti-Christ, you're the Anti-Christ.* It grew louder and Nicole stopped singing, an alarmed look on her face. Paul pulled Rick close to him.

"Let's go inside," one of the actors said, but it was already too late. A group of men stormed through the crowd and started attacking them.

Get those faggot bastards and get the Anti-Christ, Rick heard before a fist hit his chin. *Fuck, that hurt,* he thought. The guy who hit him raised his fist, ready to strike a blow again, but Paul kicked him in his stomach, making him double up and fall to the ground. Rick turned to see a screaming Nicole: she was being swung around by a man whose arm she was biting. The whole street descended into mayhem, with the Children of Abraham fighting a group of actors. Rick took in the spectacle. Most of the fighting actors still had stage make-up on their faces, and he suddenly thought they must look really funny to bystanders. Probably nerves were getting the best of him. Sirens started to come from all directions: the police had arrived. *That was quick*, Rick thought, giggling to himself.

Dozens of uniformed men appeared and started pulling the fighters away from one another.

Rick managed to punch one more man, before he was held down himself.

Let him go, Rick heard, lying face down on the pavement, he tasted blood in his mouth. *This is Rick Favier you are holding down, officer. Please help him up.* Rick recognised the voice.

"Are you okay? We got here as soon as we could," Martin said.

"Thanks, but how did you know? And you're very quick

indeed," Rick said, massaging his aching chin.

"I never told you, but we have agents following you for your protection. I decided that after the press-conference. So if you've felt paranoid lately, now you know you weren't going insane. You *are* being followed. And, after your fight with Simon earlier, we kept a few police cars close by, for just in case. But by the looks of it, you guys were doing a pretty good job defending yourselves," Martin said.

"Am I glad you did that. My hands ache, my chin is hurting, I think I'm going to have a black eye again and I can taste blood."

Martin smiled at him. "Let's buy you and your friends some alcohol whilst we take your statements and get the paramedics to look at you all. Those other guys will be arrested and taken to the police station."

"What would we do without you?" Rick said, hugging Martin.

"Stay out of trouble. Because I'm going on holiday for a week next month. I need some well deserved rest. I have a feeling I'll be extremely busy soon."

"You are? You deserve it. Where to?" Rick asked.

"Not sure yet, somewhere with a beach and where they don't know me, and it must be hot and sunny."

"Oh, I know. Isadora has family, a sister, in Rio de Janeiro. I could get you in contact with her. She can show you around. Rio is great, we've been there often, and with a guide you'll be safe and see a lot of interesting things," Rick said. He wanted to do Martin a favour: give something back.

"Yes, Rio sounds good. Will you contact her for me?" Martin asked.

"I will, you book your tickets and I'll sort things out with her. You'll have a good time there."

19. Your country needs you.
(October year 1)

Jiang sat in front of his computer, sipping a steaming cup of tea. He had examined several reports submitted to him by his scientists. More than a month ago he had been contacted by the Indian spy Pranit. Jiang had a lot of information to process, as many scientists had taken their tasks much more seriously than he had requested; they felt very strongly about attacking and destroying the Cube. Twice he had to give them new and better instructions, after more detailed information had been sent to him by the Russians.

The Cube appeared to grow quicker the closer it came to Earth: each side was now estimated to be over 100 by 100 kilometres and was approaching much faster than anyone had anticipated. He continued adjusting the 50 page proposal. He did not want to make the paper too technical; he knew the decision had already been made for the Republic to contact the other two countries. Still, he had to finish: the proposal had to be handed to the Indian and Pakistani Governments, and needed to look realistic.

Pranit had left him an email twice, asking him about the progress. As Jiang's minder, Agent Tuan, had been very pleased that the Indians stayed in contact and he had instructed Jiang to let Pranit know the scientists had made very good progress on calculations for the attack. They were close to finding a workable and successful solution.

The calculations made Jiang realise that they would be needing most of the combined arsenal of the three countries, and he had made sure his conclusions appeared very prominently in his proposal. He added his calculations, explaining the fire power required, and the ideal distance between the Cube and Earth for the attack. Jiang included estimates of the time the engineers would take to convert the missiles suitable for a flight into space. He felt proud of his proposal and confident the attack could work.

Jiang reminded himself to call his wife and tell her he would be working late again. "Hello baby, how are you today?"

"I'm good. You're calling, so I'm guessing you have to work late again," Kim said.

"Yes I do." Jiang sighed into the receiver. "I have to finish the proposal tonight. Agent Tuan is coming round tomorrow afternoon and I'll have to present it to him. I can't tell you more than that honey, you know that."

"I do, but I don't feel connected to you any more. You're home late every night and we can't talk about anything. I sit here at home all day, bored. I don't like watching the news. It is all about the Cube and it depresses me. And I'm worried for our baby."

"Listen, you're having a hard time because you're pregnant. I am doing this for our future. Only tonight and tomorrow will I come home late and then we'll have more time together. I promise you."

"Come home soon please," Kim pleaded, "I'm so lonely."

"I'll hurry. I love you," Jiang said. After he hung up the phone he tried to finish as fast as he could. On his way home, he bought her favourite flowers.

***

When Jiang stepped into his office the following morning, he was surprised and annoyed to see Tuan sitting at his desk: typing on *his* computer. He noticed his cabinets had been opened and paperwork had been spread out on his desk. His office was a real mess.

"Good morning, Mr Sook," Tuan said, not even looking away from Jiang's computer screen. "I decided to come in early today, because we are submitting your proposal to the Indians."

"I know. I finished it last night. I made a file for you, it was on the desk. You could've read that."

"I have. It's very good. But I had to make several adjustments and redact information. I don't want to give the Pakistanis and Indians anything sensitive. I also reduced the number of our nuclear weapons by 100, so they are under the impression we have 250 available. I believe we'll still have more than enough firepower to blow up the Cube. — Oh, and fetch me a cup of tea," Agent Tuan said.

He still had not once looked at Jiang, who could not believe how rude and obnoxious this man was. Having had to deal with him for the last month had been frustrating and upsetting. Jiang hurried out of his office to get that tea. He knew he would be better off being away from this monster and let off some steam, otherwise he could end up strangling Tuan. When Jiang returned, he was alarmed by the sound coming from his office: Tuan was shredding documents. "What the Hell are you doing?" he screamed.

"Don't worry, these are only the documents that relate to the proposal. I also deleted the files from your computer. And to be safe, I also wiped your hard drive."

"You what? You stupid, stupid man. My research is on there. I could fucking kill you." Jiang shook with anger. He wanted to throw the cup with hot tea in the man's face.

"Be careful what you say. I can still have you arrested. The contact you had with that Indian spy is considered treason. Don't you forget about *that* my dear friend."

Jiang felt shocked. After all he had done for the Party and his country, he realised they would always use this as leverage over him: he was at the mercy of a very cruel man. "I'm sorry, I'm loyal to our nation. I would never jeopardise our future."

"Now, listen closely," Tuan said, whilst shredding more

documents. "I've emailed Agent Pranit and arranged a meeting at eight tonight at that restaurant again. I wrote in your name, so *you* told him you're bringing me along."

When Tuan had finished shredding, he ignored Jiang when he put on his coat and walked out of the office. Before he left, he turned to Jiang. "You'd better get to work. A car will pick you up at 7 tonight. Call your wife and tell her you'll be home late. You know how emotional she gets."

Jiang saw Tuan smile for the first time since they had met. He found it bizarre Tuan thought an emotional woman was funny.

"Thank you for the tea," Tuan shouted from the corridor.

Jiang looked at the cup; Tuan had not even touched his tea. As soon as Tuan was out of sight, Jiang threw the cup down the corridor. He felt much better for it.

***

The car pulled up in the forecourt of the restaurant. The building was dark and old rags blacked out the windows. Above the entrance a broken neon sign swayed, producing a grating noise. Jiang did not remember that the place looked this bad last time he had been here, but then he had been very scared and had not paid much attention.

"That's just so typical of the Indians. They managed to rent the most dilapidated building in Hong Kong, it's so cheap and tacky, just like them and their smelly food," Tuan said.

Jiang shook his head in disbelief, *what a racist.*

As they walked towards the door, Pranit appeared and smiled at them. Jiang suspected they were being monitored, but he did not see any cameras.

"Welcome Jiang. And Agent Tuan, I'm very pleased to meet you," Pranit said.

Tuan ignored him and pushed Jiang through the door. Inside, in what used to be the dining room, a man, who Jiang had never seen before, sat at the only table. He seemed busy looking at the screen of his laptop; the glare was one of the few light sources in the room and made his face look pale and blue. Pranit introduced the man as Agent Syed from Pakistan.

After they sat down Agent Tuan took the documents out of his briefcase and handed both men a copy. "Gentlemen, here is our proposal. Read it and present it to your Governments. All future meetings shall take place in China. We decided that to be best, considering the history of hostilities between your countries. Our proposal is final and non-negotiable. I included my contact details and from now I expect to be contacted by your Government officials only. And Agent Pranit, do not seek contact with Jiang. We will incarcerate him if he goes behind our backs again."

Jiang felt a chill go through his spine and he wanted to be anywhere but here. Tuan's tone was aggressive, and the two other men did not seem happy with him either.

Tuan stood up, ready to leave and gestured Jiang to follow him. "It's a real pleasure working with you to save our planet, the People of China will be forever grateful to you. Oh, and if I ever see either of you set foot in this country again, I will have you arrested and executed for spying. Good night gentlemen."

Jiang could not wait to be back home and to see his wife. He was exhausted and needed a good night's sleep. He never spoke to, or looked at Tuan during the long journey home.

**

The sound of breaking glass woke Jiang. Darkness. Noises in the distance. Boots, were they boots he could hear in the corridor? He pulled the sheets over his face, too afraid to look when he thought he heard his bedroom door open. Kim was sleeping; he heard her soft breathing. He had to find out who had entered his room, but he did not want to wake and alarm his wife. The noises had stopped. Should he try a quick peek perhaps? He did, and the faint light on his clock said 04.55. A flash of light and a bang at the same time knocked him unconscious. A slap in his face woke him up again, everything was still dark. He was still in bed, but couldn't move. He heard sobbing: the sound came from his wife, but he could not turn his head and look at her. Someone switched the light on. Jiang was shocked to see Agent Tuan's face.

"Good morning Mr Sook. My apologies for waking you up this early. You see there is this matter of National Security — you breached it, by leaking classified documents. You are hereby charged with treason."

Jiang couldn't believe what Tuan had just said: he had not leaked anything; Tuan had been monitoring him constantly for the last month: the man knew he had behaved properly. "I never did that, you know that," he shouted in terror. Someone held him in a tighter grip and an arm pushed on his Adam's apple. The pain in his throat was excruciating.

Tuan hit Jiang in the face. "Silence, you traitor. Do not speak to me, unless I tell you to. You and your wife need to be re-educated."

"She has nothing to do with this." Another blow in his face: a fist this time.

"Shut the fuck up, traitor. The journey to your new home is long and cold, so I'll give you both a shot with a mild sleeping medicine, to make it more bearable."

"No, not my wife, please, she's pregnant, we'll lose our baby. I beg you," Jiang was crying. He heard his wife crying too; she had been awake all along.

"Pregnant? Mmm, I *like* pregnant women. Their breasts

are firm and feel oh so good. I think I'll put you to sleep first and then the boys and I shall have a bit of fun with her, before we travel," Tuan said, as he stuck the needle in Jiang's arm.

Jiang felt himself go limp. He heard his wife scream. He was conscious long enough to hear Kim's nightgown being torn to pieces and Tuan admiring her breasts.

***

Jiang woke up in a plane, only to be given another injection and fall asleep again. The next time he woke up, he was in a car, but his wife was not with him. He kept quiet, pretending to be asleep.

Wanjia Re-education Through Labour Camp, Harbin City, Heilongjiang Province the gate read. Jiang shook from fear; he had heard stories about this place. Political prisoners were put together with rapists and murderers, and the political ones often became rape and murder victims in here. He feared for his wife. He knew protecting her in this prison would be difficult. *He hadn't seen her since they —* he didn't want to think about what had happened at home.

The camp looked deserted, except for a handful of guards walking in the courtyard. Everything was covered in a thick layer of snow. The car stopped in front of a building that looked like an old factory. Jiang pretended to sleep when they dragged him out of the car. He was still in his underwear. His wrists were hurting from the cuffs and his feet were cold from the snow when he was thrown in a small cell. There was no window, no furniture, and no toilet, only a bucket. His cell smelled of piss and shit, and a small lamp in the ceiling lit the smears of excrement on the walls. Jiang was all alone. He cried.

23. Propositions.
(November year 1)

A week ago Gustavo's Aunt Isadora had contacted him through his mother. A good friend of hers, Martin, would be vacationing in Rio soon. He had been under a lot of stress recently and could use a friendly face. Could Gustavo please show him around? So when three days ago a friendly and handsome middle aged man had met up with him, Gustavo had been pleasantly surprised. The man clearly looked after himself and Gustavo judged him as a farmer would livestock at a market. Martin had hard muscles, clearly from a rigid gym regime, good teeth, a neat greying beard and a great haircut. And the way he smiled at Gustavo: the man was clearly gay. Business was hard right now, with all the troubles going on, and Gustavo needed the money, so he decided Martin would be his trick this week. He arranged to take him to Ipanema beach the following morning: there would be a good place to start seducing him. Gustavo could show off his muscular and tanned body, and wear his revealing designer swimming trunks.

***

The beach was packed with tourists and hustlers, and Martin seemed to enjoy the sun and sea. Gustavo decided he needed to get his trick a bit drunk, to get things going, so he offered to get them the local alcoholic speciality.

The sand burnt Gustavo's feet and he tried not to spill the Caipirinhas. Gustavo hurried back; he could not leave Martin on his own for too long. Martin had a very pale skin, a clear indication that he was a new arrival: fresh meat, and there was a real risk of other professional boyfriends trying to chat him up.

The alcohol did loosen Martin up. He told Gustavo he lived in London, not too far from Isadora. He could only take one week off work, and needed to get a bit of rest and recreation before, as he called it: *the shit would hit the fan*. Gustavo liked the man, but something was not right; he always seemed distracted, never willing to tell him what that *shit* would be, and after flirting all day, Martin still had not indicated he wanted sex, which Gustavo didn't really mind, but they would have to do it soon, otherwise there would not be enough time to make the man fall in love with him. He suggested they should go for a meal tonight. Martin agreed: he liked Gustavo.

***

The beach restaurant was set up to cater for lovers and was Gustavo's favourite for that reason: here he worked his magic on his tricks. The setting was romantic, fresh roses and candles placed on the tables, a pianist playing love songs, the soft sound of waves breaking in the background, and the rays of the moon and stars lighting up the beach.

Martin did not speak much during dinner. He seemed stuck in his own world, only interested in the waves. Gustavo thought he would not get anything out of this relationship, but after Martin paid for the meal and they left, he had told Gustavo he was having a really good time with him and was enjoying his company — so could they meet again at the beach tomorrow?

***

Most of the morning Martin had kept himself busy reading his papers and writing notes. Gustavo decided that today he would be a bit more aggressive in his approach of seducing Martin, and again alcohol would play a big role.

"There you go. You'll love this one; she put extra alcohol in this Caipirinha," Gustavo said, sitting himself down close to Martin.

"Thanks, I think I'm getting a bit drunk. These drinks are dangerous. How many have we had already?" Martin asked.

"Not enough." Gustavo winked. "You're getting very red Martin." Gustavo needed to get things a bit more sexual; things still weren't going the way he wanted. "Let me put some lotion on you." Gustavo stood up in front of Martin, making sure his crotch was right in Martin's face. Gustavo was a very well-endowed man and he had chosen his swimming trunks carefully: his bulge looked massive in them. He touched Martin's face, and he adjusted his penis from left to right. Martin was staring at his tool. Now he had his attention. "Lie down on the towel." Gustavo massaged the oily lotion all over Martin's back. He sat on top of him and pulled down Martin's trunks, massaging his buttocks. "All done, turn around." Martin turned over and Gustavo was relieved to see Martin's penis was erect. There was the interest! Several Caipirhinas later Gustavo suggested they should get back to the hotel for a shower and a nap.

**

"I'm tipsy," Martin said as he opened the door to the room. He shivered for a moment and was not sure if he felt the cold air through the door, or if the shiver came from the anticipation of having sex with a 24 year old Brazilian stud.

Gustavo took seconds to get undressed. Martin looked at him: this was the first time he saw him totally naked. The man was big, hung like a horse, and Martin was intimidated and aroused at the same time by the sight. "I need a shower. I'm covered in oil and sand," he said. He had not undressed yet, secretly hoping Gustavo would take control.

He had so much responsibility back home and he needed someone, anyone, to look after him for a while, to be in charge of him. As if Gustavo had read his mind, he walked up to Martin and undressed him. They walked into the shower and kissed passionately under the streams of water. Gustavo turned out to be a real gentleman and Martin felt relaxed for the first time in many weeks. After the shower Gustavo took a towel and dried Martin: the soft cotton gave them both goose bumps. Martin was pushed to the bed and Gustavo caressed him with his big soft hands.

"I want you Martin," Gustavo said to him. "I want to make love to you. Will you let me?"

"Yes, please," Martin said, almost a whisper. Martin noticed Gustavo worked very hard to make sure he enjoyed himself.

When Gustavo had brought both of them to completion, Martin felt overwhelmed: his whole body shook and he felt as if his orgasm had lasted for hours. When his body finished; Martin kept on shaking and he felt tears on his face: he was crying and could not stop himself.

Gustavo seemed alarmed. "Martin, did I hurt you? Did I do something wrong?"

"No, you didn't. You were fantastic. I — I'm just so sad right now. The world is about to end and everything will be gone. And so many people look to me for answers and I don't have them."

Gustavo kissed his lips. "No, you silly man. I've heard about the object in the sky, but they're only rumours. It's not real."

Martin pushed him away and leapt out of the bed.

"No. You're being ignorant and stupid. It's fucking real!" Martin took his folders out and threw all the papers at Gustavo. "Read them you imbecile. I work for the British Government. I have all the information. There *is* a big object coming to Earth from another star system. It's coming so fast that we can't even measure its speed. It will be here in a few months and we won't have enough time to prepare. We're stuck here on this planet, like sitting ducks and we can't do anything but wait for that thing to kill us. Fuck it, fuck it, fuck it!"

Gustavo looked shocked after Martin's violent outburst. He took a few minutes looking through the mess of papers that lay around him on the bed. "I've never believed the stories, but you're so passionate and you look so sad. Now I'm scared they're true. What am I looking at?" He asked, holding up a picture.

"You're looking at the object that is heading towards us," Martin answered, feeling calmer now. "Sorry I shouted at you. You're not stupid, just misinformed. I've been under a lot of pressure. And I feel I'm the one who must save the world. And I cannot."

"The object? Is it not a meteor? I still don't understand."

"It's classified information, but it's going to come out soon anyway, so I might as well tell you. You're looking at an alien object in the sky. A few months ago we discovered it and we've been investigating it ever since. It's flying towards us and it will be here in June or July next year. When you look at the various pictures you can see it's a green coloured Cube, we estimate each side is hundreds of kilometres long. It's travelling so fast we think it will destroy Earth when it hits us." Martin noticed the tears on Gustavo's face. "I'm sorry I upset you so much."

"No it's not that. I haven't been totally honest with you. I'm in love with a woman. Her name is Zaira. I want to grow old with her, but now you've told me our lives will end soon. And that makes me sad."

Martin had not expected this answer: Gustavo had been deceiving him all this time. Anger filled his thoughts again. "I *knew* you weren't really gay. You've been toying with me. I paid for your drinks, food, everything. You're one of those whores that targets single men. And I can't believe you did this even though I'm a friend of your Aunt Isadora, and all this time you must've been laughing behind my back. I can't believe I fell for it. I'm such an old fool." Martin walked to his desk and picked up his wallet. "I did like you, you know? I can't predict what will happen to you when this thing lands, but you've got great survival instincts. Here's some money. Spend it and live happily for as long as you can. I've decided I'm flying back home today, so I need to pack. And I really want you to go now."

Martin looked at Gustavo as he got dressed and he wondered what had happened to him to make him live such a sordid life. Martin almost fell sorry for the poor chap.

"Martin, I'm sorry. I wasn't going to ask you for money. Please don't tell my Aunt. Can we stay in contact?"

"I could lie to you and say yes and then you'd feel better about yourself for a while, but we both know I never want see you again. And you're not even really gay, so what's the point?" Martin asked. He turned away from Gustavo and started picking up his papers. He did not look when Gustavo picked up the cash and left.

***

The sun hit Gustavo's face, and hot sweat tickled his forehead when he walked along the boulevard. He loved summers in Rio, but then he realised this would be his last summer ever. Feeling defeated, he sat down on a bench and looked around. He wanted to savour the moment, see life — no — *feel* life happening and never forget. He felt sad his memories and his love would die with him, and with everybody else on the planet: such a waste.

People walked along the beach, laughing and drinking. He saw children eating ice cream: their faces covered in chocolate. He realised he wouldn't have enough time to become a father. And there were so many other things he still wanted to do. Gustavo cried. His tears and sweat mixed and the big beads ran down his cheeks, he watched them fall on the pavement: small black speckles on grey slates. He needed to see Zaira and tell her he loved her. Confident his voice would sound normal again after his long cry, he dialled Zaira. Gustavo imagined her smile.

"Hello meu amor," her voice sounded good to him. "How are you? Hey, can you take tonight off? We've been invited to a beach party on Copacabana. It's an end of the world party and we need to dress up as aliens," she said. She sounded excited.

Gustavo laughed, he felt happy she was unaware. "Zaira, my gatinha, of course we'll go. Anything for my lady. I'll get costumes and will pick you up from work later."

He took the cash from his pockets. There was a lot of money: hundreds of American dollars and as many British pounds. Martin did care for him after all, he thought.

***

When they arrived, the party was in full swing: the music was loud and people were dancing, and laughing, and kissing. The beach was lit with coloured lights and fires. Portable bars were selling alcoholic drinks. Everyone had made a real effort dressing up as aliens and they looked fantastic. Gustavo and Zaira waved at her friends, who were dancing around a fire.

"It's good to see you guys. Let me buy all of you a drink," Gustavo said. "Tonight we're celebrating. It will be the best party ever."

Zaira looked at him, puzzled. He chose to ignore her look, winked at her and walked off to the bar.

After he made sure they all had a full glass, he gestured Zaira to stand next to him. "Gatinha, I love you so much," he said, loud enough for all their friends to hear. "A toast for my lady. She makes me the happiest man in the world. And I promise she'll be happy for the rest of her life. Now, let's dance."

Gustavo thought that Zaira behaved very amorously when they were dancing; she kissed him and ran her fingers under his shirt, playing with his chest hair and pinching his nipples. He enjoyed her smell and grabbed her bum, gently massaging both cheeks. He made her giggle: she was slightly ticklish. Her lips tasted sweet from her drink. He loved everything about her. Her breasts were pressed up against him and he felt his penis grow hard. "Let's go for a walk," he said, holding her hand. As they walked off, their friends cheered and whistled. Both of them smiled at each other. After a short walk they found a quiet spot near the shore. The sea was calm, there was a slight breeze and the moon was shining. Gustavo's outfit had a big cape, so he took it off for them to sit on. For a while they sat in silence next to another, holding hands. Peace.

"Gustavo — I," she said.

He kissed her before she could continue; he did not want them to talk, not yet. Gustavo felt nervous, never had they been so intimate before and Zaira seemed in the mood to make love to him for the first time. She unbuttoned his shirt and kissed his chest. He liked Zaira taking control and he let her undress him.

"Lie down," she whispered. She sat herself on top of him and took off her dress. They were both naked now. He could see her breasts in the moonlight, and as gently as he could, he held them in his hands, and he heard her moan: barely audible. She kissed him and her soft skin brushed against his hairy chest. Her nipples were hard. Gustavo was hard. She moved her hips and let him slowly slide inside her. It was easy: she was ready for him.

"Whoa, you are big." She smiled and moved up and

down. Slow at first. Gustavo matched her rhythm. Delicately he played with her nipples and she ran her fingers through his chest hair. Sand rubbed his skin, very uncomfortable, but he made an effort to ignore the itching sensation. Zaira increased her movements, and Gustavo held her by her hips to help her moving. He looked at her, the breeze caught her hair. She was most beautiful to him. Zaira was nearing her climax and Gustavo had to hold back. He wanted to wait for her so they could orgasm together, and have a perfect first time.

Zaira's breathing became irregular and her movements indicated she was coming. Gustavo groaned and came too. Dripping with sweat she smiled and kissed him. After a few minutes she got off him and he took her into his arms holding her as close to him as he could.

"I love you so much."

"I love you too."

Gustavo listened to the sound of the waves falling on the beach. He looked at the moon, brightening the sky, and at the stars of the Milky Way, twinkling above them. The light breeze teased the hairs on his arms and chest. The salt on his lips mixed with her essence. Gustavo experienced a moment of total serenity and bliss. He sat up. "Zaira Matos. Please will you marry me?"

"Yes, I will." She kissed him.

"I love you so much. I will be the best husband and I will give everything you need." Gustavo smiled; he wanted to shout his love for her from the highest building, but for now their friends at the party would do. Oh, and tomorrow he would tell his mother: she would be so pleased, his mother liked Zaira and had already suggested he should marry her. He knew he had to hurry to make it happen: there was not much time left.

29. Secrets and lies.
(December year 1)

WebNetLeaks:

In December WebNetLeaks was sent the following information. The document is a proposal by the Chinese Government to attack the object, now known as the Ophiuchus Cube, before it reaches Earth. Many details were redacted, below are excerpts of the document:

People's Republic of China proposal for the pre-emptive attack on The Ophiuchus Cube. By the Pan Asian Ophiuchus Project. Report by Dr Tuan.

*_redacted_*

The combined nuclear arsenal of China, India and Pakistan shall be used for the attack. Using the Intercontinental Ballistic Missiles _redacted_ , a total of 368 warheads. The _redacted_ facility will convert missiles for optimum escape velocity.

*Changing flight course towards the object gives missiles an altitude of 400km after boost phase, adding the middle phase, gives an altitude of 1800km, with missiles reaching 12km/s after 16 minutes. _redacted_*

Missiles to travel at 12km/s for 55 minutes to a distance of 41,400km, taking them beyond geostationary satellite orbit.

redacted contact with the Cube after 71 minutes. Missiles to detonate on impact: resulting in the destruction of the Cube.

*_redacted_*

"Yes Prime Minister — Yes Sir. I understand. Yes I have spoken to all three ambassadors, but they knew nothing about the nukes either — I agree, the risk of retaliation will be great. — Of course Sir. I'll arrange an emergency meeting with the UN Security Council immediately." Within minutes after the leaks had appeared, Martin was on the phone with the Prime Minister. People had been very nervous; riots had broken out across the globe, and in Britain, and Martin had difficulty keeping shops supplied as people had started bulk buying in their panic. So having to deal with the Chinese plan was the last thing he needed on top of all his problems. He sat for a moment, contemplating the difficult meetings ahead. He buzzed his assistant. "Diana, can you get me a car to Heathrow Airport? Book me the first flight available to New York and get me that nice hotel, book it for a week please. Oh and get me the President's office on the phone. Thank you, Diana."

Martin had a suitcase with clothing and his passport in his office: he was prepared for days like today. He felt they happened too often nowadays. He was saving Earth. *But who is saving me*? he thought. Diana probably could, but she always went home to her husband. He had his good friends, but they all had partners, they had intimacy. He had no one. When Earth was back to normal he would have to find a less busy job and someone who really loved him, not another Gustavo.

***

In his Manhattan hotel room, Martin found a pile of documents waiting for him. He would not have time to go through all of them: his next meeting was in two hours and he needed a shower and a shave. After he finished grooming, he had a quick skim through the papers; he wanted to appear prepared, but he fell asleep on his bed instead. His phone rang, waking him up and making him wonder where he was. The voice told him his car was waiting outside. He hoped traffic would be bad, so he could read a few pages on the way.

The tall United Nations building loomed over him. He had always found this monstrosity to be one of the ugliest buildings in the world: too tall and without any architectural features. Maybe the building had to look as neutral as its organisation wanted to be perceived. When he stepped out of the car, he felt intimidated by a crowd. Over 100 shouting men and women were protesting in front of the entrance — the Children of Abraham. Before he stepped into the safety of the building, he noticed a scuffle: the Children were using their placards to attack a street preacher. Police officers stood nearby, but did not intervene. Martin dreaded to think what might happen to the man next. Martin couldn't figure out if the police seemed too scared of the Children nowadays, or if the Children had infiltrated the police. Both thoughts disturbed him. Martin decided he wouldn't get himself involved: he was needed elsewhere now. He felt he would have a rough night ahead.

The documents stated that the President of the United States had made a declaration: the USA regarded the proposed Chinese attack on the Cube an act of war, and would seek UN condemnation and veto this plan. Martin was being asked to help the American Government persuade the rest of the world to buy into their policy.

Tonight, Martin was going to meet his American counterpart: Colin Andrews. He was one of the President's closest advisers and they had spoken on the phone several times. Colin seemed a pleasant and understanding man and he had a deep masculine voice with a slight Texan accent, which Martin liked.

Two armed security guards checked his identification and let Martin into the meeting room. Normally there would be dozens of officials in a meeting, but except for one man, reading at a desk, the room was empty.

As soon as he noticed Martin he walked up and gave him

a lingering handshake. "Hi Martin. I'm Colin. It's really good to finally meet you, I've heard many great things about you. And some interesting facts too. We're very similar you know," he said with a big grin, and winked.

"If you liked what you heard, then the rumours are true. If not, then I strongly deny everything." Martin was stunned: what a handsome man; Colin was taller than him, chocolate skin, dark cropped hair, a short beard and brown eyes. He was wearing a suit that showed off a gym-fit physique. He noticed Colin did not wear a ring; that was a good sign, together with the ambiguous remarks. Martin fancied him. "I expected more people."

"The official meetings are not on till tomorrow. You and I have to prepare our joint statement for the Security Council and for the meeting with the Chinese," Colin said.

"Ah, that information must have been in the documents I didn't read. I fell asleep earlier. Sorry."

"Don't worry. We're only going through the motions. There's no way we would attack China if they fired their missiles at the Cube. The statement is to make our politicians look good and keep the public happy."

"So, all our efforts will amount to nothing, but it's our job to do it," Martin said, as he shrugged. "Okay, let's start, we have a lot of information to go through."

"I think this is it," Colin said when they finished their work four hours later. "I could do with a drink. You want to join me? I know a great place in town."

"Sure, but don't you have someone to go home to? I understand if you do. We might not have long left, so it's normal that you want to spend as much time with —" *What should I say? Him, her, loved one?* Martin thought frantically, "— them as you can." Yes, *them*, he decided, was very safe.

"No, there's no one there for me. All single," Colin said smiling and waving a ring-less hand. "Let's go. I'm taking you to my favourite cocktail bar, it's a hoot in there. I hope you like frozen Margaritas."

***

The next morning Martin woke up with one of the worst hangovers he had ever had. He had to be sick and stumbled to the toilet to empty his stomach: he felt as if the contents travelled all the way up from his toes. He vaguely remembered last night. Had he been flirting with Colin? He couldn't remember; actually, come to think of it: he did not want to remember. He looked for painkillers in his wash bag. Thank God Diana had packed them. After his shower, the pills had kicked in and he felt a lot better. When he got dressed he found a note on his dresser: *I had to take you to the hotel. You passed out. I had a great time last night. See you at the UN. Don't be late. We can't keep the President waiting. Colin.*

Martin felt shocked and ashamed. Had he really passed out? He must have done. He had no recollection of getting back to the hotel. And how come he was stark bollock naked when he woke up? How embarrassing.

When Martin walked into the meeting room at the UN, he saw Colin talking to an Asian looking man. Martin did not know who he was, but knew he would soon find out. He heard Colin excuse himself. He had a big grin on his face when he walked up to Martin.

"I see you made it to the meeting — after last night I can honestly say I'm impressed."

Martin felt his face heat up and he knew he was blushing. "Well, we Brits can down a few drinks. But, did I embarrass myself last night?"

"Yes you did, but only a little. You got very drunk. I thought it was cute. You were probably jet-lagged. I shouldn't have taken you out. Anyway, it was fine with me.

You had to let off a lot of steam. I bet you'd behave yourself much better if you were on a date," Colin said. After a quite deliberate short pause he continued. "You wanna go on a real date with me tonight?"

"You want that? After the way I behaved last night?"

"Yes, if that was your worst, then it can only get better. And tonight you'll get that kiss you asked for. You're sweet and I like you," Colin said, smiling. "By the way. You see that guy I was talking to? That's agent Tuan, he's the one that works for the Chinese Government, it's his plan we're against. He's dangerous, keep an eye on him. The other guy there in the corner is Pranit, from the Indian Intelligence. He won't admit it, but we found out that it was he who contacted a Chinese scientist with the original plan. The quiet one behind him is Syed from Pakistan."

Martin made a mental note for British Intelligence to investigate all three agents. "Let's get this meeting over and done with."

The meeting was brief. Martin was amazed how rude some of the delegates were. His translators accurately translated every profanity, and there were lots of them. Tuan was resisting and protesting everything Martin and Colin said for most of the meeting, but when Tuan realised most of the world opposed the Chinese plan, he asked for a short break, so that he could make a phone call.

Colin walked up to Martin. "Tuan is a good actor, let's see what he does in act two of this charade."

Tuan returned to the room after three minutes. "Gentlemen, the People's Republic of China has listened to your concerns. Also, we have recently found out the Cube is larger than we anticipated. It is not 500 kilometres, but over 3000. We understand our calculations to destroy the object are not correct and that is the reason why we cease preparations for the attack."

Pranit let out a cry. Syed banged his hands on his desk.

Martin was aghast. *One simple phone call with all this new information and they change their plans just like that? That couldn't be true, could it?*

"You see," Colin said, "it's all bullshit. I know how they play their diplomatic games. But for now our President and your Prime Minister have won, so they can play the heroes. But I know China will go ahead planning the attack anyway and I won't be surprised if they still go ahead with it."

Martin was not sure what to think of what had happened. He noticed Pranit, who seemed particularly distressed. When Tuan got up to leave, Pranit kicked over his chair to follow Tuan as fast as he could. Agent Syed was right behind them. "I hope you're wrong Colin. Did you see how Pranit reacted? I don't think he was informed."

"Wait and see, Martin. Now let's get out of here and have a good night out, while we still can."

31. Best friends forever.
(December year 1)

The divorce papers covered the table. Isadora looked at Rick while he read them.

She had separated from her husband recently, always having thought she had been in a happy marriage, despite the stressful times her autistic child had often caused. She had loved her husband very much, she still did, but he had ended their marriage in an abrupt way. One evening, after work, she came home to find two suitcases in the hallway.

Her husband was sitting in the living room, his coat on. He told her he wanted to be with another woman he had met and he was leaving Isadora to be with her. The children were staying with their grandmother for now, he had said. Isadora was speechless; her whole world had been turned upside down in less than two minutes. She had felt numb as she stood in the hallway looking at him as he picked up his bags and opened the door. He could not face her when he walked out. Isadora was not quite sure if she heard him speak or if she imagined it, but she thought she heard him thanking her for the good times they had spent together.

After her husband had left her, Rick had been a very good friend to her and the kids. Rick would come over at night to cheer her up whenever she had felt lonely. He comforted her when she had to prepare for the impending divorce. She knew she was going to have a difficult time in court: her ex wanted full custody of the kids, since he felt that having a fiancée, and thus being a two parent family, he could give them a better home. Isadora could not let him have the kids, especially not Thomas.

"God, I didn't think he would go this far. I'm so sorry for you Isadora," Rick said after he put the papers down.

"That arsehole shags another woman and now she's going

to look after my children? How's that fair?" Isadora's eyes were red. She had been crying since she had opened the envelope earlier, crying when she asked Rick to come to her home, still crying when Rick walked in. She had never stopped. "I'm so upset. One weekend a month just isn't enough. I can't be without them for that long."

"This is only his proposal. Of course he'll start like this, it's how custody battles are fought, and the divorce proceedings haven't started yet. You're a great mother and Thomas isn't even his child. I can't see any judge deciding against you. You'll have plenty of time to prepare your counter proposal. And you're not alone in this, I'm here for you and I'll stand by you throughout. You know what? I'll stay here tonight," Rick said, getting up to get glasses and a bottle of vodka out. "Let's have a drink."

"You read my mind — pour me a big one. I need to get wasted," Isadora said. "And you know what the worst part is? They're moving to Manchester next week already and he's taking the kids with him to stay there for a week. At least Sally stays here with me."

After hearing her name, Sally jumped on Isadora's lap and started licking her face.

Rick tried to think of anything to say to cheer Isadora up. "You know, I'm sure you're going to have them most of the time, but if they are with him, and you miss them, then Manchester isn't that far away. And you can phone and video call them on the internet. It's going to be much better than it seems to you now."

"I guess you're right. I'm just so shell shocked. I loved him very much and now he fucks me over so bad," Isadora sighed. "And I'm very worried for Thomas. I know Karen can adjust, even though she won't like being away from me and her friends, but Thomas, this could send him into his own world again. I'm not sure if he'll cope with such a change, especially if she's trying to be his mother too. It will confuse him too much."

"He's older now than when he had his last episode and I feel as if his autism seems to affect him less nowadays. You can't stop this, so you'll have to deal with it day by day."

"But I can't believe judges might decide that having the care of two parents outweighs the stress of change. He was never a good parent and she will never be his parent. Fuck it. I'm afraid I might lose the battle, lose them."

"We haven't even started the proceedings yet, so let's stay positive for now. Okay?"

"I guess so. Hey, I feel like getting high. Did you bring any — powders?"

"Sorry, no, I didn't think it would be appropriate tonight."

"You're too much of a gentleman. Oh. Hang on a minute," Isadora said, winking at Rick. "I might have some grass stashed away, let's get stoned like the good old days."

***

Isadora and Rick had met a little over 20 years ago at university. During their final year she had lived in the same student house as he had. Rick had fallen head over heels in love with her: she had the most amazing brown eyes, long dark hair, long legs and big breasts. But he was a very confused man then: he thought he might be gay, but he had fallen for a woman. Their final year together turned out to be one of the best in their lives. Isadora had fallen in love with him too and they spent a lot of time together. One thing in their relationship was missing though: they were never intimate.

One night, at a club, Isadora suggested they should get high to celebrate their graduation in style. Many ecstasies and powdered noses later, they ended up having hours of magnificent and passionate sex. Not soon after that night Isadora noticed a subtle change in Rick's behaviour. She insisted he should tell her what was on his mind, but she knew already what he needed to tell her: he was gay, but also in love with her. Isadora loved him back, very much, but knew if they did not stop being lovers, they would stop being friends.

One month later she had missed her period: she was pregnant by the man she could never truly have. Isadora had panicked and she had made the decision to leave: for her own sanity. In less than a day she had organised a flight, packed her bags and had flown back to Brazil, to stay with her family. The taxi to the airport was waiting when she stood outside the door saying her goodbyes to Rick. She told him she loved him, but she had to leave England, because the winters were too cold and she felt lonely. She also told him she would be in his way if he wanted to figure out who he really was. Rick was devastated and told her he was afraid he would never see her again, but she promised him he would.

She made sure they stayed in contact: they wrote letters almost every week, but she did hide her pregnancy from him and never told him she had given birth to a little boy: Thomas, his child. One day she phoned him: *I made a mistake, I got pregnant from a bad Brazilian man. I can't raise the baby in Rio. I'm coming back to London. Please come and pick Thomas and me up from the airport tomorrow.*

Rick had been so happy to see her again. He had missed her very much during those lonely 18 months, but all was forgotten as soon as she had walked through the doors. They cried and hugged for minutes. After she handed the baby to Rick, he couldn't move, afraid to drop him. The little boy stared at him. Rick thought he could see him smile. "You are beautiful little Thomas. Say hello to your uncle Rick."

Their friendship had never ended, and throughout the

years they became even closer and were always there for each other. Isadora was there when he got married to Paul, she was there for him when he got cancer and she was there for him when he became depressed. And Rick was the best man when Isadora got married, he was there with her husband in the hospital: waiting for her daughter to be born. He was there for her when Thomas was diagnosed with autism. They had gone through a lot together and now he was going to be there for her during her divorce.

**

Half an hour later their mood had improved.

"I feel as high as the night we had sex. You were such a great kisser," she said and moved forward to kiss him. "Your lips still look as soft as I remember. But you're still gay and you have a wonderful husband." Mentioning *husband* stopped her. Her mood changed back to sad again during a moment of awkward silence.

Rick held her hand and smiled at her, not knowing what to say.

Isadora proposed each of them should make a list of the most annoying features of her ex-husband. Both of them were giggling when the top three turned out to be nagging, nagging and nagging.

"God, did he know how to nag: *where's my laundry?* The time I spent in the laundry room with his knickers," Isadora said.

Rick laughed so hard, he almost fell off his chair; spilling his vodka all over him. He was happy to see his best friend laugh again.

Isadora had taken her phone out, typing a message.

"You're not sending him obscene messages are you?" Rick asked. "He can see your number, you know."

"No, my boob pictures only go to attractive men from

now on, not to that nagging wanker. He never knew how to treat them anyway — no, I ordered us a taxi."

"Us? Where are we going?"

"You'll see. A bit of fun."

***

Rick did not know where the taxi had dropped them off; the area was a quiet leafy suburban neighbourhood.

"We're a short walk away, but be quiet," Isadora whispered. "Let's have another joint."

They walked into a street and Isadora pointed at a big detached house. "Look, her house, this is where he lives with that bitch."

Rick felt slightly alarmed. "We're not going to break in or something? I don't want us to get into trouble."

"No, just a bit of fun. Revenge. And it's not as if I could fuck up the divorce or something, he's already fucked me over big time."

Rick knew she had made her mind up, so he would not try to argue with her, whatever her plan was.

They walked into the garden to the back of the house. Isadora found a brick and played with it in her hands.

"No, you're not going to do that," Rick said. He could not help smiling.

Isadora threw the brick at the big living room window and with a loud noise the glass panel shattered.

"Run, run for your life!" Isadora shouted, laughing. "Don't let the witch catch us."

They ran as fast as they could. Sally ran after them, not understanding what had happened, but barking from excitement. Two streets later they stopped, both of them out of breath.

"That was fun. I needed that. Now I feel I can move on and be strong when I face that prick during the divorce. And they can move to Manchester for all I care, good riddance," Isadora said, still laughing.

"He'll nag her now to clean it all up," Rick said, giggling, feeling high from the grass and happiness.

37. Junk food is bad for your health. (January year 2)

"Good evening. These are the latest headlines from the World Wide Live News Channel.

"In London the Metropolitan Police has called in the army to deal with the thousands of Children of Abraham protesters, who two hours ago stormed the Houses of Parliament. Our reporter, who is inside the Parliament buildings, has informed us that dozens of MPs and members of the House of Lords have been killed and several of them are being held hostage right now. No demands have been made as yet.

"Earlier today protesters broke away from the rally, led by Simon Waltz, held at Trafalgar Square, killing many police officers and bystanders on their way to Parliament. At the moment the Square and the area are secure again, but the Police urge everyone to stay away from the area.

"We will keep you updated with the events in London. We expect the army to storm the Parliament buildings soon, in an attempt free all hostages."

After the attempt by the Children of Abraham to kill them, Paul and Rick had been driven by the police and Martin to the Accident and Emergency room in a nearby hospital. A nurse had assessed Paul's leg and they were relieved to find that the bullet had only grazed him. A few stitches and he would be fine, but Paul and Rick were told they would have to wait for a few hours to see a doctor. Outside, ambulances queued up with dozens of wounded Police Officers and civilians. Inside, piles of the wounded and dying added to the chaos of the overcrowded department.

***

"I'm so happy you're going to be fine. I don't know what I would do without you," Rick said, holding Paul's hand. "Anyway, it's not so bad we have to wait. We're safe here. I was so scared earlier. I'm not sure what the worst was. Hearing the screams of the Officers when they were murdered outside our door, or being chased ourselves and shot at."

"I know. When they broke our door, everything went too fast to think. I just acted on instinct. I didn't even realise I was hit," Paul said.

"I'm just glad it's over. Hey, I'm quite hungry. I'll look for something to eat. Is there anything I can get you?"

"I could do with some water and a snack. Can you get me some sweet stuff?" Paul asked Rick.

"Sure, I saw a vending machine with chocolate and crisps in the corridor. I'll be right back."

Rick walked past many injured people; he saw blood everywhere. Most of them were moaning, but some were worryingly motionless. He felt helpless and responsible. Had all this violence been his fault? Was the rally on Trafalgar Square organised as a ruse, so they could send the killers to get him? He had been thrown into a dangerous world of politics and religion and he didn't like being a pawn in this game. He wanted out, but he knew there was no chance of escaping.

Outside the waiting room he noticed Martin, who was talking to a doctor.

As soon as Martin saw Rick he turned to him. "Hey you, how are you and Paul? I haven't had time yet to come over and check up on you both. It's been crazy in here."

"I'm okay, and thank God Paul is fine too. The bullet only scraped his skin. He'll need a few stitches, but we have to wait till after the seriously wounded have been treated.

There are so many of them — I think I saw a few dead officers in the corridor. I feel this is all my entire fault."

"No, it isn't. Most of them stormed Parliament. They had it all planned."

"So, what's the situation out there?"

"Not good," Martin said. "The Prime Minister ordered the army to come in. They were on standby, so it didn't take them long to get there. They're sweeping the streets now, but there's a lot of resistance and they've been shot at. We think we'll have it under control in an hour or so."

"I should've never pissed them off. I should've handled the press conference better, or come out with a different statement when they started to become so powerful. I could've done more to avoid this from happening."

"Now, now, stop it. It's really not your fault. These extremists won't listen to reason. Religious people have always looked for people they could hate. In times of distress and fear it makes it easier for them to hate and you are one of their targets. Don't worry, they'll forget about you soon. Appeasement won't work."

"But I never asked for this and I never did anything wrong to deserve this. What's going to happen to Paul and me? Where do we go after this?" Rick asked.

"You happened to be in the wrong place at the wrong time. It all started when Simon attacked us in the taxi. And I've decided, you're going to stay at my place for a few weeks, I have a spare bedroom. It's safe, and to be honest I could do with the company. I feel a bit lonely when I'm at home. I hardly see Colin, and we're both so busy that sometimes we don't talk for a week."

Rick was taken aback by his honesty. Martin had turned into their guardian angel and thinking of him as another vulnerable human being was difficult. "Thank you so much. You have no idea how much I appreciate this. I wouldn't feel safe at my home after today." Rick hugged Martin.

"Hey, I'm getting a snack. You want anything from the machine?"

"Yes, I'm famished actually, can you get me an energy bar?"

"Sure, I'll be back in a moment."

***

Rick walked down the corridor to find a vending machine. More people had been brought in and they were on stretchers left in the corridors and he had to be careful not to bump into anyone.

When Rick looked at the choices in the machine, he saw the irony in the fact that the only food one could buy in this place was very unhealthy. *Well, at least if it gives you a heart attack, a doctor is nearby,* he thought as he grabbed a couple of chocolate bars.

When he walked back down the corridor, a man, lying on a stretcher, grabbed his arm. His leg was twisted in an unnatural way and dried blood stained his trousers.

"I thought I recognised you. You are Rick Favier, aren't you?" he asked.

"Yes, I am. Your injuries look bad. Do you want me to find you a doctor?"

"No, I'm good, thank you. Actually I am *very* good." The man sat up, smiled and pointed a gun at Rick. "Gotcha!"

A deafening blow followed and Rick instinctively fell backwards. He landed on his elbows and butt. His left elbow was hurting an awful lot, he thought he must have been hit there, but his chest hurt too and he had difficulty breathing. He did not dare looking at himself.

"Fuck me." Martin squatted in front of him. "Are you okay? For a second I thought I was too late."

"Huh? What do you mean?" Rick shouted, his ears ringing from the blast.

110

"The guy. He almost shot you. I was just in time to save you."

Confused, Rick looked at the stretcher. The man was lying motionless. A big red splatter of blood and pink gooey stuff was spread on the wall behind him.

Martin sat in front of Rick with a gun in his hand, shaking slightly. "Did you get me my energy bar?"

Rick heard the goo drop on the floor and he felt the urge to throw up. "Honestly? You're thinking of food? Now? How can you keep your cool like this? And since when do you carry a gun?"

"Just now, in the van on the way here, they gave me one. And I know how to shoot, I get training every few months. But we need to get back to Paul. I think we need to stay together to keep you safe. And I'll get them to treat him now, so we can leave. It's too dangerous here and I don't want to shoot anyone else."

Police officers were filling up the corridor, their weapons drawn. Martin explained to them what had happened. Rick was amazed to see what authority he had.

"Have someone clean this mess up and have a doctor treat Paul now. I need to get this gentleman and his partner to safety," Martin said as he led Rick back to the waiting room and to Paul.

41. This is not what you want to hear. (January year 2)

Presidential address to the Nation, the United States of America.

White House, Oval Office. 9pm. January.

President William McGee:

"Good evening. Tonight, I regret to bring you grave and disturbing news, which will affect every person in the United States.

"Scientists from all over the world have been observing and investigating the object: known as the Ophiuchus Cube.

"It has become clear that the Cube is on an intercept course with Earth. My fellow Americans, this is not where the bad news ends. I have been informed the Cube is on course to land on American soil. The Cube is estimated to be 5,000 kilometres per side. By comparison, the United States is 4,600 kilometres at its widest. Most of our country will be covered by the Cube. Alaska will be unaffected, as will the extreme north-east and the south-west. The Cube will also cover parts of our good neighbours, Canada and Mexico.

"We expect the Cube to land this coming July, which will give us almost six months to evacuate our population. It will be an immense task, but we shall achieve this. We promise to send every citizen to safety before this tragic day is upon us.

"Never in the history of our great Nation have we been faced with a threat on a scale this immense and so destructive, but we will work together as one and overcome this problem.

"My administration has been working on an evacuation plan. All of you will be asked to leave your home and your community. I pray you will comply, as the alternative is certain death.

"Our allies have offered us their lands, their homes and resources. I am deeply grateful for their help. The details of the evacuation will be released and posted to your homes from tomorrow. The information will be printed in all newspapers and on the internet. Most of you will be living in foreign lands, but you will remain American citizens forever. Every single one of you will be an ambassador for our great Nation.

"The entire world will be watching us. So let us seize this moment to show why the United States of America is and shall remain the greatest nation on Earth.

"Thank you, God bless you, and may God bless the United States of America."

Colin Andrews lip-synced the address the President was reading out, as he had written the dramatic statement himself. He felt very emotional: he heard his President predict the death of his country. Ten minutes ago only six people knew this terrible news, now over 300 million Americans, and the rest of the world knew too.

Colin heard shouting outside. Through his window he noticed people running down the street. Opposite his apartment, a convenience store's window was smashed by a group of young men. He watched them entering the shop, careful not to be cut by the glass. What happened in front of him was exactly what he had expected: the rioting and looting had started. He had tried to persuade the President to declare martial law in his speech, but to no avail. The President expected only sporadic violence would happen.

The sounds of sirens and shooting came from the streets, and they drowned out the repeated speech on his television. People had started to panic much faster than he had anticipated. He phoned the White House, but the telephone network seemed overloaded: the absence of the dialling tone hurt the inside of his head. This was getting serious. If people could not phone 911, then anarchy would certainly break out immediately.

More shots came from outside. He looked out of his window again, and saw the skyline of Washington DC. His beautiful city, the place he had loved from the first day he had moved here, had a threatening look: there was an orange glow shining in the background, growing in intensity and he felt the intense hellfire was about to swallow his town and himself.

Colin wished he had a car, so he could drive to the White House in relative safety. The President needed to go back on television, to declare martial law, and Colin had to tell him.

Outside, the young men ran out of the convenience store; all were carrying bags and boxes. Behind them an older man ran out. Colin could not make out what he was shouting, but he could see the man was angry: he was probably the store owner. The man carried a shotgun and fired several times at the young men; one of them dropped all he was carrying and fell on the floor. The others kept running and Colin wondered if they were his friends. Unable to turn away, Colin kept watching as the older man walked up to the youngster, who looked to be about 15 and was holding his hands up and shaking his head. The shotgun was an inch away from the young man's head. A bright flash and a bang. Colin had never seen a man die in front of him, but now he had a front row seat, and the street lights forced him to look on, as a red lake around the boy grew. The store owner grabbed the items the younger man had been carrying and put them back in the bags.

A police car drove into the street and stopped next to the man and the store owner seemed to speak to someone in the car. A few moments later the police car drove off and the man went back inside his store. Colin was stupefied by the apparent lack of action by the police.

He tried to call the White House again, but the line was still dead.

The news channel had live reports of rioting breaking out in many major cities throughout the country, and the presenter advised everyone to stay indoors. The news ticker at the bottom of the screen announced the President would be addressing the Nation again shortly. Colin was pleased when he read it. Not knowing what to do until he could contact the White House, he poured himself a drink and sat slumped in his chair watching his country go up in flames on television.

***

"Hello? Colin Andrews here," Colin said into his phone, amazed someone had managed to get through. He hoped the White House was calling him.

"Hey you. It's Martin. We're sitting here in the Cabinet Office. We can't believe what we're seeing. Are you okay?"

"Yeah, I'm safe — thanks. I can't get to work though. I need to wait till a car picks me up. I can't go out on the streets right now — you know, being black. I know police or anyone else will shoot me, but I'm sure a car will arrive soon. But for now I'll stay put. Anyway, how are you? I saw you had quite a big riot in London."

"Yes, blimey. Today was mayhem. Those Children of Abraham attacked the police and stormed Parliament. They killed people from the Government, but luckily the Prime Minister was not there. And — you remember that guy Rick Favier I told you about? Well, they attacked him again and almost killed him and his partner. I got there in time to get them to safety, but we had to go to hospital, because Paul got shot."

"Oh my God, that's terrible."

"Yes, but that's not all. I shot a man today," Martin said.

"When we were in hospital, he tried to shoot Rick, so I had to kill him. I feel terrible. I shot without hesitating. There was a hole in his chest and blood was everywhere. And his brain was splattered on a wall. I've never shot anyone before."

"Jesus, that's intense, but you had no choice. You needed to save a friend. You're always saving everyone. I wish you were here with me now, so you could save me."

"Ah you're so sweet. That's why I love you Colin, you always say the right things. I wish I was with you too," Martin said. "But — that's not why I'm calling you. I'm going to have Rick and Paul stay with me for a few weeks and I want you to stay with me when you guys evacuate. You don't have to stay in a hotel. I'll look after you."

"Thank you, I would really like that, but the President changed his mind and we're going to Hawaii instead and I need to go with him."

"Resign, I will look after you. Both of us are trying to save the world, but we're not looking after ourselves. Please think it through," Martin pleaded.

"Okay, I'll think about it. Oh, hang on, I see the President is on television again. I need to listen to this." Colin was glad they could focus on the President. He felt uncomfortable after Martin's proposal; his loyalty was with his country, but he did not want to disappoint either of them.

"Yes, we have him on the screen here too, let's watch this," Martin said.

On each side of the Atlantic Ocean the two men were listening in silence when they heard President McGee declare martial law, recalling every reservist to the barracks and announcing that the army would be entering the cities in order to restore order. Colin heard the crackle in the phone line, knowing that Martin was on the other side, and he felt a lot less lonely.

***

"Here look at this." David Pilling waited in anticipation as his wife Jo-Anne read the memo.

"NATO Base Geilenkirchen-Teveringen, internal memo.

To all personnel:

Follow up on the President's address to the Nation. NATO has declared DEFCON 2 status.

Instructions for David Pilling, pilot.

All pilots and crew of the Boeing E-3 TCA (NATO Trainer Cargo) Aircrafts will be assigned to the Great Evacuation. Our base will be responsible for the relocation of an estimated 20 million US citizens, their personal belongings and all the necessary supplies.

Logistics will be looked after by the ground personnel and the spouses of all NATO employees at the base.

The US are grateful to our friends in Germany, Belgium and the Netherlands who will give our US citizens refuge in their countries.

Please stand by for further instructions at the briefing."

"Well, I expected something like this after the President's speech," she said.

"You know honey, I won't be home much for the next few months. I'll be flying constantly back and forth."

"They'll keep us both busy. I can't believe the Government expects us to process 20 million people through this base. Where are we putting them?"

"I don't know, but I guess the Government needs to tell our people it can be done. If anyone thinks they'll be left behind, well think of the panic," David said.

"It's going to be chaos. So what do you think is expected of me?"

"You'll be part of the team that will process the civilians when I fly them in. Put them in buses and send them on their way. But we'll hear the details at the briefing."

"David, I'm scared and I feel homesick. We should be back home with our families for the time being, so we can help them."

"I feel that way too, but we're here and we have been ordered to help, but I know it's the right thing to do for our country. And maybe we can get our family to stay with us here. And I promise you I'll be here with you when the Cube lands."

"Really? You promise?"

"I do my love. But hey, we need to go. The briefing is on in a moment. I already know that I'll be sent out later today to start flying all sorts of machinery, medical and food supplies back to the base. We need to have enough here before we start evacuating our citizens in a few days' time."

"We'll hardly have time to say goodbye. I will miss you."

"I'll miss you too, but I'll make sure that every time I land, we'll see each other. I will always be flying home to you."

43. The beauties and the beasts (February year 2)

When was the last time she had food? Too long ago for her to remember. Kim felt hungry and cold. Her cell was dark. After they had taken her to the prison she had been on her own for most of the time. Except for water and the occasional food given through the door hatch, there had been almost no interaction with a human being, except for *him*. What were they trying to do? Break her spirit? She felt they were close to succeeding. But why? She was ready to sign anything if they asked. Kim believed her husband Jiang was in the cell next to her. She was certain she could hear him scream occasionally. Her stomach ached. Was she still pregnant? Even though she had a bump, she was not sure anymore. How many weeks had she been here? She had lost count a long time ago. Was it day or night? She could not tell. Nothing seemed real to her. She remembered terrible recurring dreams, but she knew they were not: she knew they were *him*.

***

Agent Tuan felt happy: he was only an hour away from Kim. He loved her very much. Many times in the last few months he had travelled all the way from Hong Kong to see her. *His* child was growing inside her and her bump was getting really big, and thinking about her made him feel really horny. As soon as he would see her, he would fuck her again. Her breasts had grown bigger too every time he had visited her. She was almost ready to love him as much as he loved her, he was certain of that.

Tuan had never known what love had felt like until he had met Kim. His mother had left her abusive husband when he was very young, and then he had to endure the abuse from his father every single day; he couldn't remember anything else. They had moved in with his paternal grandmother, and she had been indifferent to him. His father drank a lot, and in his drunken state would hit Tuan, with his grandmother watching. Tuan was not liked at school either. He was overweight and smart, two reasons to be bullied. There was a third reason too: his father was the mayor and a member of the Communist Party and had a reputation for being corrupt — and he was, very much so. They had lived in a very small town and Tuan felt he was surrounded by stupid and ugly farmers and their families. Later in his life he would use the Communist Party to get the hell out of there and move to a proper big city, where the people were attractive, clean and intelligent.

When he was 14 he was seduced by his teacher, easily twice his age. She became pregnant and soon his father had found out. The next day she had disappeared. Tuan still often wondered what had happened to her, and the child, *his* child, she had been carrying.

The car pulled up outside the building. The cold air outside hit his face. Tuan's cock was hard. Any minute now and his cock would be inside his woman. He had his own keys to her cell. In the last few months he had arranged for her to have a proper bed with sheets, and he had made sure she was given proper food; she was eating for two now, after all.

***

Kim was sitting in a corner of her cell when she heard the keys in the lock. She knew what was about to happen to her again. She started feeling sick.

Tuan smiled. "Hello Kim. I'm so pleased to see you. I love you very much. Pull up your shirt for me. I want to see your tummy."

"I'm glad to see you too." Kim smiled. She tried to hide her disgust. "Where have you been? It's been ages."

"The preparations for the attack have been keeping me busy. I had to travel to America, India and Pakistan many times. I think we're ready for the attack. The Cube will be destroyed. — Wow, your breasts have grown. I want you Kim. I want you now."

Kim had to undress and spread her legs. She felt very vulnerable, but the deceit had to be done. Tuan needed to feel she loved him back and enjoyed being with him. He was disgusting. He smelled of old sweat and he was fat, but at least his cock was small. Any second now he would fuck her, but because she was not excited, she was not wet enough and when he entered her it really hurt, making her scream. He took only two minutes to come.

When Tuan had finished with her, he lit up a cigarette. "The Cube is going to land on America they think."

"Really, but are they not sure?"

"Their scientists say it will, but we're still going ahead though. America will be forever indebted to the People's Republic."

"What's the latest information then?"

"Well, now we have come to believe the Cube is at least 5,000 kilometres big, so it has an area of 25 million square kilometres and America will no longer exist when it lands there."

"Why won't you let it land on them? They're not our friends, are they?" Kim asked. She tried to make him believe she agreed with him.

"Even though the Cube might land on the Capitalists, it will still land on Earth. It will be best for the Republic if it never reaches Earth."

"Yes. You're right, as always. What will happen to me when all of this is over? And what will happen to Jiang?"

Kim regretted mentioning Jiang: Tuan had an annoyed look on his face now.

"For fuck's sake. You never stop asking about him. Don't you remember? I told you. He's dead. He died when we transferred the both of you to this facility. Stop asking about him. If you keep annoying me I won't come round any more and then you will be here all alone, and I'll take away your privileges."

"I'm sorry. You know I like you. I like you a lot. I'll forget about him. You and I should be together. Please take me home with you."

"You know I want to, but I can't, not yet. The Party wants to keep you here, but I'm trying very hard to get you out before our baby is born."

Kim knew he was lying to her, but for now she needed to keep him happy and she kept hoping. Tuan told her that soon he would be able to give her a happy life. He told her he felt horny again. One more fuck before he had to go, and he wanted her on her hands and knees this time. She knew he liked taking her from behind. He kept on whispering in her ear that he knew she loved it too, and how the way she moaned and groaned sounded like she was singing to him. Kim tried to imagine she was asleep.

***

Simon Waltz could not stop feeling angry. *Why the fuck can't these idiots do anything right?* Ever since Rick had punched him at the theatre he had been plotting to get that cunt killed. His speech at the Square had been a success, but for the last month the aftermath had been messy. He needed a new plan to reach more people. He was thinking he should reach a lot more Americans. Plenty of them were devout Christians anyway and were familiar with the Armageddon concept, and now they were very scared. He called a meeting with his friend Aziz at the mosque.

The mosque was packed again. Many followers had shown up to see Simon. He knew they had enough faith in him to follow his instructions without questioning him. Simon felt he was more popular than Jesus had ever been. "I am both happy and disappointed with last month's gathering at Trafalgar Square," he said. "We have shown the world we are a force to be reckoned with, but I am not happy with the fact that the Anti-Christ was not dealt with." Simon stood up. "I have an idea my brothers and sisters. The Americans are in a state of shock. Soon the Cube will land on them. I shall travel to America to give them my support in their time of need. I have decided to go to the city with the largest population of sinners, Las Vegas. I will show them God shall be there for them and send all believers to Heaven. I want to be there as soon as possible."

The crowd applauded. Simon smiled: the fools, he had them right where he wanted. He was their true leader now.

Simon took Aziz aside. "Aziz, I need you to organise a private plane for me, one that can fly non-stop from London to Las Vegas. When I'm in the US, I'll stay there till the last minute, but I'll pretend I'll stay there till the Cube lands, so the Americans know they can trust me and I'll make them join the Children of Abraham. Book me a good hotel on the Strip. I need a big suite with a few rooms, so I can hold assemblies. And get me a good couple of thousands of dollars too. And I cannot stress enough that we need more followers. I hope I can count on you to achieve this whilst I'm away."

"Simon. I'll guarantee you hundreds of thousands more followers. I know it is paramount this is taken care of when you are out of the country and I'll see to it myself it shall be done," Aziz said.

Simon had to go home and pack. He would tell his bitch wife she should stay at home to look after his kids. But first he would drive past Anne. He had secured her a new job as a reporter for the WWL News and she would be the one that could announce his departure for Las Vegas. And of course he would fuck her.

47. The great American Evacuation. (March year 2)

"Good evening this is the six o'clock news, with Anne Goodman reporting for the World Wide Live News Channel, live from Heathrow Airport. Behind me you can see the many US planes that have landed. Since the start of the evacuation, at the beginning of March, an estimated 40 million Americans have already been flown over to several host countries. Around three million people a day can be evacuated every day by airplanes. The United Nations has thanked all the countries who have offered their buses, ships and planes for the American evacuation effort and all countries who have offered to take in refugees during this unprecedented event in human history. However the UN is concerned by the Mexican Government's decision to close its US borders, soon after riots had broken out when thousands of Americans attempted to enter the country.

"In related news, I can announce that Simon Waltz, the leader of the Children of Abraham, has flown to Las Vegas to support the faithful in these dark days.

"Viewers, I need to tell you, I have spent all day in the arrivals hall, and I have never seen so many people with so much despair in their eyes. I have seen too many children crying. Families carrying only their clothing and a few personal items, all of them distressed, not knowing what the future will hold for them. I find it heart breaking to see this much suffering. There are happy stories too though. British families have been reunited and I have witnessed reunions of parents who haven't seen their children for years.

"We are witnessing the largest logistical operation ever coordinated on Earth, and we desperately need your donations. Please send as much money as you can to emergency555evacuate.com or text E555E to 21555342 for *a five pound donation.*

"This is Anne Goodman reporting from Heathrow Airport. Good night to you all. And God bless."

White House meetings last too long, Martin thought, after the President informed them they were done for the evening. The Americans always discussed, never agreeing or deciding. But then their country would cease to exist soon, so he should not be too hard on them. At least he had Colin close by now. "So how are you?" Martin asked him.

"I feel terrible, I don't think I've slept in five days," Colin said.

He did look it: Martin could see his hands shaking when Colin tried to put his coat on. During the meeting he had explained that things were not going well: the Mexican Border Agency had shot at American civilians and killed more than a dozen today.

"So, what are you going to do about the Mexican situation?" Martin asked.

"We're advising people not to illegally cross the border. There's not much more we can do, and it makes me really angry. When things were good we let millions of Mexicans in and now they turn our people away. Fuck, they are even shooting at us now. They're only letting Mexicans back in. But we estimate at least 25 million Americans have crossed the border. Together with the estimated 12 million Mexicans I think over 15 percent of our population is safe there."

"It's not good, but at least the Canadians are letting you guys in. And Europe and Australia are taking the bulk in, so I think you will manage to evacuate everyone on time."

"Yeah, when the shit hits the fan, then you find out who your real friends are. Funny, the Arabs turned out to be good friends too. They're letting many people in. Well, mainly the rich and famous are flying there. I hear

128

Hollywood is empty."

"I can't believe how many are refusing to go though. What is it? About a 100 million?" Martin asked. He had seen the reports. Most conspiracy theorists and Children of Abraham had decided to stay. Even Simon Waltz had decided to await Armageddon in Las Vegas. *Good riddance* Martin thought. "Well, you're going to get everyone who wants to, and everything you need to, out on time. You still have two more months."

"Thank God for that, we've had so many offers for help. You know, more than 10,000 planes are being used right now, both civilian and military. And we have all the cruise ships, that's a big help too — but I still can't believe my country will be gone soon. I feel so sad. My home, my mother's home, my dad's grave, all my memories, everything will be lost forever." Colin sobbed.

Martin noticed the last few months had taken their toll on Colin. He hugged him. "I'm glad the President decided to come to London now. And I'm even more glad you're staying with me. I love you Colin. We'll get through this together."

"The sheer vastness of this disaster is wearing me down. If it weren't for you, I don't know what I would've done. I see so much suffering every day and now everything I know is falling apart. My mother — I'm scared for her. She's never been out of the country. She's too old for this, it shouldn't happen to her. All I want for her is to have a good life until she meets my dad in Heaven."

Martin loved Colin very much, but he did not like listening to all this religious stuff. He felt frustrated that Colin was still committed to his religion and would pray to God several times a day: asking God to make the Cube go away. Martin felt sad to see his lover so distressed. "It will all be fine. Your mum is flying to London tomorrow and Rick and Paul, who are staying at my place, will pick her up and look after her till you and I fly back in two months. And then you'll have your mum and me all together in my home, our home. And we'll take it from there. Stay strong. And let's get out of here. I don't want the President keeping us here all night."

***

Martin and Colin had a brief walk to their waiting car. Clouds covered the evening sky, but Martin saw the green hue behind them: the Cube was always there. Now visible day and night: hanging there, too low, the green squared threat, a very inappropriate sight: the constant reminder of their impending doom. He had so much to do, but so little time left.

Because of the evacuation, the electricity companies had shut down non-essential power usage. All street lights had switched off, offices and buildings were dark and elevators had stopped working. Driving back to Colin's apartment gave Martin an insight into how big of an event the evacuation was. There was almost no traffic on the streets; the odd person was walking quickly down the road. A lot of people were still there, but no one kept lights on in their home, so as not to attract attention. Even though Washington DC would be one of the last cities to be evacuated, the town already looked deserted. A ghost town.

Colin's apartment was seven floors up. Martin was exhausted by the time they had climbed the stairs. He did not feel right, having to meet his future mother in-law under these circumstances, but it would have to do.

"I must warn you," Colin said, as they were catching their breath. "My mother is much more religious than I am, and I've found leaflets from the Children of Abraham in her room. Also, I've never officially told her I'm gay. And she doesn't know yet that she is going ahead of me tomorrow, alone, nor that she's staying at your place. So, be prepared for a fight."

"Hi Mom, how are you feeling today?" Colin asked when they walked into the living room.

His mother sat in her rocking chair: one of her few personal items they had moved to his place, after he had decided it was safer for her to stay there after the riots. She had her Bible in her hands. The half dozen candles placed around her made her look pale and tired. The dancing shadows and dark corners gave the room an eerie atmosphere. Martin felt as if someone or something was ready to jump out of the dark. Sometimes he felt the aliens were already hiding on Earth.

Colin's mother stood up and rushed towards Colin and Martin, making them jump. "I've been praying for you my son. I fear you're not on the right path and I'm afraid your father and I won't see you in Heaven. You're working against God's plan for us."

"Mom, not again, we've been over this before. I believe Americans have the right to choose whether or not they want to stay. And for those who do not want to die, but leave, I'm helping them."

Martin felt uncomfortable. He cleared his throat, so Colin would get his attention.

"Mom, this is my friend Martin Germain. He's from England. He works for the Prime Minister there and he's here to help us with the evacuation effort."

"Nancy Andrews, pleased to meet you Mr Germain." Her grimace made it clear she disapproved of him.

This is not going well, Martin thought as he shook her hand. "Mrs Andrews, so good to finally meet you too. Colin has told me a lot about you."

"Really? He hasn't mentioned you once," she said and turned away from them. She sat back, rocking her chair, reading aloud from her Bible.

"Mom, please put the Bible down. I have important things to tell you. I'm putting you on a plane to London tomorrow. I need you gone from here. The Cube is coming closer each day, and I need to know you're safe. You'll stay with friends at Martin's, we've made arrangements for you already. When I am done here, Martin and I will follow."

"No, I'm just fine here. I don't want to stay with strangers."

"Martin is not a stranger. Mother, we're lovers. And we're very much in love," Colin said and took Martin's hands in his.

"You boys are faggots?" she shouted. "I've suspected it. Colin, my son, I've prayed for you many times. Don't give in to your temptations or you'll be beyond redemption."

"Mother, please. Shut the Hell up now. I've had enough. I'm sick of you judging me. You hide behind your Bible, but ask yourself. What would Jesus do?"

Nancy threw her Bible at her son. The heavy book hit Colin above his left eye. Blood streamed from his eyebrow over his cheek and dripped onto the floor in front of him.

"I'm not going to London and stay with faggots. Do not disrespect me. End of." Nancy turned round and stormed off to her bedroom. She slammed and locked the door.

Martin heard her sob. "Leave her for now. We should let her sleep on it. Tomorrow we'll try and talk some sense into her. And if necessary we'll drag her on the plane."

"Yeah, you're right. It's all a bit too much for her. She has never said anything bad about gays before. She loves her gay hairdresser, but she has become more extreme in her religious views recently. And — I need you to sleep in the spare bedroom tonight."

"I understand, I'll see you in the morning. Sleep well," Martin said, as he hugged Colin.

Martin, wake up. Wake up now. Martin had no idea where he was. Not at home, that was for sure. When he opened his eyes, Colin was standing over him, his eyes red and wet, snot running from his nose. He had a piece of paper in his hand.

"What's this?" Martin asked.

"It's from my mother. She's gone. Look at what she wrote. She's travelling to Las Vegas, to wait there for Armageddon and die for my sins, together with all the other Children of Abraham, and Simon Waltz, who, she believes, is there to lead them to Heaven." Colin was shaking. Tears were dripping from his face. "Her bag is gone, and she took all my cash. I've looked everywhere for her. She's really gone Martin. I phoned the police, but they won't try finding her and bring her back. They said there simply isn't enough manpower, or time."

"The only way she can travel across the country is by bus, so she'll be travelling for days. We'll have to wait till she is there and then we'll find her and put her on a plane. I'll help you," Martin said.

"Really, you would do that for me?" Colin asked.

"Of course. I would do anything for you."

"Thank you, we'll do that," Colin said. He wiped the tears off his face and a small smile appeared. "Let's get dressed. We need to get to the White House, we have a lot to do."

53. Why won't you be my baby?
(April year 2)

Shouting did not seem to work. The prison guards had taken three hours before they opened her cell and taken Kim to the hospital ward. Yesterday evening, one of the nurses had given her medicines to induce labour. Her water had broken and she had contractions every three minutes now. Her baby would be born one month early. Kim missed her Jiang. She wanted her husband to be with her now, but the guards had repeatedly denied her requests to see him. The last couple of months had been unbearable: Tuan had kept raping her, and it had taken her a long time to convince him the baby was his. A lie, but necessary for her, *their*, survival. She had thought out her plan months ago and was relieved that everything would come to fruition today The contractions were very painful and she found concentrating on the task ahead proved very difficult. Her plan was full of dangers; not only could she die today, but she could kill her baby too. And if Tuan found out what had really happened: he could have all three of them executed. Another contraction. The baby was due very soon.

During the last few weeks the medical staff had grown very fond of Kim. It had been no big secret Tuan had raped her time and again, and often afterwards Kim had been taken to the hospital ward covered in cuts, burns and bruises. His behaviour disgusted them, so she had had no problem asking them for their help, and even though the nurses were afraid of Tuan, they had decided to do so. Kim was only worried because it had taken them very long to contact Tuan and she did not want the baby to be born before he arrived: that would ruin everything.

Another contraction. "Get my husband in here please, I need to see him. Please, just this once. Only for a minute?"

she asked the nurses.

After a few minutes Jiang entered the room. "My sweet wife. I'm so happy to finally see you. I have been very lonely, but thinking of you and our child has kept me alive. And soon you will give birth and I am here to support you," he said.

Kim had not witnessed Jiang's gradual deterioration, and she was shocked to see her husband looked like a moving skeleton. Months alone in his cell had taken its toll. Rags hung off his shaking, thin limbs. His eyes were bulging out of his jaundiced face, his hairless skull looked like cheap leather, and when he spoke: only a few lonely grey whiskers above his thin lips moved.

Kim had decided she could not tell him about her plan, because if Tuan told him the news, she needed Jiang to be genuinely heartbroken. She prayed Tuan would believe the deception without any doubt.

Another contraction. And more excruciating pain. She was screaming for oxygen, *I need more oxygen.* Why did she feel as if she was pushing out a bulldozer? She had to concentrate. Jiang was not holding her hand any more, she opened her eyes to see the nurses rushing him out of the room.

"Tuan has arrived. I must hide, I will see you later my darling. I love you," he said before he was led out. His smile revealed stained and chipped teeth.

She couldn't answer him. She tried to smile, but it was much too painful to see him suffer and she knew he would suffer more very soon, but once over, everything would all have been worth the pain.

More contractions. She had lost count. The pain was too much, but they would not give her painkillers, as they could ruin her plan. In and out of consciousness. Dark, light, pain. The cruelty was never ending. Pain, dark.

You need to push harder. Kim had woken up again. Tuan

was standing over her. His face was fraught with genuine concern. The nurses were trying to keep him out of the way. Her doctor gave her a knowing smile and wink; everything was still going to plan. She trusted them, she had no choice.

Kim felt as if someone had put a broken glass between her legs and was wiggling it when she was pushing. Plop, she felt as if she plopped: the bulldozer had come out. Relief. She wanted to see her child, she didn't even know if she had a boy or a girl. What if the plan went wrong and she or her baby died? She would never have this moment ever again. Kim felt the prick of a needle in her arm and her doctor stared at her, his eyes smiling. Her vision blurred and the voices became echoes: she was falling into the darkness.

***

The doctor and the nurses created a chaotic scene in the room, thereby confusing Tuan. Everything had to be done very fast. First the doctor had given Kim an injection to make her look as if her heart had failed and she had died, and as soon as Tuan turned his attention to her, the doctor would inject the tiny newborn and make her die too.

***

"Look at her, this is your daughter," a nurse said as she handed the tiny child over to Tuan.

Tuan couldn't believe his luck. He was a father. He was certain: because *she* had told him so. That little rat Jiang had not made her pregnant, no, he knew this little baby was his daughter as soon as he looked into her eyes. He recognised her as only a father could. There was no doubt in his mind that eight months ago he conceived this child with his Kim. He felt very happy. Now he could have that rat Jiang killed and marry his Kim, have a beautiful family and live happily ever after. He would never let her out of his sight and lose her like he lost his first love. Someone was pulling at his arm. Whoever was spoiling his moment, they would regret having done so: he would have them shot.

"Sorry Sir," the doctor said, "I think we have a problem. She — she's not breathing."

Tuan felt confused, how could his perfect moment be ruined like this? He handed the baby over to a nurse and looked at his lover. She was silent, not moving. No, this couldn't be happening to him. He had it all figured out: the three of them would be together forever. The contrast between fantasy and reality was too big for him to understand. He saw blood everywhere: on the sheets, on her breasts, on the floor. Red on everything, except for her face: she was pale; as white as virgin ice, never been touched by anyone but him. How could this be? He felt her wrist, but could not find her heart beat. He leaned over close to her mouth, but could not feel her warm breath on his lips. Tuan heard a woman scream. Surprised, he looked at Kim, hoping against all hope she had opened her eyes and mouth, and she was screaming, but she was not.

"The baby is dead too," a nurse cried.

Tuan turned to her. She was crying and holding a limp baby in her arms. Both of them had died, this reality was too much for him, this was not part of his plan. He did not want this type of failure in his life. "Get rid of them. Burn them in the incinerators. I have to go. Don't ever mention them to me ever again, or I will have all of you shot. You hear me?" Tuan yelled, as he stormed out of the room; he wanted to cry, but did not want any of them to see. He would have the whole medical team executed soon. He wanted these horrible events and thoughts gone from his mind. His heart hurt too much thinking about what had happened to him. He never wanted to set foot in this prison camp ever again. There was only one more thing he had to do before he could leave this horrible place. Make someone else suffer more than he was right now. Make *him* suffer; all alone in his cold and damp cell: that little rat Jiang. The thought cheered Tuan up, thinking of the pain he would inflict on him. Make him live with this devastating news for as long as possible. Tuan made his way to Jiang's cell.

"Are you here to shoot me?" Jiang asked as Tuan walked into the cell.

Tuan looked at the small pile of stained clothes in front of him, and at the pathetic creature, crouched next to the pile: cornered and scared.

"I know she's giving birth right now," Jiang said, a defiant look in his face.

Tuan walked up to him. He hated that man so much. He wanted to shoot him right here, right now. But it gave him more pleasure to think that the little rat would be suffering very soon; he had no idea his whole world would be destroyed in the next minute.

"The People's Republic of China hereby informs you that your sentence has been altered. You have been sentenced to life imprisonment for treason. I hope you live long and rot here," Tuan said. He could not stop himself smiling.

"So you have what you wanted. You have my wife and my child now. And you leave me here. Fine. As long as my child has a prosperous and happy life, it doesn't matter what happens to me."

And now I'll go for the kill, Tuan thought. This little rat was going to get what he deserved. He betrayed my country and tried to lay claim on *my* baby. "Yes, you'll be here. I'll go now and will never come back to this godforsaken place. Oh, and just to inform you. You had a daughter, but both she and your wife died during childbirth. The People's Republic of China would like to thank you for

139

all the help you have given. Goodbye."

Tuan saw Jiang's face change into a prolonged primal scream. He saw the life energy being screamed out of Jiang's mouth. Tuan felt pleasure as he left the cell. And he felt pleasure as he walked out of the prison. He still heard Jiang screaming as his car drove off towards the mountains.

***

Something was very familiar, and safe. Kim had never felt as content as she did now. She could not explain why. Then she understood. Kim had woken up and the doctors had put her baby in her arms. She could feel tiny warm and moist breaths on her face. A new odour, but very familiar, she took a deep breath through her nose and she felt her whole body tingle. Slight movements and tiny coughs. She had a baby in her arms: *her* baby. She looked around. Her plan had worked. They were safe. *Where is Jiang?* She needed to feel complete. Ah, there he was, next to her: where he belonged, sleeping in a chair. His looked happy and calm. No matter how emaciated his face was, to her he looked handsome again. All would be fine now. They were free.

"Kim," the doctor said, "everything went according to plan. Tuan believed us and he has left. You have a lovely daughter. It was very hard for your husband though. Tuan told him you had died and it broke him. He didn't respond to us, he was catatonic. We had to carry him out of his cell, but as soon as we got him here and he saw you both, he improved. I gave him something to sleep, he is exhausted. We'll move you to a safe place tomorrow. Have you thought of a name for her?"

"Yes, her name is Jia-Li. After my grandmother."

"That's a beautiful name for a beautiful girl and I'm sure, with her loving parents, she will grow up to be good too. You chose wisely."

59. Viva Las Vegas.
(May year 2)

"Go, go, go," the Marine shouted at Colin and Martin. The plane was still moving on the runway when they were pushed out. The Nevada desert night felt cold on their faces. The sky was clear and the stars were competing with the Cube for attention. Half a dozen Marines led them to a waiting army vehicle.

The Intelligence Agency had taken two months to pinpoint exactly where Colin's mother was staying. The Children of Abraham had taken over every hotel on the Strip to house their followers. Most of the hotel owners had left the US, and the ones still here did not have the resources, nor the will, to oppose The Children. Las Vegas was ruled by armed Children of Abraham Militia, who were now the de facto authority.

According to the report, Nancy Andrews was in a small motel on the old Strip, close to a chapel. She did not know yet, but tonight she would be lifted from her bed and be liberated.

***

Colin was happy to have Martin with him. The last few months had been tough; the evacuation had run into many problems, and not being able to reach his mother had been nerve-racking. Martin had always managed to reason with him, calm him down and convince him they had more than enough time to save his mother too. It had taken them a lot of effort to persuade various people for help: they had called in old favours, and had the Intelligence Agency search for Nancy. Diverting a military plane, and acquiring a team of Marines had turned out to be more difficult, but they had managed and the Marines had boarded the plane at Washington DC. Colin had used his status and his connection to the President to achieve all this, but without the President's knowledge, and Colin would get into real trouble if anything went wrong in the next few hours.

On a normal day the Strip would be buzzing with people; even early in the mornings. Drunken newlyweds, gamblers and showgirls in glitzy outfits would roam the streets, surrounded by garish, flashing lights, loud music and big advertisements enticing everyone to commit every legal and illegal sin. Today was different. No happy faces. No flashing lights. No banners. No one in this city wanted to sin and the streets stayed empty.

The Marines checked their machine guns one last time as they approached the motel where Colin's mother was supposed to be asleep. *In and out*, they had said. A simple rescue mission.

There was no receptionist at the motel, but Colin was not happy. They might have to check every room. Kicking in doors and waking up dozens of people would certainly attract unwanted attention from the Militia.

A Marine was going through paperwork left on the desk. "Got it. Mrs Andrews. Room 27."

Trying to be quiet, the group ran up the stairs. All was going well. A Marine picked the lock and opened the door. Easy. Colin exhaled, relieved. He did not want them to frighten his mother. There were four beds in the room; in one of them a person was sleeping. They pulled the blankets off. A young woman woke up and screamed until a Marine put his hand on her mouth.

"Shit," Colin said. "It's not her." Two months of living in fear he would never see his mother again, two months of looking forward to this moment, and now he felt utterly disappointed. "Where the fuck is she? Where the fuck is my mother? Her name is Nancy. Tell me bitch." Colin had lost control.

The woman looked at him. Her face was full of disdain. "The Lord shall be your saviour. Your mother told me about you, you are queer. She doesn't want to see you."

Colin punched her in her face, he made her lips bleed. She smiled at him, with blood on her teeth. Colin felt a rage he never knew he had inside him, he needed to vent his anger on the woman. He grabbed her thumb and twisted until it broke. He did not notice her scream. "Tell me where my mother is, or I'll break all your fingers."

The woman grimaced. She saw in Colin's face he was serious. "Please don't hurt me. She's in the Catholic Chapel, it's two blocks down. They're having an overnight pray-in. I swear."

The Marines and Martin rushed out of the room.

Colin turned to the woman. "If she's not there, I'll be back to finish you off." He wiped her blood off his hand on a towel and joined the others.

***

The young woman picked up the phone as soon as she heard the truck leave. "Connect me to Mr Waltz's room now. I have to report an emergency. We're under attack."

***

The presidential suite had great views over Las Vegas and the mountains in the distance. But Simon was not interested in that, or the marble floors, or the gold plated bathrooms, or the six feet tall crystal chandeliers. He was interested in the four virgins in his bed and the cocaine on the nightstand. The girls would be barely legal in Britain and he was not sure if they would be here in the US. He didn't care though; they had told him they were over 21, but more importantly: they were willing. There had been a daily stream of young women since he had arrived here over a month ago. He loved pussy and now he found himself in the land of plenty.

A security guard walked into his room unannounced. He had not even knocked at the door. Simon hated being interrupted when he was *eating*.

"Scuse me Sir, we've problems," the guard said.

Simon pushed the girl he was busy with off him and sat up. He did not bother to cover himself up; the guard had seen him having sex before. "You know never to disturb me when I'm with my followers. What the fuck is so important?"

"There's them soldiers in town and they're on their way to the Catholic Chapel. They're looking for this woman. Dunno, some dumb ass bitch told me, said they broke her fingas."

"Well, why the fuck are you still standing here? Get to the fucking car park, grab some guns, organise a couple of guys and wait for me outside the entrance. Go!" Simon got up and dressed himself. He snorted a big line and made his way to the lobby. If he could not fuck, he could kill. He enjoyed doing both.

***

Las Vegas Catholic Chapel. Children of Abraham. Pray together. All Children welcome, the sign said outside a nondescript concrete sixties building. "Well, that's easy," Colin said as they drove up to the abandoned entrance.

"We don't have much time. You," a Marine said to Colin, "point her out, but do not engage her. Leave the chapel and do not look back. You," the Marine pointed at two others, "when identified, grab the subject and if you have to, lift her off the ground and carry her out. The rest of you, keep us covered."

The men rushed into the chapel and over 200 peoples' prayers were interrupted. Gasps and screams filled with fear echoed through the room. Not a single person moved or protested, though.

Colin gazed at the effigy hanging above the altar: a giant green cube with a bleeding Jesus on a crucifix in front. Colin was shocked when he realised what he really saw: Jesus was a real person, and dead. He needed his mother away from these lunatics. Frantically he ran between the pews, looking for her. "There she is. Mother!" Colin shouted and pointed at his mother, who stood up and fled towards the back door, but the two Marines ran faster than she did. Colin watched in horror as they lifted her up. She started screaming and shouting, and tried to kick herself free. A handful of men stood up. *Wannabe heroes*, Colin thought.

"If you want to live. Sit back down," a Marine shouted.

"Mom, I'm sorry," Colin whispered as she was carried past him. She spat in his face.

Colin was pushed into the truck by the last Marine. His mother was on the floor, two Marines were trying to restrain her. Martin looked at the scene in horror.

Colin felt a bang and heard loud scratching noises, and everyone was tossed around the cabin. He landed on Martin. Had someone crashed into them? Before he could ask, their truck accelerated. He could hear car tyres screaming on the tarmac. Were they being chased? He heard too many different noises at the same time and hoped one of them had not been a gunshot.

***

The military truck had no problems keeping enough distance from the pursuers, and except for several shots fired at them, the drive to the airport was fast and easy.

The plane's ramp into the cargo bay stood open and its engines were running. The Marines leaped out of the truck. Two of them picked up Colin's mother, the rest stood outside: pointing their guns at the approaching chasers.

"Stay here, both of you," a Marine shouted at Colin and Martin.

"Mom, I love you," Colin shouted as the Marines carried her out of the truck and towards the ramp.

I hate you, I hate you, I hate you, he heard her shout, but then her voice was drowned out by the firing of several machine guns.

The plane accelerated on the runway with the ramp still down. Colin felt relieved when he saw the plane close the ramp and take off. His mother, whether she liked it or not, was on her way to London. She was safe. Tonight he would sleep a lot better. Martin squeezed his hand, smiling, almost as if he had read his mind.

The marines jumped back into the truck and they drove back to the military airstrip in the desert, where their plane to Washington DC was still waiting. And the pursuers were chasing his truck again.

***

David Pilling felt exhausted after having flown non-stop for the last three months. Every day his aircraft had been flying between several European airports and the US. *You can take turns and sleep eight hours each flight*, they had told all the pilots, but David found out that was not the reality: he managed to get two to three hours maximum, and that was on a good flight. He had to endure his ordeal for as long as it would take; his friends and colleagues needed his help. His country needed his help. However, he felt the Government was holding him and all military personnel to ransom: some clever dick in the White House had decided that the families of the military would be the last ones to be evacuated. David understood why the decision was made, and as much as he hated the situation; he did respect the man who had come up with the idea.

Today's flight was different; instead of flying from Houston to his base in Germany, he had been ordered to divert the plane to Washington DC and pick up Marines and two civilians. The civilians had instructed him to fly to Las Vegas and pick up several people, whilst waiting for the Marines who would be rescuing an *important* person, and then he would have to fly to London.

They had made David land the plane at a landing strip close to the city and the Marines, an American and a British civilian had left in a hurry. Hours later they had returned with a crazy old woman, and a truck chasing them. The Marines had carried her onto the plane and had run back to their truck. As he took off, his plane had come under fire several times and he was unsure if he had been hit, but he would not find out until they gained more altitude. He tried not to think about what might happen mid-flight.

The sun had risen, and David looked at the half blue and half green sky. The Cube floated over him and the sight made him shiver.

David's plane had never been so heavily loaded: civilians, supplies and provisions were competing for space, and being over the maximum payload, David had difficulties controlling his plane, and after an hour of piloting he had to ask his co-pilot to take over.

Exhausted, David took his time to walk around the cabin; he needed to stretch his legs before he could have a nap. He looked at his passengers, but could not focus on their faces. A mechanism in his brain made him shut down his humanity and compassion: noticing their faces would make them real. The evacuation was going to plan, but the consequences and the suffering the immense displacement was causing had not been addressed yet: they would have to deal with that later. *He* would have to deal with that later too.

David tried to find the particular crazy screaming lady. His co-pilot had told him her name was Nancy Andrews. She was the mother of a Presidential adviser, and she was the reason his plane had been diverted. Why did she deserve the extra care? All Americans were being displaced, all were scared, all had the same rights. He needed to know. "Mrs Andrews?" he asked. He stared at an old frail woman. She looked tired, but wide awake; the fear in her eyes made it evident to him that she had never flown before.

She looked at him. Her eyes locked into his, asking for answers, asking him to tell her everything would be just fine.

"I'm here to help you. How are you feeling?" he asked her. He took her hand in his. She accepted the gesture and put her other hand on his, holding on tight.

"I'm scared. They left me all alone. I've never been outside the country before and I've never flown. And now they're taking me to stay in the house of my son's lover. You see, my son's gay and I've to stay in a gay house in London. I was happy where I was, with my own kind. I never asked to be rescued. God was going to take me to Heaven and now I don't know what will happen to me. I am very afraid."

"You know, they stopped everything they were doing. We paused helping other Americans to safety. They risked their own lives, and everyone on this plane, and mine. They had my plane diverted. All for you," David said. "And you worry you have to stay in a gay house? What the hell does that mean anyway? A *gay* house? You should count your blessings that you have a son who is so devoted to you." *How could someone be so ungrateful?* He did not like her and pulled his hands from her. He needed to get away from her.

"But you see." She wanted him to understand. "Simon told me Armageddon is coming. I have to stay in America and die for my son's sins."

"You stupid woman," David said. "The Children of Abraham are a silly cult and Simon Waltz is a dangerous charlatan. He's a wife beater. And you listen to him? You're deluded." He had made her cry, but he didn't care. She had to understand how stupid she had been and how lucky she was. He heard her pray when he walked off. "I hate religion," he muttered, hoping she heard him.

*****

The diversion had worked. They were still under fire by the pursuing Militia, who seemed to think they were more important than the plane and its important package. The sound of bullets bouncing off the truck was deafening. Colin had never been under fire before, and this was certainly not something he ever wanted to experience again.

Rays of sunshine caught his eye: the promise of another beautiful day. The Sun: she never judged, regardless of what humans were up to. The dance between her and Earth had always been a welcoming and happy constant in his life. He looked out of the window: small flowers made the desert burst with colours. The sky brightened with radiant shades of yellows and oranges, with daytime blues pushing in from behind, itching to take over. He could not see the green Cube from this angle. For a brief moment Colin felt wonderful. He winked at Martin. "You okay?"

"No. We're still being shot at," Martin said. "And I found it very disturbing to see your mother in that state. She's been so brainwashed by this cult, she didn't even seem to recognise you. I hope she'll recover soon. And did you see that dead guy hanging on the cross? They're all nutters in there."

Colin agreed. He put his hand on Martin's knee and squeezed gently.

Fire in the hole, Colin heard a Marine shout. He remembered the phrase from movies he had seen. Movies — would new ones ever be made? Would he ever see one again at the cinema? Eat popcorn till his stomach hurt?

A massive bang that seemed to last forever, so loud it made his ears ring, shook Colin back to reality. Martin seemed fine, a shocked look was on his face, but he did not seem hurt. He could still think and move, so he was not hurt either. But what had happened?

The Marines were cheering and shouting. "We hit 'em. They're burning."

Colin looked out of the back window. A few metres behind them, the Militia truck was lying on its side. Black thick smoke rose up high into the sky, spoiling the Sun's dawn dance. He could swear he felt the heat radiating from the fire. He heard screams: primal noises of terror and pain, and he felt sick and wished he had not listened.

A Marine suggested they should get out and see if they could save survivors.

"Leave them. Let them burn and meet their maker," Colin heard himself say. He had not planned on saying something this nasty and the harsh sound of his voice made him feel uneasy, but dark hatred dominated his thoughts. He was too ashamed to look at Martin. Soon he would be back in Washington to help the President, and then he could forget about this horrible episode. He did not care any more for those crazy religious Americans that had decided to stay. He wished they would die like rats on a sinking ship.

No one spoke as they drove on through the desert to their waiting plane.

61. O God, where art thou?
(May year 2)

Simon did not see or hear it coming: the grenade flew towards him in silence and landed on the canvas top of his truck. A bright flash and a loud bang followed, but Simon did not notice either. Neither did he notice the fire that followed the explosion. Neither did he notice the screams of his dying security guards, who sat with him in the back of the truck. Neither did he notice when the flames engulfed him, burning his clothes and singeing his long hair. He was also unaware of the smell of burning flesh: his own flesh.

Darkness.

Simon was not on Earth anymore. He was alone, yet he did not feel lonely. He did not understand where he was, but he was not lost. He did not feel alive, but he was not dead. He had felt at war before, but now he was at peace.

Light.

A white light, no, a white tunnel beckoned him. Ecstasy hit him and he felt the urge to enter the tunnel. Simon knew he was on his way to Heaven, he had never been more certain of anything else before, all his senses told him so. The lights shone bright and were pleasantly coloured. He heard birds and children sing. A slight breeze felt warm on his skin. He smelt flowers: lavender. He was a good man: God would be pleased with him and he could not wait to finally meet Him; he had worked towards this moment all his life. A familiar face was waiting for him at his final destination. Although he did not recognise the man, he knew who He was: God, his Creator.

"Welcome Simon. Come with me. I have to show you the Truth," He said.

Simon fell on his knees and bowed his head in front of Him. "Yes my Lord. I am your servant."

He led Simon to another place: and he found himself at his home. Simon's wife was there with their three daughters. She was cooking dinner and the girls were reading books: their Bibles.

"You have forsaken your daughters. They need their father. They need a safe future and I shall show you where you have to go. Follow Me," God said.

They travelled towards the green Cube. Even though, he did not see an entrance: Simon was pulled inside. He could not see inside the Cube, but he felt safe. He belonged here.

"This is where you shall take your three daughters. Your journey shall end here. You have been chosen to start anew. You are my new Adam and you shall have three Eves. You are Alpha and Omega," He said to Simon. "And you must stop the Children of Abraham from entering the Cube. They are not worthy, they worship false gods. This shall be their fate," He said.

Simon found himself above Earth, witnessing the End of Time. Churches filled with his followers were being swallowed in the earth, the lava burning them alive. Simon recoiled when he heard them scream. Locusts swarmed the land, devouring all plants and animals. Humans ran around with boils on their faces, screaming in agony, dying a slow and painful death. Simon smelt the fire and brimstone raining down from the skies, reminding him of rotten eggs. Tidal waves drowned the cities. Lightning set forests on fire. When God's wrath had finished, nothing but wasted lands, bare rocks and lava spewing mountains were all that was left of Earth. And the Sun rose from the west.

Simon did not feel afraid of the future. God Himself had chosen him and had given clear instructions. Simon felt pleased that God had included his daughters in His divine plan.

An unpleasant feeling began to appear in his mind. He could not understand what could ruin his beautiful experience. "My Lord, I'm afraid. Something is happening to me. I feel pain. Are You punishing me? I feel confused."

"Simon. It is time for you to go. Remember what I told you. You have no time to lose. Do not disappoint me."

Simon felt he was falling backwards. Against better judgement he looked over his shoulder and he saw Hell: scorching flames and choking smoke were pulling at him. "My Lord, help me please, I beg You."

But He was not there.

Darkness.

Simon could not see who pulled him out of the burning truck; the flames had glued his eyelids together. He could not see the blackened flesh on his body, but he did feel the pain. He wanted to scream, but he had no voice.

Simon knew he had woken up again, but he felt he was trapped inside a dream. He could not open his eyes and when he tried to touch them, he noticed his hands were bandaged. The air around him felt liquid, but he did not drown. Somewhere in the distance he heard his name.

"Simon, you're in a hospital. Please don't be alarmed, but I've bad news," the voice said. "You were attacked. A grenade was thrown. Your truck burnt and you were the only one we could save."

Simon did not want the voice to continue, but he could not speak and tell the voice to shut the hell up. He remembered being with God. He wanted to be there again, where he had felt safe, but that had happened an eternity ago, and the joyous feeling was slipping away from him.

The voice continued. "You've been burnt. It's very bad,

153

but you'll live. We've given you morphine, for the pain and will do so until you have recovered. Go back to sleep, you must rest."

Simon felt a small prick on his arm and a rush through his veins. He fell asleep again.

When he woke up, another voice spoke to him "Simon. You may open your eyes now. Try it. We managed to save the sight in one. Praise the Lord."

Slowly the whiteness became bright and for a split second he thought he was back with God, but when his one working eye focused, he felt disappointed to see he was in a hospital room. Several people dressed in white gowns stood next to him. He looked at his hands, they were still bandaged. He had tubes coming out of him. Some machines were making sucking noises and others were beeping.

"How are you feeling Simon? Is there anything I can do for you?"

"No. Thank you doctor. I am feeling great. I've seen the future, and it's wonderful," Simon said.

Light.

67. Only 71 minutes to save the world. (June year 2)

"Good afternoon, this is Anne Goodman reporting from Beijing for the World Wide Live News Channel. It has just gone eight o'clock in the evening here. I am with Doctor Tuan, the architect of the Pan Asian Ophiuchus Project. As you are aware, seven months ago a document was leaked exposing the proposal of a joint effort to prepare a pre-emptive strike on the Ophiuchus Cube before it reaches Earth. This proposal was extremely controversial and the United Nations tried to condemn it. Many things have happened, since this proposal was leaked. America has been evacuated and Britain attempted to assassinate Simon Waltz.

"There has been no contact from the Cube. Scientists and amateurs from all over the world have tried to make first contact, but to no avail. The silence from the Cube is deafening.

"Let me introduce you to Doctor Tuan — Hello Sir, you have been accused by the international community, of starting an intergalactic war. What is your reply to that?"

"Hello Anne. Well, I am aware many leaders do not approve of our approach, but we never intended to attack without good reason. Our plan was to have a back-up plan to save Earth in case the alien object identified itself as aggressive. When we became aware this object was travelling towards us, we needed to make many decisions. We can sit and wait for the aliens to make themselves known and make their intentions clear to us, or we can prepare for any eventuality — and that is what we did, because we all know what happened to the Indians when the Europeans came to the Americas, and that is exactly what we try to prevent happening to mankind. The Cube has not responded in any way to our scientists, nor anyone else here on Earth to make its intentions known. The three Governments of the Pan Asian Ophiuchus Cube Project have waited until today, hoping for a response, indicating the aliens in the Cube are not hostile, but they have heard nothing. So, today is the last day we can take preventative measures, without endangering ourselves. Today, the People's Republic of China, India and Pakistan have declared war on the Cube and are executing their plan to save Earth from an alien invasion. Six minutes ago, 368 intercontinental ballistic nuclear missiles, especially adapted for this mission, have been deployed to engage the Cube and destroy it."

"Are you not afraid they might retaliate? Wasn't that the exact reason why the United Nations decided not to endorse any actions that might make them attack us?"

"We are aware of these concerns, but you have to understand, all nations on Earth have tried to make contact with the Cube and failed. If they had friendly intentions, they would have made the effort to contact us and explain we do not have to fear them. They have done nothing, and see what has happened in the USA during the evacuation — thousands of people have died, hundreds of thousands are suffering and millions are displaced. Does that seem friendly to you? If they can travel between stars, you'd think they would let us know their intentions. Our Governments have decided the aliens are hostile and we have taken it upon ourselves to save our planet."

"You said six minutes ago? When will we find out if your plan has worked?"

"In just over one hour from now."

"What are the reports saying?" President McGee asked.

"We have confirmation Sir, not the exact numbers, but it seems many missiles are on their way and should be engaging the Cube in an hour," Colin said.

"So, all we can do is wait. If anyone feels the need to pray, I suggest you do it now, and you do it hard."

Martin sat himself down next to Colin. "You all right there?" He had to whisper: everyone in the room had gone quiet and Martin did not want to upset them.

"No. I dread to think what happens if the Chinese don't succeed. I don't like it, but we have to pray now that the Cube is destroyed. The alternative is too horrifying to think about. Please hold my hand and pray with me."

Martin did not pray, but he did squeeze Colin's hand as hard as he could.

"Fifty five minutes to go."

"This looks like something out of a movie," Zaira said to her colleague. Both of them were staring at the television. They sat in the staff canteen at the hotel, as they had no work to do: all the tourists had either cancelled their stay or had left for their homes early. Her uncle had sent most employees home, but Zaira and a few others had decided to come in. She did not want to stay at home with her parents; they had become unhappier and more afraid every day with the impending arrival of the Cube. Now, she wished she had stayed at home after all, because she knew she could not travel back to her parents in time if things did go wrong during the attack.

Gustavo had been travelling to work and as soon as she had phoned him and told him about the missiles he told her to stay at the hotel no matter what happened: he would hurry there to pick her up and take her home. She needed him to hold her now, and a sudden rush of loneliness came over her.

On the screen she saw a blue sky with several missiles, their flames and smoke billowing out from below. On the

157

bottom was a news ticker with a clock counting down the minutes. "It's just so silly," she said to her colleague. "Aliens are coming from the other side of the Universe and we are trying to kill them. I'm scared what they're going to do to us after we explode all the bombs on them." Zaira had not noticed her colleague had left the building too.

"Fifty minutes."

"Can you believe that prick? As if he figured it all out," Jiang said to Kim, spitting at the television.

For the last two months they had been living in hiding. Kim's plan had worked out exactly as she had wanted. Tuan had believed she and her baby had died and had subsequently disappeared. Nobody at the prison would miss them, so the day after Jia-Li was born; their doctor had moved them 50 kilometres away from Harbin City's camp and had housed them in his basement.

Kim pointed at the screen. "Look, there's the countdown to the time of impact. Just under an hour and then we'll know if it's gone or if we're going to be in a war with them."

A sudden blast: lasting for a full minute, quaking violently, as if a chain of cars was crashing against their building, and was followed by another, and another. A wall of wind rattled the small cellar window, and Kim's ears popped. "What was that? This wasn't like an earthquake, it felt different."

"I'm not sure, let me go upstairs and see if the neighbours are fine," Jiang said as he got up.

The baby was crying; she had also felt the three shudders and the change in air pressure, and it had upset her.

"Oh my god, oh my god, Kim come, quick," Jiang shouted down the stairs.

Kim put Jia-Li in her cot and ran up. What she wanted to see was a sky with bright oranges and deep shades of red, sent from the sun's last rays before dusk. And a few bright stars poking out, announcing the imminent arrival of the dark blue of the night, and maybe the moon up there too: shining its silvery light. But instead in the distance, was a big green square hovering above the horizon, dominating the sky, replacing the cosy and warm and familiar colours with its cold green. Screams, coming from behind her, filled with horror, made Kim turn her head. And as if she was watching a painter painting a picture; she saw three bright white mushroom shaped clouds growing, right where Harbin City should be. In a perverse way she thought they looked very beautiful. "Has it started? Are they attacking us?" she asked her husband.

Jiang looked at her and pulled her towards him, holding her tight, his body shivering. "I don't know, but I'm scared of them. We need to go inside, be with Jia-Li."

She heard the pain in his trembling voice. He had not been able to keep them safe, first at the prison camp, and now, when the aliens were attacking them. Life's problems had become too much for him to handle, and she realised he had lost the ability to make important decisions. "Yes, let's be together and wait," she said. "The news will tell us what to do."

"No! — I don't agree. The Party will not be honest with us. We can't trust them. The radiation from the blasts will be too much for our baby. We need to leave."

"Where to?" Kim asked.

"Away from the big cities. They will be targets and where the fighting will take place. We need to get to the mountains — I know where. We're going to my hometown Nyalam. It's safe there and we're close to Nepal, in case we need to flee the country."

"It's going to take us months. We can't fly there."

"I know, but if we leave now, we'll make it before winter sets in. You won't like it there. It's a very small village. It's

159

nothing compared to the big city you grew up in. But there's no alternative. Sorry," Jiang said.

"Don't worry. Your idea is good. It's the safest option for us. Let's pack. We should leave tonight."

"I have reports coming in from north-east China. It appears nuclear bombs have been fired at various cities. I repeat. They have nuclear bombs. People, may God be with you. Forty minutes remaining. This is Anne Goodman reporting live from Beijing."

Rick and Paul were watching the news programme.

"So, they finally did it. Humankind is its worst own enemy. Shoot first, ask questions later. And now the enemy is bigger and stronger than us, and they're firing nukes back. Crap. Baby, I don't want to die just yet," Rick said "You think we should find cover somewhere in case they attack us here too?"

"There's nowhere to go. We'll have to wait and see what happens. Maybe they'll only attack the areas where the bombs came from. Come here, sit with me," Paul said.

They held hands and listened for noises from outside, not knowing what to expect, not knowing what a nuclear explosion would sound like.

"You think we'd feel it?"

"A direct hit? No. We wouldn't be aware. Zap, and we're gone in an instant. Turned into dust."

"Oh bugger. I need to call my mum. You should do the same."

"Anne Goodman here. There are now confirmed reports of 19 nuclear attacks. They range from north-east China into Mongolia and the latest reports came in from Kazakhstan. Thirty minutes before we hit the Cube."

"Are we under attack? What's happening? Are the aliens nuking us? And should we deploy any of our weapons?" President McGee asked, to no one in particular.

Martin was perplexed to see this much confusion and panic. He nudged Colin. "What's going on you think?"

Colin shrugged.

"Did they attack us?" the President asked again.

No one in the room seemed to have an idea. Most of them watched the news, displayed on several screens, coming in from various sources from all over the globe.

Martin noticed all attacks seemed to be centred around central Asia. Why was this happening now — and already? Then the logical explanation dawned on him. He needed to explain his idea to the President, before any terrible mistakes were made.

"Sound the alarm in the country. We must notify the people that are still in the cities, they need to run to the hills. To safety," McGee said.

"Hold on. Hold on," Martin said. "You'll cause a terrible panic and many people will die. This is wrong, it's not them, these are our nukes. The timing, it's not right you see. It would mean they fired nukes at us before we fired at them, and our satellites would have noticed and alarmed us by now, so it can't be retaliation." Martin picked up a pencil and walked up to a wall. He sketched a circle and a square on the wall and whilst he was talking, lines appeared: representing flight paths towards the square. He added lines going back to Earth. "You see, most of our nukes are still on their way to the Cube, these explosions are us, they are nukes that have fallen down, back on us, they never made it." Martin had a quick look at his watch. "Mr President, I believe we have to wait less than 25 minutes for our bombs to reach the Cube. Then we'll know for sure."

"Twenty minutes."

161

Nancy was glad she had made the two gays leave Martin's home. She did not want to be around atheists, especially not now: not after the newsreader on the radio had told her Armageddon had started in China. They always interrupted her prayers. Colin would be with her and her husband soon, in Heaven. She had asked the Lord daily to forgive her son's sins. Nancy had cramps in her fingers and her knees ached, but her pain would soon be over. She decided to pray more, in case a bomb would explode over London.

"People, I can now confirm over fifty areas have been bombed. The first hits were in north-east China, and then they moved west wards through Mongolia, China, into Kazakhstan, Georgia and Turkey. Earth is under attack. Please get yourself to safety. In five minutes from now, our weapons should reach the Cube and, please God, hopefully destroy it."

Hundreds of millions went outside to have one last look at the green monster that was hanging above them. Last minute prayers were said. Loved ones embraced each other. They witnessed over 300 hundred explosions. The flashes were as bright as the rays of the Sun: lighting up the sky more powerful than the most violent thunderstorms and many had to avert their eyes. Cheers went up from crowds in many towns and villages, but they soon died out when the blast clouds dissipated, and it became clear the Cube had not been destroyed. Euphoria descended into panic. Millions scrounged for places in shelters and in underground bunkers. Many feared the Cube would take revenge and send a rain of nuclear bombs down on Earth.

"Doctor Tuan, the Cube has not been destroyed, can you

tell us why not? And I hear you also have an explanation as to why the bombs have fallen down?"

"Yes Anne. Unfortunately the Pakistani Government didn't modify their missiles properly and most of them failed and subsequently fell back to Earth. They sent 90 up, and so far 60 of them have come down. This is most unfortunate. We do not know why the Indian and Chinese missiles have not been able to destroy the Cube, as we hoped. Maybe it has a force field protecting it. We can however confirm no missiles or other attacks were launched from the Cube. We know it has now passed the geostationary orbit point and we still anticipate it will land next month on North America. Goodbye Ms Goodman. I have to leave now."

"Oh my God, to all you people in America, please leave too. You have less than a month to get to safety. May God be with you."

"It didn't work. They're still coming for us. At least they aren't nuking us. Well, that's it folks. We still need to evacuate. Pack your things, we're flying to London," McGee said. He stood up and rushed out of his room, tears in his eyes. Colin, Martin and the others remained silent.

71. London calling.
(June year 2)

NASA press release June.
Subject: International Space Station Evacuation.
Due to the latest developments involving the Ophiuchus Cube, NASA has decided to de-man the International Space Station as a precaution for the safety of its six astronauts. The two Soyuz escape modules currently docked to the station will take the astronauts back to the surface and will land in Russia. Preparations are underway and it is expected the astronauts will leave the station within the next 12 hours. Several experiments are being terminated and the findings are being sent by signal to various space agencies. The decision to de-man the ISS is made due to the risk of collision with the Cube in one to two days.

"Paul, listen to that. What's going on?" Rick asked as he walked into the living room. Rick had been in the kitchen preparing lunch when he heard loud siren noises coming from outside.

Paul was watching television. "I'm not sure. I'll switch over to the news channel. Look — again it's Anne Goodman yakking away on the screen, she's outside Downing Street."

"I don't think I like her, she's one of Simon's, but she's always where the action is."

"That's true. I can't really hear what she's saying, the sirens are too loud. Look — Martin just walked out of the entrance. Let's try listening to what he has to say," Paul said as he turned up the volume.

They watched Anne desperately trying to interview Martin over the deafening noise, but they could hardly hold a conversation. Martin tried to look calm, but Rick knew him better than that and saw him grinding his teeth. He was clearly nervous.

A roar and whistle, followed by a burst of light and a loud bang, came through the television speakers and at the same time through the window, shaking the coffee cups on Rick's table.

They saw on their television screen Anne looking up, and pointing at the sky. The camera followed her gaze. Three giant fire balls were crossing the sky and trails of thick white smoke followed them.

They saw Martin grab Anne and pull her towards the entrance. The camera was dropped and the television screen was filled with running feet.

Paul and Rick ran to their terrace and looked in horror at the fire balls flying past: all of them as bright as the Sun.

"Fuck, it started. They're attacking us," Rick screamed. "We need to find a safe place to hide."

"Come on, we're going to the Tube station, the one that goes deep underground. We should be safe if there's an impact," Paul said as he ran to the front door.

***

People ran screaming through the streets, many were bleeding from their heads. Shattered glass from buildings littered the pavements: sparkling like little diamonds. Cars had crashed into each other. Alarms and sirens howled continuously. Big streaks of smoke filled the blue and green sky, and the air was thick with the acrid smell of gunpowder. London was under attack.

Paul and Rick managed to reach Westminster Underground station in less than three minutes. They ran into a chaotic scene. Hundreds of panic-stricken people were trying to get into the station at the same time. The staircases were littered with people prostrate on the steps; and no one seemed to notice, nor care: they were stepping on them and crushing them in their haste, trying to find safety deep under the ground.

When they entered the station, Rick noticed a little girl halfway down. She was squatting, trying to protect her head with her hands, but every time someone kicked her, she fell down a few steps. Rick grabbed her, held her in his arms and carried her down. Paul was behind them, protecting them, using his body as a shield.

In the ticket hall the staff tried to keep the masses calm, but no one paid attention: people needed to get to the lower platform levels fast: survival instinct had taken over and they kept crushing each other.

Paul and Rick managed to shuffle themselves to the side of the hall, where they thought there was less risk of getting hurt. The girl was crying, and blood was streaming from her head; making her ginger hair dark red and sticky.

"Honey, what's your name?" Rick asked.

She stared at him, frightened, but did not answer.

Paul tore off a piece of his shirt and made it into a bandage. When he reached for her head she flinched. "It's okay. I'm not going to hurt you, but you're bleeding and I need to stop it. It will make you look pretty. Do you like the flowers on my bandage?"

She smiled and nodded. "I'm thirsty and my head hurts."

They staggered to an abandoned food stall and grabbed a few bottles of water and chocolate bars.

"We might be here for a while, so I think we should go down even further. We might not be safe enough when the bombs drop," Paul said as he gave the girl a bottle and put the improvised bandage on.

Rick noticed that the escalators going down to the platforms were as chaotic and deadly as the stairs. Layers of injured and dead people had made it impossible for them to descend; especially now they had the girl with them. By now, the staff had disappeared and Rick assumed they had given up and were hiding themselves.

Paul pointed at a service door not far from them. "Let's go there, it's ajar," he said as he picked up the girl.

Inside was a dark and empty corridor. They used the lights from their mobile phones to find their way. At the end they saw stairs: going down. Jackpot!

Hundreds of people were crammed against each other on the platform. As luck would have it, there was a train in the station, so people could not be pushed onto the tracks. Rick noticed how quiet everyone was, some were whispering, a few were crying. They found themselves a corner to sit down.

The girl was hugging Paul. He gave her a chocolate bar. "So honey. You're not alone here, are you? Did you come with your mummy and daddy?" he asked.

She did not answer, but sobbed.

"Please tell me your name and what happened to you. You're safe here with us."

She could not manage more than a whisper. "I'm Florence, my mummy took me shopping and then the sirens came on. My mummy and me went down the stairs and then all these people came and then they pushed us and then I lost my mummy and then this man hit my head. And then I don't remember anymore."

Rick smiled at her and stood up. "Okay Florence, I'm Rick and that's Paul. He will stay with you and I will look for your mother. Is that okay with you?

Florence nodded. "Yes, please find my mummy."

"Can you tell me what your mum looks like and what she was wearing?"

"No — my head hurts too much."

Rick tried not to step on people's toes as he walked around the platform. He searched for women who, in his logic, looked like a distraught mother of an eight to ten year old girl. He didn't want to shout to ask if the mother of a

Florence was on the platform, because he was concerned he might upset the little girl if she heard him. Rick had asked at least 100 women on the platform and in the train, but to no avail. He tried to go up the escalators, but they were too overcrowded; there was no way he could walk up them to search any further. When he returned an hour later, he felt exhausted and sad he had failed. "Florence. I couldn't find your mummy here, but there are lots of places I can't get to right now. We'll look for her later. Okay?" He noticed she had been snoozing in Paul's arms. She looked up at him, nodded and closed her eyes again.

An eternity later, the public announcement system switched on: first a crackle, then a voice.

"Attention please. London was not under attack. I repeat. London was not under attack. The police have given the clearance to leave the station. Please make your way to the streets, using the emergency stairs only. They have been cleared for you. Stay calm and do not rush out. Take care on the stairs. If you are injured or have lost a person, please make your way to the main square in front of the station."

People cheered and applauded. Some cried again, but this time from relief. Rick was amazed by the fact people did not rush for the exits: it seemed they felt safe underground, for the time being.

"Let's go upstairs too," Rick said. "We need to find her mother."

Paul agreed and took a sleepy Florence in his arms.

***

Anxious faces of all ages, waiting to be reunited with their loved ones, crowded the square. Rick was reminded of the television documentaries, where wives of prisoners of war waited at a train station to see if their husbands had survived to come home again.

Paul put Florence on his shoulders. "Florence, you have to look for your mummy now. Can you see clearly from here?"

She could.

Rick let Paul deal with Florence and he walked off, trying to find a police officer. In the surrounding streets stood dozens of ambulances, and the paramedics were treating the many wounded. There were dead bodies on display in another street, with weeping men, women and children slumped next to them. Rick could not believe how much carnage this mass hysteria had caused, but he remembered his own fear when the sirens deafened the city. He did not dare to imagine how the public would behave during a real attack. "Officer, we have found a little girl in the station, she's slightly hurt, and she's lost her mother. Can you help us?"

"Are you kidding me?" he said. "Look around, it's chaos. I don't have time to help you. You'll have to go to the square, that's where people must go. If you can't find her mother, come by the station tomorrow and we'll take your details." The officer walked off towards a man arguing with ambulance staff.

Rick was perplexed, but not totally surprised, by the answer — but *come tomorrow*? As he walked back to Paul and Florence, he wished her mother would be standing there too.

After two hours of searching, the square had become almost empty, but Florence had not found her mother. The few people who were still waiting and hoping to be reunited, were being approached by police officers, and led to the street where the bodies were on display.

Rick and Paul were approached too. Rick didn't want Florence to see dead people, but the officer insisted they had to follow him. "I'm not happy about this," Rick said to Paul. "Can you keep her on your shoulders? So she won't be too close to them."

170

"Florence, I'm very sorry, but the police man wants us to look for your mummy, but you will see horrible things, dead people, and maybe your mummy is too. But we will stay with you," Paul said.

She shook her head. "No, I don't wanna go there. Please take me away."

Rick asked the officer to give them a bit more time to prepare her and calm her down. He agreed and approached the next person, who soon would go through some of the worst minutes of her life.

Paul understood Rick's idea and walked off in the opposite direction, away from the bodies, towards their home, still with Florence on his shoulders.

***

Florence had not asked for her mother since they had returned home; instead she had rummaged through their DVD collection and had found a couple of children's films she had insisted on watching.

She did not seem to be sad, or upset. Rick and Paul wondered if she had a concussion, or was too traumatised to remember what had happened to her. Either way: she seemed to have lost most of her memory.

"I don't understand her," Paul whispered.

"Neither do I, what are we going to do with her? I'm not sure it's legal to look after a child that isn't yours. And she's so different to Karen — but I do like her, she is sweet."

"Yes, she is. We'll go to the police tomorrow and see what happens. But what if they can't find her mother? We might have her around for a while."

Rick agreed, but the prospect of having to look after a wounded child he knew nothing about frightened him almost as much as the aliens did.

During the third film, she had fallen asleep on the sofa.

Rick woke her up and took her to the guest bedroom. "Florence, we're all very sleepy. This is where you'll sleep tonight. I'll leave the door open and the lights on. We're in the next room if you need us. Okay? And I'll stay with you till you fall asleep."

"Good night," she said and gave him a quick peck on his cheek. Within a minute she was sleeping again.

***

The next morning, during breakfast, they watched the news. Anne Goodman explained that the International Space Station had collided with the Cube and this had been the cause of the previous night's panic; the debris had burnt up above the London sky. Under different circumstances people would have considered the fireworks a spectacular display.

The interview Anne had held with Martin was repeated and only now did Rick notice what a big scare the loud explosion had given his friend. No wonder people had panicked when they saw him and the others running into 10 Downing Street for cover. The other news consisted of stories of casualties the false alarm had caused.

After breakfast the three of them went to the police station, besieged with distressed inquirers. The officer at the counter suggested that, after he had taken Florence's picture and the few details she could remember, they should return in a week's time to see if any relatives had shown up.

Florence knew she lived in North London with her mother and father, close to a shopping centre. Her ninth birthday had been last week and her mother had given her a doll. Her mother had long hair and her daddy worked on a boat. She missed her parents, and her doll, and she cried again. Florence's distress upset Rick and Paul, and since they were not achieving much at the station, they decided to leave.

On the way home, they visited a few shops. Florence needed clothes, a toothbrush and the most beautiful doll she could find: for her birthday. It dawned on them they might have become foster parents. Florence's mood had improved and she liked the idea of calling them Uncle Paul and Uncle Rick. They liked the idea too: very much.

73. The day the Earth stood still. (July year 2)

New York, July. Statement by the Secretary-General of the United Nations.

This is the final emergency announcement by the United Nations. To all world citizens. The threat to Earth has grown daily and very soon will reach its conclusion. What we feared most is going to happen: we are certain the Ophiuchus Cube will land on Earth. As we all now know, previous calculations of the landing site proved very wrong. We did not anticipate the Cube to slow down as much as it did, so new trajectory calculations give us a different and highly accurate landing site.

Each side of the Cube is estimated at 8,893 kilometres, meaning 79 million square kilometres of land and water will be covered. We are certain the whole of the continent of Africa will be under the Cube. There is a good chance the eastern coastal areas of Brazil will be covered. Southern and Middle Europe will end up under the Cube. Most of the Middle East will be covered and the west coasts of India and Sri Lanka are also at risk. Antarctica will be affected too. Your Governments have been informed and they will inform you about the appropriate action they have taken to secure your safety.

We know there is not much time left, but we advise people to stay calm and assemble at the designated evacuation areas. The UN has commandeered vehicles, ships and planes to help the countries affected and rescue as many of you as is still possible. For anyone who cannot leave: we urge you to find refuge underground. Find basements, caves, mines, bunkers or anywhere else suitable. Bring with you enough water and food and await the UN rescue missions.

Dear citizens, it hurts me to issue this statement to you. We are faced with humanity's greatest threat and we may have to fight for our survival; our future is uncertain, but we shall stand together as one. I wish you all strength and courage, and may God be with you.

"Mayday, Mayday, this is US Air Force plane: E-3 TCA , en route from the Gulf of Aden to Geilenkirchen, carrying US military personnel. Pilot David Pilling here. We are trying to escape the Cube. We are flying at 2,000 feet, but we are descending rapidly, to avoid colliding with the Cube. It is above us and descending fast. We do not know if we can reach the edge before the Cube touches down. I believe we are flying over Nuremberg. Please advise a preferred route."

For weeks, most of Earth had been in a green twilight each night. The Cube covered the sky and its eerie green light shone many times brighter than the Moon. Today was different: it was the middle of the afternoon and pitch black outside, and David was having trouble keeping his old plane under control. The sheer size of the descending Cube meant the atmosphere was pushed down with such a great force that cyclones had developed underneath. Winds of over 250 kilometres per hour toyed with his plane, sweeping in from the back. David felt as if a giant hand had grabbed the tail and was shaking the plane up and down in a violent frenzy. The howling wind and the rattling plane deafened David, and he had difficulty staying focused. The visibility through his cockpit windows was close to zero, as the rain clouds mixed with smoke, and flying debris had turned the air into a black soup with bits in it: lethal bits. His radar had become unreliable, so he had to rely on his eyes and experience to avoid colliding with the numerous other planes, which were also trying to escape: just like him.

"E-3 TCA stay on your current route. Do not deviate from your route. Over." Air Traffic Control were no help to David.

They were too busy to give him personalised advice. He was on his own. David missed his wife and had no idea if he would ever see her again. He imagined Jo-Anne would be worried sick at the base, and he had no way of contacting her.

Noises came in from the back: the soldiers in the cargo bay were screaming. He thought he heard them shout *evade* and *plane* and *starboard*. He felt confused, was there a plane to starboard or was he to evade to starboard? The shouts from the back became more frantic and more difficult to understand. *Fuck it*, he thought as he pulled the yoke and made his plane plunge down towards the left.

***

Armageddon had begun.

Today was the day the Earth stood still. From today our history would be different, unrecognisable to us all. An alien object had landed on Earth: the massive Cube towered over us and it was the most terrifying sight. Its colour was an unnatural green. Its size was larger than anything any person had ever seen. Each side measured 8,893 kilometres. From every corner of the world people were gazing at a green square of 79 million square kilometres in size. The Cube was so wide, there was no horizon. And was so big, a whole continent was gone: Africa no longer existed. And was so long, its corners reached deep into Europe, Asia, and South America. And was so tall, its top was covered in violent storm clouds and too far away to see. And was so high, for many people the Moon had gone. And was so colossal, for most people the Sun had gone: forever.

Nothing would, no, nothing could ever be the same again. And everybody knew this: everybody mourned the loss of mother Earth's innocence and virginity.

Today was the day humankind faced its own mass extinction event. Today was the day over two billion humans died.

Today was the day the Earth stood still.

For too many there was no escape from the green beast. The sky went pitch black as the Cube descended upon them. Their day had ended and they would never see another sunrise again: for this was the day they died. In horror, the condemned watched as the Cube touched the mountains and flattened them, continuing its catastrophic descent. The scene they witnessed was too much to take for the human brain, they could not process and hysteria ensued. People ran away, but had nowhere to run to and chaos followed. As more and more destruction, fires and deaths surrounded them; a feeling of utter helplessness came over them, and then came the acceptance of their fate.

Many tried to escape by hiding underground, in cellars, tunnels and caves, but that would not save them: they would find themselves trapped, and if their place of refuge did not collapse under the weight of the Cube, they would slowly die, gasping for air, in the dark.

Many tried to escape in their ships, but that would not save them either. Their vessels would be engulfed by the angry seas, and waves, higher than the tallest buildings, battered down on them, sinking their ships and drowning them.

Many tried to escape in their planes, navigating the darkness, through the thick soup of smoke, rain and debris, but it would not save them. Their flying coffins, forced down by the ever closer Cube, would crash into mountains and buildings, and if the impact did not kill them, the flames would.

Many prayed, but their Gods were not listening and their Gods would not save them when the Cube touched the roofs of their homes, and kept on coming down, trapping and crushing them.

The Vatican was not spared. A frantic Pope, who had lost his faith, tried to keep the million gatherers in St. Peter's Square calm. He promised them Heaven, but he knew there was none to go to. When the building collapsed under the weight of the Cube, and the marble crushed him, the Pope felt thankful his life would soon be over and he would not have to witness the death of the million people in front of him.

Jerusalem was not spared. Thousands of Jews prayed at the Wailing Wall and thousands of Muslims prayed at the Al-Aqsa Mosque atop the Temple Mount, but no matter how many worshippers had gathered: their prayers could not save them or their holiest places.

Mecca was not spared. Millions of Muslims decided to be there for their last pilgrimage, but praying inside and outside the Grand Mosque did not prevent Mecca from total destruction.

***

A family of four in Doha, Qatar, had decided they needed to be in their mosque with their family and friends for their final hours on Earth, and not hide somewhere in a basement. As soon as they opened their front door, the sand hit their faces and eyes. The storm had grown much worse than the news had announced; their journey would be rough and they had not much time left.

It was daytime, but the sky was darker than any human had ever witnessed. The dim light of the street lamps tried to provide small beacons of hope: guides to the places for peace of the soul. Throughout the whole city the faint calls for prayer from the mosques tried to compete with the howling winds.

The family of four were devout Muslims, but had recently joined the Children of Abraham in a nearby mosque. They liked it that the men and women were allowed to pray together, and the women did not have to cover themselves up inside. The religious authorities had tried to stop their citizens joining the new sect, but after members of the ruling family had joined, they had given up and encouraged people to do so too.

The father of the family, Ali, rushed his wife and their two daughters; trying to arrive at their mosque in time: before the end. He looked at the dark sky, and he was frightened, but he didn't want his wife and children to know: he had to be strong for them. His children were too young to understand what was going on, but they did notice the panic and fear around them. It was almost time and Ali did not know if they could reach their own mosque. The Cube was descending faster than he had anticipated.

The strong winds almost pushed them over and Ali could hardly breathe and see with all the sand hitting his face. The sound of explosions made him look back and then up: the Cube had reached the tallest buildings, its force tearing them apart. Big burning chunks of concrete and metal hurtled towards the streets. Windows exploded, turning into millions of lethal razor sharp pieces. Cars were crushed, and people, unaware, were caught under the pieces of concrete and the shards of glass. Ali decided not to head for their own mosque, but head for the one at the end of the street, as they had almost run out of time.

When they reached the door, an imam welcomed them. "Children do not be afraid. We shall soon be in paradise. Let us pray."

Ali took his family towards the main prayer room, but the imam blocked their way.

"What do you think you're doing?" he asked them.

Ali was confused. "We're going to pray," he said.

"Women are not allowed in the main room. She and your daughters need to go to the side entrance and pray with the other women."

"I don't want them to die without me, my daughters are afraid."

"Men and women must be separate. It is the way Allah wants it."

Ali could not believe how stubborn this man was. He wanted to punch the imam, but that would only upset his family more. "You're a shoe and the son of a shoe. I hope you end up in Hell."

He led his family out into the storm again. He wanted them to be together. His wife and daughters were crying. They tried to walk down the road again, but the wind was getting too strong and the sand was hurting them. His wife fell over and sat down, holding their daughters. The violent wind blew off their head-scarves. Today was the first time he saw his wife and daughters' hair wave free in public, free from the restrictions that were imposed on them. He thought they looked beautiful. Why had he made them cover up for all these years? He felt ashamed.

His eldest tugged his arm. "Daddy, I'm scared."

"I know you are my dear, it will be over soon and then we will meet again in paradise," he said to her, but Ali did not believe any more. How could Allah be the God of all beings in this universe and send His alien children to kill His Earth children? The streetlights turned off and total darkness surrounded him. The noise of explosions deafened him. The strong wind hurt his eyes and he could not open them anymore. Sand and thick smoke filled up his lungs. He could feel the Cube was closing in on him: the Cube was only a few centimetres above him now and was not stopping. This was it: the end had come. Ali had to stretch his arms to embrace his wife and daughters, he hugged them as hard as he could till the last second.

***

Not only had the people who were caught under the Cube perished that day. The enormous winds, clouds and debris that blew away from each side of the Cube created perfect storms: speeding across the seas and land for hundreds of kilometres; blowing houses away, as if they were made of paper, and killing their frightened refugees. Tsunamis rushed towards coastal areas and colossal waves engulfed entire regions and cities. Many drowned when they were washed away.

The Cube slowly pushed down the Earth, to make them fit, and as it flattened an entire continent, the planet had to release its stresses, and earthquakes shook every corner of the world. Many houses came tumbling down: nowhere was safe.

Animals were not spared either. Birds were trapped under the Cube and others perished in the storms; not even an albatross could out-fly the violent winds. Fish died as they were swept along with the destructive waves. Violent whirlpools pushed whales and other sea mammals to the bottom of the ocean, too deep for them to swim back to the surface, and, gasping for air, they drowned. Dead sea creatures would wash ashore for many weeks to come.

***

Simon's bed shook. Was the morphine playing tricks on him? Panicked, he looked around him. They had told him the Cube would not land on Las Vegas, but the shaking grew more intense and did not seem to end. Had they told him lies? So he would not panic perhaps? Simon did not like not knowing, and he felt scared, and being high did not help him much either. He was alone in his room, how come at a time like this everyone had abandoned him? Had they forgotten he was their leader? The rumbling made him feel sick. He needed information, so he switched on his television and found Anne's news channel. She was reporting from a studio in London. In the background he saw the Cube. During her report the windows blew in, from the sound shock-wave. Pieces of glass hit her on the back of her head, but although Anne looked shaken from the explosion, she kept reporting.

Simon thought of her pussy. He wondered if she would still be sexually attracted to him — now he had many scars on his body. He should arrange a meeting with her, fly her over, or fly back to London. She would have to have sex with him; she was still in his debt. Anne reported the Cube had landed and had touched British soil near Eastbourne. The rest of the country had been badly damaged, but initial reports suggested the population had been prepared and there had not been reports of many casualties. Simon panicked. His daughters. Were they safe and unharmed? He needed to call his bitch wife and find out if she had been looking after them properly.

***

Florence had kept Paul and Rick sane the last few days. They had explained to her what the landing would mean, but she seemed underwhelmed by the whole situation, she was more interested in meeting Paul's parents. Three days ago they had packed their overnight bags and suitcases with tinned food and prepared their home to withstand any damage possible due to the landing. Then they had driven

100 kilometres to the small Hampshire village where Paul had grown up.

His parents had prepared the spare bedrooms and had taken out all Paul's toys from the attic: they finally had a granddaughter.

Paul's parents told Florence many stories about the Blitz during the Second World War and they explained why they had put sticky tape on their windows, kept their curtains shut, and why their cellar was full of drinking water in bottles. Florence had listened in awe.

Today, all of them sat in silence in front of the television when the Cube landed. There had been no immediate noise; that came later. So did the wind, with the debris, and a chunk of a house had landed onto Paul's parents' car, but their home was spared. No windows were broken, and the slight earthquake had not done any damage either.

Rick was in shock. He didn't like the new situation on Earth: this new reality. Everything had changed, forever. So many things had broken today. So many people had died today. And he was afraid of the aliens: when would they come out and attack? Rick was not sure if he would ever sleep again. He had never been so scared.

After his initial shock had gone, Rick tried to call his mother and his friends; but the network was overloaded, so he sent them text messages. His mother should be fine: the Cube would have landed far away from her. He knew Martin and Colin should be fine too, after all they were deep underground in the Downing Street bunker, but he needed confirmation. Rick was more concerned for Isadora and the kids. Everyone had tried to convince Thomas that anywhere outside London would be safer for them, but he had refused, forcing Isadora and Karen to stay at home.

His phone buzzed and Rick saw messages appear from the people he loved: they were all alive.

**

From the canteen on the airbase Jo-Anne had a perfect view of the ongoing disaster. The room was full with army wives, but she felt very much alone: David had not yet returned.

The actual landing of the Cube had felt like an anti-climax. She expected thunder, lightning and an earthquake that would knock her off her feet, but that had not happened. But she realised things were very wrong, when, after a short while, the sound shock-wave started to rattle the windows and, after that, the smoke and debris-filled winds reached her. The floor under her feet started shaking and Jo-Anne feared she might die soon, without her husband at her side, under the rubble of the collapsed canteen.

Planes were still landing at the base. Each time all the women would rush outside into the storm and debris, not caring about the dangerous conditions. Some women would cry from happiness, others from despair, as they identified the plane and, with it, who had come home and who had not. Jo-Anne knew what plane David was flying and as soon as she recognised his, she ran out onto the tarmac. The wind almost blew her over, but she did not mind, her eyes were fixed on the door and when it opened and David walked down the steps, she could not stop her tears. "I'm so happy to see you. I thought you were — you had —."

"Hush now, I'm here my love," David interrupted her as he hugged her. "Let's go inside, it's dangerous out here."

Jo-Anne rubbed his chin; he had not shaved for days and his stubbles felt good on her fingers. She felt like pinching herself to make sure she was not dreaming, because for the last few months she had, and she had been in a nightmare.

Armageddon had ended.

79. Back and Forth.
(August year 2)

"Good evening. This is Anne Goodman for the World Wide Live News Channel. I'm here with Doctor Tuan in Beijing, for this special report on the landing of the Cube. Good evening Doctor. After all the chaos and terrible loss of lives, you and your Government have new details about the Cube. Can you please share them with us?"

"Thank you Anne. Yes, the loss of life has been catastrophic. We had our best scientists study the recent events and we have this report for you. The Cube came from the Ophiuchus constellation, from the area of the star Cebalrai, its official name Beta Ophiuchi. This star is 82 light years from Earth. We first noticed the Cube obscuring this star one year ago and we do not know how long it has been travelling from there. But we understand the Cube has travelled as fast as the speed of light for most of its journey. I know we say it is impossible to travel this fast, but unfortunately we have the proof right here. My scientists are working on new theories, but hopefully soon we can ask the inhabitants ourselves how they did it."

"Thank you Doctor. So what happened since the Cube entered Earth's orbit?"

"As you know, fortunately, the Cube did not collide with the Moon. The Cube slowed down before it landed, and its speed, seconds before landing, was almost zero and therefore caused relatively little damage. I know it sounds bizarre to say this after the disasters, but if the Cube had landed with a higher speed, then our planet would have been destroyed. We believe the inhabitants intended to cause as little damage as possible and that the Cube was custom built for landing on planets."

"So tell me, I didn't see any big rockets, or smoke coming

187

out of it, as I would see in a science fiction movie. How do you believe it moves?"

"There is no evidence of a propulsion system. We believe it uses magnetism to travel and land. We think the Cube detected Earth's magnetic field and therefore chose to travel here and used our iron core to land. We believe the Cube can change its magnetic poles in order to be attracted or repulsed by another object, in this case Earth. In quantum physics there is a theory that the exchange of photons can change magnetic fields and the galaxy is filled with photons. The Cube could be one giant, magnetic solar panel."

"That is awfully technical. What can you tell us about the Cube itself?"

"It has sides of 8,893 kilometres, its volume is 703 billion and 300 million cubic kilometres and I use the American term for billion. For you to understand the sheer size, one could easily fit the planet Mars inside the Cube and still have enough room left for more than 100 Mount Everests on top of each other."

"Phew — that's big. Is there more information available?"

"We tried to determine the Cube's age, but the results that came back were inconclusive."

"What does that mean?"

"Carbon dating is not possible, because the Cube is not organic. So we've tried to use other methods, including measuring radioactive decay. But as I said, all were inconclusive."

"Can't you give us any idea of its age?"

"All right then. We believe the Cube is at least 100 million years old, and it is very possible that it is a lot older than that. But as I said, we cannot be certain."

"Gosh. That's hard to get your mind round. It was built before the dinosaurs were wiped out? — Doctor Tuan, what effects did the Cube have on Earth?"

"When it landed, it flattened the earth underneath and

our planet is no longer a sphere. Its four outer corners start at Eastbourne in England, going south-west through the North Atlantic Ocean, touching land at the east coast of Brazil near Recife, missing Salvador and then east of Rio de Janeiro it goes back in to the South Atlantic Ocean where the next corner is 300 kilometres east of Florianopolis. The most southern point is south-east from South Africa in Antarctica. The last corner is located south-east of Sri Lanka in the Indian Ocean.

"As you can see on the map, Anne, the whole of Africa is covered, so are the southern, middle and eastern parts of Europe, including the Vatican, only leaving small parts of Galicia in Spain, Brittany in France, Northern and Eastern Europe, Scandinavia and the British Isles uncovered. It shaved Brazil, touched India on the southern west coast, destroying Goa. It covers the Middle East and the whole Arabian peninsula, including Mecca. Half of Iran and the whole of Turkey are covered. Jerusalem is gone, which is a major blow for the followers of the Children of Abraham. We estimate over 1.5 billion people were killed instantly when the Cube landed, and the resulting earthquakes, storms and tsunamis killed another 500 million. And there was also a terrible loss in the animal world."

"I still can't believe this, it's too terrible for words. Two billion people died that day? Oh my God. Sorry. Give me a moment please. I can't.

—

My apologies Doctor Tuan. Please tell me. The Cube is here. What does this mean for the future of Earth and for us?"

"Every country has their military on standby, but we are in unknown territory. We have to wait for the aliens to make contact and make their intentions known, our future is out of our hands now. We do not know the mass of the Cube yet and thus do not know how this affects the gravitation of

189

Earth and the subsequent consequences for the Moon's orbit, or indeed our own orbit around the Sun. All we can do is hope and pray for the best."

"Thank you Doctor Tuan. Viewers please accept my apologies. It was very unprofessional of me to cry, but I hope you understand. It is too much for me to take in. And yes, praying would be good. Uhm — anyway viewers, after the commercial break I will return with our weatherman Daniel Lou to talk about the changes in the weather the Cube is causing and where we can expect the most rain and storms. Thank you. And God bless you."

Colin always tried to make the best of his mornings. He would set the alarm really early, so he and Martin could cuddle and have long breakfasts. Today was the same. They had a bit of a routine in the kitchen: making porridge and brewing tea together. Colin's mother Nancy always woke up after they had left for work, so they had their peace and quiet.

"The President's flying back today," Colin said. "We're going to be very busy."

"Have you told him yet you're staying here?" Martin asked.

Colin had decided to stay in London, to be with Martin, but he knew Martin still felt insecure, because he had not yet made an official announcement.

"McGee hasn't been happy with me since we rescued my mother from Las Vegas. He was annoyed when he found out we used his Marines and planes. It was fine to save my mother, but he was very angry with me when he found out Simon hadn't died. He told me, we should have checked the grenade killed him, and finished him off ourselves if it hadn't. Simon's survival has been a major public relations disaster for the President. So no, I haven't found the right time yet."

"Well, even if he fires you, with my salary, we have enough money for the three of us."

"I do think he appreciates what I do and will let me stay here."

The kitchen door opened and startled them: Colin's mother never woke up this early. She looked annoyed. "Let you stay where?"

"Here in London, Mom. Have you been listening behind the door?"

"I thought we was leaving today. That's why I woke up early and packed my things. I thought we was flying back with the President."

Martin stood up, kissed Colin goodbye and left. Colin appreciated the gesture: the next conversation would be very unpleasant.

"I'm staying here Mother. I want to be with Martin and many Americans are staying too, so there's a job for me. I'll tell the President today, when he boards the plane."

"You're so selfish. What about me? I don't wanna stay here. I hate everything about London. And that Cube — is too close. It covers half the sky and I hate it. And if you make me stay I'll hate you too," Nancy said, her voice trembling, her eyes filled with anger.

"*I* am selfish?" Colin felt unpleasantly surprised by her outburst. For the last three months she had seemed reasonably content and had never indicated she felt this way. "You ungrateful and selfish woman. We risked our lives to save you. People died because of you. And this is how you reward me?"

"I didn't need no saving by you. Jesus saved me long time ago. You did it because *you* are selfish. And you forced me to be part of your disgusting, sinful lifestyle. I don't wanna be here and I'm going back."

"Yes, it's probably better if you leave. If you are so repulsed by us, then I don't want your venom near me."

"Good. I'll be on the next plane," Nancy said, storming off and slamming the door behind her.

By carrying her luggage and bags herself to the taxi, she made it clear to Colin she did not want his help. She never stopped looking out of the window during the hour drive to the airport. Colin tried to hold her hand once, but she pulled hers away. He noticed a shiver going through her body.

Air Force One was surrounded by military vehicles and men with machine guns. The President was not taking any chances after the Simon Waltz fiasco, as the Children of Abraham had vowed to kill him, and a few had tried. People were boarding the plane fast. They looked happy; the Cube was not visible from anywhere in the States and did not cause the constant rain and wind they had to endure here in London. They could not wait to fly back home.

Colin felt reluctant having to face his boss. In the next few minutes he would lose his mother and his American life for good. He missed his old life, from before that damned Cube had arrived.

They were the next to be processed. After showing their passports, security let him pass, but not his mother. He told her to wait as he walked up the stairs.

The plane was almost full: people were laughing and drinking Champagne. A stewardess offered him a flute and canapés. Her face was pretty and her smile seemed genuine. The scene disturbed Colin, it was perverse to see the blatant happiness and joy in these sad times. He felt relieved not be part of this grotesque spectacle.

President McGee noticed Colin and gestured him to come over.

"Mr President," Colin said as he sat down.

"Colin." No smile.

"I'm not moving back, and I'd like to request a position at the embassy, so I can continue to serve my country."

"I had a feeling you wouldn't come. I'm surprised to see you here. I feel bad our relationship changed after the Las Vegas incident. But Colin, you really betrayed my trust and caused me, us, a lot of problems. But I will grant your request. You are an asset. I will also assign you as our liaison officer to the Prime Minister."

"Thank you, Sir. And I am truly sorry."

"I know you are. You did it for your mother, I would have done the same — my friend."

Tears welled up in Colin's eyes. He would have preferred if McGee had stayed angry with him; it would have been much easier for him to say goodbye.

"I have one last request, Sir. My mother. She's very unhappy here and wants to go home. Can she take my place?"

"Of course." A smile. Their goodbye had finished.

Colin passed his mother on the stairs. She never looked at him. There was no one to wave goodbye to and Colin did not feel the need to see the plane leave. He left the airport in a hurry. As soon as he stepped into his taxi, he phoned Martin. "My mother, she's gone."

"I'm sorry. I suspected she would leave. She thought the both of you would today. Did you explain why you didn't?"

"I tried, but she wouldn't listen. I managed to get her on the plane, but she never spoke to me. Have I lost her for good?"

"No you haven't," Martin said. "Give her time to calm down. She'll be happier at her home. And the President?"

"He was so nice to me, I still feel like crying. In a way he gave me his blessing. And I have the job."

"Good, come to Downing Street now. I don't want you to be alone."

***

The roars of jet engines woke Simon up. The constant noise had been going on for more than a week: every few minutes a plane landed or took off, all day and all night. Las Vegas was being repopulated with the same Sinners, and they disgusted Simon. He had a terrible headache, but his painkillers were not working; he had been on morphine since they had *killed* him. He did not use the drugs for pain control anymore, but to make himself feel happier. He had not spoken with God since his resurrection, but often at Him: thanking Him that He had kept to His plan. Simon knew he had a difficult task ahead, convincing his followers of the new plan. He had not made an appearance or statement since the Cube had landed. He knew the press would mock him for predicting the wrong type of Armageddon on the wrong continent, but he was not bothered. His near-murder had messed up his plan to fly back to London in time, but that did not upset him: the Cube had not landed on him, so he was still alive and could still execute God's plan.

Simon's penthouse suite felt abandoned. He didn't get many visitors nowadays: his followers had left him in peace to recover and his women had stayed away, because his burns had made him less attractive. His face had, for the most part, been spared and his hair had grown back, but most of his body would be scarred for the rest of his life. At least his cock still worked. He hated the British Government, and especially that faggot Rick: he was responsible for all that was wrong in the world.

Simon felt he had healed enough to travel back home, where his followers were loyal, unlike the Americans: who had all but abandoned him, and he would be taking back his role as their leader and he would make them suffer the consequences of their betrayal.

He had phoned Aziz and had arranged for a private plane to collect him. Simon could not stay here in Las Vegas, even if he wanted to: the authorities had returned. The law enforcers were back too and he had found out that they were planning to arrest him. Some moron, one of his security guards, had gone to the police and told them how he had people murdered and how he used to have drug crazed sex parties with underage girls in his penthouse. Simon had a few more hours before his plane was due to land, so he would have enough time to pack his belongings: especially his money and drugs. He had arranged for four cars to be ready in the car park, with keys in the ignitions. To make certain his close staff would not suspect he was about to flee, he had sent all of them out on errands. No one would see him leave the hotel.

This time tomorrow he would be reunited with his daughters. He would use the flight-time to prepare the speech, through which he would convince his followers Satan was waiting for the heathens inside the Cube. He needed to keep the false Children out of there: there was no room for them in New Eden — only he was the true Child of Abraham.

83. From Russia without love. (September year 2)

The techno-music beats were pumping loudly at the Rasputin nightclub in Solntsevo, Moscow. The music was so loud you could feel the bass throbbing in your stomach. But Yuri Manelyuk was not interested in dancing; he was vomiting in a cubicle in the toilets. And his nausea was made worse by his body-guard banging on the door, and his girlfriend Eva screaming in the background. Five minutes ago, when he was flirting with Eva on the dance floor, he noticed something hot and wet on his face. When he licked his lips he tasted blood, and right after that he doubled up, lost the feeling in his legs and collapsed on the floor. His body-guard, Stanislav, had carried him to the toilets, where Yuri had locked himself up in a cubicle to throw up.

Yuri knew why he was sick: since the nuclear bombs had obliterated parts of Central Asia, the steady stream of drugs had almost dried up, and his choice of drugs, ketamine, had not been available for weeks, not even for him: the leader of the Solntsevskaya Bratva, otherwise known as *The Brotherhood*. So tonight, in order to get high, he had been snorting copious amounts of very pure cocaine and now he was paying the price.

"Yuri, you need to come out now. The Defence Minister has arrived for the meeting," Stanislav yelled through the door.

"Give me a moment," Yuri said. He was still retching. "Someone get me a bottle of water and some mints. Minister Kovalev can wait." After one last intense throwing up he felt good enough to face everyone again. When he appeared, Eva stood in front of him, crying. "Don't be so hysterical, I'm fine." She did annoy him sometimes, but she was pretty and a good fuck, and he did love her. He noticed the cocaine had kicked in: he felt wide awake and aware, and, looking at his girlfriend, very horny, but now he had a meeting with the Minister.

Thick dark wallpaper, low lighting and ambient music gave the VIP area a relaxed feel. Cheap perfume battled with cigar smoke. In most booths sat, mostly, fat men in suits, accompanied by Yuri's girls. He would have a word with them later. Tonight, he found their perfume smelled too strong. He was pleased to see the Champagne bottles on the tables; his girls were making their clients spend a lot of money. Business had been good since the Cube's arrival.

The booth at the far end of the room was occupied by the Minister. A girl was entertaining him, her hands caressing his hair and groin. She was whispering in his ear and they were both laughing. As soon as Yuri sat down opposite them, she got up and walked off. Yuri would offer one of his girls to the Minister later, as a freebie. He knew about the importance of keeping his business associates happy at all times. "Minister Kovalev, good to meet you. I hope you have good news." Kovalev smiled, exposing his yellow teeth. Yuri could smell his breath, a combination of alcohol and garlic. Cocaine had heightened his senses too much: all smells were too strong for him tonight. He felt sorry for his girls; one of them would have to kiss and fuck the man later.

"Yuri, yes, excellent news. Because of the evacuation chaos, the Americans don't patrol South America any more, so we have new routes established for the cocaine. It's much better quality and cheaper for us to buy. Our profit margins will be much higher. And I have personally taken care of your request, the ketamine route from India has reopened. The first shipment is in your warehouse, together with the guns I had delivered last night."

Yuri felt a tap on his knee. He reached down and the Minister put a small package in his hand. When he looked, he saw a small plastic bag with *ketamine* written on it. "Thank you Kovalev," he said. His cocaine induced nausea almost forgotten. Kovalev had no idea how grateful he was for the gift. "And as a thank you for our continued business," Yuri waved at his girlfriend, gesturing for her to join them at the table, "you may take our best girl home tonight, on the house of course."

Eva was by far the best of all his girls and although he felt horny for his girlfriend tonight, he would be better off having her out of the picture, as she had been distressed earlier and would certainly nag him later about his episode. He needed to go to his warehouse and check the latest drugs and weapons delivery. One big line of ketamine first, and then he would be off to his warehouse to inspect the goods.

***

The cocktail of drugs in his blood made him feel paranoid. Stanislav was driving him, and in the car behind them was his security detail. Yuri kept on looking behind him. He wasn't sure if the car behind belonged to him or not. His eyes could not focus, and he thought he had lost sight of the car several times when they had gone around corners. Time had almost stopped for Yuri, and he felt the drive was taking them forever. Yuri tried to call his security, but he could not get his phone to work; his hands were too sweaty. Damned drugs. Feeling agitated, he looked back again, but he could not trust his own judgement and decided to give it a rest. He was sure his body-guard would notice if anything out of the ordinary had happened.

Yuri always enjoyed the night drives to his warehouse, a quick whizz down the M3 motorway and then through the forests, and up and down a few hills. He opened his window and the scent of pine trees filled his head. His senses felt incredibly strong. He loved being this high, and so he decided to have another line.

The sound of the gravel under the tyres woke Yuri up. He was not sure how long he had been asleep, but the car's headlights lighting up his warehouse announced he had arrived. Yuri and Stanislav stepped out of the car, and his security car pulled up behind them. He noticed they blocked the exit. His body-guard walked up to the other car and called for the others to step out. The passenger window opened and a shot was fired. Yuri saw his body-guard fall to the ground. *Stanislav, no!* He pulled his own gun, fired shots at the car and ran into the safety of the dark woods. He had no idea who had shot at them, but he knew this was an assassination attempt on him. In an instant he felt sober again and his survival instinct kicked in. Never before had he run as fast as he had now. He felt happy a full Moon lit the forest, otherwise he certainly would have fallen many times and maybe broken a leg by now.

After an hour of staggering, he found himself at the banks of a small river; he knew it was the Protva. Yuri felt exhausted and allowed himself a short rest. The adrenaline still pumped through his veins and made his heart hurt. He listened for his pursuers, but the woods were silent. He felt sorry for Stanislav; dozens of times his body-guard had saved his life, but today he had paid the ultimate price. Yuri had no idea how he could cope on his own, without the trust and protection he had relied on for years.

He tried his phone, but he had no reception. That was a good thing actually, he decided: because if the Government was behind the attempt on his life, at least they could not track him down. He had to find a nearby town and use a pay-phone, so he could contact his associates at the club and find out what was happening. For now, his mobile had to stay switched off, just in case.

He followed the river for half an hour and reached the M3 again. He recognised the stretch of road and he remembered a petrol station a few kilometres away. The walk had taken him longer than he expected, as staying off the road and in the safety of darkness slowed him down. He was astonished to find a working pay-phone at the station.

He phoned his nightclub and was relieved to hear Igor, the manager, answer.

"Boss, you're alive! I'm so relieved to hear from you. We had a shooting at the club. Members from a rival gang came in and said they killed you, and then everyone drew their guns. They're all dead, we have a few dead too. Eva had already left with Kovalev, we have spoken to her and she's safe. Are you?"

"Yeah, I'm safe, but Stanislav is dead and our warehouse has been compromised. Igor, take a car and pick me up at the first petrol station after you pass Obninsk. And assemble a big team to secure our warehouse. A rival gang, you said? Okay, anyone they find there. I want them dead. And call Eva, tell her I'm okay, but don't tell anyone else where I am."

***

Yuri's body was shaking from the cold when his car arrived. He had been hiding in the bushes for over an hour, and his drugs had worn off. The warmth of the car embraced him as soon as he stepped inside. During the journey Igor told him the details of the attack. It had come from another gang from Moscow, who, because of the shortages, had been searching throughout the entire underworld for drugs, and apparently had heard Yuri's brotherhood were hiding a good amount. A couple of guys were already on the way to their headquarters to take revenge and kill the competition. Yuri felt pleased he had a good team to rely on. He told Igor to drive him to Kovalev's apartment. He had a plan to keep himself and his team safe and for that he needed the Minister's co-operation. He switched on his phone and told Eva he was on his way to pick her up.

Kovalev lived in a block of flats behind the Kremlin, an ornate and old building, built many years before the Revolution, but well maintained. The rich and famous lived here. Yuri noticed the armed guards outside the building. He knew this was unusual; normally the guards would only be inside at the reception desk. Evidently there were many nervous people in Moscow tonight, and a few of them would be dead by the morning. He would instruct Igor to find out if any of his enemies lived here; he might as well have them shot too.

Eva hugged him as soon as he walked into the apartment. "I was so worried. Thank God you're here. Take me home please. Kovalev is disgusting."

"In a moment babe. I have to take care of business first. Please wait in the bedroom. And get dressed."

Kovalev sat in his underwear on the sofa in the living room. He was drinking straight out of a vodka bottle. It was not a pretty sight: the man was fat and extremely hairy. Yuri's stomach turned when he saw yellow stains on Kovalev's underwear, and dirty toes sticking out of holes of even dirtier socks. He regretted assigning Eva to him. Maybe the time was right for her to retire. "You know that special offer you made me last year? I accept it now."

"I — I'm not sure I can. It's not that easy anymore. Things have changed since the Cube landed, you know," Kovalev said.

"Yes, everything changed, and even more so after tonight. I was almost killed and now I need your help. We're friends, and I don't want my friend to be exposed to the President. You know what the penalty is for people like you, the traitors who work with the Mafia. I must safeguard my position and I need my backup plan as soon as possible. Organise it and I will keep you safe too. I know you can deliver. Get me the bomb."

"Please promise me you won't nuke Moscow."

"Of course I won't. My business is here. My parents live here. I'll only use it as a deterrent. I know you have it stored somewhere here in Moscow. Have it sent to my club tonight, I'll be there, waiting. And for fuck sake, clean yourself up man. You're disgusting."

***

On a normal night his club would have been packed with revellers, business men, politicians and prostitutes, but now no music played, all the lights were on and except for his employees the place was empty. Nine bodies lay dumped in a corner; three of them were his men. Bar staff and some of his girls were busy cleaning blood off the walls. Yuri slipped a few times on the bloodstained floor. The scent of blood and gunpowder filled his nose. When everyone noticed him, they cheered, and hugged and kissed him. No matter what: they were loyal to him, he would never forget that.

"All right. I'm deeply sorry for what happened tonight. We're taking care of the problem now. All you girls, and bar staff, thank you very much for helping with the cleaning, but I know you're all shaken and tired, so I'm sending you all home."

As soon as Yuri was alone with Igor he told him to prepare the cellar for the arrival of the bomb. His manager had known of the plan before, so he knew what to do. Yuri would get rid of the bodies and clean the rest of the club himself: it had been ages since he had got his hands dirty.

Five hours later, Kovalev and a few soldiers delivered the package. The bomb came in a wooden crate and was much smaller than Yuri had expected, and a lot lighter too: around 40 kilos he guessed. When he opened the box, the writing said: *RA-115s;* exactly what he expected to see, although he thought a *suitcase* nuke would be just that and not be a wooden crate. When the bomb was safely stored and hidden away, he took a few pictures of his new toy on his phone, making sure the lettering was readable. He sent out a picture message with a warning to a few of his enemies: they would know what this meant.

89. First Contact (?).
(October year 2)

Three months had passed since the Cube had landed on Earth. Nature proved strong and fought back: seedlings sprouted on every continent, birds nested in trees, fish spawned in seas and mammals gave birth again.

Still in shock, mankind too, started recovering from the initial disaster, and slowly but surely parts of life returned to normal. Farmers fed their cattle, and fields were harvested. Babies were born, birthdays were celebrated, people fell in love, couples got married. Hope proved to be a tough emotion and had survived the ordeal.

In the United States, ships had returned to the ports, and planes had been flying day and night: the country had mostly been repopulated. The Government had almost re-established itself: law and order was nearly restored and swift justice had been served to many criminals. The economy had not yet fully recovered; many hungry people relied on relief efforts from the government, and there were still riots in city centres from time to time.

***

President McGee was going through his daily army reports: they were monitoring the Cube from various locations on three continents and via their satellites. Today again, no news meant good news. The Cube just *sat* there, on top of Africa, seeming absolutely dormant. So far, several attempts by scientists and civilians to open channels of communication had led to nothing: except for an unnerving silence. McGee felt frustrated by, and angry with, the aliens: he felt it was very arrogant and rude to half destroy someone else's planet and not have the decency to explain why. But he was told by his top scientists not to attribute human emotions to aliens; their thought patterns could be very different from humans, and they might not have a concept of what was considered good or bad.

McGee felt tired and he was looking forward to a good sleep, but not to waking up, because tomorrow he would have the same tedious problems to deal with.

His phone woke him, McGee looked at the clock: six o'clock in the morning. This could only mean bad news. He felt reluctant to answer the call.

"Mr President. Sorry to wake you up, but you need to hear this."

Colin was on the other side. He missed his assistant and was happy to hear his voice.

"There's a development. The Cube has opened up, on the Brazilian side. The opening is a circle and it is about two kilometres from ground level. It's not big, less than 20 metres in diameter."

"Has anything come out? Can we look inside it with cameras?"

"Nothing — yet. A helicopter with cameras is on its way now. They should be there in about 15 minutes. They're broadcasting on the secure channel. It's on now."

"Thank you Colin," McGee said. "I'll switch it on here. I pray this is not the beginning of the end."

"I'll be praying too Sir."

"Colin. Are you happy in London? I miss you — uhm — your knowledge and support."

"I miss you too Sir. Yes, I'm very happy here. I had to stay. I wasn't sure how much time I had left to find love."

"I know you found him and I'm happy for you. Now, let's see what today has in store for us." In less than three minutes McGee had dressed himself, ordered a pot of coffee and started watching his television in the Oval office. His phone rang again: this time his Secretary of Defense telling him he had heard the news and was on his way. McGee looked at the screen: the helicopter had not arrived yet. For a moment he didn't know what to do. He was on his own, had no one to talk to, no papers to sign. He decided against waking up his wife; he did not want to alarm her. In a way he felt relieved that something was finally happening. The waiting had been very frustrating all these months.

He was sipping his second coffee when the camera pointed at the opening. It was difficult to see much: like the outside, the hole was green inside. After a few minutes, a strong searchlight shone into the hole. McGee could make out an empty tunnel, which seemed not to have an end. And again, nothing was happening.

His Secretary of Defense walked in. "Morning Bill, how are you?"

"Michael, good to see you. I'm a bit frightened. So what's going on?"

"Nothing much. I was on the phone on my way here and found out that every side has been surveyed and they've found only this one opening."

"So what now? Can we send a probe in?"

"The Brazilian Government wants to wait and see. They're afraid that if we antagonise them, they'll bear the brunt of any attacks. If you don't care — I can send a drone in."

"Well, I *do* care about them, but I think we might have to override their concerns. Send one in. We must find out what's inside there at all costs. I'll deal with the Brazilians later. Are we on high alert yet?"

"Yes, and our navy is at a safe distance and so is our air force."

***

The drone was sent, but did not arrive in time. Six hours

after McGee had ordered an investigation, something came out of the Cube: a green orb, around 17 metres in diameter. The orb fell towards the ground, gaining speed. It did not crash, but adjusted its trajectory and started its journey a metre above ground and at a speed of 320 kilometres per hour. A short while after, the opening closed, leaving everyone wondering what had happened.

* * *

"Damn, that orb was fast. We almost missed it," Michael said to his President as he rewound the video. The orb plunged down too fast for the camera to keep up.

"I think I had a heart attack just now. Is anyone following this orb?" McGee asked Michael. "Could it be a bomb?"

"Not sure, but I'd suggest we go on highest alert and go underground again."

"Good idea. And let other leaders know what just happened and that something might be heading their way," McGee said as he picked up the phone to alert his wife. He wanted her safe.

* * *

<Local language and metrics adopted>

Accelerate. Atmosphere found. Analysis completed: 78.09% nitrogen. 20.95% oxygen. 0.93% argon. 0.039% carbon dioxide. 1% water vapour.

Organic compounds found. Analysis completed: carbohydrates, lipids, nucleic acids, proteins.

Decelerate. Submerge. Accelerate.

Liquid found. Analysis completed: 96.5% water. 3.4% sodium chloride. magnesium. sulphur. potassium. carbon. bromide.

Organic compounds found. Analysis completed:

carbohydrates, lipids, nucleic acids, proteins.
Accelerate. Climb. Atmosphere.

***

"Sir, the orb has emerged from the ocean and has made landfall in Florida at Fort Lauderdale. It's travelling over US soil. We're receiving reports from all over the State and they're very disturbing. People are witnessing strange things happening," Michael said. He was not looking at his President: he had his phone in his hand and was typing a message.

"What is it? Just tell me, and what's more important on your phone than talking to me?" McGee said as he pulled the phone out of Michael's hand.

"The orb is cutting through everything in its path. Buildings, cars, trees, people. It leaves a round hole where it has been."

"It cuts through? How?"

"We don't know. Whatever it touches has vanished. Big holes through buildings, and people, where they were standing, only their feet and legs are left — cut off and the rest of their bodies — gone. No burn marks, just gone. I'm receiving picture messages, have a look at them."

McGee looked at the phone in his hand. He stared at buildings with perfect circles cut out. He saw trains, cars and trucks with a part of a circle cut out. Legs standing up, but without a torso. Heads lying around: their bodies gone. "What the hell?" he shouted, handing the phone back. "Do we have our air force nearby?"

"Sir, yes there are a few bases. I know what you're going to say, but we agreed with other nations, not to show aggression towards them." The Secretary wriggled his phone in his hand, not dialling.

"I don't fucking care anymore what we agreed on, or

what they might do. This is an attack on the US. Shoot it down. Make the call. That is an order!" McGee stood up and threw a cup his coffee through the room, missing the television by a few centimetres, leaving brown stains on the screen. "And have somebody clean that up. I'm taking a break, let me know when that thing is destroyed." The door slammed behind him, as he ran out of the office to his private bathroom. After he locked the door, he took out a pack of cigarettes from behind the toilet. He calmed down after he had inhaled a few puffs of smoke. He hated not being in control of the situation, or in control of his temper.

***

For five days the orb had travelled over continents and through the oceans, leaving a trail of destruction behind. Many jets tried to shoot the orb down, but to no avail. The orb never responded to the attacks. A few hours before the orb reached the opposite side of the Cube from where its journey had started, an identical opening had appeared, and the orb disappeared into it. It never made it known why it had come. It never made it known why it had gone.

Decelerate. Full stop. Cycle completed.

97. Where did everybody go?
(November year 2)

"Good afternoon. This is Anne Goodman reporting for the World Wide Live News Channel. I am in Eastbourne, East Sussex, England, only a few kilometres away from the Cube. We have been reporting live since last night, when very large blocks started protruding from the Cube.

"For those of you who have just joined us, here is a small recap of events. Yesterday evening around eight o'clock rectangles started to come out of the Cube very slowly. Today the pace has been speeding up. The blocks are around one and a half kilometres above ground, and are approximately 40 kilometres wide, five high and at least 15 kilometres deep. Reports from all over the world have confirmed there are 17 of these blocks on each side of the Cube. The army and air force are present with helicopters and fighter jets monitoring for any perceivable threat.

"One moment please. I think something is happening. Yes, I can see a change. The block, that is above Eastbourne, seems to have detached itself from the Cube and is hanging in the sky. I have been told by my producer, through my earpiece, that all blocks have detached now.

"Oh dear — I can see something coming out of the bottom. It's white, but doesn't look like smoke to me. The white stuff is travelling down towards the surface, and it seems to be going faster as it's coming down. I can see the stuff engulfing the top of buildings and it's not stopping there. It's going all the way down to street level now. I have no idea what it is. I just hope everyone is safe. I can't really see what's going on. It's too far away for me to see.

"Viewers — the block seems to be moving forward now and the white stuff is moving with it, staying underneath. It's all moving towards me. It's very fast. I'm still not sure

what it is made of. It doesn't look like smoke, it looks like foam. Yes, it's foam. I'll be swallowed up in it any minute now. It is coming closer — I'm a bit nervous, but I will keep on reporting if I can from inside the foam. Any second now.

"This is Anne Goodman reporting live from Eastbourne, bringing you the latest news from the Cube. I can see the foam clearly now. It looks like bubble bath foa—"

The white took over the screen, but Anne was still visible through the foam. She did not move, and did not speak into her microphone. In less than five seconds her body turned bright red, lost its shape, formed into a red bubble, streamed up the foam and disappeared. Her clothes fell on the floor, as did her microphone, making a muffled sound. No trace of her was left.

"Am I seeing this right? Did she just break up in little pieces and get sucked up? What the hell happened? Are we under attack?" the Prime Minister asked. He stood up, looking around the crowded room; looking for answers. "Where the fuck did she go? Someone call that news station and give me some fucking answers." Silence. Not one person moved, adding to the PM's anger. "You," he pointed at one of his cabinet ministers, "pick up the phone and call them now. And are we safe here? Can anyone just bloody well answer me?"

"Yes Sir, we are. Downing Street war bunkers are air tight and we're running in nuclear attack mode." Martin tried to keep his voice in check. If anyone heard his voice tremble, they might realise how scared he was.

"And someone please call the fucking air force. How the hell did they allow this to happen? I need information and a live feed and see what is going on there — is anyone left in Eastbourne? And is anyone actually *fighting* that thing?" The Prime Minister barked his commands, not to anyone in particular.

Martin noticed the panic in the Prime Minister's eyes and walked over to him. "Sir, we also need to know where this block is heading. We must warn people to get out of its path."

"Yes, you're absolutely right. It looks like she was vaporised and then sucked up. Can you find out for me please? I feel my head will explode soon. And I'm working with fucking morons. I hope I can count on you."

"I will. I'll call the air force now. Sir, please remember, we're all very shocked by what happened just now. Waiting for information is frustrating, but I need you to stay calm, otherwise everyone in this room will start to panic," Martin said. Before he picked up the phone, he indicated to one of his assistants to bring him and the others a cup of tea. *A bit of sanity, we're British after all,* he thought.

The call lasted less than a minute, and Martin was not looking forward to relaying the information to the Prime Minister. "Sir, I have the report from the air force. They're following the block and it is travelling at a speed of around 400 kilometres per hour in a north-north-westerly direction. Apparently we've been firing missiles at it already, but to no avail."

"What the hell does that mean?"

"Well, it's going over West London at the moment and it's on its way towards Manchester and we cannot stop it." An electric shock went through Martin when he had said Manchester out loud: he remembered Rick and Paul were there right now. He had to call them. Warn them. He could not figure out how long the block would take to get there. His mind failed and he couldn't calculate. *Dammit, don't waste your time: call Rick now!*

"You," pointing to several assistants, "start calling the police, city halls, fire brigades and hospitals of every town that is in the block's path. Warn everyone to evacuate. Get them out of the way. Do whatever. I don't know, think of

213

something." Martin sat down and dialled his friend. *Please pick up.*

***

"Hello? Ah, good to hear from you — yes, we're okay — yes, we're still in Manchester, having a bite to eat in a restaurant before we head back to London. Why?" Rick asked. He mouthed *Martin* to the rest of the group. "Yes, we have the kids with us. Their father was quite happy for Isadora to look after them for a couple of weeks. He was tired of Thomas and his new wife always arguing. But, what's up Martin? You sound agitated." Rick's face turned white as he listened to Martin telling him about their looming death sentence. "Oh God — yes you be careful too. I'll tell the others. Bye."

"What's wrong?" Paul asked.

Rick's distress affected everyone on the table. They stared at him, waiting for an answer. Thomas rocked in his chair, feeling something was wrong. In the background people's phones rang, a cacophony of ring-tones. A woman howled and fell on the floor. A group of businessmen stood up, throwing over their chairs, and ran out of the restaurant. Screams came from outside. Sirens yelped: there were many, close by and in the distance.

"It's bad. I'm so sorry. Something horrible is coming our way. A block — it came out of the Cube and it's killing everyone in its path. It'll be here in about half an hour, max."

"That's terrible. What should we do?" Isadora asked.

"I don't know. Martin said they're telling people to evacuate. But it's going to be mayhem outside. We won't have time to leave the city."

Karen stared at her phone. "Guys, you need to have a look at this. It shows what happened a bit earlier and what's going to happen to us. I'm scared."

The last minute of Anne's news broadcast was on a continuous loop. Again and again she transformed into a red blob, dissolved and was sucked up by the foam. No one spoke as they could not take their eyes off the alien scene playing out on the small screen.

Thomas let out a prolonged cry. "Too much. My head hurts. Make it stop. Can't leave Sally alone." He ran out of the restaurant.

"Thomas, come back here," Isadora shouted as she ran after him.

The others followed them out. Thomas had untied Sally from a tree and held her in his arms. He stood frozen in front of a man and a woman who were lying on the street. The man was shouting at her and had his hands around her neck. She was not moving. "Why does he hurt her? Everybody is going crazy," he shouted.

Isadora grabbed Thomas. "Come on, we're not safe here."

They ran into a side street. "How long before it gets here? And does anyone have any ideas on what we should do?" Paul asked.

"Less than half an hour. We need to get underground, in a bunker or something similar. But I don't know Manchester. Do they have an Underground system here?" Rick asked

"No," Karen said. "It only runs overground. But there's a bunker close to here. An old Cold War telephone exchange. Maybe we could go there. I know where it is, only five minutes away."

***

They were not the only ones that had thought of hiding in the bunker. A crowd stood outside the closed iron doors. Several people had tried to climb over the wall, but got stuck in the barbed wires.

"This isn't going to work. We need an alternative. Where can we be safe? And we only have 15 minutes tops. Come on, think! Karen? You always come up with ideas," Isadora said.

"Please Karen, help me." Thomas looked at her, desperate for his little sister to save him and protect him, as she so often did.

"Uhm — we need a place that is hermetically sealed," Karen said.

"Huh? What does that mean?" Isadora asked.

"Airtight. It needs to be airtight. That foam seems to behave like regular foam, so it can go under doors, through keyholes and stuff. That's why we need to go somewhere with a seal. Like a fridge. Oh my God, I've got it!" Karen smiled. "We need to find a shop, a green grocer or a butcher or something and sit in their fridge or freezer. There are shops a few streets away. Come on."

***

The butcher wielded a knife at them. "We're closed. Get out. I have no money in the till, go and loot somewhere else."

Karen walked up to him. "No, we're not after your money. I have thought of a way to save us from that block that's coming. We need to sit in your airtight fridge and wait for the block to fly past."

"I have a walk in freezer that's airtight, but I'm not sure it will work." The butcher did not look convinced and kept his knife pointed at them.

"If you have a better idea, now is the time to tell us. But she's very clever and her idea makes a lot of sense. Please help us and open your freezer for us," Paul said, as the whole group walked towards the freezer door.

"I turned it off. With the six of us in here it'll warm up a bit," the butcher said, after he closed the door behind him. "How long do you reckon we need to stay in here?"

"I'm not sure. I tried my phone, but have no reception in here," Karen said. She seemed the only calm one in the group. She smiled at Thomas. "You know we will be fine, yes?"

Thomas smiled back at her. "I'm turning into ice cream" He hadn't spoken much since he had run out of the restaurant. Nerves made the others laugh at his little joke.

"I think we'll be out before you freeze, Thomas. Help me out here, you're good with numbers. If I remember right, it's 160 kilometres long and it goes about 400 kilometres per hour."

"Uhm, oh that's so easy," Thomas said. "It passes us in less than half an hour."

"So, if it arrives here in about ten minutes, add half an hour, give it another 20 minutes to be on the safe side, then I believe we can get out in an hour," Paul said.

They all agreed and stared at one another in silence, waiting.

"I'm not ready yet. Let's wait a bit longer," the butcher said.

"It's been over two hours now," Paul said, "I'm opening up. I'm freezing and I'm pretty sure we're running out of oxygen." He opened the door. No foam attacked them. They walked into the shop: totally empty — not any fresh meat was left at the meat counter.

"You think it's safe?" Isadora asked as they peered out the windows.

"We'll find out soon enough. Come on," Paul said as he opened the door and walked out.

It did not feel appropriate for them to break the silence, and the contrast of the panic stricken streets from before and now was too grotesque for them to compute. Nothing moved. Empty streets, empty shops and empty buildings;

no people anywhere, no trees, no birds, or any other living beings. The streets were so silent, they all tip-toed; anxious not to make a noise. All cars were abandoned; a few of them had collided or run into buildings. All the timber in buildings had been sucked up too, so a few had collapsed, and others seemed close to collapsing. Street after street had the same scene. And still not one single person was around. They noticed clothes on the streets, some with watches and glasses lying alongside. Behind shop windows there were more abandoned clothing lying around.

Around a corner was a church, its wooden roof collapsed. An empty space in front of the church: the ground a dull dark colour, had no evidence of the trees and the flowers that used to be there. A handful of metal benches stood in the centre, the sole reminders that there used to be a small park here. An abandoned pram stood next to a bench, a bundle of clothes in front. None of them dared to speak. Rick felt numb, his brain had been replaced with cotton wool.

Rick's phone rang and made all of them jump. The happy music of the ring-tone sounded perverse. He had forgotten about his phone. He stared at the screen, for a moment he was unable to figure out how to answer. "Hello?"

"Oh my God, oh my fucking God. I thought you were dead. I'm so happy to hear your voice. Are you all okay?" Martin asked.

Rick heard him sob. "Yes we are. We hid in the freezer in a butcher's. How are you?"

"I feel like shit. It's absolute mayhem everywhere and people are dying all over the world. I spoke to Colin in the States, they're evacuating people now, but everyone is panicking and it's chaos. We're receiving reports from all over the world. These things are sucking up everything in their paths. Many of them are going over the oceans and emptying them too. And we have no idea how long they'll be around. You must hurry back to London. I can keep you guys safe here for as long as these things go round — but your car won't work, petrol and tyres are also being sucked up. You must follow the railway to the east of Manchester and go to Hyde where the train station is. The block did not go over there. There's a car dealer there. Take a car, just steal it, and hurry back here."

Rick told the others what they had to do.

With tears rolling down his cheeks, the butcher told them he had to go home to see if his wife was still alive, but there was no hope in his voice. He turned around and walked off, not saying goodbye. The others watched him.

They walked to where their car was parked. Someone had driven into it. Rick hoped for the best as he tried to start the car, but of course it wouldn't.

"All right, let's get our stuff and go east," Rick said.

They found it difficult to work their way past parked and crashed cars. They did not make much progress. When they walked past a bicycle shop, Karen suggested they should borrow some bikes, so they could be out of Manchester before dark.

The tyre-less wheels of the bicycles rattled on the road. No one came out to see what the noise was, no dogs barked, no birds were startled and flew away. Even Sally stayed quiet. Throughout Manchester they did not encounter one other living soul.

***

They found the car dealership a little after sunset. And as they expected, there was no one there. Rick broke into the office and walked out a few minutes later with his hands full of car keys. They found a big car with a full tank of petrol and without speaking a word they got in and drove off. No one spoke much during the journey back home.

There were a few cars on the roads, their occupants surprised to see them on the road as much as they were. Karen watched news clips on her phone and occasionally ran a commentary. The radio was on; all stations had the same emergency broadcast repeated over and over again: *hide from the blocks, hide from the blocks, hide from the blocks.*

101. Rio(ts).
(December year 2)

Gustavo was glued to the television, watching the reports of the blocks that had dissolved people, animals and plants all over the world. Tensions had been high in many areas in Rio: people were attacked and shops were looted, so Zaira and Gustavo had decided to live at her parents for the time being. Her upper class area was safer than his favelas. They were lucky the blocks had not flown over Rio: they had destroyed life in other cities, like Sao Paulo and their capital Brasilia. The Government had lost most of its ministers and the whole civil service had problems keeping the country running at a minimum level. Hysteria had taken control: no one knew what was going to happen, and if they were going to be next to die.

Gustavo felt a hand on his arm and looked at Zaira and smiled. She looked as if she wanted to say something, but before she could start, his phone rang.

"Mum, what's up?" he asked, his voice trembling. "Calm down please." He paused. "Yes, stay there, we'll come and pick you up now." He put his phone down and looked at Zaira. "We must get my mother. There are riots in the street and there's a big fire near her, but there's no fire brigade coming. She's scared. We must go now."

Zaira's parents handed him the key to their car. That Gustavo did not have a driving licence did not matter to them, these were extreme times. And they were happy to take his mother in too. Gustavo was relieved they still believed he worked in a bar; if they found out how he really made his money, they would never let him, or his mother, stay anywhere near them and their daughter again.

***

The big green Cube loomed over the city, and the streets were almost empty, as most people were afraid to leave their homes. However, the Cube was not the most immediate threat: people were. Gustavo had thought humans would look after each other with an alien object on Earth, but he had been very wrong: rapes, murders and burning houses were a daily event in many Brazilian cities. Martial law was enforced in Brazil, so the police could shoot to kill, but that had not stopped the criminals looting his beautiful country. He felt uncomfortable driving an ostentatious German car into the favelas, but his mother needed him, and his money was hidden in his bedroom: thousands of dollars, pounds and euros.

He noticed the fire was about four houses away when they pulled up in front of his mother's home. Neighbours were running up and down the street with buckets of water, trying in vain to douse the fire. The poor souls didn't know the fire brigade was overstretched and would go to the wealthy neighbourhoods first, or only. Nobody cared about the favelas.

His mum leaped up from her chair when they came in. She gave him the biggest hug he had ever had. He loved her very much, he had been incredibly stupid having left her here for so long, but till now she had been too stubborn and too proud to be moved. He instructed Zaira to help his mother to pack her belongings. He did not want her to see him filling up a suitcase with foreign money. They did not have much time, as the fire could reach the house in minutes. He was relieved to see his bedroom was untouched and he opened his secret vault. After he secured all his cash, he filled up a bag with clothing, pictures and a few personal items. Gustavo heard a commotion from the other part of the house. Disturbed, he ran to the living room to see his mother and Zaira standing opposite four men with guns: who were pointing their guns at the two people who meant everything to him.

"So, what's a rich man like you doing here? Give us your cash and keys," one of them said.

Gustavo felt a sharp pain in his chest: his heart was ready to explode. The car! It was too posh, they had noticed the car and assumed they would find rich people, money, and with it hope — a way out of there. He needed to think of a plan to turn the situation around and make them leave.

"I stole this car to get my mother. I'm like you. We have no money," he said. "Please leave us alone, we'll leave now and you can have anything from this house." Gustavo approached the man closest to him, his hands opened, trying to resolve the stand-off, but he tripped and almost lost his balance. He tried to regain balance, but the man with the gun was startled, and a flash of light with a loud blast followed. Did the Cube attack them? Or had he heard the gun go off?

Gustavo was confused. His ears were ringing, he could not make out the sounds around him, were people screaming or talking to him? Events played out in slow motion in front of him. He saw Zaira and his mother were hugging, and the men had turned around and were running for the door. From somewhere he heard screams, but they were muffled. By now, the men had run out and Gustavo shouted at them as he tried to chase them away from his house. When he returned, he saw Zaira sitting by his mother who was not moving. He did not understand Zaira, she was crying and talking to him. What was going on? He felt a sharp pain on his cheek and he was brought back to reality. Zaira had slapped him.

"Gustavo, your mum — she's shot. Do something, don't just stand there, help me," she said as she sat next to his mother.

He wanted to say something comforting as he knelt next

to his mother, but he could not: his mother had died. Her dead eyes stared at him, but her tears still ran down her cheeks. He wiped her face dry, hoping she might react. When she did not: he went back inside his dream, his nightmare.

"Gustavo, we must go now. The fire, we'll burn if we don't get out," Zaira shouted at him.

Gustavo could not move. No, he did not want to move, he wanted to tell his mother he loved her and he wanted her to hear him saying those three little words, and he wanted her to say the same to him. He wished he could stay here and die with her, in their home. Nothing mattered any more to him. But then why should it? The world was coming to an end and now his mother was dead. It was probably better to die here right now with his mother, than to die at the hands of the aliens; who knew what had happened to all those people who had been sucked up? Every second the future looked bleaker than ever and he did not have the strength to endure more horror. Another slap.

"Wake up. We must go. Pull yourself together. Gustavo, I'm pregnant," Zaira shouted.

Her eyes stared at him. Gustavo tried to understand. Pregnant? Wake up? Gustavo realised he wasn't dreaming, he was awake and everything was real, he had to act. A father? He was going to be a father? How? But this is not the right time, the world is too dangerous. *Move you bastard! You also want to lose your unborn child?*

Gustavo kissed his mother on her lips and closed her eyes with his fingers. *I love you mother, always.* He needed to look after Zaira and his child. *His* child. "Just a second Zaira." He stood up and ran back to his room to collect his bags. "Come, it's not safe here," he said as he grabbed Zaira and pulled her to the door.

The heat overwhelmed him when they ran for the car.

The fire had started eating the neighbour's house. The car was left untouched, the invaders had gone: there was nothing of interest for anyone here. He would leave the favelas for the last time.

"Pregnant? I thought something was up. How are you feeling? Are you throwing up? Is the baby okay?" Gustavo asked. He tried to keep his attention on the road; there was not much traffic, but his mind was racing and he couldn't concentrate. He had so many more questions to ask her, but did not know where to start. His emotions started toying with him and made him paranoid: the whole world was after him and his wife, and his baby. Confusion dominated his mind. He had to tell her about the money, he had to tell her he could protect her — but how? He could not tell her the truth, not now whilst she was carrying his child. If she found out he had been having sex with men for money she would certainly leave him and they would never see one another again.

"I was just about to tell you when your mother rang — oh God, your mother, I'm so sorry. I only found out this morning. I'm scared, I don't want a baby, not now, not here in this crazy place. We must go somewhere Gustavo, tell me, what do you say?" Zaira pulled his hand to make him feel her belly. She sobbed.

"Let me think. I have some money, we can move to anywhere we want. Away from the bad people, but I don't know where it's safe. Let's get back to your parents first and then we'll discuss it. I need to think, give me a minute please." Gustavo realised he would never spend time with his mother again. He missed her already. She had been a good mother to him, never hit him, or shouted at him, and had never judged him. It was not fair she was gone, but she had peace now and she would not have to face the aliens.

**

There was no evidence of any trouble in the wealthier areas of Rio. Their big car had no problems being let through several checkpoints; yes the rich were safe, they were organised, and they had the money to protect themselves.

Zaira's father was standing outside, holding his gun, as they drove up the driveway. He had seen news reports from the favelas and his relief showed as soon as they stepped out of the car, but his faced turned to sadness when he realised only two had arrived.

Zaira's mother brought in coffee. Her living room looked pristine, as usual, with expensive paintings on every wall and *objets d'art* in every corner: she was very sophisticated. Zaira must have had a hard time from her, falling in love with him, a guy from the favelas, not owning anything, only working in a bar. But Zaira's mother never showed any signs of disapproval: she seemed to have welcomed him into their family with open arms.

Zaira's mother hugged Gustavo when Zaira told them what had happened earlier. Her warm embrace made him feel sad and happy at the same time. He had lost everything of his previous life, yet here he was, loved by his new family. Time to tell the parents the other news. "Zaira, why don't you tell them the good news," he said.

"I'm pregnant," she said flatly.

Zaira's mother smiled and winked at Gustavo: she loved him.

Then an argument ensued. Zaira and her father were disagreeing and agreeing over the same subject: they both felt it was not safe enough to raise a child in Rio, but neither could come up with a plan. She accused her father of wanting her to abort the baby. How could he suggest that? This was a love child and no matter what happened in the world, her child would be safe. That was not what he meant, she was twisting his words, her dad said, he only wanted the best for them.

Gustavo felt the argument would end with words that they both would regret having said. "I have thousands of dollars and pounds and euros and I have an aunt in London, she's my mother's sister. Isadora. I'll take Zaira there. It's safe and they have good hospitals."

They looked at him, their eyes asking him to explain himself more.

"I've been saving up all my tips and wages for many years. I've always been very careful with money. I know where I'm from and I know people look down on me, but I'm honest. I've never stolen anything in my whole life and I've never harmed anyone. I'll look after your daughter and grandchild." His response was very emotional, but they did not know his shame. They didn't know how he had really earned his money. *Don't tell them, stick to your story.* He opened his suitcase and showed them the money.

"It's decided then. You'll fly to London and come back when this is all over. This isn't a discussion. Zaira, go to your room and pack your bags now," her father said as he stood up and walked to a cabinet.

Zaira's mother was crying. Zaira was crying. This was all happening too fast for them.

Gustavo felt he was not a hero and he had not really thought the plan out; he had not seen his aunt for years, he had her current address, *he hoped*, but she might not be home, or be dead too.

"Take care of her," her father said as he put Zaira's passport in his hand.

Gustavo looked at the packed bags and knew they were about to say goodbye. He had no idea how he would take care of her, but he had to, he was now a father and the protector of his family.

Zaira's parents stood outside the car as Gustavo put her

one bag in the back. Zaira didn't want to leave, her mother was in tears, but the men had decided. A goodbye, which felt to Gustavo lasted more than a lifetime, followed. As they drove away from the house, Gustavo looked in his rear-view mirror at two people who had grown ten years older in the last hour and he realised they might never see them again.

***

They parked the car close to the terminal; they were not supposed to be there, but there was no one around to challenge them. Several police and army vans stood outside the entrance, but no uniforms were anywhere in sight. Gustavo thought it was odd not to see security outside the airport; given these exceptional circumstances.

Clearly, they had not been the only ones with the idea of flying away from Rio. The queues at the check-in desks were enormous and no one was moving. Gustavo decided they had to change their tactics. He noticed a British airline customer service desk with only a few customers standing in front.

After a short wait an overworked and irritable employee turned to them. She had made her mind up already: Gustavo did not look rich enough to pay for a ticket. "We have no tickets for you people."

"What, there are no tickets for any flights?" Gustavo asked.

"Oh, of course there are, but they're very expensive, and we do not take credit cards. I don't think *you* can afford them."

"I have cash. We need two tickets on your next flight to London. Name your price, I'll pay."

She quoted an outrageous price for two first class tickets, smiling whilst she spoke: knowing she had won. *The bitch.*

Gustavo didn't flinch. He took out a bunch of 100 dollar bills from his suitcase, casually counted them and threw them on the desk. "As I said, two tickets to London. And keep the change, my dear." This was what a man did to take care of his family. He felt proud; he could not remember ever feeling like this.

There was no border control; all uniformed people seemed to have disappeared. Gustavo and Zaira were lucky; the flight they had booked would leave in three hours, but the airline crew had already started boarding passengers. An armed man, who seemed to wear a pilot's uniform, stood outside the gate, overlooking the operation; every passenger was scrutinised: their luggage opened and inspected; they even had to empty their pockets.

Gustavo felt nervous. What would they do if they found all his money? After a short wait, it was their turn to board. He handed over their passports and tickets. First class, so he hoped for good treatment. The armed man told them to open their cases. This was it. If they were perceived to be thieves, all would fall apart and they could lose everything and not fly to safety. His face itched and sweat beads ran down his face when he opened his case. *Stay calm, you can only make things worse.* The man looked at his clothes and the bundles of cash and did not seem to be impressed or upset at all. He smiled as he waved them through. Gustavo was perplexed, he had not seen that coming, but nobody knew where he got the money from, nobody was judging him. He would walk away from the favelas forever as a new man: no more slums for him, no more stigma, ever.

The Cube had caused storms for hundreds of miles around the globe, and they ran into heavy turbulence during the flight. Zaira felt sick throughout, but the seatbelt lights were kept on, so she was not allowed to use the toilets. Discreetly, she threw up in the sick bags. Gustavo tried his best to comfort her, but she did not want him to make a fuss. Eventually she fell asleep for the rest of the flight and he managed to relax a bit too.

***

England was wet, cold and grey, and so were the people. The weather patterns had changed and it had been raining most of the time in Southern England since the Cube had landed.

During landing Gustavo had looked out of his window and noticed what the absence of organic material looked like: no trees, plants, or birds. No colours. He was thankful Rio had been spared from the foam. And that big green Cube again: it was much closer to the horizon here than it had been back in Brazil. The sight disturbed him: where a blue sky with scattered white clouds used to be, was now that green coloured monstrous *thing*. Not exactly a wall, but it felt like one to him: a wall he could never climb. He could not see where the sky started or where the Cube ended. He felt his eyes played tricks on him and he could not remember how the sky used to look before.

The official at border control would not let them go through. They were singled out and taken into an office, away from the crowd. Even though they had bought return tickets, to show they were planning to return to Brazil, the official did not want to let them in. Gustavo was so close to his destination, yet felt he would never reach it. He hoped the man wanted a bribe: it seemed too obvious to him, so he decided to offer one and the official accepted without hesitation. Money was power, and Gustavo had more than enough. But when he opened his suitcase, he did not think to hide all his money from the official. Gustavo's new found cockiness had made him sloppy.

The man saw the notes, his eyes lit up and he pointed at the cash. "Yeah, that'll do nicely. Thank you, and have a nice stay."

Gustavo was astounded: he had been outsmarted and defeated; how could he have let his guard down? He was supposed to be street smart. Thousands and thousands had been lost. Only the money they had in their wallets was left: a few hundred pounds.

**

The complex London Underground system intimidated Gustavo and Zaira: dozens of lines spun under London like a spider's web, trapping her citizens in cold metal coffins. As they waited for their long journey to end they watched the other passengers: drab and sad, not talking, not smiling and trying to avoid eye contact. Unfriendly people in London, but that suited them right now: they were ignored; nobody seemed to want to know strangers.

In the dark, cold and wet streets only a few houses had their lights on. Gustavo tried to find the house of his aunt, but he wondered if he had made a mistake. He did not know much about Isadora: he had only met her when he was a small boy. She had left Rio many years ago and had only maintained contact with his mother. He was worried his aunt wouldn't like them turning up to ask if they could live with her. What if she said no? What if she was not at home? He had no idea where to spend the night: London was not a welcoming city. Doubts were running through his mind, he had lost his money, and he did not want to be a failure and have to fly them back to Rio so soon.

A dark building with a big black wooden door greeted them, with a big window alongside with its curtains drawn. Gustavo thought his aunt might not want to attract unwanted attention, probably in case the aliens would come out of the Cube. He could not see if lights were on inside, he did not know if she would be home, and he was not sure if she actually still lived here. This was perhaps the most nerve wrecking moment ever in his life. He kissed Zaira and rang the doorbell. A dog started barking behind the door.

"Sally, stop it — hello, who's there?"

"Auntie Isadora. It's me, your nephew Gustavo. I need your help," he shouted at the big door.

The door opened and a woman, holding a dog, appeared. Light shone over her shoulders, highlighting her hair, almost creating a halo.

"Gustavo? Oh my God, it *is* you, and what have you grown! And who's that pretty lady with you? Quick, come on in, you look wet and cold. We're just about to have dinner."

The room felt warm. Soft cushions were scattered on the sofas and paintings filled the rich red coloured walls. Dozens of Christmas cards were placed around the fireplace, and a small fire was burning. A Christmas tree stood in the corner, decorated with multi coloured baubles, twinkling lights and tinsel on every branch, and a fairy on top completed the perfect picture. Over a dozen gifts had been carefully placed under the tree.

Two teenagers sat at the dining table, with steaming food on their plates. The smell made Gustavo's stomach rumble. The kids were staring at him, and a drenched Zaira, who stayed in the corner.

"Karen, can you get some food from the kitchen? I believe your cousin and his lady are joining us for dinner — and let's get you changed into something dry," she said as she smiled and winked at Zaira.

Blood does run thicker than water, Gustavo thought. He actually had achieved a good thing: he had found a safe place for his wife and his unborn baby.

When Isadora and Zaira returned, Gustavo felt sad and began to cry.

Isadora stretched out her arms, gesturing him towards her with her smile; she reminded him of his mother. Her embrace was warm, genuine and heartfelt. Gustavo held her tight, he didn't want to let her go. He wished she would hold him forever, for this moment to never end, but he realised that was impossible. Gustavo kept on crying and he felt good, and for a moment he forgot about everything and he imagined his mother was hugging him.

"Oh my sweet boy. It's all right now, everything will be fine," she said.

No, nothing would not be. She did not yet know her sister had died. She was the only family he had left. He pushed himself away from his aunt. He held her hands and looked into her eyes. His tears made it difficult to see her beautiful face. He could hear Zaira crying in the background: she knew what he was about to tell his aunt.

"I'm so sorry Auntie, it's about Mum."

103. Go green.
(January year 3)

Two weeks into the new year, without an announcement, or any fanfare, the Cube opened itself up. Around 50 metres above ground level, vast openings appeared, on each of the four sides. Doors, over a kilometre high and a 150 kilometres wide, slid slowly open. The event lasted four days and four nights: *they* did not seem to be in any hurry.

Military forces from all around the world were put on their highest alerts and millions of people fled from their homes, trying to be as far away as possible. But that was two weeks ago and no little green men with laser guns had come out to vaporise us, or put anal probes into anyone. The Cube sat there, with its doors wide open, towering over us, threatening us, taunting us — maybe inviting us? All attempts to communicate were met with silence. Cameras peered inside and the whole world tried to make sense of what they saw: big empty green halls. The world was in agony for not knowing what would happen next; something had to be done.

***

We have to force the issue, Prime Minister Marchant had said.

Martin sat at another emergency meeting. Yet again. He had not slept in his own bed for the last two weeks. Makeshift beds had sprung up all over the Downing Street bunker, to provide well needed rest for the Government, army and Ophiuchus Task Force officials. The showers had broken down over a week ago and had not yet been repaired; even the Prime Minister couldn't hire a plumber right now. The smell of unwashed men made sleeping almost impossible. Martin felt he needed to go home and have a proper shower himself. He missed home, his normal life, and sleeping next to Colin — ah, Colin: he was the lucky one; he attended a few meetings during the day and was allowed to go home at night. *I'll tell them I'm going home for one night. Fuck it. I've done enough and nothing is happening anyway,* he thought.

"Martin, what do you think of this proposal?"

"Excuse me?" Martin had been daydreaming again. He had no idea what was proposed. He felt ashamed for his momentary lapse of attention. "Sorry, I wasn't listening."

The Prime Minister grunted. "We need to send a small military team, in a helicopter. Not too big, so we won't appear aggressive. Only for a reconnaissance mission. We must know what's in there and how to prepare ourselves."

"Do you have anyone in mind who's willing and crazy enough to fly into the lion's den?" Martin asked.

"I know a pilot who can fly in difficult circumstances. He flew us into Las Vegas and also managed to escape from under the Cube. His name is David Pilling. I can send for him, so we can do this tomorrow," Colin said.

"Good, that's sorted — Martin, you get a military team together and arrange the mission," the Prime Minister said.

"Yes Sir, but I feel we need a civilian in the team too. In case of first contact. No offence General," Martin said to the General, with a smile on his face, "but civilians talk first and then shoot, unlike your men, who do it the other way around."

"None taken."

"Ah, Martin, yes you're right. Prepare yourself, you just volunteered," the Prime Minister said, "and think of something to say when you meet the aliens. Your speech needs to be official, but also informal. I'm certain you'll come up with something good."

Martin had not expected to go himself. "In that case. I'll

have to go home now. I think best at home, and I need a very long hot bath and a good night's sleep. I stink and I don't want to scare the aliens."

Colin winked at him. A little smile on his face, intended only for Martin. No one else noticed.

"And just like at the movies, the aliens have of course chosen to speak and understand perfect English," Martin whispered in Colin's ear. "Let's head home together."

***

Dawn was dull at the military airport. The rain clattered down, again as always, and Martin got soaked during the short walk from his taxi to the helicopter. He noticed the wind direction had changed: today it was very strong, and blowing in the direction of the Cube. David Pilling and three Marines were waiting for him, checking their handguns. Martin noticed radios, grenades and cameras in the cabin.

"Here's a gun for you Sir," David said, handing him one.

Martin refused. "I won't be needing that, but thank you. I'll have a camera and a radio instead."

"Yes, you're allocated those. Are you ready to leave? Or do you wish to say anything first?"

"Yes — when we encounter the aliens, I don't want you guys to shoot at them and risk having us killed. I want to attempt communicating with them first. This is a civilian operation, with your military expertise as a back-up only. We need to gather as much information as we can in a very short time. If we lose someone — we will not turn this into a rescue mission. Let's go."

There was no chatter through his headphones during the flight and Martin felt lonely. At least he had had a good night's sleep and had found himself cuddled up against Colin when he had woken up. The helicopter approached the Cube, and the green colossus towered in front of

Martin. The strong winds pushed the helicopter forward with a violent shudder; Martin thought David would have a difficult time flying in a straight line. He imagined that if aliens were watching them now, it would probably seem to them as if a drunken fly was trying to get into their home. *Do they have flies?* Martin thought. He was shocked when the oblong aperture appeared very close in front of him: they were almost there, almost inside. As they approached the entrance the lack of activity made him feel uncomfortable. Were they watching him? Waiting for the right time to shoot him out of the sky? Or were they teasing him, letting him enter their domain, only to capture him and to not kill him, but to do things worse than death would be?

David's voice made Martin jump, as he informed them he had decided to land the helicopter on the left side at the periphery of the opening. After David switched off the helicopter engines, and the rotors stopped spinning, they all sat in silence waiting; expecting to be seized by aliens at any minute, but nothing happened.

Martin looked through the windows, into the vast space. Although sunlight did not shine into the hall, and Martin could not see any lamps, there seemed to be enough light emanating from the ceiling, the walls and the floor for Martin to see clearly. Primal fear almost paralysed him: this hall was too enormous, and from somewhere deep inside his brain he could hear himself scream that humans were not supposed to be here and experience this. He tried to make himself feel safe inside his bubble, the cocoon around him that was part of humanity, the last defence for his sanity: the helicopter cabin. Stepping out, would make him the first human being ever inside and in contact with something not from this Earth, and the importance of this moment overwhelmed him. Martin noticed he was playing music in his mind. A classical piece by Gustav Holst: *Mars,*

The Bringer of War.

Quite appropriate, he thought, and a wry smile appeared on his face. *Maybe I'll meet some Martians today.*

David instructed them to start the mission. Martin opened the door and put his foot on the flat surface. He had almost forgotten to breathe and the first time cool air flowed into his lungs, he was pulled out of his dream-like trance. He almost fell over: gravity was less here and he felt half as heavy as he should be. Through the sound of the blowing wind, Martin noticed the absence of familiar noises: there were no birds.

One small step for man, one giant leap for mankind, he heard one of the Marines say as they jumped out of the cabin. The comment made them laugh. The sound of their voices felt inappropriate to Martin: an innocence had been broken. He noticed the absence of an echo.

The ambient level of the green light seemed to be the same as dawn on a clear spring morning. There were no shadows, nothing lurked in the dark, there was nothing around to frighten him. There were no objects or beings in this mammoth vault.

The quartet looked around, trying to capture everything on their cameras, but there was nothing interesting to record. Martin suggested they spread out, explore, walk to the wall they were closest to, and look for anything or anyone.

Martin became aware of the colours, or rather the lack of them: all he saw were shades of green. He was fascinated when he noticed how this colour spectrum seemed to be going from almost white to almost black, but only used the colour green as shading. He felt relieved his green military outfit made him blend in.

After walking for a few minutes in the low gravity he managed to keep his balance. He noticed something on the floor: three strips of various shades of green were running along the wall, from the entrance towards the centre of the Cube. He estimated each one of them was about a hundred metres wide. He approached the lightest one and set one foot on the strip. Nothing happened. *Could these be traffic lanes?* He wanted to radio the Marines that it was safe to walk over the strips, but he noticed they had crossed the strips already and were approaching the wall. Martin decided not to follow the strips to the centre, but to follow them towards the entrance. After a short walk he noticed a big square on the floor: a very light green, almost white. He stepped inside the square and again nothing happened. The three strips he had noticed before started in this square. As he was thinking what this could mean, he stepped onto the lightest strip.

***

"Martin, can you hear me? Come in Martin. It's time for us to leave and we're going home now. If you can hear me — please look after yourself," David said through his radio for the last time as the helicopter took off. They had waited for six hours for Martin to reappear, but as he had instructed them: they were not to go after him. Martin was gone, he had vanished into thin air, and none of the Marines had seen it happen.

107. Fantastic voyage.
(January year 3)

Hang on, what happened just now? Martin said to himself after a second of confusion and total disorientation. He looked around and at himself, not quite understanding what had happened to, or *with* him. Good, he was still standing upright and he felt no pain, so there was nothing wrong with his body, but he was moving. Yes, he felt he was in motion and he was moving forward and was going damn fast too — but he was not walking. *Ah, this is like a conveyor belt or a travelator. Nice.* Martin looked in front of him and saw a corridor that seemed to disappear into infinity. Various green shades and green shapes flashed past him, and when he looked back he saw the familiar blue and grey sky-colours disappear: the exit back to Earth was diminishing into nothing.

He felt rather excited. Here he was, still alive, into the unknown, and on his own. He had to make the best out of his situation and discover as much as possible, before he would meet the aliens — or they would capture him — or worse. He remembered to switch on his camera and started recording. He had no idea how long he had been travelling, but he did feel he had to try to make his way back to the others, or the others might start to worry about him. Martin turned to his left, a clumsy move; he had forgotten about the low gravity, and he fell to his side, but something made him bounce back: an invisible barrier had kept him on the strip. *Be more careful Martin.* He noticed different green coloured markings, attached to the walls, flying past him. Intuitively he reached out for one. A sudden stop. He noticed he was standing on a similar square as before.

"Hello all. Well, this is turning into an exciting exercise. I've found a way of travelling, but have found no aliens as yet. Strangely, I don't feel afraid, even though I think I should be. I'll try to get back to the Marines, so we can explore together. I feel there is plenty more to see," he said, smiling into the camera. He felt like a child would at summer camp on the verge of an adventure.

Martin noticed his surroundings did not look very different from before, everything was a shade of green. He was at a junction of sorts: several corridors interconnected here, all had many coloured strips. He looked up, and noticed a corridor above him, and another one was hanging askew behind him. All corridors seemed to lead to infinity.

Martin had more than a few dozen strips to choose from, and he had no idea which one would take him back to the Marines. How *did* their traffic system work? He stepped on a strip closest to the one he travelled on before and wished for the best.

Travelling again. Even faster this time, the markers passed him at an alarming rate. Martin didn't see the Earth's sky approaching, and he realised he was not on his way back to the Marines. He felt he had to make a decision soon, to get off this travelator, or otherwise he could end up anywhere. Before he had decided to reach out for a marker, and stop, he realised that the corridor he was travelling in had a light at its end. The brightness increased as fast as he moved towards the light, so he decided to stay on the travelator to investigate.

A sudden stop. He had arrived at the end of the corridor without having reached for a marker. He gazed up to the light source that had drawn his attention. He saw a bright white light that looked familiar; reminding him of the Sun, but this light was much smaller — a little star, with a few tiny clouds moving around it. The light did not hurt his eyes, but his instinct made him look away. The rays of this Sun felt warm on his head. He noticed the Sun was connected by six large columns that went to each side of the — hang on a second — where was he now? What exactly was he looking at? He took a few seconds to take in his surroundings. He was inside a sphere: an enormous sphere, with the Sun hanging many kilometres up in the centre. To the sides and all around him was a lattice of triangles: they were plateaus of flat land and plateaus with buildings. Triangular pieces of empty land and triangular cities with triangular kilometres high buildings.

"Oh my God."

He tried to find the horizon, but there was none: the ground curved upwards instead. He noticed the buildings in the cities leaned over, pointing towards him, and the cities farther away leaned over even more. When he gazed into the distance, the cities and plateaus started merging into each other and disappeared into a monotonous green nothingness. First he thought he was looking at a green sky, but he soon realised that the side above him would have the same buildings as those he was seeing around him. He felt strange thinking about the cities that were built above his head, where the creatures would be living upside down. He tried to count the number of cities, but there were too many, they were all over the sphere, and most of the buildings in the cities seemed kilometres high. He knew he was in the purpose-built habitation area of the Cube: tens of billions of aliens could live here — he had not seen one yet and he wondered where they were all hiding.

Martin felt thirsty and also needed to pee, so he decided to head for the nearest building in search of water. And his stomach had started rumbling, so maybe find food too. He walked for half an hour and reached a triangular building. He *really* needed to pee now, but he felt embarrassed to go anywhere outside: what if the aliens were watching him? He did not want to be caught with his trousers down.

He looked at the wall and floor and wondered what material they were made of. He put a finger on the floor; it did not feel cold, it was not rough, not sticky, it was smooth, but had good grip when walking on it. He also put his finger on the wall of the building and it felt exactly the same. He took his pocket knife and tried to carve into the surface, but the material did not scratch. Everything appeared to be made of the same material, with an opaque appearance he could not see through, but light did seem to shine through, and emanate from within. Throughout his expedition he had noticed various green colours: the material reminded him of a toughened version of quartz. *Could this be a purpose-built — or grown, crystal quartz cube for the aliens to travel and live in?* Martin could not find any seams between the floor and the building, and he thought this planet sized object was an amazing feat of engineering. He felt he needed to show real respect to whoever had built this: when he would meet them.

A triangular opening, approximately five metres wide at its base, and four metres high, interrupted the vast green wall and Martin assumed this had to be the entrance, or a doorway, but he could not find a door behind the opening. He looked at the other buildings near him and noticed none of the openings had doors in them. On higher levels he saw more triangular openings; he thought they might be windows. He tried to find the top of the building, but it was taller than the highest structure he had ever seen on Earth and he hurt his neck trying.

Martin prepared himself for being attacked by tall aliens as he entered the building. He found himself inside a giant green hall with many triangular benches of around a metre high. The ceiling was over ten metres high. He peeked through more doorways, leading to more halls and rooms. He explored the various rooms, and each one he had been in, also had a triangular shape. All rooms were empty except for the benches. He could not find staircases, or lifts. He wondered how the aliens reached the upper levels. *Do they fly and where the hell are they?*

Martin still needed that pee, but had not found toilets either, so he decided to use a wall outside. He reached a corner; not a right angle, but as he suspected, a 60 degree angle, in keeping with the triangular theme inside the sphere. He noticed a light green triangle on the floor. When he stepped on it, he hoped he was correct in thinking it could be a? — yes, he was — the triangle was an elevator. The platform travelled upwards and markers passed him, they looked very similar to those on the travelators and he assumed these represented the floors. Martin didn't like heights too much, but he did want to know if the elevators also had an invisible barrier. His hand bounced back after he stuck it out, and he breathed a sigh of relief. As he went higher, the view became more magnificent. At ground level he had been overwhelmed, but that was nothing compared to what he was seeing now.

Martin was surrounded by vast empty triangular plateaus; around half of them were too deep to see the bottom, and all were various shades of green again. On many plateaus were the big cities, their high buildings, all triangular too, towered like cathedrals, with their spires trying to touch the Sun. Martin felt dizzy looking at this inverted Earth. Satisfied he had ascended high enough, he waved his hand at a marker. The elevator stopped and Martin stepped into a small triangular hall, with many doorways. He walked through one, and found several interconnected rooms. He felt this could be a living quarter, or an apartment. There were several benches inside and a doorway which gave access to a terrace, where he relieved himself, as he was bursting by now. He walked right up to the edge to admire the interior of the sphere. The view made him stop breathing for a moment. He wondered if there was an invisible barrier here; his bouncing foot confirmed there was. *These aliens are serious about health and safety,*

Martin thought. He estimated he was two kilometres above ground level, and the view was magical: he felt he was inside a giant snow globe.

Back inside, he noticed two small triangular alcoves in a wall. He stuck his hand in one and water streamed out. Martin was pleased, he felt dehydrated and he did not doubt the water would be clean enough to drink. When he finished quenching his thirst, he tried the next alcove. Green slurry came out; reminding him of green custard. He didn't like the flavour: it tasted similar to cheap mashed up vegetables in baby food, and the film *Soylent Green* popped up in his head. The thought made him shudder.

He had no idea how long he had been inside the sphere, but he did feel tired and sleepy. He decided to have a quick nap on one of the benches. Before nodding off, he listened to the silence and it dawned on him: he would not find any aliens in here. He was all alone.

***

When Martin woke up, his back ached from sleeping on the hard surface. For a brief moment he thought he was at home and had experienced the most vivid dream, but as soon as the cold green surrounded him again, he realised he really was in this alien place. He missed his bed and Colin. After his so-called *breakfast* he went out on the terrace, to scan other buildings and areas around him, but still he did not see any signs of aliens: there really was nobody here. If he was correct, this information had massive implications. So, who was attacking them and where were they hiding, if at all? He decided against trying to find his way back out, to Earth. First he needed to make absolutely certain he was correct. He refreshed himself in something resembling a shower room, left his apartment and took the elevator back to ground level. The most logical place to find aliens would be either a power plant, or any type of manufacturing area. He decided to visit the nearest column, also a triangular shape, which was attached to the Sun. If he could not find another travelator, he estimated he would have to walk for at least three weeks. And he was not looking forward to being in this oppressive monochrome sterile space: without any trees, shrubs or flowers: without any life.

Martin found a circle on the floor at the corner of the city, he stepped onto it and, as he hoped for, he found himself at a junction again. Full of confidence he stepped on a strip and after about 20 seconds stopped himself at the first marker. When he stepped off the circle, he noticed he was at the corner of another city and was heading in the right direction towards the column. It was difficult to estimate distances without a horizon, but he thought he had travelled over 100 kilometres. He would have to be careful and repeat the procedure often, so not to overshoot, but he was pleased at the speed he was travelling. This circle shaped travel method appeared to be ten times faster than the square travelator, and Martin baptised it the Inter-City.

When Martin found himself at a point close enough to the column, he noticed he was at the converging point of a city and several empty plateaus, and one of which had the column at its corner, so he could not use the Inter-City circle any more. He estimated he was at least 30 kilometres away from the column and he would take a few hours to walk there. The air was quite warm and he thought the heat would slow him down, but the low gravity would speed him up again. He hoped his goal would be worth the hike.

The column was massive, each side over a kilometre wide and thousands of kilometres high; disappearing into the Sun. He walked around it twice, but could not find an entrance: there were no circles, triangles, squares or any other shaped indicators to go inside, or travel up. The sheer frustration of having wasted his time made Martin stamp his feet. He was tired of walking, and tired of being on his own. He wanted to go home.

Whilst walking back towards the circle, Martin heard a noise in the distance. This was the first time he had heard something since he had entered the Cube, and the noise was growing louder by the second: turning into a roar. He ran towards the noise, still kilometres away, and when he got close he noticed it came from the bottom of one of the deep plateaus: from many kilometres below. Martin realised he was looking into a basin filling up with water. The water appeared to be boiling hot and was spitting upwards, and thunderous upside down waterfalls and fountains created angry vortices and whirlpools. Martin noticed more roaring noises coming from different directions; other basins had started filling up too. The Cube was creating lakes inside the sphere. He knew where the water had come from: the Cube had been syphoning from the oceans. This explained the strange currents and the receding coastlines that had started a few days ago.

Martin had to go home and tell everyone immediately, but first he had to find his way back — it could take him days to figure out how to get out of the sphere first.

Martin started walking back to the converging point, so he could step on the circle and take things from there. He felt a tingling on his face and arms. He wondered what it could be and noticed a rain cloud, high in the sky, was passing over him. Tiny raindrops were falling down, gently and slower than snow flurries. The small drops on his face refreshed him. Water had been brought into the sphere and now the mini Sun had initiated a hydro-logic cycle similar to the Earth's.

After walking for a few hours, Martin needed to sit down to rest and think, but he fell asleep again. After he woke up he decided to walk on. But something unusual caught his attention. He had almost missed it, but he noticed a tiny movement from the corner of his eye. His heart jumped a few beats and adrenaline rushed through him. Had the aliens found him? Did they try to make first contact? He turned towards where he thought the movement originated from, but he only saw an empty building. Why would they hide? Boldness, encouraged by anger and frustration made him almost run up to the building.

Martin heard a sound, only once; difficult to hear it over the distant roars, but he was certain he had heard something. The sound reminded him of a bird chirping. He found it very confusing, but familiar enough to calm him down. And again: he heard more chirps. He followed the sound with his eyes and at the bottom of the nearest building he saw two tiny birds — blue tits, he thought. His presence startled them and they flew off. It was great to finally see different colours inside the sphere. Martin's eyes welled up with happiness. This world did not feel so alien to him now and he was not all alone any more either. Martin ran after the birds and saw them fly to a nearby dark square hole, and they disappeared inside. He recognised the hole when he looked into it: another entrance to the sphere. He found his way out.

Martin stepped into the hole, onto a strip and again travelled at high speed. This time, he decided, he would not stop at a marker, but stay on until the end; hoping this travelator would finish at the Cube entrance where he had started his journey a few days ago.

Hours later, a sudden stop. When he stepped off the square he found himself in a familiar giant hall again. There was no sign of the Marines; he had not expected them to be there, but he still felt disappointed. Martin walked up to the ridge and looked out. All he saw were waves and clouds, but he felt fantastic seeing the ocean again. The saltiness of the sea-air tasted good on his lips. He knew he was not at the correct exit, but now he understood how to travel, so it would only be a matter of time to find the right exit. Third time round: he was lucky. He walked to the ridge and looked at the familiar buildings and landscape of his England.

In the distance he saw a helicopter. Martin waved both his arms frantically and screamed his lungs out. "Here, I'm here, I'm okay." He was almost home.

109. Prime yourselves.
(February year 3)

"— due to the reduced yield, the Government has decided not to allow farmers to renew their livestock. Farmers are now advised to plant high calorie vegetables, root vegetables and potatoes. Consumer groups have welcomed the news and believe the food crisis can be overcome by turning the Nation into vegetarians —.

"My apologies, but I hear from my producer that we have a live report from the Cube."

"Look. It's Uncle Martin. He's not dead at all. Look at him waving. I'm so happy he's alive," Florence shouted at Paul and Rick, as they watched the morning news. Since Martin had disappeared they had been mourning the loss of their good friend, and since no one else had been brave or stupid enough to venture into the Cube, there had been no rescue mission or attempt to find him.

The army had reported Martin as missing in action, but the news reporters had already declared him dead, because the army had mentioned that a type of deadly zapping beam might have vaporised him. But now a news helicopter was streaming live pictures from the same opening where Martin had disappeared days ago and Martin was there now, waving and smiling. A military helicopter appeared on the screen: flying into the opening, almost blowing Martin over. Its rotors did not slow down when Martin jumped in, and the helicopter flew out of the Cube less than 30 seconds later.

"Gosh, that was fast. I'm happy Uncle Martin is safe. You were so sad, I didn't like that — oh, and you should ask him over for dinner. I want to know about the Martians," Florence said.

Rick wondered if Martin would have a message from the aliens. He couldn't wait to see him and ask him all about his adventure, but he knew Martin would have to debrief first, and see Colin second.

Rick's phone rang: Isadora. Rick expected her to tell him Martin was on television, but instead she told him Thomas was insisting on seeing them today. He had to announce something very big, but it was a secret and he would only tell if Uncle Rick was present.

Rick asked them over for dinner, all of them. He asked her if Thomas was experiencing another autism induced episode, but Isadora told him this time was different. Rick had to find out later, but all was good, he did not have to worry.

***

"Uncle Rick," Thomas shouted, "I've discovered the Cube's secret." Thomas ran into the living room where Rick was sitting. He threw a notebook on the table and hugged and kissed Rick.

"A secret? Tell me," Rick said and he glanced at Isadora who was smiling at him, as she walked in with Karen, Florence and Paul. Gustavo and Zaira followed, and Rick noticed the small bump on her belly: she was starting to show. Rick had invited them too for the evening; they were part of his extended family.

Thomas started talking before everyone had a chance to sit down. "Okay. So I saw this pattern, but I couldn't figure out what it was. It was making me go crazy. So I've been calculating. And it was too simple to even think about it."

"Yes, you drove us all crazy," Isadora interrupted, winking at Thomas. "Go on, tell him. We all want to know now."

"So they say each side of the Cube is 8,893 kilometres long, and that orb that came out was 17 metres in diameter. And then there were the foaming blocks that came out and then there were the air openings. Yes?" Thomas was out of breath and he started fidgeting. "They're all sums of prime numbers! Uncle Rick. I know their secret." Thomas walked around the table, stepping on Paul's toes, but he didn't notice. The tension was showing on his face. He tried to pick up his notebook, but it kept falling out of his hands.

"Calm down Thomas. You're doing great. Sit down and explain everything to me please," Rick said as he picked up the notebook. He knew how to talk to Thomas and calm him down.

"So the Cube itself is 8,893 kilometres each side," Thomas continued, "I don't know what unit of measurement the aliens are using, but if I use kilometres then it's very simple to calculate. I know it sounds too good to be true, but it works out the way I do it. They could, by coincidence have a unit that is more or less one kilometre, but it doesn't matter what they use for me to do the calculations. So, as you should know, number 1 is not a prime, but 2, 3, 5, 7, 11, 13 and so on are. When you add them all up: starting with 2, so 2 plus 3 is 5, plus 5 is 10, plus 7 is 17 and so on, and the last prime number to add is 311, then you come to 8,893. The orb that flew round Earth is 17 metres in diameter. That is 2 plus 3 plus 5 plus 7. I'm not sure how high that hole was it came out from, but they said it was about two kilometres. If you add up to number 137, then you come to 1,988 metres. That's pretty close. The blocks with the foam are done the same way and you get in kilometres: 40.28 wide, 4.888 high and 14.8 deep. I can predict the exact measurements for the air vents too: they were 58 metres up from the ground, 1,060 metres high and 148 kilometres wide. In the news they always round numbers up or down to make it easier — Uncle Rick, you work for the Government, have them measured. I'm sure you'll find these numbers are correct." His voice became loud and high pitched from excitement and he couldn't sit still on the sofa. A big grin was on his face though. He seemed very proud of himself.

"And you did all of this on your own? That's impressive," Rick said as he took his phone out. "I'm calling Martin now to tell him, he'll be very interested. You're a genius! Not one scientist came up with this. Let's have a beer before dinner to celebrate."

***

As soon as Martin was told of the discovery, he and Colin had rushed over to Rick's place. He was excited to see him, and more so to hear from Thomas. After they walked into the room, Florence was the first to hug him. When he looked around to greet everyone, Martin froze and wanted to disappear into the Cube again: Gustavo was sitting on the sofa. He could feel blood rushing to his face. How on Earth did they end up in the same room? Had Rick or Isadora told him Gustavo was in London? He had had too much on his mind to remember. This guy could mess everything up between him and Colin. And the shame it could cause, if his friends found out he had paid for sex.

Martin tried to look casual when he greeted Gustavo. He was relieved when Gustavo did the same. His anxiety subsided and he remembered how Gustavo had prevented him from having a nervous breakdown back in Rio. In hindsight, he owed him.

"You know Thomas, your theory sounds very interesting. Rick told me to bring along the exact measurements of the Cube, so if you want we can check them now," Martin said as he took out a big folder, stamped *Top Secret*. "Or do you want to hear about my adventure inside the Cube first?" He winked at Rick.

Everyone yelled. "Adventure first." Even Colin joined in, who had heard it before, but loved the story.

Martin told them all about the travelators, the elevators and the Inter-City, the lack of colours other than green, the big triangular buildings in the cities, and the immense emptiness of the sphere. He told them about the Sun, the rain, the food, the lakes and the two birds. *Did he see any aliens?* No — no aliens at all: the Cube's emptiness was the biggest paradox and frightened Martin much more than if he had found them.

"It sounds wonderful inside, I want to see it," Karen said. "Take me there please."

"If she can go, I want to go too. I discovered the secrets," Thomas said.

"I'm not allowed to let people go in. Officially, it's still too dangerous. Our Government is meeting with other Governments to decide what we do next. For all we know, the aliens might be hiding somewhere. Someone must have flown the thing. It's a giant spaceship."

"They sound like space tourists and their camper-van is using Earth as their parking space," Florence said.

"Good point Florence, but where's the driver? All right Thomas. It's time to crunch those numbers," Martin said, noticing the disappointment in Thomas's eyes.

All nine people were very impressed with Thomas's mathematical skills. Every calculation corresponded with the measurements. He explained how he had reached the conclusion and now he was showing them how his predictions exactly matched the measurements Martin had brought along.

***

Rick and Florence served dinner and everyone sat down to eat, but Colin's phone rang: it was President McGee. The disapproving tone in Colin's voice made the others uncomfortable; they knew something had to be wrong. Colin hung up and they sat silent, waiting for him to explain.

"Uhm, you guys, switch on the television. You might want to see this — Brazil is going in."

East of Rio de Janeiro, Brazilian builders had positioned a crane next to an opening and, using a basket, hauled people up into the Cube. Soldiers were busy constructing a more permanent structure, made of scaffolding and a wooden ramp. The opening was less than 60 metres above ground level, similar to a seven-floor building. A reporter interviewed several men who were next in line for the basket. They told him they were going to loot the Cube, as compensation for the destruction of their homes.

Gustavo jumped up as soon as he saw the men. "These are very bad men, they're from the favelas." He looked at Martin. "Martin, you can't let them go in. They'll ruin everything. They have weapons. Please do something."

"I can't control what other countries do."

"No, you don't understand — I am begging you Martin. It's really important. Zaira, you know what they can do. Tell Martin." Gustavo's voice was trembling. He moved very close to Martin. His hands squeezed Martin's shoulders and their eyes locked. "Please, for me," he whispered in his ear.

Everyone in the room wondered what scene was playing out in front of them: Gustavo was behaving intimately, and Martin looked uncomfortable. Rick coughed to break the silence and end the awkward moment.

Martin stood up, pushing Gustavo away. "I need to make a phone call," he said as he walked off.

Colin followed him. "What was *that* all about?" he asked.

"Rick told me Gustavo's mother was shot dead by thugs. I think that's why he's so upset. Maybe they're the same men he saw just now. Just leave it please and let me make that call," Martin said as he dialled the Prime Minister on his phone.

"Yes Sir, I know. Good to see others are keeping to the agreement not to enter." The sarcasm in Martin's voice was clear. "Agreed Sir, I shall see to it forthwith. Goodbye." Martin returned to the living room. "It's arranged, I'm going back in. A car is picking me up. We've decided to return with a team of scientists to investigate more. We can't have other countries taking an advantage over us. Although — I will need help from the cleverest man on the planet." Martin winked at Thomas. "Isadora, I would like to take Thomas with me. I could really use his skills. It is safe inside, I truly believe the Cube is empty," Martin said.

Thomas jumped up and danced around the room. "Mum, can I? Can I?"

"If Uncle Rick goes as well, then — okay," Isadora said. Her smile at Rick was her approval.

"Sure Thomas, let's go on an adventure," Rick said.

Whilst waiting for the car to arrive, they watched the news. Reports came in from the Ukraine and Iran. The Ukrainians were co-operating with the Russians and allowed the Russians to fly to the openings. The Iranians were not happy with the Chinese, who violated their airspace with their planes, as their air force was escorting a big cargo plane towards the Cube.

Russia and China were still a few hours away from the Cube, and though the Brazilians had already gone in, they would not yet know how to operate the travelators, nor how to find the sphere. But nonetheless Martin felt they had to hurry. The Cube had become less mysterious and even less threatening now he understood the inside better, and soon many others would make similar discoveries and then feel the same way too. Martin had to go to the bathroom. When he came out Isadora was waiting for him.

She positioned herself close to him and whispered. "I need to have a quick word. You must *really* look after

Thomas."

"Of course I will. He'll be safe."

"But, I mean, nothing can happen to him. And you need to look after Rick." Isadora poked him on his chest.

"Of course." Martin felt annoyed by her intensity. "Don't you trust me?"

"Yes I trust you. I'm letting my son go with you, aren't I? But there's something you should know. Rick is Thomas's father."

"What?" Martin was stunned. "When?"

"At university."

"I knew something was up. But you left him and then lied to him. I remember he was devastated when you left — heartbroken."

"I was young and scared. I needed a husband for my child, and Rick couldn't be."

"And he doesn't know. Does he? Why are you telling *me* this? I'm stressed enough as it is."

"I'm sorry." Isadora was crying now. "I'm scared I might lose the two most important men in my life. Please don't tell Rick. Promise me. I'll tell him soon. Now that he and Paul are looking after Florence, I know they're good parents. But the right moment never seems to come up. Not today either, so *uncle* will have to suffice for now."

"Promised, and I won't let anything happen to them."

The goodbye was more emotional than Martin expected: Isadora cried again, and so did Karen, Florence and Paul. They were all hugging and kissing Thomas and Rick.

"Be careful my baby," Isadora said to Thomas, as she kissed him on his cheek.

"Oh Mum, you're embarrassing me," he said, smiling as he pulled away from her.

Martin kissed Colin goodbye and the three of them were ready to leave for the airport: where their helicopter was waiting.

Gustavo ran after them, he took Martin aside before he could step into the car. "Sorry about earlier. Us, it's our secret, I won't tell. You know, I really liked you then."

"There never was any us. And please don't ever, ever do this again. I love Colin and I won't have you fuck things up."

113. The Room of Revelations. (March 03)

Thomas had never been in a helicopter before, but he was enjoying himself during this flight. He had flown once, but he had been a baby then, so he couldn't remember. He did not understand why his mother always told him he wasn't ready to fly yet. She always told him about a lot of things he could not do. That bothered him sometimes, he did not know why though. He could also not understand why his little sister was ready to do many more things than he was.

Sometimes when he was bothered by his feelings everyone around him got really stressed. Only Uncle Rick seemed to treat him as normal, no matter how he behaved himself. He felt happy Uncle Rick was here with him in the helicopter: he felt safe and really liked being high up in the air. The noise of the rotors interfered with his thoughts and made it harder for him to think, but that was good, he had fewer thoughts in his head now.

Martin had told him how important he was, how he would solve more mysteries of the Cube. Earth was counting on him. He thought it was funny, how his mother and others always treated him as if he were disabled, but he was actually the smartest man on the planet. How could everyone else *not* have seen the obvious solution by using the prime numbers?

We're almost going to land. Hold on tight Thomas, he heard the pilot say. The Cube did not frighten him: nothing in the world had ever made more sense to him. He noticed trucks and workmen at ground level; the work on the permanent ramp had started and in a few days more people could go into the Cube, but today the only people inside would be him and his small team. The Marines and the pilot had been very nice to him. They were joking around, but did not make fun of him. Instead they made fun with him. They were so manly and they had guns and they were dressed really cool. He liked their helmets and he was thrilled when they told him he would wear the same outfit as them. He decided he wanted to become a Marine, but he knew his mother would tell him he was not ready for that either.

"Thomas, be careful when you step out. Have fun with the low gravity", a Marine said to him after they landed.

"Yeehaw!" Thomas was running and jumping inside the giant hall, and he could leap twice as high and more than twice as far as on Earth. He loved it, and he could do this forever. He saw Rick fall over a few times. His uncle's clumsiness made him laugh. "Imagine being on a trampoline," he shouted at him. He saw his uncle and Martin were laughing too. One of the Marines performed a somersault, and others were jumping over each other. Uncle Rick seemed to be moving better now, jumping up instead of stepping.

"All right you all, that's enough mucking about. It's time we did some work," Martin yelled into the wind. "Follow me," he said, jump-walking towards the square on the floor.

"Thomas, we're off to the sphere now using the travelator, as I explained to you. I believe the entrance is about halfway down, so if you can calculate after how many markers we need to get off and tell me, that would be great."

"Okay, I won't make us miss the sphere," Thomas said. He felt excited, now he could start to impress them.

Martin made sure the group stepped on the lightest strip together. Thomas felt disoriented; he moved so fast. He almost missed the first marker. The others were chatting, but he made sure he was not listening in. He visualised the numbers in his head. Counting. Counting. The travelator seemed to go on forever. "It's the next one Martin."

"Everyone, reach for the approaching marker now," Martin shouted.

A sudden stop and Thomas found himself in the middle a science fiction film. The beauty of the sphere's interior almost overwhelmed him. The rays of the small Sun warmed his skin. The air felt quite warm and humid, but not uncomfortable. He could not find the horizon, the landscape curved up into the distance where it merged into a green nothingness. He looked at the patchwork of triangular plateaus and he loved the logical pattern. What really took his breath away were the big buildings: the imposing skylines of the enormous cities. His neck hurt as he tried to look all the way up.

The buildings in the distance reminded him of The Emerald City; maybe he would find the Wizard of Oz. He had so many questions to ask, and there were thousands of cities, thousands of wizards maybe, with thousands of answers. He wanted to run to the buildings and explore. He noticed his uncle, who was standing still, with a big grin on his face. "Isn't this amazing?" Thomas asked.

"Yes, it is really beautiful. I never expected to see anything like this in my life," Rick answered.

***

One of the Marines started taking measurements with a long-range laser. After a couple of minutes he announced his findings. "Thomas, the diameter of the sphere is about 7,699 kilometres. And I'm impressed with you, because that's a prime number."

"I knew it!" Thomas shouted, smiling. "Martin, can we go to a building now? I want to go up one of those awesome elevators." Thomas had never wanted anything so much in his life before. He wanted to know all the heights of every

263

building, he was certain they would all be prime numbers too. If Martin would not let him go there, he did not know what he would do. The idea of not going made him feel unhappy. He felt his breathing becoming difficult. He didn't want to hyperventilate. Uncle Rick — he needed to get to Uncle Rick quickly.

Rick noticed Thomas fidgeting, "Martin, can we go there please?"

"Of course we can, but only for a moment, because I want us to explore much more. There are many parts we haven't seen yet." Martin shrugged at the Marines. "Guys, we need to keep Thomas happy." He turned to Thomas. "Okay you, lead the way to the closest building, and we'll go as high as we can."

Instantaneously the elevator travelled at a lightning speed, but Thomas did not feel any acceleration. He did not feel his stomach go down the way it would in one of those fast lifts on Earth, so he didn't feel scared. The invisible barriers kept him safe and gave him a fantastic view of the sphere's landscape. Very high up, the lift went through a small cloud, but Thomas did not feel rain. Soon afterwards, the lift reached the top and stopped. Thomas stepped inside the building and he was in an alien home. He had often wondered how they lived, and now he could see for himself. There was no one inside and he felt slightly disappointed. Everything looked pretty in there though. The walls were a very nice green colour. There were many benches, although they were a bit too high to comfortably sit on: the aliens must be taller than humans. And the windows were massive; he enjoyed the view. Everything was made of green triangles, and he liked that. And Martin was right, he thought, it is all empty in here. Where are they? Hiding from us? But they are brave enough to come to Earth. Why? It does not make sense. Maybe they are ashamed of what they did to us. Or? A chilling thought made the hairs on his neck stand up. "Martin," he said, "what if the aliens aren't hiding, but are invisible to us?"

His question stopped everyone in their tracks.

"Thomas has been right about everything else, so why not this?" Rick looked around and rubbed his shoulders, as if to wipe them clean.

The Marines took the safety off their guns; they looked nervously around them.

"I think I would have noticed them last time, and we would notice evidence of their presence now. We haven't seen any elevators go up or down, nothing else is moving, or has been moved," Martin said. "Even if they had some sort of cloaking device, I'm sure they wouldn't let us walk around like this, touching all their things, or going inside their homes."

The group huddled close together and Martin proposed they walk up to the terrace to look at the views.

Thomas walked up to the edge and the invisible barrier stopped him from falling. He thought the aliens were very clever builders. The Sun was much closer now, and he noticed the warmth on his skin. He saw the small cloud they passed through before, now moving between the buildings at a gentle pace. He looked around for more clouds and noticed some of them were rain clouds and the ground underneath was wet. He liked the rain. He was happy there was rain in here. He did not want to go home. Everything at home was miserable now. There were storms and the wind was noisy and the sky was always grey. And everything was broken and the people were very unhappy. But here, inside, felt like a quiet spring day. He liked spring, he loved to see the birds with their little baby birds flying in the garden. There were no birds here though. Thomas felt tears on his cheeks. He was sad. So much was lost. Nothing was the same and he didn't like change, especially what had changed during the last months. He walked up to Rick, who took him in his arms and gave him a good hug.

"Hey you, what's the matter?"

"Everything is broken, the Cube broke it, but it's so beautiful in here. I don't understand why something this wonderful can be so cruel and it's upsetting me." Thomas looked at his uncle, who also had tears in his eyes.

"We're all upset. It's fine how you feel. I feel the same. But look at the wondrous world in here, really see it," Rick said.

Thomas turned back to look at the view again. He saw the other cities and the green empty plateaus and the big lakes. He was inside a big Christmas bauble with a fairy light in the middle. Thomas felt better already. He heard Martin call them back inside. When they arrived Martin stood next to two holes in a wall. "These are water and food dispensers. Anyone want to try? Let me warn you, the food is a bit bland — to say the least."

Thomas put his hands in and green slush dropped in his palms. The *food* did not look appetising to him, but he licked it anyway. He had never tasted anything like this before in his life. He was not sure if he liked it or not. It reminded him of thick pea soup, but he could also taste meat and fish.

***

Thomas decided they had to go back to the travelators; Martin had brought him here to do important work after all. They asked Thomas to think where he thought the auxiliary areas might be, so he took out his notebook and sketched a model of the Cube and sphere, and drew a map. After walking a while they reached the exit and walked into a square. Thomas took a moment to get his bearings. He pointed to a strip that seemed to go diagonally up.

The corridors were long, many markers passed and

Thomas had trouble counting; they were travelling very fast again. He told everyone to get off at the next marker. "I think we travelled over 1,000 kilometres, but I'm not sure. I have to calculate."

They were in a big hall, at a junction, with many squares on the floor. Martin asked Thomas to come over. When he walked towards him he noticed two massive doors at the far side; they were high enough to let the Eiffel Tower through. They took 20 minutes to reach the doors. Thomas noticed a panel with markings, about two metres up, where the two doors met. He knew this was a lock, without a keyhole, but with a keypad. He was sure he could find the algorithm to open the doors, as long as they gave him a bit of time. He started sketching the markings on a page.

A thunderous boom came from one of the corridors. The noise made him jump. There was activity somewhere. He saw the Marines draw their guns. He forgot about the lock, and wanted to investigate. The door would still be there later.

All of them wanted to find out where the boom had come from, so Martin asked Thomas to lead them into the right direction.

Markers, markers, markers. "Next one," Thomas shouted. They stepped off and were in another great hall with two doors. There were some differences. The doors were much smaller, the size of double-decker buses. At their centre was a blackened scorched area.

"It looks like a grenade exploded here. Someone must have tried to open these doors. And failed," a Marine said.

Thomas looked at the lock. He had to wipe off the soot. He could smell sulphur. Humans had done this. The lock was not damaged and he noticed this lock had similar markings as the one on the previous doors. "The lock is fine. I'm going to finish drawing these markings in my pad, so I can solve the puzzle and open the doors," he said and he went back in his own mind again: calculating. Sudden movements and noises made him look around. He didn't like being interrupted.

"Agent Tuan. Fancy seeing you here. I see your failed attempt to nuke the Cube has not deterred you from trying to blow things up in here," Thomas heard Martin say. He saw 12 Chinese Soldiers and Agent Tuan standing 50 metres away, blocking the way back to the square.

"Mr Germain. How is your exploration going? Any luck with the lock? I see you now employ children to do your hard work." Tuan was grinning. His hand was on his holster, he seemed ready to draw his gun.

"Can you open the lock?" Rick whispered to Thomas, "I have a bad feeling about this."

"I don't like that man, he's horrible. I want to get away from him." Thomas felt a rush: the lock-markings started rearranging themselves in his head. "I'm going to need a while Uncle."

"Take your time. I know you can do it."

"I think you should move on, you've tried this area. Now it's our turn," Martin said to Tuan. Behind his back he gave signals to the Marines, and they moved closer to the door, now surrounding Rick and Thomas, with their weapons drawn.

"Mr Germain. May I *please* have a word with the boy? It seems he is attempting to open the doors."

"No, you stay away from him," Martin said.

Thomas heard Tuan shouting something in Chinese. He saw them move towards him. But the Marines were standing around him: they were protecting him. He could not let them down now, he liked them. He tried his best guess and typed in a combination on the keypad. The doors slid open and he was pushed inside by the Marines.

Loud bangs, gun shots. He wanted to hide, run away, but someone held on to him and pulled him to the side of the opening.

"Thomas, we're all in. You must close the doors before they come in too," Rick said.

He found it was hard to think, because all the men were shooting and there was a lot of noise. He typed the same combination and the doors closed. The shooting noises were gone, replaced by the Marines cheering him on. They hugged him and patted him on his back. He felt very proud.

The place they were in was darker than the corridor and Thomas took a minute to let his eyes adjust. The room was long, and high, and reminded him of a cathedral. On the left and right sides stood massive columns, as far as he could see. There had to be hundreds in here. He walked up to one and touched it, he felt a slight vibration. "This is a pipe, something is running through it," he said.

All of them felt several columns and concluded the same.

"Maybe we're close to the engine room," Rick said.

One of the Marines looked through his binoculars and told them there were doors at the far end of the room. The walk would take them a long time.

Thomas had no problem opening the next doors. The following hall was the largest he had ever seen and was very bright. Dozens of corridors, with squares in front of them, led out of the hall. Thousands of triangular shaped benches stood arranged in perfect rows, facing a giant empty light green wall. On the opposite side was a wall with two colossal doors. These doors were different; instead of being one single colour, they looked like a monochrome painting to Thomas. The doors were filled with intricate symbols, and they were connected to each other with curves and lines and the whole spectrum from white, via green, to black was used. In an instant he knew this hall had great importance and he expected this to be the place where the aliens would have their meetings. And these doors were the reason why. He had to open them and find out.

"These doors — we must go behind them." Thomas could not say more, his senses overloaded with excitement. He needed to distract himself, do calculations and solve the next puzzle. He hoped the keypad's algorithm on the special doors would be more difficult to crack.

***

The doors *did* have a more complex lock, but of course Thomas managed to open them. He would have to write the solution down; otherwise even *he* might forget how to open these doors next time. He heard mutterings and gasps behind him: this room was the brightest yet and very different from anything they had seen so far. The walls were high and, as always, green. There were over a dozen benches and they were placed in front of blocks that were higher: there had to be a purpose to this set-up. The most exciting thing about this room was the tremendous wall in front of him, made up of many small squares; all different shades of green and a lot of them seemed to be lit up.

"This seems to be set up to sit and look at the wall and work with the squares. Are these consoles perhaps?" Martin asked.

"But there's nothing on these consoles. They're smooth, no buttons, no touch screens," Rick said as he ran his hands over a block. "This could be a, or the, control room, but what does it control and how?"

"Maybe it's switched off, or in hibernation mode like a computer," Thomas said.

"Good point Thomas," Martin said, "Okay, shall we go through this room and look for a very big *ON* switch? I think we might have to look for something — err — green?"

Thomas had to laugh. Martin was funny. Oh, hang on — He noticed a square, on the right and almost at the bottom of the wall: it looked darker now. He was certain its light had gone off. He asked the others, but none of them had noticed a difference.

Martin instructed the Marines to focus their cameras on the wall and record. He asked Thomas to write down the keys to the doors and sketch the wall with the illuminated squares, in case there was a code to decipher. When Thomas finished, he walked to the wall. It was big, not too high, but many hundreds of metres wide. A checker-board of squares, repeating itself too many times towards the right for him to see. Each square in the board was less than a metre by a metre. Each board was 23 rows high and 89 columns wide. On the left of each board was one more row of 23 squares, but they were different: they had symbols on them, similar to the ones on the entrance doors: *symbol-squares*, he thought. Most of these symbol-squares were dark green, but some were very light, almost white. Thomas thought they must have a great significance.

On the far left board almost half of the squares were much lighter than the others. Thomas could draw a curved line in his head from left top to right bottom, with the lighter squares positioned on the left of the curve. He walked closer to the wall. The boards on the right of him were all dark green, except for a few white symbol-squares. Was this a message board? A clock? Or some kind of instruction manual? Unless he could find out what they meant, this important wall would stay a mystery. But these symbols looked a million times more complex than the most intricate Aztec or hieroglyphics symbols. There was something logical about them though, similar to the keypads. This had to be their written language. Thomas sat down in front of the wall and started calculating again.

"Thomas, this reminds me of the charts we use in project planning, you know, with the shaded bars signifying activity within a time frame. A Gantt Chart, you know what that is?"

271

Martin asked.

"Yeah, I know what that is." Thomas felt annoyed at being interrupted. *Duh*, of course it was some kind of planning chart. If they wanted him to solve this, they would have to leave him alone.

"Look, the square on the left of the previous one has just gone dark," Rick said.

"Do we know how much time has passed?" Martin asked.

"At least ten minutes, maybe more, I'll keep track of the time now," a Marine said.

Thomas looked at the column where the other square had gone dark. Interesting. This one was on the 14th row and only two squares on this row were still lit. The 13th row had 41 lit squares. He looked at all the rows above them. He had an idea, but needed a little more time. The top row had two lit squares, the second row had three. Okay, the pattern was clear: again all were prime numbers. Each row had the next prime number in its column and the squares were switching off at certain intervals.

"This is a clock, and it's counting down. The symbol-squares are events and the ones that are light are important ones, it's counting to the next one above it. And if you look at the lower rows and at the boards on the right side, you see the light symbol-squares — those events have already happened. I need to know how much time there is between each switch-off, and then I'll know when something is going to happen next. And I can do that by looking at what already happened. It's like a tick of a clock, but I need to wait for the next few ticks," Thomas said.

As he expected: the next square went dark after just over ten minutes and the one after that too. Now he was waiting for row 13. All 41 squares were lit. In about ten minutes he expected, well — hoped, the 41st would go dark. Uncle Rick offered him water and a power bar. Only now did Thomas realise how famished and tired he felt.

"Light off at nine minutes and 12 seconds," he heard a Marine shout.

This complicated things: each prime number had a different time, too. Nothing he couldn't cope with, but it would take him more time to make his calculations, no biggie: *40 times more of nine minutes, and then in six hours it will jump to row 12.* He scribbled more notes in his pad; some pages looked like a map, others were filled with mathematical equations, or solutions to opening doors. Thomas yawned. "Can we sleep here? I'm tired."

"Good idea," Martin said. "Whoever is on watch, also notes the countdown."

When they woke up, Thomas felt disappointed that the countdown had not moved on to row 12. The active row was still the 13th. He had been wrong, or — unless it had to count itself down 41 times before moving on. *Oh my God!* He felt so silly. Of course it had to.

Dark thoughts and troubling ideas started to develop in Thomas's brain. He needed to make sure about something first, so he walked along the wall. Only the board on the right of the current one had white symbol-squares, exactly as he expected. After passing many boards without markers, and having walked for more than a kilometre, he found two boards that were exactly the same as the current one, but with no light squares to count down; all were dark.

Oh crap, he was right again. Thomas felt the strength in his legs go. He wanted to sit down, but slumped against the wall. He saw Rick and Martin running towards him. When they got closer he saw the worried looks on their faces — had they figured it out too? He noticed he was crying: he was so upset with what he had discovered. Everything would change, and he does not like changes; it makes his brain go all funny. He felt he was about to lose control of himself. He needed Uncle Rick to hold him. It was always good when Uncle Rick told him everything was okay. Why were they taking so long? Be here. Please.

"Hey you, you want to tell me what's upsetting you?" Rick asked him, and sat down and took him in his arms. "Whatever it is, I'm here. You can tell me."

"I — found out what's going to happen next — it's not good." Thomas was welling up again. "This is a clock, a countdown clock — and it's almost finished counting down." His speech was interrupted by heavy breathing. "It's going to go away — in five months and a few days. Then it goes. Gone. What will happen to Earth then?"

"Are you sure?"

"I think I am, no, of course I am. But we must have someone else check this. I don't want to be wrong and scare people for nothing," Thomas said.

"I will do that for you Thomas. Write down what you think and why and I will send a team of scientists here," Martin said.

"Uncle Rick, please take me home, I want to see Karen and my mama."

"Yes, I'll take you home now and I won't leave your side," Rick said.

"Thank you. You are always there for me. And I like it that you are looking after Florence. She is very happy. And I feel I have two little sisters now."

Rick looked surprised.

"I really wish you were my dad."

"Hey you, me too. I really wish that too. And I do love you as if you were my own son."

127. Time to choose.
(April year 3)

"Good evening. In a moment Prime Minister Christopher Marchant will address our Nation on all television and radio channels. Speculations about the content of the message have been rife since the second British expedition, led by Martin Germain, returned from the Cube last month. We understand similar messages will be broadcast in most countries throughout the world today.

"Viewers, here is the Prime Minister."

"Citizens of the United Kingdom of Great Britain and Northern Ireland. I shall start with a quote from one of our greatest leaders, The Right Honourable Sir Winston Churchill. 'Now, this is not the end. It is not even the beginning of the end. But it is, perhaps, the end of the beginning.'

"Please hold on to this thought while I address you.

"Nine months ago everything changed with the arrival of the Cube. Earth's history and future have irreversibly changed beyond anything we could ever have imagined. We had to rethink everything we thought we knew about ourselves and the universe. We know now we are not alone.

"On the day the Cube landed we lost over two billion people and many more have died in subsequent attacks. Animals and plants have been killed and our fragile ecosystem is almost destroyed. We do not know if Earth, or life itself, can survive this disaster.

"Our second expedition inside the Cube proved that what appeared to be alien attacks were instructions that came from a machine instead: a machine instructed not to do evil, but to do what it was built for by its makers.

"We have discovered the Cube is empty inside. There are no aliens. We do not know where they have gone. There is an inhabitable space inside, which we refer to as the Sphere. Inside this empty Sphere are lakes, giant empty plateaus and thousands upon thousands of empty cities, with skyscrapers many kilometres high. The Sphere has a small Sun and has a moderate climate. It is habitable for humans. It is ready to be settled.

"This is where I come to the next part of my address to you, and I cannot find an easy way to bring you the news. Our top scientists have calculated and verified that the Cube will leave our devastated Earth four months from today. Tomorrow every household in the country will receive an information pack, which will also be available on the internet and in every newspaper. Together with all the information we have gathered we ask you to make a choice. Perhaps the hardest choice ever to be made in the whole of mankind's history.

"You will be asked to make the choice of staying on Earth when the Cube leaves, or joining our programme of settlement in the Cube and leaving Earth with it.

"We shall never know which choice will have been the best one. We will never know whose life will be harder, but we are explorers. And, these difficult choices will double the chance for the survival of mankind.

"I would like to make something very clear. The people who decide to leave are not traitors for giving up on Earth, but they are true pioneers and ready to face unknown dangers, and will most likely never return.

"Likewise, the people who decide to stay behind on Earth are not cowards, have not given up hope, are not afraid of change and the unknown, but are determined to rescue Earth and rebuild her for all life. There is no right or wrong choice for you to make, but you will have to make one regardless.

"One member of our Royal family, a Prince whose identity will remain unknown for now, has volunteered to travel with

276

the Cube and the British citizens. He will make himself known after the Cube has left Earth. We have decided to name the part of the Cube we lay claim to in honour of our great Nation: it shall be New Albion and the Prince will be the Viceroy.

"Preparations are underway for an easy and speedy settlement. We will bring in supplies and resources to give the explorers and citizens of New Albion the best possible start and best chance for survival.

"The people who stay behind will not be forgotten. Life on Earth will continue, our farms, factories and hospitals will keep on working. Government will stay in place and law and order will be enforced.

"We are parents and children, brothers and sisters who must say our farewells. It will be difficult, because we did not want to be put in this position, but we are here now. We have seen great challenges in the past, and will have great challenges in the future, but we always have overcome them, and so will we again.

"I would like to quote Sir Winston Churchill once more. 'Every day you may make progress. Every step may be fruitful. Yet there will stretch out before you an ever-lengthening, ever-ascending, ever-improving path. You know you will never get to the end of the journey. But this, so far from discouraging, only adds to the joy and the glory of the climb.'

"Thank you. I wish you all the best for the future. And may God be with us all."

Agent Tuan hated London. He had expected the city to be full of white people, but all he saw were blacks, Indians and queers. London was a multicultural cesspit, full of whores who would sleep with anyone. He felt sick when he saw mixed raced couples with their mongrel children walking the streets. They should not be going in the Cube. And then there were the traitors: the Chinese who had left their country to live here in London. He did not want to see any of them inside the Cube either. If it were up to him; only the healthy young and straight Chinese would be allowed in, but it was not. He could control the Chinese, but not the rest of the world. All he could try was to limit the numbers of foreigners entering, and for that he would use Simon Waltz: whom he was about to meet.

A tacky pink fluorescent sign welcomed Tuan to Simon's headquarters: it read *Childe of braha*. To Tuan the broken sign was the evidence of a broken belief. The fuckers did not care about their image anymore, and the hundreds of millions of followers kept to themselves now, too afraid to draw attention to them; in case God would not save them on the day Armageddon would start for real. Tuan did not want them in the Cube either — there were too many Jews and Muslims amongst them.

The girl at the reception desk ignored him, though she must have heard him come in; the door had scratched over the marble floor. She was reading the Bible and chewing gum with her mouth open: just like a cow.

"I'm here to see Simon," he said.

The girl looked at him, raising an eyebrow as she seemed to assess him and then discount him. "Simon's not in." She blew a pink bubble with her gum and popped it with a loud bang.

"Yes, he is in, my darling. I spoke with him ten minutes ago. I'm Agent Tuan. He *is* expecting me." Tuan leaned over till he was almost touching her face. "You'd better use those pretty little fingers to call him, or else I'll break them," he whispered.

"Stairs. Up to the third floor."

Tuan walked to the stairs. From behind him, he could hear her talk. The black bitch was slagging him off. *Yeah, the Chinese one, yeah, you're right, he's an arsehole, he's on his way up to you now.* He would deal with her later.

"Sit down please, my apologies for the cold reception, she's pretty, but pretty useless. A good fuck though," Simon said, laughing at his own joke. "I'm glad we finally meet. I was intrigued when I heard you wanted to talk to me. I hear you've been inside the Cube already. How was it?"

"It's very impressive inside. Virgin territory, all empty and filled with cities ready to be colonised. The People's Republic of China is preparing to send in the best of our country and establish New China. We've appointed hundreds of millions of volunteers. They're all healthy young people, ready to have children. We will move the first few millions in soon. There's no room for gays, sick, the disabled or the old. The Sphere has no need for private property. Food and drink are provided for free, so our people will work towards a true and equal socialist society for the entire Sphere — and that is where I need your help. We need to be in the majority for our planned society to work, and to be totally frank with you — your people, who believe in a god, well — it would ruin our plan. There's no room for religion, it causes conflicts and wars, so we want you to convince your followers not to go in. *You* are most welcome of course."

"Ah, I understand," Simon said, "but why would I help you? It seems you only like Chinese, and I'm not, nor am I a communist. Why would I want to be under your rule?"

"The Sphere is big enough for all of us. We want to give humanity the best chance of starting fresh and new. But we don't want certain types of people in."

"Certain types?" Simon asked.

"Yes, no Jews and Muslims, and as few blacks as possible — but the Cube already took care of most of them." Tuan giggled at his own joke. "And if possible, only a few Indians and Pakistanis, they can do the jobs that are beneath the Chinese. You white people are fine. You are mostly cultured and developed. As long as you don't send gays, or mixed race."

"That's not communism, you're a plain old racist. But, I might be interested — what's in it for me though?"

"We want to reach out to the white people, so you'll be given a prestigious and high rank in the New China government. You'll make and decide policy, and you'll be rich and have everything you desire. We'll help you with promoting your message to deter your followers and use our forces to deny them entry, in case some haven't listened to you."

Simon smiled. "We have a deal. I'll write a statement, and when I'm done with them, no one who believes in God will dare to enter the Cube. And you'll pick up me and my family?"

"Of course, your wife and children can come too, but at the last minute. We can't have you leave too soon, your followers might want to follow you. We'll arrange it so that you'll accompany the London based Chinese ambassador."

***

Simon's mood improved and he felt invigorated as soon as Tuan had left his office. Tuan would do all the work for him, *the fool*. How fantastic that the Chinese asked him to do exactly what he was planning to do anyway. And although Simon knew he could not trust Tuan, for now he would work with him. He would use the Chinese to achieve his goal: punishing the Children of Abraham. They had betrayed him in Las Vegas, and now it was his turn to return the favour. He did not like the idea of the Chinese interfering with his New Eden, though. He wanted to create the perfect new society, as instructed by God, and atheists and commies would not fit into that plan.

Simon needed to contact the British Government as soon

as possible and talk to them about Tuan. If he played his cards right, he could have the Chinese in conflict with everyone else, and build his paradise uninterrupted. He should use that faggot for that. If he could save them from the commies, they would be thankful and be in his debt, and would take the heat off him. He buzzed his receptionist. "Make yourself useful and get me Martin Germain on the phone."

"That Chinese arsehole. He hit me." She was sobbing.

"Yeah, he must have heard you slagging him off. That was very stupid of you. Now, get me Martin. Tell him I have very important news."

***

Today was the day after the Prime Minister's speech and the impact had been enormous. Martin and Colin had been summoned to the Government office in Whitehall for a special announcement by the PM. Martin was shocked to see the number of people outside Downing Street: hundreds of them, their mood sombre. People moved out of their way for Martin and Colin when they walked up to the gate. They all looked at Martin, silent, the fear showing in their eyes. He could see they needed answers, but were afraid to ask them, scared of what he might say.

"I'm not going. I have to stay here," the Prime Minister said to Martin as he walked into the crowded office. Martin and the other advisers did not agree and they pleaded with him to change his mind, but he would not budge. Martin needed a private word with his PM. "Christopher, what's going on? You promised you'd come. Why the change of heart?"

"There's something I never made public. You don't even know about it. I can't go on a *lifelong* journey like this. I have diabetes, and insulin only lasts for three years, and that is when it's refrigerated, and there are no fridges there. I won't survive. I'll die as soon as it runs out. My place is here in Downing Street, to serve and help rebuild our Nation. And my wife isn't too keen on leaving anyway."

"But Sir, we need continuity and strong government in the Cube," Martin said.

"I'll check who in our cabinet is going in the Cube. One of them will be the acting PM. And I'll appoint you to oversee elections as soon as you're all settled in. And I need you to look after the Viceroy. You're still going, right?"

"Yes, I'll go. And will take care of everything. But —" The phone on Martin's desk rang. "Sorry," he said as he picked it up. The lady on the other end told him Simon Waltz needed to speak with him urgently. Martin wondered why: Simon had been very hostile towards him since the so-called *assassination attempt*. He put the speaker on, so the whole room could listen in. "Mr Waltz, to what do I owe this pleasure?" Martin almost laughed when he saw the look of surprise on Colin's face.

"I have very important information regarding Agent Tuan and his plans for the Cube," Simon said. "He forced me to write a statement forbidding my followers from entering the Cube."

"So?" Martin did not care. Good riddance. He looked around and saw a confused Colin shrug. "What does it have to do with us?"

"Tuan and the Chinese are preparing for a New China. They intend to be the majority and rule over everyone inside the Sphere. They want to turn it into a communist hellhole. And they'll use force to achieve their goal."

Martin was confused. He did not want to believe Simon, but he could not ignore the information either. "Why are you telling me this?"

"Tuan wants me to fly to China and then go in the Cube with the Chinese. He promised me I would be part of their government and rule over the non-Chinese — that means you. But I don't want to live with them. I want to stay here on Earth with my followers. And I would have to leave my wife and three daughters behind."

"I've seen first hand what a cunt you are. I don't care about you."

"But, please think of my wife and daughters. They're innocent and I want them to be safe. I promise I'll cooperate with you and stay on Earth, just as long as you keep them safe. You owe me Martin. Without this information you will be forced to live under Chinese rule."

"Give me a moment. I need to think," Martin said as he put the phone on silent. "Any suggestions?" He looked around the room; most shook their heads.

"Tell him we need time to consider this," the PM said.

"No, we can't make him wait. We need an answer now," Martin said.

"I know," Colin said. "We offer him safety and his family safe passage. We let him think he'll stay here in England, so he'll keep on providing us with useful information. But we'll hand him over to the Chinese and tell them of his betrayal. They can do with him whatever they want."

Martin noticed the Prime Minister nodding: he approved.

"Thanks Colin," Martin said and put the phone back on speaker. "Mr Waltz, you have yourself a deal. We'll protect you and your family from the Chinese as long as you keep them convinced you are playing along with their plans and you provide us with constant and useful information. And make bloody well sure your statement to the Children of Abraham is convincing enough, otherwise the deal is off. I'll contact you soon." Martin put the phone down before Simon could answer. "I think we ought to make some extra preparations then. Get the army organised and send in plenty of guns too. And Colin, I'd suggest you advise your President to do the same. Now, let's get back to work, we have a lot of scared people out there."

* * *

After a stressful day Martin and Colin rushed home and cooked dinner. They made a point of always having their evening meal together: just the two of them. Their dinner ritual had become almost sacred to them and they would never let themselves be disturbed by politics or Cube news.

After eating, they sat down on the sofa, cups of steaming tea in their hands.

"Martin, I've spoken to McGee, he will prepare the army too. He's going in and our Vice President will stay on Earth. But McGee asked me to help him organise the big move. I couldn't refuse. I'll fly back to the US tomorrow. I'm sorry."

Martin knew that Colin had waited with his announcement till after dinner and he was thankful for that. "I will miss this," he said, as he took a sip of his tea. He stared deep into his cup, avoiding eye contact with Colin. He wanted to cry. He couldn't bear the idea of losing Colin in this dangerous brave new world. "I'm so used to having you around. I don't want us to be apart, but I won't try stopping you. I know you have to do this."

"I'm so sorry. I don't want to go, but I *have* to. And I also want to say one last goodbye to my mother, or maybe I can convince her to come with me. I have to try."

"Don't be. At least we'll be calling each other all the time and we'll be living in the Sphere together. I know we both have our duties here on Earth, and we must make sure the rest of our lives will be as comfortable and safe as possible. We're strong. We've had that connection from the day we met. Remember our first night in New York? I knew right away you were the one for me," Martin said. Now he could look at him. He was pleased to see Colin smiling.

Martin decided not to fall asleep that night; he wanted to

savour their last few hours together. He wanted to watch Colin sleep and really *see* him, so that whatever happened next, he would never forget him.

Martin did fall asleep though, in Colin's arms. The next morning he woke up, still in his arms. Martin had never slept so well. Things would be fine.

131. Getting there is the easy part. (April year 3)

World Wide Live News Channel evening news.

"Good evening, this is Daniel Lou with a round-up of the headlines and a special report on the changing weather conditions.

"Fighting has broken out in Iran between the Iranians and the Chinese. The Chinese Government has been using air vents located in Iran as the entrance to the Cube and the Iranians claim their airspace has been violated. The Chinese air force has been bombing Iranian air defences to secure safe passage for their planes, raising concerns from other nations.

"The United States and Canada have signed a co-operation pact and pooled their resources to fly their citizens and resources to the Cube. The Galicians and the people of Brittany have agreed to allow the North Americans to use their territories as bases to enter the Cube. In return they accepted the offer of help with resources and settling logistics.

"The South American Governments are working together in sending in their citizens through the Brazilian entrance.

"Australia, New Zealand and Japan are co-operating to bring biodiversity to the Cube. Using Sri Lanka as their point of entry, they will bring in soil, seeds and seedlings for many varieties of plants and trees. Insects for pollination and various animals are also being brought in. The project is nicknamed Project Noah's Ark. Britain, Scandinavia and the American countries have pledged to contribute to it.

"In the Indian Ocean, the Chinese navy attacked and destroyed six Thai ships. The Chinese Government claimed their cargo ships were targeted by Thai pirates and they want to send out a strong message that all pirates will be

met by lethal force. The cargo ships in question were transporting livestock and spices.

"After the commercial break I shall be reporting on the changing weather conditions since the landing of the Cube nine months ago."

—

"Welcome back. Nine months ago the Cube landed on Earth and it had a major impact on our weather systems. The size of the object together with the dust particles have resulted in changed weather patterns. Sunsets around the world have turned a vivid red, with some people calling it blood red. Sunrises have turned green, with the Sun in certain parts of the world staying green for most of the day. This is attributed to the dust and particles blown into the upper atmosphere and carried great distances.

"The last time this phenomenon occurred was after the eruption of the Krakatoa volcano in 1883. Then it lasted many months. There are no signs of our atmosphere starting to return to pre-landing levels and another change we are witnessing is the increase in clouds and precipitation. Rain has increased 50 percent in the areas around the Cube, and up to 20 percent in other areas. The particles and dust caused a drop of around two degrees Celsius in global temperature, resulting in heavy snowfalls in northern regions and excessive ice formation in the Polar Regions. Current weather models predict this cold snap to last up to three years, but the precipitation will remain at higher levels for longer, although many think it is too early to make long term weather predictions."

Biologist Barend Trevelyan was not looking at the television screen in the background. He already knew what the weatherman was reporting today. Every morning he was woken up by a green dawn. Every evening most of his animals howled and cried at the Sun that by then had turned red. Barend felt awful that he could not explain to them why the Sun turned into these colours. And the animals did not enjoy the rain either, but that was to be expected: his animals were used to dry and hot weather in their Sydney zoo.

Australia had not been much affected by the Cube; yes, there had been more storms and rain, and during the landing day a small tsunami had swept parts of the West Coast, but the blocks with the life-swallowing foam had not hit the major cities, so compared to most of the world the continent had mostly escaped the disaster. And now life continued almost as normal again.

Barend was not surprised to hear the announcement for the Big Move. People had lost everything, they were scared and hungry, and for many there was nothing worth staying for. He feared most Earth life would not survive after the Cube had gone: there were too many unknown factors.

Barend spent most hours of the day feeding and comforting his animals, sometimes staying overnight in the enclosures with them, much to the chagrin of his wife Angelique. He and his wife had discussed moving into the Cube. She liked the idea, but he did not want to, or could not leave his animals behind. They needed him too and he could not be made to choose between her and them. His wife smiled at him and told him she expected and understood his reaction; he had too much love in him and that was why she loved him so much back. He was surprised when she proposed they should take the animals with them. Why had he not thought of this himself? Angelique was so clever.

They had taken a few days to write a proposal and present it to the Sydney authorities, who were in charge of the move. They proposed to move the carnivore animals to the upper floors of the tallest buildings, where there would be a good balance of outside and inside space. The herbivores would be set free on the nature plateaus as soon as they had grown enough fauna. Enough pairs of the chosen species would be flown in to ensure their survival and reduce the risk of inbreeding. The animals would have to get used to eating the slurry, but Barend and his wife expected this would not be a problem. When he asked for volunteers at the zoo to sign up to look after the animals, he was pleased that more than half offered their help.

After a week Barend had received a phone call: the Sydney authorities liked his plan and had agreed, but they would execute his plan last, so as to make sure there was room left for anyone who decided to go at the last minute. Barend was to start preparations, as he was made responsible for the logistics of the move. They also requested him to work with other scientists to calculate the number of trees that would be needed to offset the carbon dioxide a large population would exhale, and replenish the oxygen that would be inhaled. No one yet knew if the Cube had scrubbers, filters or any other way for preventing the atmosphere from turning toxic.

Barend and his wife attended several conventions around the country, talking to botanists and foresters, and submitted their reports to NASA and several Governments, including Martin Germain. Humans would have to bring in a lot of animals, insects, seeds and mature plants, but also a lot of soil and chemicals to make more soil. And sweet water fish and plants for the lakes. The task ahead seemed overwhelming, but Barend was thankful many countries promised to help him. He felt it was a shame only flora and fauna suitable for a moderate climate would go into the Cube, but Barend imagined that at least the polar bears would be enjoying the new weather on Earth.

***

Kim Sook never liked Nyalam: the village was small and backward. People were friendly though, but slightly mistrusting, as she was Chinese and belonged to *the enemy*. At least when they had arrived there last August, after a difficult two month journey, spent mostly in the back of damp draughty trucks, the rainy season had almost finished. Rainy season in the mountains had meant a lot of rain and coldness. And then came the winter to the mountain village: dry and sunny, but even colder. Kim felt her bones were always freezing, no matter how well she dressed. Jia-Li seemed very uncomfortable too. Her tiny fingers and toes always felt cold when Kim touched them.

Jiang's family were lovely. They had cried a lot when they saw their son again after too many years, and they cried more when they met Kim and Jia-Li. For years, Jiang had sent them money every month, but since their imprisonment that income had stopped, so the family had to live on modest wages, and now with three extra mouths to feed, the food had become very bland and in small portions. And the heating was turned off for most of the day.

Last month the family had received a letter from the State. They were notified that one family member had qualified as *young and healthy* and was selected as a volunteer to populate the Cube on behalf of the Republic. It was Jiang's 16 year old nephew Weisheng. The poor boy didn't want to leave his family, but he had to: non-collaboration would mean severe punishment for the whole family, or disappearance. Kim had phoned Agent Pranit in India, but he was unable to help a whole family. He did suggest Kim, Jiang and their baby could be smuggled to India and then enter the Cube from there. They should tell Weisheng to travel to the Indian sector and find them, so they could look after him. Not ideal, but the best Pranit could manage right now.

Today was the day they had to say goodbye to Jiang's family. Tomorrow the army would come and take the volunteers with them, so they had to be out of the village. Pranit had arranged transport for them to cross the border into Nepal. In Kathmandu they would catch a plane to New Delhi, where they would wait their turn to be taken to the Cube. Kim was very excited; soon she would start a new life with her family. Jia-Li would grow up without the fear Kim had suffered for too long. And she would be away from this cold, soulless village, and away from this horrible country.

***

"Is Auntie Isadora coming?" Florence asked.

"Yes, she is, and so are Karen and Thomas," Paul said. "Oh, and Gustavo and Zaira of course."

"Good, I like them, and Uncle Martin?"

"Yes, him too and his partner Colin." Paul and Rick looked at each other. It was clear to them Florence needed familiar faces when they moved into the Cube.

"And your friend, the lady actress?"

"Nicole Hamilton you mean? Yes, she and many other actors are going in too. They will sing for us and entertain us." Paul had to smile. Florence was actually looking forward to the move. If she were in charge, they would be moving in today.

"That's good, because without a television and internet I think I will be very bored. Will the bogeyman come?"

"No, a little bird told me he has to stay, as a punishment for his bad behaviour," Rick said. He knew she knew Simon's name, but she refused to use his.

"Good. I don't like him."

Paul had to laugh. "You know, there will be other children there, who you can play with. You'll be making lots of new friends. And the weather is always nice, even the rain is special."

"But I will miss the snow. And what about your parents? Are they coming?"

"No darling, I'm sorry, they said they're too old to move. But they, and Paul's parents too, told me they will be very happy staying here," Rick said.

Florence looked sad, her lips were pouting and she was ready to cry. Rick needed to distract her. "We will be buying new clothes for you, and toys. So you'll look like a little princess and have lots to play with. Would you like that?"

A big smile appeared on her face. She had already forgotten feeling sad. "Yes, please."

"Why don't you go to your room and make a list of things you think you need," Paul said to her. Florence ran off to her room.

"It's going to be bittersweet saying goodbye to a lot of people, but to be honest, I'm actually quite excited about the move. I've always wanted to travel to the stars," Rick said to Paul.

"Yes, it can't be worse than staying here. But seeing Florence upset because our parents won't come makes me sad. I should call them. I miss them already," Paul said.

"Me too. Let's call them every day from now on, and tell them how much we love them."

137. Stop rejecting, start accepting. (May year 3)

Statement by the Spiritual Leader of the Children of Abraham, Simon Waltz.

Children of Abraham. As you know Armageddon is upon us. God has sent the Devil to rid our Earth of the Sinners. The Devil came disguised as the Cube to fool the Sinners. But I know the truth, you know the truth and we were not seduced. As you know an attempt to kill me was made, and I died. And God summoned me and He spoke to me, and He revealed His plan to me. Stage one was to purge Earth of most Sinners: the heathens, the prostitutes, the homosexuals, the witches, and the diseased. Then He would blind the remaining Sinners and make them believe the Devil is not inside the Cube. He convinced them inside is a new start for them, but God took me inside and showed me the prison. Once they go inside and the Cube leaves our Earth, the Devil shall reveal Himself to them and they will find themselves in Hell. God is giving us, the Children of Abraham, another chance: a cleansed Earth for His children. After God had shown me His plan, He resurrected me to give you His message.

God has told me to warn you. To warn you away from the Cube. Do not enter it. Do not leave with it. Do not be convinced by the Devil to go anywhere near it. God wants you to stay on Earth and be part of His New Paradise. His New Eden.

In a few months time the Devil and his worshippers shall leave, never to return, and we shall reclaim our Earth as rightfully ours.

Stay strong my Children. Keep your faith strong. God is with you.

"Well, that takes care of the religious lunatics," President McGee said to Colin after they had read Simon's statement. "My apologies. I didn't think. I shouldn't have said that. It's disrespectful to your mother. Oh, and good morning to you."

"Don't worry Bill. It's fine. They *are* crazy. When I'm finished here for the day, I'll visit her." As soon as Colin had walked in, the statement had been put in front of his nose; there had been no opportunity for casual talks yet.

"Does she know you're back?" Bill asked.

"No, I'd thought it would be better not to call her. You know, in case she'd disappear on me again."

"She's home. We've kept an eye on her. She's gone back to worship at her normal church. Nancy hasn't been anywhere near the Children of Abraham," Bill said. He opened up files on his desk, indicating they should do some work. "This move is a nightmare to organise."

"Bill, hang on for a second. You had her under surveillance all this time? That's a lot of resources to spend on an unimportant woman. She's been back for a long time." Colin did not understand.

"I did it for you, Colin."

He was touched by the President's loyalty to him. "Thank you — and yes, let's organise this logistical hell. I'm glad the Canadians are on board. Overall, the list of available planes and ships is pretty impressive. I think we might pull this off yet."

For the next ten hours Colin tried to achieve the almost impossible: making things happen. All types of resources had to be flown in: food, cutlery, clothing and blankets, stationery, medical supplies, books and musical instruments, and much more. The army would set up a base in the Sphere to protect Americans against the Chinese. And he had to organise cargo ships to be loaded with soil, animals and plants. Colin knew he would be doing this job for months, and he was looking forward to the day he could move into the Cube. And he wanted Martin with him, they worked well together and Martin always made it seem so easy to make things happen. He would call him on his way to his mother later.

***

Colin was relieved to see the lights switched on at his mother's house. A car was parked outside. The two men inside waved at him and showed him their CIA passes. The President had not lied when he told him they had kept an eye on her. He felt good, knowing he was appreciated. He hoped his mother knew too.

He rang the doorbell and noticed curtains moving behind the main window. He recognised the shadow of his mother. She made him wait ten minutes, but eventually she opened the door.

"Colin, I didn't know you were back. Please come in. I'll make you a cup of tea. Have you eaten? You look skinny."

She reacted as if they had never fallen out, as if nothing bad had happened between them. Electricity was back to normal again, but most light in the room came from scented candles. Apple and cinnamon: her favourite, and the smell took Colin back to his childhood. Her rocking chair stood in the corner and had her Bible on. Nothing ever really changed. Colin seated himself on the sofa and waited for his mother to return.

She brought tea and sandwiches. "Peanut butter and jelly. Just how you like them."

Colin remembered his mother preparing them for him when he was a child. He would sit at the kitchen table, watching her as she took out the big jars. She never made him eat the crusts. He was so happy then. He remembered how he liked to help her hanging up the laundry in the garden. They spent a lot of time out there; she would tell him stories about exotic places and he always thought she had travelled the world, but later in life he discovered they were all loving little lies, but lovely big stories, told to open up his mind and make him inquisitive. And her plan had worked: as a teenager he had spent a lot of time in his local library, looking at pictures of those faraway lands, and reading up on the peoples and their customs. That was why he had become a diplomat; he wanted to see the countries for himself.

"Mom, I want you to come and live with me in the Cube."

"Oh my sweet boy. You know I can't do that. Besides, I've promised your cousin Jesse and his wife I would live with them at their farm. They are good Christians and they will look after me when I need it," she said.

"Please."

"Let's not spoil the moment. Eat," Nancy demanded. She handed him the plate with the crust-less sandwiches: four of them. "The men outside have been very friendly you know. They like it when I bring them coffee and cake. Thank you for protecting me. There have been a lot of burglaries and robberies in the area."

Colin tried to answer her, but she shushed him; he should have known better than to talk with his mouth full — she had never tolerated that. Chewing and thinking made him realise it was better not to tell her it hadn't been him who had sent the CIA. Ignorance was bliss, and most probably the reason why she was not hostile towards him. She still behaved very coldly though.

"Can I at least drive you there?" Colin asked her after he finished his last sandwich. He really needed to feel love from his mother; she was not giving him enough.

"No, your cousin is picking me up next week. He has a big truck and all my stuff is moving too, and I haven't even packed everything yet. I'll be really happy there with the kids and all the animals."

"You can be happy with me too, inside the Cube. We're making a fresh start. It will be better in there than here on Earth. I'm organising the move myself, so I know." He was pleading with her now.

"I'm too old for change and too much has changed already. I want to stay here. I was born here and my parents were born here. This is where I belong. This is where I will be buried and will be with your father for all eternity. You have to go my son, I understand. As a small child I saw the hunger in your eyes for new things, for the truth. There is nothing new for you here any more. In the Cube there is a lifetime of discoveries waiting for you. And you'll be with the person you love."

Colin was stunned. He knew this was as much as she could acknowledge him and Martin. He had her approval. She had allowed herself to love him again. "Thank you Mother. I love you."

"I love you too. And besides, I heard there are no churches in the Cube. How am I supposed to pray for you there? Every day I will ask the Lord to look after you on my behalf and keep you from harm. You are my boy, no matter what. Remember when it was you and me, a team, against the world? That has never changed for me."

Colin couldn't speak. Instead he embraced her as hard as he could. She had warmed to him: they were almost back to normal.

"Oh my, I can feel you're still going to the gym. You're squeezing the life out of me." She laughed. Colin enjoyed hearing her being happy: it had been more than a year.

"You should go, you have two worlds to save, and you need your sleep. Come round again tomorrow. I'll make you more sandwiches."

"Yes Mom, I will." Colin kissed her goodbye.

At the door, she grabbed his hand. She put a small silver

necklace with a cross in his hand. "It used to belong to your grandmother, then me — and now to you."

"Mom?" Colin never noticed her taking it off, she was always wearing the necklace. "Why are you giving me this now?"

"You will need it more than I do," she said. "Go and save the world. We'll talk tomorrow. And Colin, I love you very much and I am very proud of you. Never forget that."

Colin felt overwhelmed and confused by her dramatic goodbye. He wondered what she had meant as he drove home to his apartment. He felt strange when he drove into his street and saw his building. His apartment looked empty: last year he had moved his personal belongings to London. His furniture looked lost in his living room, without the pictures on the walls and without his plants. His bed looked too big and cold, he did not want to sleep on his own tonight. Suddenly he felt very lonely.

***

Colin went through another busy day at the White House. For every solution to a problem, many more challenges popped up: organising cargo planes and ships proved difficult; many owners wanted a premium price and Colin ended up commandeering most of them. Also, many people who were staying behind were not happy with the loss of their resources and staged protests outside farms, factories and distribution centres. At the New Jersey port fights had broken out overnight between the opposing camps and after protesters started shooting at the workers Colin had to call in the US Coast Guard. Everything seemed to go belly up. He could not wait for today to finish. He was looking forward to more peanut butter and jelly sandwiches.

After finishing the strenuous day at the White House, Colin made his way to his mother's. He gave her a quick call to tell her he wouldn't be long, but she did not answer her phone. It was already very late; maybe she was resting.

The CIA men waved at Colin as he walked up to the front door. He rang the bell a couple of times, but no answer. All lights were off. He walked over to the men. One of them stepped out of the car. "Hi, did you change your mind?"

"What do you mean?" Colin asked.

"We thought you were going in to check the house, or pick up your stuff."

"No, I'm here to see my mother."

"But — she's gone. A truck came by real early this morning. They loaded a couple of boxes and a rocking chair, and then she left."

"You should've called me," Colin shouted at the man.

"Calm down please. Your mother spoke with us. She told us explicitly not to phone you, because you would be very busy. She gave us the impression you knew."

Colin realised she had told him farewell last night, and she had decided to set him free. He knew she did not want to see him again and he needed to respect her wishes. But accepting her decision was difficult for him. He reached for the little cross hanging around his neck. He remembered he had pictures of her in England with Martin. He had to talk to Martin: he had to hear his voice. It was the middle of the night in London, but he knew Martin was always there for him. "My mum has left me again," he said, sobbing, as soon as Martin picked up the phone. "Now I understand that she made it clear to me yesterday that we'll never see each other again."

"I'm so sorry for you. But clearly this is what she wants. Let her be happy in her own way. It's tough, but you have to let her go. And you know I'm here for you. Only a few more months and then we'll start a new life in the Cube. We'll be happy together."

"Yes, but now I feel I'm leaving everything and everyone

301

behind. I'm lonely Martin. I won't even see you here on Earth any more."

"You what?" Martin sounded upset. "I won't see you here any more?"

"Sorry, there's so much to do, I can't make it to London before we leave. I need to set up inside the Cube fairly soon. We're settling several cities inside the Sphere."

"What about our plan to go in together? And as soon as you are in, how will we stay in contact? And how will I know where you are? I might not find you. Don't do this to me."

Colin could hear the fear and anger in Martin's voice, and he was certain Martin was holding back. He did not want to fight with him, not now, he felt bad enough already. "Let's not discuss this now. I don't feel right. I don't want to argue with you."

"Sorry, you're right. I'm sure we'll find a way. When are you going?"

"In a month's time. We estimate 50 million Americans will move. And now with the plants and the animals going in too, we'll have a lot more to organise inside the Cube. And deal with the Chinese threat of course."

"Have you decided what areas you'll be using to transport the extra goods? Damn, I miss you so much already."

"I miss you too, very much. And yes, what's left of France, Brittany and that bit of Spain, Galicia. We're building ramps there right now and oil tankers with resources are already arriving."

"You'll make sure we find each other. You hear me?"

Colin thought he heard Martin cry. "Of course. You're all I have left. I love you."

"I love you too. Call me tomorrow."

"I will, oh and Martin, please make sure you pack my pictures. My mother is on them."

139. Fantastic Fun Facts.
(June year 3)

Extract from The Relocation Guide for Kids. Age group 6 to 11: Fantastic Fun Facts and more about living in the Sphere. Issued by the New Albion Government.

Hello to you, Boys and Girls. It is Super Duper you are with us inside the Sphere!
We love having you and want to tell you the Fantastic Fun Facts about living here.
Always keep this little book in your pocket at all cost.
So you know where you are and you'll never get lost.
Are you ready to learn what it's all about?
Sit down, and you will soon find out.

So Boys and Girls, are you ready to learn some great things? Here are a few really Fantastic Fun Facts:

The city you live in is inside a Sphere, and the Sphere is inside a big Cube. And we call it: The Ophiuchus Cube. It travels through space and it goes very fast. It gets its energy from all the stars outside the Cube. The stars are the same as the Sun in the Sphere, but they look much smaller because they are very far away. You cannot see them from where you are, but they are all around you. And they are important, because they make our Sun shine and keep you warm. Don't look at the Sun for too long, or your eyes will hurt. The Sun is held in the middle of the Sphere with six columns. These columns end in the centre of each of the six sides of the Cube and all the Sun's energy runs through them.

Everything in the Sphere and the Cube is made with Prime

Numbers.

Do you know what a Prime Number is? It is a number that you can only divide by 1 or by itself. Can you name the first 15 Prime Numbers?

Here is the answer: 2, 3, 5, 7, 11, 13, 17, 19, 23, 29, 31, 37, 41, 43, 47, but they don't stop here. Can you count more? Try it now, it's a lot of fun!

Now come a few difficult facts and it is fine if you do not understand them yet.

The Sphere has a total surface of 186 million square kilometres. The surface of the Sphere is divided into triangles. All of them have the same size.

The official way of saying what the Sphere is called, is with very difficult words: it is an Icosahedral Geodesic sphere. If you can't remember this now, don't worry! All you need to know is what it means: The Sphere is round and made up of a lot of triangles.

All triangles have three sides and each side is about 29 kilometres long (a Prime Number again) and that means they have on average a surface of 361 square kilometres. And that is almost as big as the Isle of Wight back on Earth. A triangle like this is called an Equilateral Triangle. Do you know how many triangles are in the Sphere?

Here is the answer: The Sphere can be divided into 20 areas: they are called faces (like the patches on a leather football). Each face has 25,921 triangles, so there are a total of 518,420 triangles. Now, that is a lot! Each face has 1,993 cities, so there are 39,860 cities in the Sphere. And you know what? Every city is surrounded by 12 triangles; just under half of them are water and the rest are land.

In each city are enough buildings to house at least 15 million people. That is big!

Because you and your parents came from a country that is

called Great Britain, you are now living together with everyone of that country in our city: New Albion.

And there are over ten million of us here!

The person in charge of New Albion is called The Viceroy. His name is Albert Windsor and when you talk to him, you say: Your Excellency. He is very important and makes all the decisions to keep you safe.

The red, white and blue flag you see on all the buildings is called The Union Jack. It is the same flag as Great Britain and we liked it so much we took it with us, and now it is the flag of New Albion too. And there are people wearing t-shirts with the flag on it: they are the guides, and they keep you safe and can help you with everything you need to know.

The Sun shines all day in the Sphere, so there is no day and night, but we do keep the time. We have 24 hours every day. In many buildings are the Timekeepers. They are very good at keeping time and they chime the bells every hour. If you are close enough to one of the buildings, you can hear them. These are the most important hours for you.

8 chimes are for waking up, have your breakfast, brush your teeth, have your shower and get ready to go out, because:

9 chimes are for school.

12 chimes are called midday and then we have lunch.

15 chimes, you will like: that is when school finishes and you go home or play with your friends.

18 chimes are for dinner time.

20 chimes are for bedtime.

24 chimes are midnight, and that is the end of the day, but you should be sleeping then.

Travelling in the Sphere is a breeze.
You'll find your home with ease:

Walk. This is the best way to get around in, and close to, the city. You walk home, to school, to the playing areas and to your friends, and always look and learn the markers, so you always know where you are.

Triangles. Going up and down the buildings is done with the elevator: you find the triangles on the outside of the buildings. Remember to memorise your floor-marker and when it comes up: stick your hand out.

Circles. Do not step in one without an adult. This is the Inter-City and will take you to other cities and you might get lost. If you did go and want to go home: get off at the first marker, stay in the circle and step on the same colour strip, but on the opposite side from where you came from.

Squares. Also do not go here without an adult. A square takes you away from the Sphere in the travelator and it is really difficult to find your way home. If you did go and want to go home: get off at the first marker, stay in the square and go on the same colour strip, but on the opposite side from where you came.

Here is an important tip for you to know.
Always tell an adult where you go.
Don't go too far from the city. And if you do get lost then look for a New Albion sign.
Follow our instructions. It's easy peasy, you'll be home in a doddle, and you'll always be fine.

How to get home rules.
In New Albion, find someone you know, or if you can not, look for someone who wears the Union Jack: they are the guides and they will help you.

If you have walked out of the city: turn around and look at

the buildings. On the outsides big Union Jack flags hang: that is where your home is.

If you find yourself in an empty city or on land you have not been to before: do not panic. Look for a Union Jack, it will tell you where the nearest Circle is and in the Circle look for the instructions and go on that strip. And don't forget to look for the right marker to get off on time.

Sometimes things that happen in the Sphere can be very bad,

But if you are careful, and listen to us, you will not get sad.

If you feel sick, or got hurt, or maybe you fell over, you cut yourself, or had any other accident: go to the hospital building in the centre of the city. If you don't know where it is, find someone you know, or a guide and they will help you.

If you see something bad, look for someone you know or a guide and tell them about it.

If you are alone and lost, do not go with strangers. If you see strangers, hide till they are gone, and then find your way back using the How To Get Home guide.

Outside the City you might find animals. Some are nice, some are not. If you are not with an adult, stay away from the animals. We don't want you to get bitten and get hurt.

We have told you all we know to help you, but we need one more thing from you to get you back.

Please write your name and where you live and if you need help, show it to a guide in the Union Jack.

Hello, my name is: _____ ,
I live in building: _____ ,
on floor: _____ , in New Albion.

"Careful with those pigs," Tuan said to the peasant. He started to get very annoyed with the farmers. They had no idea how much money pigs would be worth in the Cube. Crap, he could not believe he was going to live in a place without electricity and this disgusting slurry to eat. He felt as if he had stepped back in time and was living in his nightmarish little village again. Tuan's body shook, as he expected his dad to hit him on the back of his head, and his grandmother, sitting in the corner, watching him being abused, and not helping him. But that had happened a long time ago. Today he had to ensure the pigs and chicken were all housed and settling in. All the animals were clearly distressed; they had been in trucks and planes for days, and now the change in gravity made them panic. The chickens had found a new freedom — they could fly in the Sphere, unlike on Earth. They managed to jump much higher and stay in the air, their wings clumsily flapping. Many tried to escape and farmers, helped by soldiers, tried to catch them. Tuan found the whole scene terribly funny.

He himself enjoyed his new weight; he felt almost half as light and he enjoyed how easy walking felt. If everything worked out to his plan, the animals would eat the slurry and then the Communist Party could provide the people with real meat, so they would stay happy and easier to control. But Tuan would make sure he would have the best cuts of meat for himself.

In a few hours his shift would end and hopefully the animals would be locked up in their assigned apartments. They and their farmers would be in buildings on the other side of the city: far away from his own home. Tuan was looking forward to his new home; it had taken him a lot of effort finding the right place, but he got exactly what he wanted: his penthouse overlooked the lakes and the plateaus that were assigned to become nature reserves, and all his furniture and clothes had arrived today. He was glad he had brought his own mattress.

Outside the farm building he saw a truck being unloaded and more pigs jumped out. He noticed two frail and very old women standing in front of the truck; they were so old they could hardly walk, even with the low gravity. Tuan felt outraged and raced towards them. What the hell were they doing here? They were not supposed to be here — China only allowed in the straight, young and healthy people. Old, or gay, or disabled were forbidden here.

When he confronted the women, a farmer ran up to him. Tuan started shouting at all three of them. It turned out that the farmer, who was assigned as a volunteer to live in the Cube, had smuggled in his two aunts. The farmer tried to explain that they were dependent on him for food and housing, and they would die if they had to stay behind. Tuan was not interested; what they had tried was against the rules. He gestured soldiers over to him and when the three *criminals* were handcuffed, he led them back to the entrance of the Cube.

During the journey, the women cried and pleaded with Tuan, but he ignored them. When they stepped off the square, close to the entrance, Tuan saw a news crew and made them come over. He instructed them to film what would happen next. "This is what we do with people who do not belong in the Cube and the people who smuggle them in," Tuan said into the camera. He pushed all three of them over the edge. He heard them scream when they fell back to Earth. "Make sure this makes today's headlines," he said, smiling at the camera man.

***

Yuri Manelyuk checked the list one last time before he gave the go ahead to the convoy of over 100 trucks and buses. All his weapons, gold, drugs, his girls and his most trusted members were accounted for. Over 700 men and women accompanied him. Solntsevskaya Bratva would leave Moscow and Earth behind and start anew inside the Cube. He decided they would use the Ukraine entrance near Odessa to avoid being detected by the Russian Government and army. The journey would be long and tedious: at least 24 hours to get there. Yuri had heard from Kovalev that some generals in the Russian army had found out about his nuke, and they wanted to arrest him and seize the bomb, so he needed to leave right now.

Yuri felt excited as he walked to his truck. He noticed Eva sleeping in the cabin; he was pleased to see she felt comfortable. His body-guards opened the back of his truck and they showed him, again, that the nuke was still there. Yuri felt the cocaine made him more efficient, but he realised the drug also made him borderline obsessive compulsive. Once inside the truck, he gave the order over the radio for the convoy to start the journey. *Goodbye to you, rat-infested Moscow.*

The journey was uneventful, except for the weather worsening the closer they got to their final destination. Yuri snorted a lot of cocaine, because he wanted to stay awake and alert. He did not like the look of the Cube at all, staring at him for the whole journey and growing larger by the minute. Moscow had been spared most of the destruction, but he felt unsafe. No matter what the government had told him, somehow he still expected some kind of attack. He hoped his anxiety would stop as soon as they were inside the Sphere. He always needed to see things for himself so he could believe them.

Traffic had been bad at Kiev and Odessa, but when they reached the entrance to the Cube Yuri was pleasantly surprised to see the area was fairly empty. It took Yuri 15 minutes, one kilo of gold and 25 packets of cocaine to jump to the front of the queue. Not bad, he thought; it had been a lot easier than he expected to bribe the officials at the gate.

Yuri and his convoy were instructed to drive up the ramp. Once inside the Cube; Yuri had to do a lot of explaining and organising to make sure everyone and everything would arrive at the same location, and he was surprised that his trucks and buses could use the travelators. He had not thought about what would happen to his vehicles once they reached the Cube, so he was pleased they did not have to carry their goods and risked being found out by the authorities.

The journey to the Sphere was fast, and comfortable. The sight of the interior overwhelmed Yuri. He had to step out of his truck to get a better view and the low gravity tried to make him fall over forwards; instinctively he held out his arms and he rolled over twice. Behind him he could hear Eva laugh.

Feeling lighter was sensational and Yuri jumped up a few times. He flew over two metres high and landed gently on his feet. It was almost as if he was jumping on a trampoline and for a short moment he felt like a boy again. He would enjoy himself in here. When he looked around, his stomach turned. He had seen the pictures and videos on the news, but nothing had prepared him for the enormity and vastness of the Sphere's interior. The greenness played tricks on his eyes and he had to look at his hands and clothing to lose the feeling his eyes could only see one colour.

He looked at the scattered cities, and the farther away, the more their tall buildings pointed at him; the more they reminded him of guns and canons. The Sun, with the clouds around it, was not bright enough and felt too small: a tiny dot compared to the real Sun, but yet looked too big and too close to him. And not finding the horizon unsettled him too; he would take a long time to get used to this new reality. Green had never been his favourite colour, and he especially disliked this green: everything looked too artificial — he thought this was a soulless colour.

His thoughts were interrupted by a young Ukrainian man.

"Hello Sir, welcome to the Sphere, let me guide you to your new home."

"Thank you, I appreciate your help," Yuri said. He was pleased with the innocence of the guide, who clearly had left the corruption of Earth behind. It seemed the optimism of the settlers had made them fantasise about a new glorious, honest and free world, without guns and criminals: this should work to his advantage.

"Ah, I hear you're Russian. We welcome all Russians too. I'll explain where your fellow countrymen are settling and where the Ukraine settles, so you can make up your own mind," the man said, smiling, as he handed out a bag with papers to Yuri. "I have important and useful information for you to read. When you enter the Circle you can travel, with the Inter-City, to various cities. If you take the light lane on the left and get off on the fifth marker, you will be in the Ukrainian area. And the light lane in front of you will take you to Russia. Just stay on that one till the end. There are lanes on the right too, but they lead to empty cities, so there is nothing there for you. I wish you all a happy new life," the still smiling Ukrainian guide said.

"Thank you and I wish the same to you," Yuri said as he walked back to his truck. He instructed his convoy to follow him into the Circle and drive onto the light lane on the right and stay on the strip until the end. He wanted to be as far away from any authority, so he could run his empire from a secret and safe location.

After his truck arrived at the edge of an empty city, he waited for the rest of his convoy to arrive and gather in front of him. "Ladies and gentlemen, let me introduce you to your new home. I shall call this city Solntsevo, so we will never forget where we came from," Yuri said to his people. Eva chirped and kissed him, she had a little bag in her hand. He had great plans for the future, but first he wanted to get high and share a very fat line of cocaine with his woman.

149. Exodus.
(July year 3)

Kim loved living in New Delhi. She had never left China before, but was happy she had been forced to. The Indians were fantastic: they had a completely different skin colour, a warm brown — and their food: she just loved their food. The Indian curry spices were unlike any flavour she had ever tasted. And everything in India was so colourful too. The women's garments were bright and exciting and their jewellery looked very intricate and elegant. And Pranit had been the perfect host; he had introduced them to other Chinese ex-pats and he had taught them about Indian customs and his country's history. Kim had even started learning a few Indian words, but everyone seemed to speak English. She was very sad they had to leave the country today, but she knew why they had to go.

The plane had taken them to an airport where Goa used to be and a short drive had taken them close to the Cube entrance. Kim was shocked to see the Cube, reaching higher than the clouds. The green was overwhelming. She felt nervous, because in a few hours everything she knew would be gone forever. Pranit was waiting for them at a checkpoint. They were searched, their documents were checked and they were allowed to enter the embarkation area. The makeshift waiting room was busy, with long lines of families carrying as much as they could, patiently waiting in a line to be taken up one of the many ramps. Military personnel were directing traffic: heavy trucks loaded with goods, with, according to Pranit, enough curry spices to last a thousand years. Kim estimated over 100,000 people were present, but everything seemed to go in a very orderly fashion. And even though the rain soaked them as soon as they stepped outside; Kim started feeling in a better mood.

Pranit whisked them to a small bus. They were VIPs, so they would not have to queue. Even their luggage was carried for them.

Before they boarded, Pranit walked up to Kim: "This is where I say goodbye to you for now. I have much more work to do here on Earth before I can join you. I promise that we will look after you. And we will find your nephew." Pranit kissed Kim and Jia-Li and gave Jiang a firm handshake. He turned to look back and waved at them several times when he walked off, smiling all the time. Kim cried a little bit when she realised she wouldn't see Pranit for a while. She liked him, and she knew he still felt very guilty for being responsible for getting them imprisoned.

Women with jewellery and bright coloured dresses, and men with big bellies and gold watches sat in the front of the bus. In the back were the more ordinary people. Kim had learnt about the Indian caste system. This bus was filled with high caste families and their servants. She thought it was a shame they were taking their old bad habits into the Cube, but she felt it was not right to judge the people, or the culture, of the country that had decided to take care of them.

She noticed a few other Chinese people in the bus; their clothing looked drab compared to the rest of the passengers. Kim realised she and Jiang were wearing Chinese clothing too and she felt she needed to make more of an effort to look more feminine and proud, just like the Indian women. She was not in China any more. Jia-Li stirred; she was hungry, and Kim decided to breastfeed her so that she would stay quiet during the final moments on Earth.

The ramp sloped gently, and even with the heavy traffic the bus had only taken 15 minutes to reach the entrance. Once inside, the driver reminded them of the low gravity and not to wander off, but to stick with their assigned guides.

Jiang stepped out of the bus first and jumped up and down. "This is great Kim, hand me Jia-Li, you'll jump higher than a ballerina."

Kim tried to keep her dignity, but she fell face down. She was used to Earth gravity and her instinct made her hands plunge towards the floor to break her fall, but she ended up bouncing up backwards, landing on her butt. She heard Jiang laughing. Two posh Indian ladies from the bus tried to hurry to her and help her up, but they ended up falling over as well, and tears from laughing ran down their cheeks. At least all the people were in good spirits.

The porters finished unloading the luggage onto the carts and the bus passengers were directed to their guide. Kim noticed the blandness of the Cube was broken by the vibrancy of the people's clothing and luggage, and loud conversations. She felt the Indians were importing the essence of India and she liked that a lot.

Their guide warned them to expect a slight disorientation when stepping from the square onto the travelator and again at the end of their journey.

He was right, Kim thought. Jia-Li felt the unfamiliar feeling too and started crying. Kim's eyes were telling her she was moving, but her body was not. Luckily she didn't get sick.

"You'll get used to it, but you'll hardly need to use the travelators later, unless you find work outside the Sphere," the guide told them. "We're almost there. Nothing will prepare you for what you're about to see, but don't worry, overall you'll be amazed by what you're about to witness."

The transition to the full stop was instantaneous and Kim's senses overwhelmed her. The Sun's rays warmed her face. The air was damp and warm, but not uncomfortable and was a nice change from the horrible weather in Nyalam. There was a faint odour of freshly washed linen. The lack of the horizon and the buildings hanging over her head would need getting used to, but she didn't mind, nor was she alarmed by the view. And everything was made of triangles: that felt the oddest to her.

Jiang's hand touched her shoulder and he kissed her neck. "It's so beautiful in here. I love the green, it's such a happy colour. And the buildings are so majestic the way they try to reach the Sun. I'm very excited, because soon we'll see our new home. Are you ready for this my darling?"

She smiled at him. "You know what Jiang? I am. We've had such a terrible time. Let us make this a new start and create a great future for Jia-Li."

"And maybe a little brother for her?" Jiang winked.

The Indian Government had decided to settle close to a Sphere entrance, so they and the other colonists were driven, by waiting rickshaws, to the closest city, located next to a lake.

The guide called their names from a list. "Hello, and welcome to New Goa. Your apartment is in the building on the left; its name is Hope and you're on floor 289. Your porter will show you how the elevator works. Enjoy your new home."

Kim noticed Jiang enjoying the view the higher they went up. The porter showed them the force-field and Kim felt safer for it. He told them to memorise the symbol on their floor, as there were no stairs anywhere in the Sphere and finding the right floor could prove difficult.

They were the first family to arrive at their allocated floor, so they could choose from five apartments. Jiang ran in and out of all of them and every time he came out of one he became more excited. "My lady, I have found us our new home," he said as he pointed to the first entrance on the left. "This one has the largest outside terrace with the best views and enough bedrooms for a few brothers and sisters for our Jia-Li. Please follow me in, my lady."

The porter coughed to attract their attention. He had unloaded their luggage and he was unpacking a large bag that did not belong to them. "Before I leave I'll explain how your apartment works and what the Indian Government has issued you." He led them into an empty room. "This is your shower and toilet. Unfortunately they are the same. You can shower here by moving your hand over this area on the wall to switch on and off the water. It comes out of that high point in the opposite wall. And when you have to go to the toilet afterwards, you do the same to clean yourself and wash away your — well you know what I mean."

Kim waved her hand and a steady stream of water came out of a hole four metres above them, and it was lukewarm. *Not bad*, she thought.

The porter led them back into the main room. "This is your family room, there are the benches to sit and sleep on, and in that wall over there," he said, as he walked to the wall with two small alcoves, "are your food and water dispensers."

Kim looked at the contents of the bag. The porter noticed. "Ah, yes. As you can see we have provided bowls, cups and cutlery. A dozen of each, but please be careful not to break them, as we won't issue extra ones. A sharp knife. Blankets, pillows and extra fabric sheets. Pencils and paper. Needles and thread. And, because we haven't figured out how to drill holes in the walls, glue, so you can hang up fabric in front of your door, to let people know this is your home and have your privacy.

"This last item is a tin with curry spices. You have to get used to the food, so we advise you to start mixing the spices in and reduce them over time. Ah, and when you explore the city later, do walk towards the tallest building in the centre of the city. This is where the Government for New Goa is located, and that is also where you can find work. In its main hall the town meetings will be held. I have to go now — new citizens are arriving all the time. It was a pleasure meeting you and I wish you a happy future as

Cubists. Goodbye."

Kim liked the term. A Cubist: the new name defined them.

After the porter had left, Kim prepared food for them. She tasted the slurry first, and she was pleased they had the spices. Jiang took a blanket to the terrace and spread it on a bench. They sat down with their food and water. This was the first meal of their new life.

"Kim, just look at this fantastic view. I have you and Jia-Li, and we have food and a fantastic apartment. Okay, there's no electricity, no television, or computers, but I don't mind. I already like it here. It's simple, but peaceful. I'm happy. I love you baby."

Kim smiled at him; the horrors of Earth were already forgotten. She looked at the clouds moving at a gentle pace around the Sun. "After the Cube leaves next month, we'll find Weisheng and he'll live here with us. Let's eat, and after dinner we'll go to bed. I think we'll sleep well here. And tomorrow — is the start of our exciting and happy future."

***

"Did you get it?" Simon asked his wife Erica when she walked in. She had been away for hours. He had asked her to buy a few simple things and even that had proved too difficult for her. Many shops were supposed to be open during night-time in London, so what *was* her problem? He was running out of time: in less than an hour the car, sent by Martin to pick up his wife and their three daughters from home, would arrive. Martin had agreed to send only one driver, at three in the morning, so it would be less likely any of the Children of Abraham would notice his family leaving.

Erica handed him a bag. "I couldn't find coloured contact lenses. Only the hair dye. As you requested, black."

"It'll have to do." Simon grabbed the bag and rushed to

the kitchen. He had to dye his hair and beard. When done, he would ask her to cut his hair short. And he would shave most of his beard. "Tell the girls to get dressed, and get my suit and shirt ready on the bed. And hurry back here, we don't have much time. You still have to cut my hair."

"Yes, but why are you doing this?"

"Shut up woman. You don't need to know anything, just follow my instructions and it will work out for us." *For fuck's sake, the bitch never shuts up*, he thought as he stuck his head under the tap and let warm water run through his hair. In front of the mirror he applied the dye. The instructions said it would take half an hour to set. He didn't have that long. Erica returned with scissors and cut his hair. She was covered in dye, and so was he. She made a real mess of everything.

"You forgot your eyebrows."

"My my, you said something useful. That makes a change." Simon put the dye on them. He shaved most of his beard, leaving only a black handlebar moustache. No one should recognise him. "When the doorbell rings, open the door and ask him to come in and help you with your luggage. Direct him to the living room. Stay outside and make sure the girls stay upstairs."

At exactly three o'clock the doorbell chimed. Simon heard Erica open the door and talk to the driver. Simon had placed the suitcases at the opposite side of the door in the living room. He hid behind the door, waiting for the driver to enter.

The door opened and a man in a black suit walked in. He did not notice Simon sneaking up behind him, nor did he notice Simon preparing to lunge a crowbar at him.

With all his strength Simon hit the back of the man's head. A thud was followed by a crack and the man slumped on the floor: unconscious. Simon took the man's keys, wallet and chauffeur's cap, and some paperwork: they were the instructions from Martin. He was pleased the man also carried a gun. Simon had felt naked without one ever since he had left Las Vegas. He looked at the man and a rush of adrenaline went through him. The palms of his hands were wet from sweat.

He looked at them and again at the man. *Should I? — It's been so long.* Before he could answer his thoughts, he had his hands around the man's neck. He used his body weight to crush the man's larynx. His fingers felt the heartbeat fade in the arteries. Simon felt strong. God would be pleased: another heathen was sent to Hell. He noticed his penis pumping and hardening. He had killed another human being. Simon rushed to the kitchen sink, got his erect cock out and without touching himself ejaculated.

After he dressed in the driver's suit, he left the living room and closed the door. He called his wife and daughters down. As instructed, they carried their bags. He hurried them to the car outside.

"Where's the driver?" Erica asked.

"We came to an agreement and he let me go. He is a Child of Abraham. Get in the car and let me drive, without you distracting me as usual."

***

Five Chinese men found the door to the house ajar. They had their guns drawn. In the living room they found a half naked corpse, and it was not Simon. "We're too late. Agent Tuan will not be pleased," one of them said.

***

The drive to Eastbourne was uneventful, as the roads were mostly empty. Simon's daughters were sleeping in the back and Erica did her best not to speak. Simon drove up to the checkpoint at the Cube's entrance. He waved the paperwork and the chauffeur's identification at the guard. "Sir, could you confirm who it is you are transporting?"

"They are Erica Waltz and her three daughters Judith, Sarah and Esther."

"If you could open the trunk for me please, I need to check Mr Waltz is not hidden in the car."

"Understood," Simon said. The guard had not recognised him. Everything was going to plan.

At the bottom of the ramp they were told to leave the car and keys behind, and use a trolley for their luggage. They would have a long walk up, but at least the ramp was not too steep. The girls would not like walking and probably demand their father would let them sit on the trolley and be pulled, but that was fine; like him, they were the Chosen ones. They joined a long line of people heading towards the entrance. Even in the middle of the night the place was crowded, and progress was too slow for Simon's liking.

Simon noticed a large group of men standing close to the bottom of the ramp. They were cordoned off by the military. He recognised a few of them: they were Children of Abraham. They were shouting profanities at the people going up the ramp. Simon decided to walk next to his wife, away from them. Maybe they would not identify him. He was in disguise, but he didn't want to tempt fate.

"I know you," Simon heard a man shout. His heart sank. He was discovered.

"You're Erica. Simon's wife. You Jezebel." Others joined in and more men from the mob started shouting at her.

Simon's daughters were crying and his wife started tugging his arm. Crap — why was this happening to him?

A few men tried to break through the cordon, and, despite the soldiers' best efforts, they succeeded. They ran up to Erica and one of them slapped her in the face.

She screamed. "Simon, please help me."

"Shut up woman, they can't know I'm here," he whispered.

Simon looked at the soldiers fighting the men. A flash of light caught Simon's eye, when he looked in the direction, he saw a man waving a gun.

The man was shouting at him now. "Look 'ere, it's Simon innit. He's gonna go in there too. He's betrayed us. I'm gonna get him."

Simon grabbed his wife and pulled her in front of him. He heard a blast. Blood splattered in his face. He licked his lips: they were warm and salty. He felt the full weight of Erica's body in his hands and as he let her go he noticed half of her head had disappeared. He ran his fingers over his face and through his hair, and when he looked at them they were covered in pink goo. The girls were screaming, and the sound reminded him of the noises the young women made when he pleased them back in Las Vegas. Soldiers fired shots, not at him, but at the man, who fell to the floor. Fighting broke out between the mob and the soldiers.

"I'm sorry Sir, you have to move on. It's for your own safety. We'll deal with your wife later. Get inside the Cube. Now please," a soldier said.

Chaos was all around Simon, men were fighting and he heard more gun shots. His daughters were still screaming. Bystanders ran in all directions, away from the danger. He shouted at his daughters and told them to follow him as he pulled the trolley with all his strength. He had to make it into the Cube. God had chosen him for His plan. God had saved him, again.

The welcoming committee directed him, and the others, to the entrance of the Cube. Normally everyone would be re-checked at this point, but due to the incident, all that seemed to have been forgotten. It suited Simon well.

A Government representative gave him a sheet of paper. It read: *New Albion, Tower DF, level 56.*

"This will be your new home Sir," the guide said. "Please hurry to get yourself to safety. Follow the British flags and the instructions of the other guides, they're wearing the same outfit as I am." He pointed at his Union Jack T-shirt and baseball cap. The guide handed four boxes to Simon and his daughters, marked: *Compliments of the British Government and the Viceroy of New Albion.*

Rushing, they followed the others on to the travelators. When Simon recovered from his disorientation and saw the markers and corridors flying past, he wondered if the beings that built this wondrous object also believed in God.

His three daughters were sobbing. "Your mummy is in Heaven now," he said to them, "you'll see her again, but God has a plan for us and very soon I shall tell you what it is." For a short moment he felt uncomfortable with the thought that he had to take their innocence in order to achieve God's plan for mankind, but he knew his daughters would understand. And anyway, all teenage girls liked having babies.

When they arrived inside the Sphere, Simon doubted himself for a moment and he wondered if he had made the right choice in coming. *God, you did not lie to me?* The triangles looked like pieces of a complex puzzle only the Devil could design. The Sun was hot and the air was hot. He hated this place already, and it was full of Sinners. But God had told him to be here. He saw people walk onto a circle and disappear. "What's happening to them? Are you killing them?" he asked a guide close to the circle.

"No Sir, this is the way to travel to your home fastest. Otherwise you would have to walk for months. Please enter the circle and step on the lightest strip. A guide will help you."

"Why the lightest?" he asked.

"That is the strip that will take you to New Albion, Sir."

"Thank you, I know enough."

Simon led his daughters into the circle. The other travellers stepped on the lightest strip and off they went. Simon guessed this was the best time to cut his ties with the rest of mankind and find his New Eden. He instructed his daughters to sit on the trolley. He chose the darkest strip, opposite to where everyone else went, and he hoped he would end up farthest away from them.

"Daddy, you're going the wrong way," Esther said.

"No darling, those people are the Sinners. We can't be near them. God has a plan for us. We need to be far away from them. We're going on a pilgrimage to find our own home and we shall call it New Eden. And we'll be just like Adam and Eve."

151. Farewell my good friends.
(August year 3)

"*Prime Minister Christopher Marchant is about to address the Nation on all television and radio channels. Please stand by as we switch over to 10 Downing Street.*"

"*Citizens of the United Kingdom of Great Britain and Northern Ireland, citizens of New Albion. As you know the Cube has started the process of leaving Earth. Departure is expected in the next few days. I am happy to announce that almost everyone who chose to settle in the Cube is now relocated there. Around ten million Britons chose to take this new life, and many people from all over the globe have moved to the Cube, almost 500 million in total.*

"*Those remaining on Earth have had to say goodbye to families and friends. I have too, and I was saddened. Farewells are always more difficult for the people who stay behind. But even though our loved ones will be gone, they will live on and double the chances for mankind to survive the ordeal we have been through.*

"*I had to say goodbye to many, but I would like to mention a special man who has kept our country as safe and sane as possible during these hard times. He also made sure our country is well prepared for the difficult times ahead. His name is Martin Germain, and I shall forever be in his debt. Thank you, Martin.*

"*I want to mention another great man: Viceroy Albert Windsor. He has made great efforts to ensure the continuation of our great Nation and to keep the spirit of the British alive. I am certain he will stand up for democracy and freedom for the citizens of New Albion.*

"*Extreme efforts have been made to make sure the citizens of New Albion have a good start and a fighting chance to stay safe and alive on their journey. We have* installed medical supplies and daily items such as cutlery, blankets, pen and paper, because there is no electricity in the Cube.

"There has been another huge undertaking initiated by a brave and visionary man from Australia, Barend Trevelyan. He co-ordinated many countries to bring animals, fish, insects, seeds and plants into the Cube. Also soil, so the travellers can plant forests and have fresh air to breathe and forever be reminded of our beautiful Earth. I am delighted Barend and his wife have set up the first, of many, zoos inside the Cube and are already looking after many animals.

"Those leaving us have also been given instruments and sheet music, so they can play music and sing songs to remember their loved ones and the planet they left behind.

"Maybe one day, they or their descendants will return to Earth and find that we, the ones who stayed behind, succeeded in rebuilding our beautiful planet, our home, their real home and welcome them back with our arms wide open.

"We shall miss you. Farewell my good friends."

"All right, we have a problem." Martin's voice was loud and hurt Rick's head, he hated being woken up by his mobile phone. What time was it? Still dark, he should be sleeping. Paul stirred next to him, turned over and went back to sleep.

"Hey, what's happening?" Rick asked, switching on the light.

"The doors are closing. I think the Cube is going to leave soon."

"But I thought we still have a week or so."

"Yes, I thought so too, but now we believe the Cube is working towards its next marker in the control room, and when the doors are closed is when the next symbol-square will light up. Rick, we can't take the risk, if the doors are closed, we'll miss the ride and we'll be stuck here. And an hour ago we lost use of the ramp at the Eastbourne entrance. By this time tomorrow, we won't have access through our territory any more and then we'd have to travel to Belgium or Germany to get in. This is causing all sorts of problems," Martin said.

"What do you propose we do? We were assigned to go in a few days," Rick said. He prodded Paul to wake him up and put Martin on speaker phone.

"Okay, I have helicopter seats reserved. You have to make your way to the Northolt air base. It is near Ruislip, just off the A40, it's easy to find. I'm there now. We're evacuating personnel. You have to be very quick though. I still have enough authority to get you inside the base, but the situation will become more chaotic by the hour, as people start to panic. Traffic shouldn't be too bad right now, but in a few hours when people have woken up to the news, I expect many will come and then you might not make it through. And then I don't know what will happen. And I really want all of you with me, I don't want to go in there on my own. I haven't heard from Colin for weeks. I don't know what's going on."

"I'm sure Colin is fine and waiting for you. But bugger, it's happening so fast. I'll call Isadora and we'll get to you as fast as we can."

"Good. Two hours should be more than enough for all of you to get here. I'll be waiting for you, but please hurry," Martin said and hung up.

Paul woke Florence, and Rick phoned Isadora. She told him they had packed their bags weeks ago and had been on standby for a rapid departure ever since. They agreed Isadora would come to their home and then they would drive there together in both their cars. Rick could hear her running around and waking up the others. She was wasting

329

no time.

Rick looked at the suitcases and rucksacks in the hallway: they had been prepared and ready to go too. It was hard to have to leave almost everything behind. Except for plenty of clothing and books, they had packed a few personal belongings. The pictures of his parents were in his coat pocket. "One last goodbye to our home and then we'll wait by the car for the others," Rick said.

The three of them walked around the flat in silence. Rick remembered the first time they walked into their new home. Things had been so different back then, and they were so happy. He remembered when he had come home and had to tell Paul he was diagnosed with cancer. He remembered getting married to Paul. He remembered looking at the stars and the excitement when one was missing. He remembered when the religious maniacs broke into their home and shot at them, injuring Paul and how afraid he had been he might lose him. He remembered the first time Florence came into their lives. He made sure he would remember everything he had to leave behind.

The bed they had shared for years would stay empty forever. The sofa they had sat on, with the small stains from the wine they spilt over the years. The spare bedroom, now belonging to Florence, full with all the toys and stuffed animals they had bought for her. The roof terrace, where they did their gardening, and where still now many plants had flowers. This was the end of an era. For the last time in his life Rick locked his front door, he wondered if other people, a family maybe, would ever use it as their home and make their own memories. They would not even know who had lived here before. Rick felt already forgotten for ever: just like the dead.

Before the arrival of the Cube, the Sun at this hour would often have started changing the black carpet of night, covered in many little twinkling stars, into a vibrant light blue and pink coloured rug. Not for a long time had Rick seen this spectacle, and he would not today either as thick rain clouds covered the sky. Tonight the rain dominated again; drops were racing through the beams of the streetlights. Rick couldn't remember a day without rain any more. A blue sky with its blinding hot Sun seemed as far away as a dream, and he already missed them both.

They took a minute to load their luggage in the back of the car. None of them wanted to wait inside. This was the last day they would stand under the real sky and be exposed to real rain.

There was no traffic on the street, or any people walking on the pavements, and when the car with Isadora and the others turned into their street, Rick jumped.

"I think I broke the speed limit and must have been photographed several times, said Isadora. "I wonder if the mail man will be fast enough to deliver me the fines." Isadora hugged Rick as she stepped out of the car for a quick chat and to let Sally run around for a pee.

Rick felt pleased they were all together now. He waved at the kids and Gustavo and Zaira, and gave a happy tail wagging Sally a quick hug. "Zaira looks uncomfortable and sad. She's not in labour I hope? That would really mess things up," Rick said.

"She insists she's not. Cramps only. But she's almost nine months in. Oh God, I can just imagine her waters breaking when we step into the Cube. As if we haven't enough drama already." Isadora smiled at Rick. "She's been on the phone with her parents in Rio and she's upset because she won't ever see them again."

"Yeah, I still have to call my family. I hope they pick up the phone before we get into the Cube. I hope Zaira is feeling okay, it can't be easy for her, being almost due. Anyway, let's get going. We have 90 minutes to get there, plenty of time, but I don't want to cut it too short. Make sure you stay right behind me."

***

Rick had not expected to see a big angry crowd in front of the gate, when they arrived at Northolt. Martin had been wrong. There was no way they could drive past them, or the many parked cars. Rick estimated at least 2,000 people were shouting at the guards on the other side of the fence. A horrible feeling went through Rick: they would not make it past the crowd in time and they would be stuck here on Earth. He didn't know what to do next, except to wait for Martin. Now more than ever he had to depend on the reliability of a friend's promise, and his desperation made him frustrated; he was not in control of the situation.

Paul suggested Rick should phone Martin and let him know they had arrived: maybe he could send a truck to pick them up. Isadora knocked on Rick's window: she had half expected Martin would be waiting for them and she was close to panicking.

"I'm calling Martin now, don't worry," Rick said to her. He noticed the fear in his voice made her cringe.

Martin told Rick he knew of the situation, but had not wanted to alarm them in advance and risk them crashing their cars on the motorway. He had everything under control and would hop in a truck to pick them up now. He told them to be ready and waiting for him, as things might get tense.

Ten minutes after the call, a military truck drove up behind them. Rick figured it had come from another entrance. Martin gestured them towards him as he and three soldiers jumped out. Rick and the others ran as fast as they could to the back of the truck, carrying their luggage and supporting the pregnant Zaira. Rick heard angry shouts behind him, as people started to realise what was happening and they wanted to get on the truck too. He couldn't blame them and he felt guilty for leaving them behind.

The soldiers pointed their weapons at the dozens of refugees, shouting at them to stay away. One of them shot into the air. For a moment the crowd stopped, giving Rick and the others enough time to get into the truck. Before they could close the door, the truck had started driving away from the crowd.

Rick hugged Martin. He was happy to see his good friend. "Thank you."

"I'm very happy you're all here. We're ready to go in," Martin said as he pointed to his own luggage inside the truck. "Our helicopter is waiting."

"I was afraid your plan would go all wrong. It's so chaotic out there. I feel bad for the people outside, it's like leaving them to die."

"No, no, they will all go inside too, don't worry. We're actually processing everyone very fast, they will be safe. I just wanted you here in time, just to be sure." Martin smiled at Rick and the others.

The kids were talking to Zaira; she looked very uncomfortable, but she seemed to enjoy the attention and the distraction. Rick hoped everything would work out fine. The noise of several helicopters made him pause and take in the sight: this was truly an evacuation on an epic scale, but everything looked very calm. Dozens of helicopters stood on the tarmac and soldiers were helping people board with their luggage. Up in the sky more helicopters were waiting to land. He knew the British army was well organised and he almost expected to be offered a proper cup of tea soon, just to make the picture of British perseverance complete.

Whilst walking to their helicopter, Rick was struck by the strength of the downdraught coming from the rotors. He had always found it a strange concept that blades could cut through air and lift up such a heavy machine, but he was glad they could: this was his ride out of here. It was going to be strange to fly back into the Cube again.

The entrance hall was bigger than Rick remembered. All the helicopters and people looked so small and insignificant inside. Because they had flown in farther away from the corner, they had to walk a few kilometres to reach the next Square, and Rick took up the time to chat with Martin. "So how come we had preferential treatment today?"

"The Prime Minister owed me, after all I did for the country. When the doors started closing, he told me to depart immediately and that I could ask him for a last favour, so he could show his gratitude. So I thought of all of you, and how badly I wanted you here. You," Martin paused for a moment and looked at the group, "all of you, I consider you my family, and what would my life be like without my family in here?"

Rick smiled at him. "Yes, I think this motley crew makes a good family. And you still have no idea about Colin?"

"He went in months ago. He managed to get a few messages to me, but I lost contact with him weeks ago. Now that we're here I must find him. I promised him. But I haven't figured out yet how to get to the American sector. It will be difficult, they have several cities — Rick, uhm — that's why at the next Square, I won't be stepping on the same travelator as you. I will go in a different direction, I'll be searching for Colin."

Rick had not expected having to say goodbye to Martin so soon, but he understood his friend. "And you'd better make sure you'll find us again."

"Of course," Martin said. He took a few pieces of paper from his pocket. "These are our addresses, as you can see we'll all be on the same floor in the same building. And you're holding on to most of my belongings till I'm back."

They went silent and listened to Florence and Karen, who had started singing children's songs. They were a few hundred metres from the square when they heard Isadora shout. "Her waters broke."

"Now? You've got to be kidding me," Rick said to Martin, as he looked at Zaira. She tried to smile, but she was obviously in pain. Gustavo and Paul lifted her up and hurried towards the Square, with the rest following them. A stranger came forward and offered his trolley for Zaira to sit on. They carried her on to it and Gustavo and Isadora both pushed the trolley along.

"There's a hospital in New Albion. Zaira can give birth there. The guides will help you," Martin said.

"Guys, I'm going with Zaira and Gustavo to the hospital, you take the kids, and Sally too," Isadora said.

"Of course, here's your address. We'll meet you and the baby there," Rick said. He kissed Isadora. "Now go, don't wait for us!" Rick felt sad when he saw them run off and disappear after they stepped on the Square. "Karen, Thomas, you stay close to me. We'll see your mum again soon. Okay?" The kids nodded, they seemed fine. It was a very exciting time for them and they had each other to talk to and play with.

A guide welcomed them at the Square and they received their welcome pack and instructions.

Martin cleared his throat. "Right, this is where I go in a different direction from you," he said as he pointed to a strip opposite to where they were standing. He gave the kids hugs and kisses. He told Thomas to be brave and promised him he would be part of all the exciting expeditions unlocking the Cube's secrets. Then he turned to Paul and Rick. "I don't like goodbyes, so I'll keep this short. I love you guys. And I will return — with Colin. Wait for me."

"I love you too Martin," Rick said, "and thank you for everything."

Together, Paul and Rick embraced Martin. All three of them cried.

"The last few years have been very demanding on all of us, and your friendship is very important to me. Without each other we probably would not have survived," Martin said.

"We'll be waiting for you. And hurry, you hear? And don't do anything foolish," Rick said, his voice croaking. He watched Martin step on a strip and disappear. Rick looked at Paul and the three kids. There was not much left of his *family* and he felt he might never see any of them ever again.

"You okay?" Paul asked. "We will be fine, I know that. They all have to come and find us. Look at all the luggage they left with us." He smiled at Rick.

"Yes, you're right, but I'm not happy. Let's go to our new home, the kids are anxious to see it — okay kids. Grab your bags and let's jump on the travelator," Rick shouted. He tried to make his voice sound happy.

***

The markers flew past and before Rick realised, their journey on the travelator was over. Rick and Paul, Thomas, Karen and Florence walked into the Sphere. The kids were holding hands. Sally ran around them; she was excited, jumping high and far. Rick glanced at Florence: her face was shining with happiness and she gasped from excitement when they were directed into the circle for the last leg of their travels.

The contrast between the emptiness during Rick's last visit into the Sphere, and the vibrant and colourful city that appeared in front of him, made his eyes water.

Paul noticed Rick's tears, so he winked at him and gently squeezed his hand.

Welcoming giant British flags were hanging out of many windows and the walls were decorated with colourful posters depicting British landmarks: this was their New Albion, their new home, their new future.

Happy noises came from men, women and children, happy to be reunited with their loved ones, who were running into each other's arms, and were hugging and kissing.

Rick noticed a group of older men and women sitting on benches and chairs on a square; some were enjoying the sunshine, others were playing card games and chess; it could have been a lovely summer's day in London's Trafalgar Square.

***

Rick looked at Florence. She gazed with amazement at the buildings and all the people around them. He had never doubted she would love the Sphere and he was happy to see he had been right. Her eyes followed a group of children who were running and skipping towards a man who was playing his guitar. Their hairs were all messy and spiky and they were laughing and singing and dancing along with the music. A girl with flowers in her hair waved at Florence and Karen and Thomas, gesturing them to come over and join them. Rick and Paul looked at Florence: she had a big grin on her face.

"You're smiling. Why?" Rick asked her.

"Can't you see, Uncle? This is going to be the best adventure ever."

The End.

Epilogue.

Ithaca.
By Constantine P. Cavafy,
(April 29, 1863 - April 29, 1933).
Written in 1911.

When you set sail for Ithaca,
wish for the road to be long,
full of adventures, full of knowledge.
The Lestrygonians and the Cyclopes,
an angry Poseidon — do not fear.
You will never find such on your path,
If your thoughts remain lofty, and your spirit
and body are touched by a fine emotion.
The Lestrygonians and the Cyclopes,
a savage Poseidon you will not encounter,
if you do not carry them within your spirit,
if your spirit does not place them before you.

Wish for the road to be long.
many the summer mornings to be when
with what pleasure, what joy
you will enter ports seen for the first time.
Stop at Phoenician markets,
and purchase fine foods,
nacre and coral, amber and ebony,
and exquisite perfumes of all sorts,
the most delicate fragrances you can find.
To many Egyptian cities you must go,
to learn and learn from the cultivated.

Always keep Ithaca in your mind.
To arrive there is your final destination.
But do not hurry the voyage at all.
It is better for it to last many years,
and when old to rest in the island,
rich with all you have gained on the way,
not expecting Ithaca to offer you wealth.

Ithaca has given you the beautiful journey.
Without her you would not have set out on the road.
Nothing more does she have to give you.

And if you find her poor, Ithaca has not deceived you.
Wise as you have become, with so much experience,
you must already have understood what Ithaca means.

Dear reader,

I hope you have enjoyed reading my novel as much as I have writing it.
Please let others know about my book. Tell your family and friends and everyone else that loves science fiction. Leave comments on websites and talk to your local (independent) bookshop, so others can find my novel.

This story is not finished. In the next book you will find out where the Cube is travelling to, and what happens to all its inhabitants. The finished series will have a total of six novels.

If you would like to be informed when the next instalment in this series is published, follow or contact the author, or be added to the mailing list, please visit:
www.ophiuchuscube.com

Thank you very much for reading my story.
Hendrik de Jong.